BACK
THROUGH A FIELD OF STARS

Book Two of The
Through a Field of Stars
Trilogy

BRIAN JOHN SKILLEN

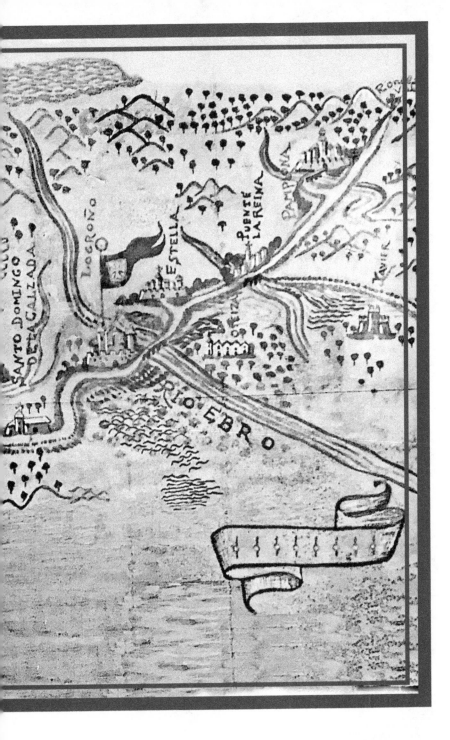

Published by: 1881 Productions
Arvada, Colorado, USA

ISBN 978-1-7353036-4-2

Design and formatting by Valeria Fox
Edited by Librum Artis Editorial Services

Printed in the United States of America

November 2021

www.throughafieldofstars.com
throughafieldofstars@gmail.com

This book is dedicated to all the pilgrims from
the Camino de Santiago
who inspired

Back: Through A Field of Stars,

especially my wife Chelsea.

I hope reading this novel inspires you
to take the adventure of a lifetime.

Buen Camino!

AUTHOR'S NOTES

On April 8, 2017, in the small town of Castrojeriz, I was first told about a secret code of the Knights Templar on the Camino de Santiago. This code inspired me to write the Through a Field of Stars series. As I hiked the Camino across Spain, the story for this novel played like a movie in my head. The things I saw, the people I met, and the experiences I had all wove together into the perfect narrative. Since that day, I have walked more than a thousand miles doing research for this book series.

The first novel in the series, The Way: Through a Field of Stars is set in the year 1306, one year before the Knights Templar mysteriously disappeared, along with their treasure. The novel follows Princess Isabella of France on a fictitious pilgrimage along the Camino de Santiago as her father, King Philip, plots to disband the Templars. Join Isabella and her companions as they travel through foreign lands, unlock the Templar's secret codes, avoid immortal Shadows, and discover the wisdom of the Camino de Santiago.

The second novel, Back: Through a Field of Stars, was inspired by a return trip I took to the Camino de Santiago in 2018. Just like the first novel, the pilgrims I met on this Camino became characters in the novel, and experiences I had on this journey wove their way into the pages you are about to read.

Being a historical fantasy, many of the characters are historical figures, like Princes Isabella of France and the Knights Templar. Though these characters are actually historical figures, I've altered certain things about them to fit the narrative. To learn more about the factual history of these characters, refer to the appendix in the back of the novel. Being a fantasy, there are also some supernatural entities you can expect along the way.

I hope this novel inspires the adventure of a life-time. "Buen Camino!"

FUN FACTS

- All the secret codes in the novel are based on symbols, ruins, and other things I saw on my own Camino. If you walk the Camino de Santiago yourself, and know where to look, you can still see all these fascinating markings today.

- The letter J came into existence in 1524, so all of the codes are based on a twenty-five-letter alphabet.

- The title of the novel, Back: Through a Field of Stars, was inspired by the saying, "There is a star in the Milky Way for every pilgrim who walks the Camino de Santiago."

TABLE OF CONTENTS

CHAPTER 1

La Manche, 1307

The mist from the sea whipped off the waves and kissed Isabella's face. She closed her eyes and enjoyed the sun—its warmth was the only thing keeping the bite of the wind at bay. Spreading her arms, Isabella felt free as they sailed over the waves. It was possibly the last taste of freedom she would have in this life. Soon they would arrive in Paris, and she would have to face her fate.

Isabella longed to be back in Spain, to be back in Etienne's arms. The whole voyage she had wondered if she had made the right decision. However, the further she got from Spain, the more she felt like she was making a mistake. If she had stayed, she and Etienne could have shared a life together. Isabella smiled at the thought of Etienne as an old man.

The smile quickly disappeared as she faced the reality that leaving was the only way to protect Etienne and her friends. If she had chosen to stay, they would've been hunted forever—not only because of her, but because of her father's obsession with the Templar treasure. She was returning to France for only one reason—to convince her father to give up his quest.

Isabella sighed heavily and placed both hands on the railing. She gripped the coarse wood tightly. It isn't fair, she thought.

She wondered how she could face her father now that so much had changed. A large wave tossed the boat, causing Isabella to stumble backward.

"Be careful, Your Highness." Isabella was steadied by a strong hand on her back. She turned to see a white mantle with the red cross of a Knights Templar.[1] Her heart raced in the vain hope it was Etienne, but as her eyes moved up, a young Templar with ginger hair came into view.

"Get your grubby hands off of her," Sister Caroline said, smacking the Templar's hand away. She put her fists on her hips as a spray of water shot up from the sea, making her look like a figurehead on a ship. "Now go," she ordered.

The young Templar fumbled with his words, but managed, "As you command." He bowed and left immediately.

Isabella smiled and curtsied to the large nun who had appeared out of nowhere. "Sister Caroline, I don't know how I ever could have survived this trip without you," Isabella jested, but there was some truth in her words. When the sickness had overtaken the ship, Sister Fransie and Sister Caroline had saved many lives, including her own. The sickness had turned what was supposed to be a few weeks' journey into several months. It was impossible to dock anywhere, and Isabella had refused to let the ship enter her kingdom's waters until the last of the sickness was gone. She wouldn't put her people at risk.

"Ever since they discovered you are Princess Isabella of France,[2] they haven't been able to take their eyes off of you." Sister Caroline shook her head disapprovingly, and her brimmed head-covering moved awkwardly from side-to-side. She dressed differently than the nuns in France. Besides her brimmed wimple—which Isabella supposed was to block the Spanish sun—her habit was made of undyed gray wool instead of black, which was the norm in Paris.

"When we get to France, I will request that you and Sister Fransie be assigned to the castle. You two have become so dear to me. I am sure the bishop will grant me this, and if not, I will go straight to the Pope." Isabella looked around. "Where is Sister Fransie?"

"She is below with the last of the sick." Sister Caroline stood fast with her hands on her hips as another large burst of water sprayed and foamed behind her.

Isabella tried to stifle her laughter. The somber mood onboard reflected her own feelings; however, the thought of Sister Caroline as a figurehead of a ship sailing over the ocean was too much to contain. Regaining her composure, Isabella realized this was the first time she had allowed herself to laugh since leaving Etienne.

CHAPTER 2

Sister Fransie dipped a rag into the bucket next to the bed, the water sloshing with the rocking of the ship. She wrung out the rag and gently placed it on the forehead of the sailor lying to her left. She tenderly stroked his face, and he managed a weak smile.

"I don't know why you're trying to cure him—he's dying," said a gruff voice.

Sister Fransie looked over her shoulder, and the shaft of light streaming in from the upper deck blinded her. As her eyes cleared, she saw another sailor propped up against the railing of the stairs.

Sister Fransie smiled gently and dipped the rag in the bucket again. "Even if I can't heal his body, I can heal his loneliness. Being abandoned, unloved, and uncared for is a much greater sickness than what his body is going through now. True, he may die. But, if I do nothing, I would have to live with the thought that I let him die alone and unloved."

"We all die alone." The sailor shifted his position and crossed his arms.

"Timothy won't. I will stay with him until he is well or he has breathed his last."

The sailor in bed feebly squeezed Sister Fransie's hand, and she turned her attention to him immediately. His eyes shone with a love and gratitude that words could never express. He took a few labored breaths and gave up his spirit. Sister Fransie continued to hold Timothy's hand as the heat left his body. In the void, the boat creaked and moaned under the pressure of the sea.

After a few moments, the sound of heavy boots descending the stairs broke the silence. With each step, little particles of dust flew up and danced in the shafts of the light. Recognizing the boots, the pessimistic sailor stood at attention. "Captain."

"At ease," the captain returned. He noticed Fransie still holding Timothy's hand. "Thank you for your service, Sister. May he rest in peace." The captain placed a hand over his heart, and after sufficient time had passed, he continued. "Was he the last one showing symptoms?"

Fransie nodded. "All the others have either recovered or left this earth."

"This sickness has taken too many of my men," the captain said. Fransie could detect a quiet mourning behind his strong voice. "We will give Timothy a proper burial and at long last continue on to Paris."

CHAPTER 3

Isabella felt a lump in her throat as they approached Le Louvre. She took a deep breath, and her shoulders slumped. The gardens and the fortified castle before her solidified her return to Paris. This was real, and she would soon have to face her father. Just before they reached Le Louvre, the sails were lowered, and the ship coasted to a makeshift dock.

"Anton, why are we stopping here?" Isabella asked the captain.

"This is as far as we go, Your Highness. Actually, this is as far as any large ship goes."

He motioned to the defensive stone wall that surrounded the bustling metropolis—two imposing turrets flanked the river, each teeming with archers whose arrows were pointed directly at them. "Your father has taken extra precautions since you left. I know it's no way for a princess to travel, but we will continue on to the palace in a small rowboat. First though, I need to inform the guards of our business."

The sailors extended a ramp to the wooden dock, and Anton disembarked. The captain had an air of confidence about him that sometimes bordered on arrogance. If Isabella didn't know better, she would have sworn he was descended from royalty.

Anton met the guards, and they exchanged a few words. One guard stole a glance at Isabella then quickly turned his gaze to the ground. A few more words were exchanged, and the guards signaled the archers in the tower, who lowered their bows.

Anton climbed back aboard the ship. "If you will accompany me, ladies." He motioned for Isabella, Sister Fransie, and Sister Caroline to follow him to a rowboat.

A large knot formed in Isabella's stomach as they approached the Île de la Cité. The small island was the heart of Paris and where her father's castle stood. From the rowboat, the island looked like a defiant ship parting the Seine River in two. Isabella closed her eyes and tried to imagine she was still on the Camino de Santiago,[3] but it did no good. The closer she got to the castle, the more she wished she would have stayed with Etienne. She couldn't shake the feeling of foreboding. To distract herself, she turned to Anton. "Thank you for getting us here safely."

"It's a Templar's duty to protect pilgrims," he said politely.

Isabella had heard this response so many times on the Camino she almost rolled her eyes. She caught herself before she did and asked, "Where will you go after this?"

"We will load up our ship again and head back to Spain. But, before we do, we will visit Grand Master Jacques de Molay[4] at the Templar commandery."

Isabella stared at Anton blankly. "He's here?" Her face betrayed a momentary look of disgust. The last time she had met Molay, she had wanted to kill him. She loathed him for the way he had treated her on the Camino—he had almost taken Etienne away from her forever.

"I was surprised, as well. The guards told me that the Pope has called all of the Templar and Hospitaller[5] masters here to discuss another crusade to the Holy Land. He mistook our ship for one of the Templar command ships. The guard also said none of the Hospitallers have arrived yet."

Isabella hoped she and Molay would never meet again. Feeling that the day couldn't get any worse, she ordered, "Quickly, we must make haste. One doesn't keep my father waiting."

The two sailors rowed harder, and Paris streamed past them. The banks of the Seine River were lined with merchants and fisherman alike. Isabella's ears perked up as their French words rose above the rushing water and the clip-clop of horses' hooves on the cobblestone streets. Those words, spoken in her mother tongue, were her welcoming committee. The Camino had taught her simplicity, and she was grateful for this humble welcome to her home—if she could still call it that.

Anton guided the rowboat to the ramp on the right side of the island, which led from the water to the raised streets above. The two sailors fastened the raft tightly and all exited. At the top of the ramp, they were met by a well-dressed young woman with brunette hair and large blue eyes, as well as a whole company of the King's Guard.

"Oh, there you are! I saw the signal from the tower and had to be the first to see you," the young woman said as she rushed to Isabella and wrapped her in an embrace.

"Matilda, I almost didn't recognize you. I should have known it was you who would meet me." Isabella returned Matilda's embrace tightly. Isabella had forgotten that her cousin was now at court—Matilda had grown so much in the year since Isabella had left.

"They would have had to throw me in your father's awful dungeons to stop me." Matilda let go of Isabella and stepped back. "My, look at you! We must get you out of these rags and into one of your favorite gowns." Matilda raised her hands and made a brushing motion toward Anton and the others. "Shoo, shoo, you can leave now. You are no longer needed."

"Matilda, that is no way to treat these brave people who delivered me from death's door." Isabella turned to Anton. "My apologies, Captain, for my friend."

"Ooo, a captain. Well, that changes things." Matilda made a small curtsy to Anton and giggled flirtatiously. "And how big is your boat?"

"Matilda! You are impertinent! Your princess orders you to hold your tongue." Matilda took a step back and placed her arms behind her innocently.

"Captain, thank you for your service. You and your men have gone above and beyond your call of duty. The king will be sure to hear of your actions."

"Thank you, Your Highness. It was an honor and a privilege to have you sail with us." Anton bowed, and the two sailors followed suit. As Anton disappeared, so did Isabella's last hope for escape back to the Camino. Her body tensed—she wanted to run, but she was frozen.

"Mmm, now that Captain Handsome is gone, I have to inform you of all the juicy gossip that has happened since you left." Matilda hooked arms with Isabella and walked her to the coach. Sister Fransie and Sister Caroline followed closely behind. Noticing, Matilda turned to them. "I said you are dismissed."

"Matilda, this is Sister Caroline and Sister Fransie; they will be accompanying us to the castle to serve as my personal spiritual council. They will remind me of the lessons I learned on the Camino"

"Oh, how common," Matilda retorted. "My, how you have changed. Very well then, let us away."

Isabella stared blankly out the window of the coach as Matilda spoke ceaselessly about the happenings in court. Isabella paid no attention—it didn't interest her anymore. As they approached the castle, the steeple of Saint Chapelle rose above the palace wall, and Isabella had the overwhelming urge to stop for prayer before seeing her father.

"And then Sylvan rolled into the cake. You should have seen the duchess's face as he—"

Isabella put her hand on Matilda's shoulder. "I must stop for prayer before seeing my father." Isabella had rehearsed what she would tell her father a thousand times, but she needed to go over it once more before seeing him. One wrong word could betray both her friends and everything she knew about the Templars' secret treasure.

On her Camino, Isabella had learned how to unlock the seven doors that protected the Templars' greatest treasure, as well as how to decode the clues in the cathedrals that led to its location. But, she had also learned that the treasure only brought death. She could not let her father possess it. She would stick with the story she had rehearsed—it needed to be perfect for her father to believe it.

"But, he said to come directly to him. He awaits you in Le Grand Salle."

"Perfect, Le Grand Salle is just down the hall from the chapel. It won't be but a moment's delay. For your love of me, do this one thing. Leave me to pray, and deliver my guests to my chambers."

"I don't think—"

"Do as your princess orders. I will answer to my father. It will be a fun surprise."

Reluctantly, Matilda knocked on the coach, and it slowed to a stop. A chivalrous-looking older knight opened the door. "What is it, my Ladies?"

"Your princess orders that you take her to Saint Chapelle."

"The orders were to enter the palace grounds through the royal entrance and—"

Matilda put her hand on the man's cheek, interrupting his speech. "*Your princess* orders it."

The knight bowed. "As you wish." He shut the door and the carriage continued.

Within a matter of minutes, they were at the lower entrance to Saint Chapelle. The coach stopped once more, and the same chivalrous knight opened the door. Isabella extended her hand, and the knight helped her descend the few small steps. No matter how many times Isabella had seen this church, she was still in awe. The stained-glass windows glinted in the sun like gems, offsetting the gray granite rock of the chapel, and gargoyles hung on every buttress, as the spires reached toward heaven. The chapel had always been her refuge—the one place she could be alone.

Isabella walked under a column-lined archway and through one of the doors. She remembered running in and out of these columns as a child, chasing after Etienne. On entering, Isabella turned to the left and walked up the spiral staircase leading to the upper chapel.

"Hmm-hmm. That staircase is closed except to clergy and royalty." Isabella turned to see an elderly priest.

"Loui, do you not know your princess when you see her?"

The old priest squinted a few times. "Your Highness, forgive these old eyes. They don't see as well as they used to."

"There is nothing to forgive. Now, if you will excuse me, I mustn't keep my God, nor my King, waiting."

Isabella continued up the dimly lit spiral staircase. As she reached the landing, she stepped through the door and stopped. Her breath was taken away as she was bathed in the jewel-toned sunlight shining through the windows. Each stained-glass window was a masterpiece. They were more beautiful than the most decadent crown, set with the rarest jewels.

"I'm home," she whispered. "I'm alive."

Isabella ran to the altar and fell to her knees. "My Lord Jesus Christ, thank you for letting me return safely. Thank you for watching over me and protecting me. I love you, my Lord. Please watch over my friends I have traveled with. Please watch over Etienne." Isabella's eyes moistened at the mention of his name. "My Lord, give me discernment over what to tell my father."

Isabella made the sign of the cross and cleared the tears from her eyes. She turned, and her heart stopped. Her father, King Philip,[6] was standing a few paces away with his arms behind his back. Isabella ran and embraced him, but Philip stood still.

"Father," she said warmly.

After a long pause, Philip responded, "You can call me Your Majesty until I have determined if my daughter has returned whole and loyal to her King."

Isabella took a few steps back and stood awkwardly, like a child who has just been shamed. She gathered what confidence she could and straightened. "What must Your Majesty know?"

"Who is Etienne?"

"A Templar," Isabella responded without missing a beat. She learned long ago that when telling a lie, one must have a small dose of the truth to be believed. She was relieved that her father didn't recognize Etienne's name. She hadn't planned to mention him. If her father knew Etienne was the boy he had sentenced to death all those years ago, he would be livid. He also would know exactly how to find him. To Isabella's knowledge, Etienne was the only dark-skinned Templar. This wasn't going at all like she had rehearsed.

"And why does this Templar deserve your tears?"

"He saved my life more than once and was poisoned in the process. He fought bravely against Tristan, who was trying to capture me and sell me to the Moors."[7]

"Tristan, your personal guard? He betrayed you?"

"It was because of him that all of the bloodshed and destruction befell so many good people."

"Why would he betray you?"

"He said you had no money to pay the guard. He said you are destitute. I think he wanted the Templars' treasure for himself."

"Silence!" Philip bellowed, sending an echo up to the rafters. His tone was a sharp contrast to the tranquility of the church. "Did you hear this from his own mouth?"

"No, Etienne told me."

Philip took a menacing step toward Isabella, but she stood fast. "I will ask you again. Who is Etienne? Why would you trust him over Tristan?"

"A Templar who saved my life on many occasions—"

"Hold out your hands."

Isabella held out her hands obediently. Philip produced a long rod from behind his back. He looked at it for a moment then brought it down hard on Isabella's hands. Isabella flinched at the pain but made no sound. Philip brought the rod down for a second blow, which split the skin. Tears formed in Isabella's eyes, but no sound escaped her lips.

"I will ask you again, and this time I want the full truth. Who is Etienne, and how has he turned you against your dear father?"

"He is a Templar." Philip brought the rod down hard again on Isabella's hands. The impact sent little droplets of blood flying in all directions and left her hands quivering. "He is a Templar who saved my life." Philip brought the rod up again, but before he could strike, Isabella said, "Father, please! I feigned love for him so I could fulfill the mission you sent me on."

Philip steadied his hand and lowered the rod. "Continue."

"In order to be believed, I made myself fall in love with him. I used his love to discover that which you asked for. But, this love has clouded my mind and judgment."

"And what did you discover, my dear daughter?"

"Did the letter I had Tristan send not reach you?"

"I never received a letter from you."

He doesn't know about the letter. Isabella wished she wouldn't have uttered those words. With that simple sentence, she had doomed them all. Surly her father would press her for information about its contents. He knew that she wouldn't have sent a letter, unless she had discovered something about the treasure.

"This truly is a sign of Tristan's treachery, Your Majesty."

Philip reached out and stroked Isabella's face. "Who is Etienne?" Philip asked again.

"He is someone I used to fulfill your ends."

Philip struck Isabella's hands hard, and she bit her lip to remain silent. "I feel there is something you still aren't telling me."

Isabella could take the physical pain, but the disapproval of her father was much harder to bear. "The Templars have a secret treasure more valuable than all others."

"I already know this, daughter. That is why I sent you on your quest."

Isabella regained her composure. "Yes, Father, but what you do not know is that its location is encoded into the cathedrals along the Camino de Santiago." Isabella didn't dare tell him about the hidden doors and the trials that needed to be overcome. She hoped that she had given him just enough to make the pain stop.

"And, I suppose this Etienne knows where to find these codes and how to decode them." Isabella turned white. Her face betrayed the one she loved most in this world. "Then we must find this Etienne. These are good tidings. This is the missing piece of information I needed."

"What do you mean?" Isabella asked cautiously.

"My spy in the Templars has told me about seven secret doors that bind the treasure. He has already located and unlocked one of them. It is only a matter of time before we find the others. With the information Etienne has, I can finally know the location of the one true treasure."

The blood drained from Isabella's body, and her knees grew weak.

"Come, embrace your father and your King." Isabella raised her trembling hands and embraced Philip, her blood-soaked clothing staining his garments. "Blood of my blood...know that if I didn't need you to marry Prince Edward, I would have you executed for your treason."

Philip turned and walked out of the chapel. As soon as he had left, Isabella fell to the floor and convulsed with tears. She brought her bloodied hands to her chest and held them tight. "Etienne, my love, where are you?" she whispered.

CHAPTER 4

Etienne sat with his head firmly pressed to the table, the world spinning again. He turned to the left and let out a large belch. The noise was quickly consumed by the clinking of glasses and the laughter of patrons at the surrounding tables. Etienne was ashamed of himself. He had become the stereotype that people had thrust upon him his whole life because of his dark skin. No one in the bar would have guessed he used to be a Templar before Isabella came back into his life. Etienne's eyes blurred with tears, both for Isabella and for the person he had become.

"Ach, there, there, laddie," Andy said, patting Etienne on the back. "I 'ave been there many times myself." Etienne's best friend, Andy Sinclair, beamed down a smile. Through Etienne's blurred vision, he couldn't tell if it was Andy's teeth or his bald head twinkling in the candle light.

Etienne's body was numb—he could barely feel Andy's touch. "I miss her," Etienne slurred.

"Aye, we all do." Andy placed his hands on his large stomach and leaned back.

"But, I love her." Etienne reached for his glass. Overjudging the distance, he sent the glass flying off the table, spilling its contents onto another patron at the next table. The man stood quickly but was slow to turn—his body shaking with rage. Two other men at his table stood as well, revealing the shell and Cross of Saint James on their mantle—the symbol of the Knights of Saint James.[8]

"Apologies for my friend. He has had too much ta drink," Andy said.

"So have I," the patron growled, leaping toward them.

Etienne shifted his head, narrowly avoiding his attacker's fist, which went crashing onto the table. Etienne sat up straight and looked in the direction of the knights. Instead of seeing three, his blurred vision now saw six.

"Andy, we're only outnumbered three to one. It is our duty to fight." Beyond duty, Etienne had a rage inside of him that he needed to let loose. He grabbed his attacker's hand, which had barely left the table, and kicked out his attacker's feet, sending his head straight into the wood.

The two other knights pulled Etienne from the stool and held him fast. The third knight regained his composure and punched Etienne in the gut.

Andy swung a wine bottle at the attackers, but he missed, sending him crashing into Etienne and the other two knights. This gave Etienne a chance to gain the upper hand. He leveraged Andy's weight and sent all of them flying out the door.

Etienne fell hard on the cobblestone road outside the bar, but he was the first to rise and draw his sword. The two knights that had restrained him inside squared off as the third came out the door. All of the patrons of the bar peered out the window, eagerly awaiting the battle.

"Gino, Michael, James, that is enough," a commanding voice said.

Etienne turned as an imposing figure walked toward them slowly from the dark street. As he entered the light, Etienne saw that he was also wearing the Cross of Saint James on his mantle.

The three other knights stood at attention. "Yes, Grand Master."

"My apologies for my knights. I don't know what has come over them." He turned to the men, "You three will serve extra patrol this week. Knights of your noble birth should know better than to get into a common fray." He turned back to Andy and Etienne. "It was brave of you to take on three Knights of Saint James."

"Well ta be fair, I didna do much," Andy said.

Etienne cut in. "It wasn't bravery, but that we are bound to our oath. Templars are never to leave a fight unless we are outnumbered more than three to one. In this situation, we had the advantage."

"So you are Templars?" the Grand Master asked.

Etienne nodded.

"And this would have been a fight to the death?"

Etienne nodded his head again. "If necessary."

"If you are Templars, where are your mantles?" demanded one of the other knights.

"Well ta be precise, we were Templars," Andy said. "We kinda had ta leave the order."

"And why is that?" the Grand Master asked.

"Love." Etienne shot the Grand Master a piercing look.

"I see," said the Grand Master. "That is why we allow our order to marry. I am Joseph Osorez, Grand Master of the Order of Saint James." Joseph extended his hand to Etienne. "I am happy no blood was drawn tonight. I insist that you join me tomorrow in the cloister of the cathedral. We have much to speak about."

"I will be there when the sun is at its highest." Etienne took Joseph's hand and they shook.

"Good, let us away then." Joseph beckoned for the three knights to follow him.

After they were out of sight, Etienne placed an arm around Andy's shoulder. "I am going to need your help home."

"I wouldna 'ave guessed that. Ya still fight brilliantly even when ya canna stand straight." Andy hooked an arm around Etienne, and they stumbled down the dimly lit street.

Etienne's heart was heavy. He had never felt so lost before. He had always had the structure of either the king's guard, or the Templars, or his desire to protect Isabella. Now though, he had nothing.

Andy and Etienne took a sharp left down a little alley. Soon, the buildings opened, and Etienne could see the Cathedral of Santiago[2] lit by the moon. They passed the large garden they had been hired to tend and continued to the three-story house where they had taken refuge.

Andy's sister Clair was waiting for them at the door. "Ach, an where 'ave you lot been?" She crossed her arms, looking them up and down. "You've been fighten' again, Andy Sinclair." Clair shook her head.

"Now, now, Clair, we didna start it. We were attacked."

"I'm sure ya didna," Clair said doubtfully. "Now, ya best get ta bed. We all 'ave work in the morn'."

Etienne awoke with his head still spinning. He shifted his body, and his whole right side hurt.

What happened last night? he thought as he shifted back to his left.

Etienne closed his eyes to stop the spinning room. Just as he was about to fall back asleep, the head-splitting sound of curtains being drawn pierced his skull and a large shaft of light filled the bedroom. Etienne tried to cover his eyes, but it did no good.

"'Tis time ta get up." Clair's voice rang in Etienne's ears, and he flinched.

Andy groaned and sat up groggily in his bed. "It canna be morning yet."

"Aye, 'tis, an' there's lots ta do," Clair said, pulling off both of their covers.

Etienne felt like a shadow of the person he used to be. He used to love the mornings and was always energized when he woke. Now, he never wanted to leave his bed, and when he did, he wanted to forget everything with a drink. They weren't supposed to be stuck in Santiago de Compostela[10]; Etienne should be back in Castrojeriz with the Templars. Andy and Clair should be in Scotland with Clair's daughter alive; Gerhart and Mariano would be with Alba, Mariano's deceased love, hustling pilgrims. But here they all were, far from home, without any money, and it was all because of Isabella's quest. Even with all they had lost, Etienne knew each of them would do it again to help Isabella. He would give anything to have her back again.

"Breakfast is-a ready. Come on down, then." Clair's words snapped Etienne out of his trance. She shook her head and left the room.

"What happened last night? I hurt all over," Etienne asked Andy.

"What? Ya donna remember?" Etienne stared at Andy blankly. "Ya picked a fight with three Knights of Saint James."

"Ahhh." Etienne placed both hands on his head. "Did we win?" Etienne peeked through his fingers at Andy.

"Aye, laddie, that we did, and ya 'ave an appointment with the grand master today at noon."

Etienne pulled his hair slightly. "I can't believe I did that. What does the grand master want with me?"

"Well ta be fair, it was-na' your fault. And, I think he was impressed with your bravery."

"It was more like drunken stupidity."

"Aye, donna be too hard on yourself. Come on, let's get some food." Andy pulled Etienne to his feet. "Clair will beat us worse than those knights if we donna hurry."

Downstairs, Gerhart and Mariano were well into their meal. Gerhart had three plates of food in front of him; even sitting down, he was taller than Clair, who was standing behind him. He was the largest person Etienne had ever encountered.

Mariano smiled at them and looked as suave as the first day they had met. His beard was well trimmed, and he still had his charisma, even after everything that had happened. Etienne managed a smile and nodded to both of them. Etienne wished he was doing as well as them.

When Etienne had first met Mariano and Gerhart, they were former mercenaries who had turned to a life of swindling pilgrims. Andy was their last mark on the fateful night they all came together. Etienne never would have guessed that they would become like family—and in Andy and Clair's cases, *literally* family, as Gerhart had married Clair.

The smell of eggs and bacon revived Etienne as they sat. He was famished.

"Ach, good, there ya are." Clair dished them up some food. "Andy, ya donna wan' ta be late again. Ya need that job so we can buy passage back home."

"Aye, that I do. I 'ave ta admit 'tis strange ta be doing accounting after all those months on the road." Andy shoveled a large bite of eggs into his mouth.

"It's better than working in the fields." Gerhart slammed his cup down heavily and wiped his lips. "What I wouldn't give to be back in battle with my axe again."

"Ye are doin' an honest man's work now," Clair said, staring at him squarely. "'Tis no shame in that. Plus, I couldna' bear ta lose ya." She leaned over and kissed his cheek.

"It isn't so bad working for me, is it?" All turned to see a pixie of a woman standing in the door, her hands firmly pressed on the frame in a playful manner. Etienne liked Chelsea. After parting ways with Isabella in Finisterre, he and the others had returned to Santiago, and Chelsea took them in.

"No," Mariano said, "we are very grateful for the opportunity to work for our room and board." All nodded in agreement.

"Good, because today we're weeding. Who's ready to get dirty?" Chelsea placed a hand on Andy's shoulder, and he turned fifty shades of red.

"I, ahh, well, ya know, I 'ave ta go." Andy quickly gathered his things and was out of the door in a flash. Etienne and Gerhart looked at each other and snickered.

As the sun was reaching the highest point in the sky, Etienne left for his meeting with the grand master. He passed the bar where they had fought the night before and shook his head in renewed shame. Ascending the stairs, he stopped in the giant courtyard in front of the Cathedral of Santiago de Compostela. Since their return, he had avoided the cathedral at all costs— every time he passed it, he felt like he had let down Saint James.[11] It also reminded him of Isabella. He didn't want to be reminded of her, nor of the failure he had become. He pulled his cloak about him tightly.

Outside the front entrance, Etienne remembered the joy in his heart when they had first arrived in Santiago. He remembered embracing Isabella on these very steps. Before Etienne delved too deeply into memories, the door opened, and two pilgrims passed. He held the large wooden door for a few more pilgrims and entered.

This was the first time he had entered the cathedral since their return to Santiago. Etienne no longer felt worthy to grace these halls. Today he would have to overcome that—he would have to answer for his actions the evening before.

The coolness in the cathedral was a welcome contrast to the heat of the fields. Etienne sighed heavily as he walked down the stairs. The cathedral seemed larger and emptier than the last time he was here. Of course, last time, he was with Isabella and his friends. Etienne reached the landing, and on either side of him, giant columns lined the pews leading to the altar. From there, the church split into two wings, each large enough to hold an entire church.

Out of habit, Etienne bowed and made the sign of the cross in front of the immense altar. Every inch of it was plated in gold, and it stretched to the domed ceiling. In the center was a statue of Santiago. Unable to look at the statue, Etienne rose and turned to his right. His footsteps echoed through the cathedral as he entered the hall that led to the cloister. At the entrance, he was greeted by a knight who looked vaguely familiar.

"I am here to see the grand master," Etienne said to a knight with a slim face and black hair that shone in the light.

The knight looked him up and down. "You seemed a lot bigger last night."

"And I thought there were six of you," Etienne said, not giving the man any room.

The knight smiled slightly and extended his hand. "My name is James Caruso; I would like to apologize on behalf of myself and my brothers." Etienne returned the smile.

Etienne took James's hand and shook it firmly. "I should thank you, I needed to let off some steam. I am sorry you and your brothers were at the other end of it."

"The grand master is awaiting you in the courtyard." James opened the door and Etienne entered.

Etienne rubbed his eyes—the bright light in the courtyard was a contrast to the dim church, and he felt his headache returning.

"Ahh, there you are." The commanding voice of the grand master filled the entire space.

Etienne walked to the center of the stone enclosure and stopped a few paces away from the grand master. He was a lion of a man with a bald head and a sandy blond beard. His blue eyes were piercing, but Etienne sensed kindness behind them.

"I don't think I got your name last night," the grand master said.

"My name is Etienne LaRue; and how should I address you?"

"Since I am not your grand master—yet—you may call me Joseph."

"So you intend for me to join the Knights of Saint James?" Etienne asked.

"Are you of noble birth?" Etienne shook his head. "Then you can never become a Knight of Saint James, but you can enter into our service. A talent like yours would be a shame to waste. Even though you couldn't stand without swaying last night, you put my knights to shame. We could use someone of your skill in our fight against the Moors. We have almost rid the land of them, but the task isn't finished yet."

"So this is what you wanted to speak about?"

"This, and your answer of why you left the Templars." Etienne's body tensed. "You said it was for love. I would like to hear more." Etienne ground his feet firmly in the dirt. "Ahh, I see. This is still a sensitive subject. This is why you are wasting a talent like yours drunk in a bar."

Etienne took a deep breath and tried to relax, but his perspiration smelled slightly of alcohol from the night before. He took another breath and was able to soften his body.

"Santiago sent me a vision of my true love on the verge of death. I had a choice to make—listen to the saint and save her, or listen to my grand master." Etienne took another deep breath. "I chose to listen to the saint and abandoned my grand master and brothers. A deed worthy of death, but I valued her life more than my own." Etienne looked down at the ground and shook his head. "Now, sometimes I wish I would have listened to my grand master."

Joseph placed his hand on Etienne's shoulder. Once again, Etienne's body tensed, and he flinched backward. Joseph removed his hand.

"That is a choice that any person would have difficulty making. Do not let this incident ruin you. A person is not defined by a single moment in their life. I can offer you stability and structure once more. I can offer you a brotherhood."

"I will consider your offer." Etienne raised his head.

"I hope you do. That will be all." Etienne nodded and walked back to the chapel.

The cool of the church was a welcome feeling once more. Etienne walked to the altar, and for the first time since Isabella had left, he knelt in prayer.

"My God, give me strength and guidance..."

When Etienne opened his eyes, he didn't know how much time had passed. He turned his head from left to right and saw a steady stream of pilgrims flowing through the church. Etienne made the sign of the cross and rose. He walked to the western exit when something caught his eye: a familiar bald head ducking out of sight behind a pillar. Etienne crept up slowly on the pillar. As he rounded it, he lunged forward and caught Andy by surprise.

Andy clutched both hands over his heart and stumbled back to a pew, hyperventilating as he sat. Etienne moved to him, but Andy held up a hand.

"And why would ya do a thing like tha'? Ya almos' killed me!"

"Come on, it wasn't that bad. What are you doing here? Aren't you supposed to be at work?"

"Well, ah, ya see, I ah..." Andy fumbled around, picking up the papers he had dropped.

"What is it?" Etienne asked, noticing Andy's discomfort. He tried to help Andy pick up the papers, but Andy shooed him away.

"'Tis alright. I 'ave it."

Etienne looked at one of the papers and noticed a symbol from the code they had discovered at the Keystone Church. He looked at the pillar, and amongst the mason's marks was the same symbol.

"What are you doing?" Even though he had asked the question, Etienne knew exactly what Andy was up to—he was still searching for the location of the Templars' most valued treasure.

The words of Ronan, Etienne's mentor and friend, came echoing back to him: *As a precaution, should anything happen to the Templar Grand Master and his Seneschal, the whereabouts of the treasure was encoded in the cathedrals along the Camino. Like a giant puzzle, each cathedral holds part of the secret that leads to the treasure's location. Besides leaving a map to the treasure's location in the cathedrals, the grand master bound the treasure, and the evil it brought into the world, behind seven doors. When unlocked, each door presents both a trial and a key. Only when these keys are united and the trials overcome, will a person be worthy to stand in the presence of the one true treasure.*

Etienne felt tears pressing against the back of his eyes. He had lost Ronan because of this treasure, and he wasn't about to lose Andy as well. Etienne hardened his features and stared Andy down.

Andy held up both hands. "Now, laddie, don't ya be mad." He looked around and whispered, "I figured if the Templars ever found us I'd be dead, so it didna' matter if I kept searching. Plus, I 'ad ta do something durn' the day—" Andy stopped himself abruptly.

Etienne continued to stare at Andy until he began to speak. "Well I, I donna 'ave a job any longer."

"And how long haven't you had a job?"

"Well, since abou' the second week we got here."

Etienne picked up a piece of paper in his hand. "So, when the rest of us have been working in the fields, you have been doing this?" Etienne shook the paper violently.

"I know you're mad. But, I couldna' bring myself ta tell Clair. I 'ave been looking for another job. Ta be honest, though, this feels more important than any job."

"And what exactly is this?" Etienne shook the paper again.

"The last code," Andy said with reverence. "I 'ave the whole church mapped out and 'ave found all of the coded letters amongst the masons' marks. I just canna figure it out—"

Etienne placed a hand to Andy's mouth. He sensed something. He removed his hand and put his finger to his lips. Andy quickly gathered the rest of the papers as Etienne leaned his back to the pillar and peeked around. Across from them, on the opposite side of the church, stood James and the two other knights from the evening before.

"Let's get out of here." Etienne placed an arm around Andy's shoulder and ushered him out of the church.

CHAPTER 5

Gaston LeBron, captain of the king's personal guard, walked heavily up the stairs from the guards' quarters to the Great Hall. He had been summoned to the king's black granite table for an emergency meeting of the small council. The captain marched out of the chamber connecting the stairs to the Great Hall and entered the enormous space. The two curved ceilings towered over him, making a double arch at least fifty feet above his head. This hall was built for grandeur; it was built for opulence.

In the center of the hall, the large granite table stood with several members of the council already gathered. Gaston made his way to his seat and pulled it out purposefully. All bowed their heads at him as he joined the table, and he bowed his silver head in return. Gaston was well respected. He had been around much longer and was also much stronger than many of the members of the council—none would dare to get on his bad side.

Gaston turned to the man on his right. "Pierre, do you know why the king has called this meeting?"

"I think it has to do with Isabella," Pierre returned in a hushed voice.

"Is our little girl back home?" Gaston said with excitement.

Before Pierre could respond, the sound of chairs moving on the marble floor disturbed them. Gaston looked up to see the king approaching and most of the other members on their feet. Gaston pushed himself up and bowed as the king neared.

"My most trusted advisors, you may sit," the king said, taking his seat. All followed suit, and the sound of chairs adjusting reverberated off the walls.

King Philip placed both hands on the table, and all moving ceased. Philip gripped the table and pressed his fingers hard on the surface.

"I am sure you all are wondering why I have gathered you here. Before rumor begins, I will be the first to inform you that Isabella may have been compromised on her Camino by the Templars. She is to be treated as a spy, but still treated as my daughter. Her quarters have been moved to the tower, where she will stay until the Templar threat is gone."

"And what threat would that be, Your Majesty?" Gaston asked, sitting up in his seat like a bear who has just sensed danger.

"Ahh, Gaston, always the first to protect. The Templars have always been a threat. They drain kingdoms of their gold, and with the crusades finished, I hear they have an eye to set up a kingdom within my kingdom." Philip slammed both hands on the table. "We cannot allow this to happen!" His voice echoed then died in the vastness of the room.

"Your Majesty, my spies haven't informed me of this," said another gentleman with a sallow face.

"These Templars are like a plague, and now they may have corrupted my daughter. France will not stand for this!"

The other advisors sitting at the table sent up a loud cheer, except for Gaston, who asked, "And what about the Church, Your Majesty? We do not want to start a war within our country, nor a war with the Church."

A wicked smile spread across the king's face. "The Pope is with us; the Church is with us." The other men let up a loud cheer again, and Gaston sat back with a foreboding feeling.

The king silenced the others with one sweep of his hand. "There is another matter—we need to find a Templar on the Camino de Santiago named Etienne."

CHAPTER 6

Isabella sat in an alcove of the circular room, staring at the Seine River far below. Her eyes were raw from tears. Matilda had found her crumpled in the church and gently escorted her to her new chamber. Isabella didn't care that she was in the tower where special prisoners were kept—she had felt like a prisoner since the moment she stepped foot on this island. Being on the Camino had made Isabella realize the freedom she had been missing her whole life. She looked longingly down the Seine to the Louvre and the wall surrounding the city. What once was a sign of security to her was now a sign of bondage.

"Ouch!" A sharp needle stab brought Isabella's attention back into the room.

"I'm sorry, Your Highness; we will be done soon," Sister Fransie said, sewing shut the cut on Isabella's hand. "These wounds are deeper than I thought last night."

Sister Caroline paced the room ceaselessly with her arms behind her back. "I can't believe your father did...Why, I am tempted to go down there and give him a piece of my mind... You are just a child... If Matilda hadn't found you, who knows... What sort of father would do something like that—" Her muttering was interrupted by the large wooden door swinging open and hitting the wall hard.

"Gaston!" Isabella exclaimed, nearly jumping out of her chair.

"Hold still, one more stitch and I'll be done." Sister Fransie tied off the string and broke the thread from the needle. "There, that does it."

Isabella ran from her seat and wrapped her arms around the silver-haired man, making sure not to press her wounds against him. "Gaston, I'm so happy to see you."

"I'm happy you made it back to us safely, Petite Fleur." He returned the embrace, lifting Isabella off the ground in a bear-hug. Setting her down, he continued, "So, it is true, your father has locked you up as a criminal."

Isabella took a step back and spread her arms. "Welcome to my new accommodations."

Gaston smiled and raised his eyebrows in a fatherly manner. "As far as I know, the only crime you are guilty of is stealing young men's hearts." His eyes rested on Isabella's hands, and his expression hardened. "What has that man done to you?"

"What he thought necessary," returned Isabella, unsure if she should defend her father or condemn him. She still felt loyal to him, even after all that he had done.

"He has become so paranoid... I'm sorry, where are my manners?" He bowed to Sister Fransie and Sister Caroline. "I am Gaston LeBron, captain of the king's guard."

Sister Caroline stepped forward and took his arm. "I am Sister Caroline, and this is Sister Fransie. We are pleased to make the acquaintance of such a handsome and kind man."

"Sister Caroline! Release that Gaston at once," Sister Fransie said, scandalized.

"It is quite all right," he said as Sister Caroline released her grip. He turned his attention back to Isabella. "I have something of great urgency to speak with you about. Can these sisters be trusted?"

"I would trust them with my life."

"Good." Gaston closed the heavy door and lowered his voice. "What I am about to say would be considered treason. If your father ever found out, all of our lives would be in great peril." He took a step to Isabella. "Are your father's accusations true? Do you love the Templars?"

"They saved my life on numerous occasions," Isabella replied diplomatically.

"Petite Fleur, I need you to answer with all honesty. It has to do with Etienne." Isabella and the nuns gasped in unison. Noticing, he asked the sisters, "Do you know Etienne as well?" They both nodded. "I see," Gaston said. "I will ask you one last time, Your Highness, is what your father says true? Do you have love for the Templars?"

Isabella responded hesitantly. "I have love for one Templar."

"Etienne?" Gaston asked. Isabella nodded. "Is this the same Etienne that you knew in childhood? My Etienne?"

"Yes, it is him. I never thought I would see him again. Then he appeared and was with me every step of the Camino. I have always loved him and always will."

"As have I—he was like a son to me. That is why I am here. King Philip is sending someone to capture him. I do not need to tell you what he does to those he wants information from." Gaston looked at Isabella's hands.

"This is my fault; this is all my fault." Isabella stumbled back to her seat, tears filling her eyes.

"No, Petite Fleur, this isn't your fault." Gaston put his hand on her shoulder. "Your father has become obsessed with...with destroying the Templars. Do you love your country?"

"Of course I do," Isabella said regally.

"If you could save thousands of your countrymen's lives, would you?"

"I would do anything for my country. That is why I am marrying Edward, and not Etienne."

"Good, then I will share with you the weight which grows heavy on my shoulders...I am a Templar."

"What?" she managed. Isabella stared at Gaston. Her father's most trusted protector was a spy? How could this be?

"It was I who got Etienne into the order of the Templars and saved him all those years ago. No one knows this secret save those in this room. Now I ask you, will you help me to save Etienne and your country?"

Isabella looked down at her newly sewn hands. "You want me to betray my father?"

"No, I want you to help me save his life, as well as the lives of my soldiers, and Etienne. Your father and Pope Clement[12] are planning to round up and imprison all of the Templars under the guise of heresy. But, we all know it is to clear your father's debt. If we do not intervene, when Philip puts this plan into action, thousands of lives will be lost. Not just the lives of soldiers—war devours innocent people as well."

"What must we do?" Isabella asked.

"We need to get a message to Jacques de Molay at the Templar Commandery—"

Isabella sighed heavily and crossed her arms.

"I didn't know you two were acquainted," Gaston said, cautiously.

"Don't worry, Gaston, my love for Etienne is much greater than my dislike for Molay."

"That is good, because we need to warn him of your father's plan so he can escape the city and avoid an all-out war between the Templars and your father's forces. If Molay leaves France, your father will have to give up his plan."

"It won't work." Isabella crossed her arms tighter.

"And why is that?"

Isabella pointed to the guard towers on either side of the Seine River at the entrance to Paris.

"We were forced to disembark our vessel at Le Louvre, and the towers were covered with archers."

"Yes, your father has doubled the guards at all the entrances to the city. He has become so paranoid that we will be attacked."

Isabella laughed and shook her head. "No. Don't you see, Gaston? It isn't to keep invaders out—it is to keep Molay and the other Templars in."

Gaston took a step back and shook his head. "You always had your father's mind. Why didn't I see this earlier? Your father has a habit of keeping his plans to himself until they are executed."

"It makes perfect sense—the guard at the entrance to the city mistook our ship for one of the Templar command ships. He said several had arrived for the meeting between the Templars, Hospitallers, and the Pope about another crusade—but, none of the Hospitaller ships had arrived yet."

"I see now; your father has blinded Molay by using his greatest desire against him. For years, Molay has been trying to gain support for another crusade."

"Men are often blinded by their ambition. When will my father strike?"

"I don't know. He said either sometime in the fall, or when he catches Etienne, whichever comes first. Why is Etienne so important to him?"

Isabella looked at her hands.

"Never mind, either way, we must get a message to Molay." Gaston stroked his beard. "It will be difficult. Your father has the castle on lockdown, and you are supposed to stay here until his plan is executed. The only time outsiders are allowed on the palace grounds is for Mass on Sundays—but, since you are trapped here, and I cannot be seen leaving—we must find another way."

"Two nuns leaving the chapel would go unnoticed," Sister Fransie remarked.

"Sister Fransie, what are you talking about?" Sister Caroline crossed her arms.

Gaston chuckled. "I forgot you were here."

"That is exactly my point," Sister Fransie said.

Isabella smiled at Sister Caroline's gaping mouth. Isabella had always pegged Caroline as the more adventurous one—perhaps she was wrong.

"Sisters, would you help us?" Gaston asked.

Both were quiet, then Sister Fransie spoke. "As long as we aren't going against God, nor the Church, we will help."

"You will be doing neither, just delivering a message—and this." He dug into his pocket and took out a gold ring with the Templar cross on it. He gave it to Sister Fransie and beckoned for them to come to the window to the right of the fireplace. Pointing, he said, "Do you see those towers to the north, just next to the city wall and the canal?"

Sister Fransie nodded.

"Good, that is the Templar commandery—you will need to go there to deliver this message to Molay, and no other: 'King Philip and the Pope are conspiring to round up the Templars. Molay must escape with the other Templar leadership to avoid bloodshed. I do not know when he will strike for sure, but a strike is imminent in the fall. Also, one of our own is in trouble on the Camino de Santiago. Etienne LaRue must be found and protected at all cost.' Do you have that?"

Sister Fransie parroted back the message.

"Perfect, thank you. This evening after Mass, I will help you to escape the castle."

CHAPTER 7

Etienne and Andy walked across the large square in front of the cathedral in silence. They descended the stairs and passed San Fructuoso, the church that sat opposite to the bar they frequented.

Just as they were about to turn down the small alley leading to their home, Andy stopped. "Come on, ya canna tell Clair that I quit my job."

"Why not? You have been lying to all of us this whole time. The others deserve to know that as we have been working in the fields, you have been in the church."

"Look, ya just canna tell them. I will get a job tomorrow."

"And where are we going to get the money that you were supposedly making?"

"Ya could take the job with the Knights of Saint James."

"I have never been paid to protect people. That would make me no better than a mercenary."

"Like Gerhart and Mariano used ta be? They arna' so bad."

"I already have enough blood on my hands."

"Ya would be helping people again. Maybe you'd get back ta your old self. I used ta respect ya more than any man I met. But now..." Etienne didn't show it, but Andy's words had struck him to his core.

"This conversation isn't about me. It is about you and your deception."

"Look, do ya wanna stay 'ere forever wallowing in self-pity? Ya lost love. It's happened ta lots of people—"

Etienne pressed Andy firmly against the wall and held his forearm to his throat. Andy turned many shades of red and purple until finally Etienne let him go.

Andy bent over and gasped for air. "See," he said, through heaving breaths, "'tis what I mean. The old Etienne would never do that to a friend. He would die to protect his friends."

"Maybe the old Etienne is dead." Etienne turned the corner and saw Gerhart, Mariano, and Clair working in the fields. Mariano was fighting with a particularly difficult weed as Clair and Gerhart struggled to pull a bluish-gray donkey forward by the reins. Before anyone saw him, Etienne turned back around the corner and faced Andy.

"Clair and I can provide a better life in Scotland for everyone," Andy said, scrunching his brow. "We just need ta get there."

Etienne put his back to the wall and took a deep breath. "I will do one paid mission with the Knights of Saint James. But, if you haven't found a job before I return, God help you, Andy Sinclair."

CHAPTER 8

After the evening prayer, the parishioners left the lower level of Sainte-Chapelle, a beautiful chapel with blue and gold arched ceilings. A few people lingered, but most headed toward the Gate of Saint Michel, the only remaining way in or out of the palace grounds. Among the crowd were two unassuming nuns—indistinguishable, and invisible to all, except the keen eyes of Father Alexander DuMond. His long fingers adjusted his clerical collar as he followed the nuns at a distance. He had observed the parishioners every night for the past month at the orders of the Pope, and was to report anything unusual.

All had been normal, except tonight. He had never seen these sisters before, nor the habits they wore. During the service they seemed tense, especially the larger one. The two nuns exited the gates, and Alexander followed closely behind, careful not to be seen. They turned left on Rue de la Barillerie and headed to Le Pont au Change, the bridge that connects Île de la Cité with the north of Paris.

The nuns stopped on the bridge and admired the sun setting behind the castle. The sky was a fiery red with highlights of purple and orange accenting the clouds. The river below reflected the sky perfectly, with its waves gently rippling. It was a true gift from God. Turning away from the view, the nuns discretely looked toward the palace tower where the king kept his special prisoners. They exchanged a few words then continued on.

After crossing the bridge, the nuns turned right and walked until they were parallel with Notre Dame. Here they changed course to the north, and Alexander had a suspicion that he knew where they were going.

He continued to follow them, and soon they were walking up Rue du Temple. Within a matter of fifteen minutes they were at the outer gates of the Templar Commandery, and Alexander's suspicions were confirmed. He lingered around a corner just barely out of sight. As they waited, the nuns looked left and right nervously. The giant gates opened, and they disappeared.

Alexander hastily retraced his steps, but instead of heading back to the castle, he made his way to Notre Dame, where Pope Clement had taken up residence. The two spires of the church were like two giant arms reaching up to the heavens. All of the gargoyles stared down at Alexander as he crossed the large courtyard in front of the cathedral. He approached the three giant archways that were carved with the saints. Every part of the edifice was a perfect picture; a religious picture.

Alexander entered through the door below the right archway, and the smell of incense lingered in the air from the evening prayer. He marched down the right side of the church and passed the large rose stained-glass window. He stopped outside of the door leading to the Pope's private chambers and whispered to the Hospitaller guard, "I must see the Pope."

"Yes, Father, I will inform His Excellency of your arrival. You must wait here."

Alexander nodded and the guard disappeared behind the door. Alexander admired the beautiful craftsmanship of the cathedral as he waited. Every aspect of it was worthy of God. He looked at the red candle burning next to the altar. *A worthy home for you, my Lord*. He made the sign of the cross and bowed.

The door handle clinked, and he turned to see the Pope emerging. Alexander kneeled and took the Pope by the hand, kissing his ring. "Your Excellency."

"You may rise, Alexander, what news?"

"It is as you said. Something unusual passed tonight." Alexander's voice was a hoarse, raspy whisper.

"Continue."

"Two nuns attended mass this evening. It was very strange; I didn't see them enter, and they looked nervous the whole time. I followed them after the mass; they lingered on Le Pont au Change and looked back at the prison tower. They then continued on to the Templar Commandery and disappeared not more than twenty minutes ago."

Pope Clement put his hand on Alexander's bowed head. "You have done good work today, my son. God is pleased with you. Now, your God and your Pope ask one more thing from you."

"Anything for the service of God."

"You must bring those nuns to me. I believe they have valuable information." Alexander smiled broadly. He was charged with doing God's work, and he would stop at nothing to complete the task he had been given.

CHAPTER 9

Sister Caroline grasped Sister Fransie's arm tightly as their escort led them through the Templar preceptory. Fransie kept her eyes down, focusing on the gray stones, silently reciting the rosary—these prayers always gave her comfort. Despite the reassurances from Isabella, something about the Templars made Fransie nervous. She had heard rumors of their mysterious ways and couldn't trust blindly. She had thought about going to a member of the clergy, but if the rumors were true, and the Pope was serving Philip, then he was no Pope.

Entering the Templar preceptory was like entering into a kingdom. A giant wall surrounded the whole compound, and its contents were almost more impressive than the palace she had just left. Their escort was leading them to the provincial master's house, where Jacques de Molay was quartered. Sister Fransie lifted her eyes to admire a church as they passed.

"She is beautiful, no?" their escort said. Sister Fransie nodded. "The chapel is dedicated to the Virgin Mary—may her grace always watch over us." Sister Fransie's body relaxed a bit at the mention of the Virgin Mary, but Sister Caroline kept a tight grip on her arm.

The Templar pointed to the left. "And that over there is the Tour de Cesar. It was the first building constructed here. Before we came, this whole land was just a large swamp."

"And what is that giant tower?" Sister Caroline asked. Sister Fransie followed her gaze to a tower with four turrets, each capped with a pointed blue roof.

"That is La Grosse Tour. After the Holy Land fell, this preceptory became the main headquarters for the Knights Templar in Europe. We needed to have something impressive here," the Templar said, smiling. "And this is the Provincial Master's quarters." He held open the door and ushered them through.

Sister Fransie and Sister Caroline followed their escort down a long hall with a velvety red carpet to a door with two guards.

"These sisters request an audience with the grand master. They insist it is of great urgency," their escort announced.

The guard on the right nodded and entered the room. He returned moments later and beckoned for the sisters to follow. The room was lit by a fire in a giant hearth and torches evenly spaced on the stone walls. Between each torch hung a tapestry of the finest quality. In the center of the room was a large circular table where several Knights Templar were seated.

"Sister Caroline, Sister Fransie. What are you doing here?" a younger Knight said, standing.

"Anton! Oh Anton, thank goodness for a familiar face," Sister Caroline said. Sister Fransie's eyes adjusted to the light and the captain's face came into focus.

An elder knight stood and all of the other Templars rose. "Good evening, sisters. To what do we owe the pleasure of this visit?" The older knight bowed, and all others followed suit.

Sister Fransie and Sister Caroline exchanged a look. Fransie could see the nervousness in Caroline's eyes. She patted Sister

Caroline on the hand and took a step forward. "I am assuming you are Jacques de Molay?" she asked the elderly knight.

"It is so."

"We must speak with you in private. It is of the greatest importance."

"What you must say, you can say in front of my brothers." Molay looked to the knights on his left and right.

Sister Fransie reached into her pocket and pulled out the golden ring Gaston had given her. She handed it to the closest knight and he passed it to Molay.

"We must speak to you alone," Sister Fransie repeated.

"I see," Molay said, observing the ring. He closed his hand into a fist. "Brothers, forgive me. I must ask you to leave." All of the knights took their leave until only the three of them remained.

"How did you come to acquire this ring?" the Grand Master demanded. "Is Gaston dead? We haven't heard anything from him in months."

"See here, that is no way to talk to women of the cloth," Sister Caroline said, finding her courage.

Molay chuckled and sat back down. "Forgive my manners, please join me."

"He isn't dead, but he risked both his life and ours so we could deliver this message to you." Sister Fransie gripped the back of a chair and remained standing. "First, King Philip and the Pope are plotting a coup against the Templars..." Fransie's voice trembled as her heart sank—had she just betrayed the church? But if what Gaston said was true, then Pope Clement was no longer serving God.

"Thank you, Sister. By the look on your face, I can see how difficult that was for you to say. I understand the guilt you must be feeling right now. Let me assure you, you haven't betrayed the church. It is Clement who has." Molay sat back and stroked his beard.

Fransie wished he would keep speaking. She needed the reassurance that she was doing the right thing.

"What is the second thing?" Molay asked.

"Gaston urges you to escape with the other Templar leadership to avoid bloodshed. He said by doing this, you can save the lives of many people. There's only one problem though..."

Molay looked at Sister Fransie expectantly.

"I'm afraid you may not be able to leave—all ships in and out of Paris are being checked, and the guards around the city have been doubled. Isabella figured out that the guards have been put there to keep you in, rather than to keep enemies out. She said that your ambition for another crusade had blinded you to her father's plan."

"And why would I ever trust her?" Molay seethed.

"Because of her love for Etienne."

Molay stood abruptly knocking his chair over. "What does that deserter have to do with it?"

Sister Fransie's body tensed as she inhaled deeply. Why was Molay acting like this? She took a few breaths before she continued.

"Gaston said the exact date of the attack is uncertain, but it will be sometime in the fall." Sister Fransie looked at Sister Caroline. "Or when they catch Etienne, whichever comes first."

Molay's face turned white. He reached down for his chair, grasping it as if he was trying to hold onto the reality from a few minutes before.

"Philip knows! Isabella told him! If I see her, I will kill her myself!"

"How dare you! Isabella is betraying her father—her country—to give you this message. You should be ashamed of yourself." Sister Caroline placed her hands on her hips.

"Why would she do that?"

"She loves Etienne. Her father had to torture that information out of her. I sewed her wounds with my own hands." Fransie felt her cheeks redden and her gaze narrow. "Also, Etienne isn't a deserter. He was given orders by an authority higher than you."

"What are you talking about?"

"Etienne was ordered by Santiago to save Isabella. He was still loyal to the Templars when we left Spain.

The fire crackled and popped, filling the silence in the room.

"There is only one choice left. We have been backed into a corner. Did Isabella tell you why Philip is going after Etienne?" Both nuns shook their heads in unison. "That is good. Ignorance of this will protect you on your journey."

"What journey?" Fransie managed.

"You must find Etienne before Philip does and deliver a message for me."

Sister Caroline sputtered. "Why us? Why not send some Templars?" She crossed her arms again and eyed Molay warily.

"If your information is true, it would appear that I am trapped here, along with the other commanders, and our every move is being watched. But no one would suspect two nuns on the Camino. Plus, Etienne would trust you. The Templars I sent to kill him for his treason have been unsuccessful thus far."

Fransie didn't know what to think. This was all happening so quickly. She'd expected to be back at the castle by the morning— to be with Isabella and settle into a new routine.

Molay dropped his head and raised it slowly. "Sisters, God entrusted the Templars with something very important. If Philip or the Pope ever possessed it, the world would be doomed. Etienne must find it first, and you are the only ones who can deliver what he needs to succeed. Will you accept this task in the name of God?"

Fransie nodded, but Sister Caroline held still. Molay beckoned for Fransie to come closer and he whispered into her ear...

CHAPTER 10

Etienne looked down at his white tunic with the shell and Cross of Saint James. *This is all wrong. It should be a Templar cross. I am still a Templar.* But something about it on his body felt right. He wasn't the person he was when he wore a Templar's uniform. He had fallen into disgrace. Actually, Etienne didn't know who he was anymore—nor where he belonged.

"That looks good on you—much better than the rags you were wearing at the bar when we first met," James said, patting Etienne on the shoulder. "Come, I want to properly introduce you to my brothers."

Etienne followed James into the Parza das Praterias, the plaza that lay outside the south entrance to the cathedral. There were several Knights of Saint James watering their horses at the fountain. Etienne immediately recognized the two who had attacked him in the bar along with James.

"Gino, don't you have something to say to Etienne?" James said, approaching the knights.

The shorter of the two had sandy blond hair and a young face. He looked Etienne up and down. "I hope you fight as well against the Moors as you did against us."

"By the looks of him in the light, he might actually be a Moor," the taller knight said.

James lunged at both knights and they wrestled to the ground.

"What's going on here?" came from behind Etienne's shoulder. The three brothers stopped fighting immediately.

"I'm sorry, Grand Master. I was just introducing Etienne to Mikey and Gino."

"And what are you doing on the ground? It is despicable for a Knight of Saint James to behave like this. If your mother wasn't Lady Caruso, I would have you expelled from the order."

"It's all right, Grand Master. I hope they can fight together instead of against each other when we face the Moors," Etienne said, helping James to his feet. He purposely left the other two on the ground. Etienne could ignore their insults, but it didn't mean he had to help them up.

"Let's get you to your horse," James said, leading Etienne to a beautiful stallion.

Within a few minutes, Etienne and the other twenty knights were mounted and armed. Etienne took a few breaths as his horse shifted its weight in anticipation.

"Come, the hunt is on! The Moors have been sighted south of Portomarin." The grand master shouted, leading the charge out of the courtyard.

It was exhilarating to ride a horse once more. Etienne watched the city fly by as the wind hit his face. He was heading back to the Camino de Santiago. He felt free as the adrenaline, which he'd so missed, pumped through his body; it was like waking from a slumber.

CHAPTER 11

Golden rays of light streaked across the Seine River as the first birds sang. Isabella's eyes stung from a sleepless night. She had expected Sister Fransie and Sister Caroline to return, and when they did not, she had spent the evening pacing her small room, leaping at every noise.

Isabella wrung her hands. *Two more deaths at my expense—I can't have two more deaths. They must return.*

Isabella had played a thousand scenarios in her head, most of which ended unfavorably for her friends. She wondered why her mind spun in these circles, fixating on these negative thoughts.

The door creaked open, and Isabella's heart leapt in anticipation, but when she saw Matilda's face, it fell to the pit of her stomach.

"Your Highness." Matilda curtsied and smiled coyly. She was followed in by two servants.

"Matilda, you know you don't have to do that."

"Good, then I must say, you look dreadful. Did you not sleep?" Looking around the room she continued. "Where are your two nuns? Did your father have them dismissed? I told you to go see him first."

Isabella raised an eyebrow, which silenced Matilda immediately.

"I'm sorry, Your Highness. We are here to dress you for the day. You are still wearing those dreadful clothes from your travels. You may be a prisoner here, but there is no need to look like one."

"You know?"

"The whole castle knows. It is all anyone is talking about. They are saying that your father is keeping you here until your marriage so you don't run back to the Camino and marry a boy named Etienne."

Isabella's heart burrowed deeper into her gut at the mention of his name. She placed both hands on her stomach.

"This will make you feel better." Matilda clapped her hands and the two servants produced a radiant silver gown.

"It is beautiful." Isabella feigned excitement. Why was she pretending? She was the princess. She didn't need to please anyone, except for her father. She had become so accustomed to being a no-one on the Camino that it was hard for her to act the part of a princess. Isabella didn't know who she was anymore, nor how to fit into this society. Their values were so different from hers now.

"So, who is Etienne?" Matilda loosened Isabella's hair and combed it.

"Matilda, you shouldn't listen to rumors." Isabella felt her cheeks redden.

"I have known you for too long—"

"Leave us!" Isabella commanded the two other servants. They curtsied and scurried out of the room.

"Matilda, we are cousins, but you have taken too many liberties. You cannot act like that in front of others."

Matilda looked at Isabella with large eyes. "Isabella, I—I apologize. It won't happen again. I am just so excited to see you and hear of your adventures. I have never left Paris. I have never met a boy in a foreign land and fallen in love," Matilda said dreamily.

"Oh, Matilda, how I love you." Isabella patted her hand and looked out the window.

Matilda attacked a particularly stubborn tangle with her brush. "When was the last time you brushed your hair properly?"

Isabella's shoulders slumped, and her eyes turned sad.

"It was in Burgos...the night before Lady Jessica died." Matilda stopped tugging and placed a hand on Isabella's shoulder.

"That could have been me." Isabella squeezed Matilda's hand.

"I'm happy it wasn't, Matilda—those were dark times. I do not wish to speak of them again." Isabella had found peace with Jessica's death but wanted to divert the subject away from the Camino and Etienne.

"Isabella, you are so different now. I don't know where you get your strength from."

If Matilda wanted to see strength, she should have seen Clair. Isabella smiled gently at the thought of her friend.

"After your Camino, have you found peace with your mother's death?" Matilda had a way of asking all the wrong questions at exactly the wrong time. The smile vanished from Isabella's lips. She had forgotten that her father had told others that Isabella was going on the Camino to find peace from her mother's death, and to see her mother's homeland of Navarre, before she wed. It was a different story than the one she had given on the Camino.

"Yes, I have." Isabella answered. She had found another mother in Clair, as well as peace and forgiveness on the Camino. "Ouch!" Matilda tugged harder, finally freeing the knot in Isabella's hair. Within a few minutes, Matilda had turned Isabella's disheveled hair into a beautiful braid.

"Now you look like Princess Isabella." Matilda walked Isabella to a mirror.

"No, Matilda. Now I look like Queen Isabella of England."

"Your Majesty." Matilda curtsied.

Isabella was ready to make the sacrifice. She was ready to marry Edward to stop the war with England forever. She hoped, with this peace, her father would give up his search for the Templars' secret treasure.

CHAPTER 12

It was late when the coach pulled into St-Jean-Pied-de-Port.[13] Sister Caroline had beads of sweat dotting her face. During the day this could be explained away by the heat, but on a cool evening in the mountain air, there was no other explanation beyond nerves. Sister Fransie felt calm, although she moved her fingers to the next bead on her rosary and said the Lord's Prayer silently. On the wooden bench across from them was a group of rambunctious Italians drinking wine. The covered wagon went over a large bump, spilling the wine, which caused another chorus of laughter.

"I don't like the looks of these Italians. I think they have been trying to undress me with their eyes since we left Paris," Sister Caroline whispered, crossing her arms over her ample bosom.

"It would seem that twenty days in a carriage with a group of Italians has cured your carnal cravings."

"Definitely; the only man for me is Jesus again."

"The Lord be praised, Sister Caroline."

The Italians hadn't bothered Sister Fransie—she actually found them quite amusing, especially the one named Stefano. He was always making jokes, yet he had solemn eyes. Fransie could tell he was the leader. There was also Luca, Stefano's brother; Michael, who was the most devout of the four; and finally Emmanuel, the prankster of the group. Fransie was happy that they were the pilgrims leaving Paris the same day as she and Caroline. Even though they made Caroline nervous, Fransie felt safe with them.

The coach came to a stop abruptly, causing even more wine to spill. A tall, thin priest with a gaunt face appeared at the opening of the wagon with a torch in his hand.

"Can we help you, Father?" Stefano said in his smooth Italian accent.

"There is nothing you can help me with," the priest replied dryly. "I only require the sisters. It has been requested by the Pope that they accompany me back to Paris."

"Forgive me, Father, but we are on urgent business and must make it to Santiago," Sister Fransie said. She had never defied an order from a priest before. On the inside she asked God's forgiveness, but Sister Fransie didn't trust this man.

"You will come with me," the priest said in a way that felt like poison. Sister Fransie's rosary trembled in her hands.

Sister Caroline stood up defiantly and placed her hands on her hips. "We wouldn't go with you if you were the last priest on earth." The priest grabbed Caroline's wrists and tugged.

Sister Caroline leaned back, resisting the priest, as Stefano and the other Italians drew their swords. Outside the wagon, the sound of many swords being drawn cut through the night; they were surrounded.

"Very well then," the priest said, loosening his grip on Sister Caroline. "If the prey chooses to stay in the den, I will smoke you out." He threw his torch in the wagon, which immediately set the wine-soaked wood ablaze. Thick black smoke filled the carriage, and heat pressed on Sister Fransie's face. Sister Caroline wrapped her arms around Fransie and together they tumbled out of the wagon. Sister Caroline absorbed the brunt of the landing, but Sister Fransie felt flesh tear away on her shoulder. To her right, an attacker let out an agonizing scream as Luca ran him through. Blood poured out all over the ground and Fransie averted her eyes.

Strong arms lifted Sister Fransie to her feet. "You must run now! Molay sent us to protect you. We will find you," Stefano whispered urgently. Sister Caroline took Fransie by the hand, and together they ran off into the night as a symphony of blades clashing filled the air.

Molay had sent them? But, aren't they just pilgrims? Fransie wondered if she had heard him correctly. These Italians weren't like any Templars she had met before, and Molay had said it was best if they traveled without a Templar escort. *Who are they? And for that matter, who attacked us?*

Sister Fransie and Sister Caroline ran deep into the woods before their legs gave out. Now, a thick curtain of trees hung around them, and all sounds from the battle were absorbed in its folds. Sweat soaked Sister Fransie's clothes, and she felt the cold night air press hard against her. A chill ran through her body, and she shivered.

"I can't take one more step or I will die," Sister Caroline said through deep pants. She leaned heavily against a tree and placed her head on her hand. "Why did Molay have to send us?"

Sister Fransie didn't reply—she was too shaken by what she had seen. The only thing that made sense to her was to pray.

Jesus, I pray for the lives of all of those men down there, both the good and the bad. Please deliver us through this dark night and forgive us our sins.

Sister Fransie joined Sister Caroline at the foot of the tree, and they wrapped their arms around each other. Fransie's mind kept repeating the scene of the carnage, and frantically wondered what the priest wanted with them. Did he know about their mission? If he did, Fransie felt in her heart that he wouldn't stop until he caught them. There was too much at stake.

CHAPTER 13

"I miss Etienne," Andy complained over dinner. "Maybe I shoulda' gone ta keep an eye on him." It had been three weeks, and the guilt of Etienne covering for him was eating Andy up on the inside. He heaped more food onto his plate, hoping to smother the feeling.

"Why would you get to go when we have to stay here and tend to the fields?" Gerhart slammed down his jug. "I would love to use my axe again. I used to be Gerhart the Destroyer—"

Clair silenced Gerhart with raised eyebrows. "The only thing ya will use that axe for is choppin' wood. I cuddna' have either of you go. Now, quit yer belly achin'." Clair looked at Gerhart sternly. "Plus, ya promised me that you gave up that life and would never return to it." Gerhart hung his head low.

"I don't know what I would do without you here," Chelsea said. "You all have been such a big help in the fields. And Andy, you are the best cook we have ever had. I love when it's your night to make dinner." She took Andy's hand. "I mean it."

The blood ran to Andy's cheeks, and he avoided Chelsea's gaze. Andy had liked her since the moment they met. She was the reason he convinced the others to choose this boarding house. Andy admired Chelsea's work ethic, and she was the kindest person he had ever met. Her father was on a voyage and had left Chelsea in charge of the boarding house.

During their several-months'-stay, Chelsea had taken in many people who couldn't pay. She also frequently gave food to the poor outside the cathedral. On the farm, Chelsea went from task to task like a hummingbird. She thrived on it, and as a result, the boarding house and fields prospered.

"Now's as good a time as any to tell you that I must leave as well," Mariano said, sitting back in his chair. "I can't explain it, but I am restless, and I feel called to go east."

Andy had noticed Mariano wasn't himself. The peaceful state he had been in while they walked the Camino had vanished. He would have moments of profound wisdom, but then would sink into depression. These days, you never knew who you would get. What had happened to all of them? Clair was the only one that still seemed sane and in her element.

"Ach, what is happening ta this family? If Isabella was here..." Clair looked down at the table.

"Right, that does it. I'm going ta the pub." Andy placed both hands on the table and stood. Neither the food nor this conversation was helping to soothe his mood—he needed a drink.

Andy walked down the dark street to the pub, the lanterns flickering and the light dancing off the gray stones. The mention of Isabella's name had struck a nerve in him. When she was with them, all seemed right in the world. She had given them a purpose. Now, it seemed everyone was stuck. Gerhart was trying to fit into a life he didn't belong in—there is no way he could be domesticated—and Mariano had lost his peace the moment they settled into Santiago. Etienne was brokenhearted and had taken to the drink, and Clair was trying to hold everyone and everything together. She was trying so hard, God bless her, but you can't make a lie work. Even with all of the misfortune they had experienced before Isabella left, he would trade it in a heartbeat for what they had now—a life without purpose is no life at all.

Andy reminded himself that he still had a purpose to hold onto. Finding the treasure was his obsession. He was holding onto that purpose like a dying person holds onto their last breath. He refused to let the mundane take him over. He would not surrender. The pursuit of knowledge was his life's purpose, and to discover the Templars' treasure was the ultimate goal. Andy had heard that this treasure might be the *Prisca Sapientia*[14]—the sacred wisdom that was revealed to Adam and Moses directly by God. Finding this perfect knowledge would be the ultimate treasure. Excitement bubbled up in Andy's body just thinking about it.

"Yeah, I heard them say they used to be Templars," a voice said from inside the bar. Andy froze just before he passed the large window.

"There is no such thing as a former Templar. There is either a dead Templar, or a deserter; nothing else," a husky voice returned. Andy peeked through the glass, careful not to be seen. At the bar were four Templars, the leader of which looked familiar. "Can you describe these two men to me?"

"Yeah, they come in here every night," the bartender replied. "I would be happy if they are the two you are looking for. They have been nothing but trouble for this place. One is short and stocky with a bald head. The other has dark skin and is young, but very strong. He is the type of person you wouldn't want to deal with one on one."

Andy's body tensed. The barman had sold them out! He thought they had been friends. Andy knew he should turn away, but he wanted to hear more.

"Those are the two deserters we are looking for. Do you know where we can find them?"

"If you wait here long enough, they will be coming in. As I said before, they are in here every night, and usually show up around this time. Can I offer you a drink?"

"A true Templar doesn't drink."

"Sir, what is that?" another Templar said, pointing in Andy's direction. Andy realized that even though he was out of view, his breath was steaming up the glass with each exhale. Andy sped across the road to San Fructuoso. He knew he couldn't outrun the Templars and hoped the church would honor the tradition of sanctuary.

Andy banged on the door and looked over his shoulder. Luckily, the exit was on the far side of the bar. That, and the fact that the Templars had to push past some patrons, bought him some time. He banged on the door again. It creaked open and Andy pushed his way inside, falling on the floor.

"Sanctuary! Sanctuary! I declare sanctuary!" Andy shouted. The priest looked at him and shut the door firmly, locking it.

"Open up! By order of the Templars we insist that you open these doors immediately," a Templar boomed, pounding hard.

"This man has requested sanctuary and we have granted it. God's law is higher than that of the Templars."

"Very well," said the Templar on the other side of the door. "Knights, position yourselves at all entrances to the church. If he tries to leave, detain him by any means possible."

Andy lay on his back, listening to the footsteps outside repositioning themselves. He stared at the ceiling and blinked his eyes. High above, at the apex of the dome, were four small Templar crosses with a larger one in the middle.

Of course, where five become one... the code! *Here I lay under a field of stars where five become one.* Andy smiled broadly. He and Etienne had gone through many trials to decode those two sentences—the Templars had hidden them well in the other cathedrals. Andy suspected there were other parts to the riddle that led to the Templars' greatest treasure, but had he accidentally stumbled onto its location? Even though Andy had passed by this church every day, he had never been inside. He had focused all of his attention on the Cathedral.

"Are you all right, son?" the priest asked.

"Aye, better than all right. Thank you, Father." The priest helped Andy to his feet.

"What did you do to invoke the anger of the Templars? Is there something you would like to confess?"

"Nothin'; I used ta be one of them. They just cuddna' let me go." Andy brushed himself off. "Thank ya kindly for granting me sanctuary."

"It is all in the service of God. Please, make yourself comfortable on a pew. The hour is late." The priest bowed and left Andy in the chapel.

Well, Andy Sinclair, how do ya get yourself out of this one? Andy stared at the ceiling and walked directly below the apex of the dome where the five Templar crosses were.

Of course 'tis the Cross of Jerusalem. Why didna' I think of it earlier? Where five become one. That means...

Andy looked under his feet and saw the circular pattern that was on the church in Astorga. He had learned from Etienne that the pattern was called the flower of life, and inside it was the tree of life.[15]

This symbol was the key to unlocking the seven doors that bound the Templars' greatest treasure. Only when all seven doors were unbound, and the location of the treasure decoded, was one worthy enough to possess it. At least, that is what Andy had deduced. But, he was open to a shortcut now that it had presented itself.

Could this be the entrance to the ultimate treasure?

Andy's curiosity outweighed his fear—he stood on a pew to see the whole of the image on the floor. From above, he saw where the ten circular objects were hidden among the larger intersecting circles to make the tree of life. Andy remembered the sequence that Charity had used in Astorga to unlock the last door, and he jumped from circle-to-circle, creating the zig-zag pattern.

Andy jumped firmly on the last circle and the ground moved below his feet. He scrambled to the side—grabbing a pew for dear life—as the circles turned into gears, and the ground between them descended into a staircase.

Andy stared down the spiral staircase, which was lit with an eerie green glow. He loosened his grip on the pew, made the sign of the cross, and descended. His whole body was shaking. The last time he'd encountered a set of stairs like this, he was with Etienne. He wished his best friend was with him now.

Andy plucked up his courage and tried to remember everything he had learned about these doors. Etienne had said that with each door there was a trial and a treasure. Andy stopped at the thought of a trial.

Courage, man. You faced your own Shadow. I canna think of anything worse than that. And Charity wasna' so bad. You are still a Knight Templar, Andy Sinclair. You can do this.

Andy reached the bottom level and was met by a large wooden door suspended a few inches in the air. He drew his dagger as the wood inside the door morphed into a face with a slot for a mouth, from which the green light poured.

"Back, back, ya beasty!" Andy yelled, brandishing his dagger. The face and the door remained still, hovering a few inches off the ground. Andy slowly crept closer for an examination. He waved his hands frantically in front of the face, but there was no movement. He walked away and turned quickly, hoping to surprise the face, but the door remained unchanged. Andy walked all the way around the levitating door and saw no room behind it, nor an indication of where the light was coming from.

There was no door handle, nor lock on the door, but that didn't matter—Andy knew how to open it. He had overheard Ronan tell Etienne that all you had to do was draw a backward Z between the eyes of the face with a dab of blood.

"Well then, let's you and I do this," Andy said to the face on the door. He pricked his finger with his dagger and traced a backward Z. The door moaned and opened to a large chamber. In the middle was a lone pedestal with something on it. Andy's hair stood on end as he crept closer. He jumped back as a severed head with leathery skin came into view on the pedestal. A tightness rose in his chest—he didn't know if this was the trial or the treasure.

"You must be Baphomet,"[16] Andy said, approaching cautiously. He had heard of the supposed Templar deity, but now here it was. Andy looked around the room and touched the head with a shaky hand.

CHAPTER 14

Sister Fransie opened her eyes with the sun. The woods, which had been so frightful last night, were now picturesque. "Sister Caroline, wake up. It's morning." Sister Caroline let out a monstrous snore that shook her out of her sleep more than Fransie's words.

"What? What is that? I don't want to go to Mass," Sister Caroline mumbled incoherently.

"Now what?" Sister Fransie asked, as Caroline continued to wake up.

"What?" Sister Caroline said, yawning.

"Now what do we do? Maybe we should wait here for Stefano and the other Italians."

"I am not going to wait around to be saved by a man. Plus, we don't really know if Molay sent them. Maybe the priest was trying to protect us from the Italians by taking us back to Paris." Sister Caroline shot up and marched forward. Fransie followed reluctantly, knowing that Sister Caroline's actions were triggered by fear and not pride.

The sisters wandered around aimlessly for hours. Even though Sister Fransie was accustomed to fasting, she felt the pains of hunger gnawing at her stomach. Overhead a falcon let out a cry and dove into a nearby grove of trees.

"Perhaps it has killed something—I am starving," Sister Caroline said, heading for the grove.

The sisters pushed through the brush and entered a clearing. In the middle was a small feast of rabbit, bread, cheese, and wine. Sister Caroline moved toward it swiftly, but Sister Fransie restrained her.

"Caroline, this could be a trap. We don't know who put that there."

"I did," said a voice unlike any Fransie had heard before.

"Over there." Sister Caroline pointed a trembling finger at a Black man with shocking white hair, and eyes glazed with blindness. On his shoulder sat the falcon they had seen dive.

"Eat, I have been expecting you," the stranger said. Even though he was a Moor, Fransie felt relaxed in his presence, unlike the priest last night—the thought of him still gave Fransie a chill. Her gut had been right about the priest, and she would trust it again.

"How is it that you have been expecting us?" Sister Caroline crossed her arms and squinted her eyes.

"I saw you coming a mile away," replied the stranger with a rolling laugh.

"But, you are clearly blind. How could you?" Sister Caroline asked.

"I will answer all of your questions, but first you must eat. You have had a rough journey, and a long night."

Sister Caroline shot Fransie a concerned look.

"It's all right, Caroline. I don't know why, but I trust him." Fransie placed a tender hand on Caroline's shoulder. She looked back at the stranger. "I don't know how it is possible, but I feel like I have known you my whole life," Sister Fransie said.

"But, he is a Moor," Sister Caroline said, tilting her head down and raising her eyebrows.

"I am neither a Moor, nor a Christian, nor a Jew. I am here and now—that is all."

"Did we die last night?" Sister Fransie asked.

The stranger let out another rolling laugh and said, "My darling, have you ever truly lived? Now, you must eat."

Sister Fransie and Sister Caroline sat by the small meal, and the old man joined them, taking powerful strides. He sat and ate a piece of bread.

"See, there is nothing to fear." He handed both sisters a piece of bread. Fransie was the first to eat. The moment she swallowed, the quiet tremors in her body of both fear and cold were eased.

The stranger poured each a glass of wine. His blind hands filled both glasses to the brim. The falcon perched on his shoulder cocked its head from side to side and ruffled its feathers. Fransie was mesmerized by the majestic creature. She had never seen a bird of prey up close.

"She is a peregrine falcon," the stranger said, answering Fransie's question before she asked it.

"How is it that she is bonded to you?" Sister Fransie turned her head, and the bird mimicked her.

"We have known each other for many years." The stranger fed the falcon a piece of meat. "She serves as my eyes."

"Are you well, Sister Caroline?" Fransie noticed her friend hadn't moved since the old man poured the wine.

"It...It's the color of their blood. I can't..." Sister Caroline murmured with a vacant stare. Fransie put her arms around her friend. "Why, why did they have to die? Why is there war? How could God allow for that?"

"Ha, ha, ha!" The force of the old man's laughter set Sister Fransie back. "Truly there is only one war."

"Have you no compassion? We lost many companions last night," Sister Fransie said.

"Compassion is all that I am," the stranger replied. "I have compassion for every person who suffers from this war."

"And which war is it that you speak of? Who is it that is after us?" Sister Fransie asked.

"It is not who, but what." The old man straightened. "The only war that truly matters is the war inside you. There is a terrible fight going on inside each person between two forces. It started when man ate from the tree of knowledge. One force is what you would call evil—it is anger, envy, sorrow, regret, greed, arrogance, self-pity, guilt, resentment, inferiority, lies, false pride, and superiority. The other is good—it is joy, peace, love, hope, serenity, humility, kindness, benevolence, empathy, generosity, truth, compassion, and faith."

"Which one wins?" asked Sister Fransie.

"The one you believe," replied the old man. "The thoughts you choose to believe empower these forces, or destroys them. I only tell you this because I can see that you have tended to the garden of your soul well, Sister Fransie. I have something to give you." Fransie nodded, and the old man placed his hands over her ears.

"Don't-a move," said someone with a thick Italian accent. Sister Fransie opened her eyes to see Stefano with a knife to the old man's neck.

"I would advise the same thing for you, my friend."

"Why's-a tha—" Metal hit metal, and Stefano's dagger was shot out of his hand by an arrow.

"Because I would kill you before you had the chance to draw my father's blood," said a strong woman with another arrow loaded in her bow. Her bronze skin was stretched tightly over her well-defined body. She looked like Artemis come to life.

Stefano drew his sword and the other Italians emerged from the woods. Sister Fransie's heart leapt with joy—they weren't dead!

"Everyone lower your weapons. We are all friends here," Sister Fransie said, raising her hands.

"But, they are Moors," Stefano spat.

"And Jesus taught us to love our enemies, Stefano. As I said, they are friends." Stefano slowly lowered his sword, and the old man's daughter lowered her bow.

"Now that we are all acquainted, let us dine before our passions consume us." The old man smiled broadly and motioned for Stefano and the others to join. Stefano nodded and they gathered around the food.

"Raphael, that means you as well," the old man said to his daughter. The young woman let out a large sigh and placed her arrow in the quiver.

"Father, I don't like this," Raphael said, eyeing the Italians.

"Well, you better get used to it." The old man let out another thunderous laugh. "You will be leading them through our lands. It is our custom to escort guests to safety." Raphael narrowed her eyes. "It is the way of things." A second falcon screeched in the air above.

Sister Fransie thanked the Lord for delivering the Italians back to her, and a guide. Fransie smiled at Caroline, but her dear friend stared vacantly at the wine in her cup.

CHAPTER 15

Mariano sat in the eucalyptus forest just outside of Santiago de Compostela. He had made camp by a little stream with a wooden bridge the day before. The eucalyptus bark in the fire gave off its sweet aroma as it burned. Mariano laid back, propping himself up on both elbows, watching the serpentine column of smoke rise. He didn't know why he had left Santiago, but he knew he had to. His soul was restless. After tasting the peace he had experienced on the Camino, he felt like he didn't belong in this world.

"Ah, so you have arrived," a familiar voice said.

Mariano scrambled to his feet, leaving trenches in the dirt from his heels. It was the Alchemist,[17] her eyes shining brightly behind her veiled face. The tattoos on her cheeks raised as she smiled. Once again Mariano was captivated by her eyes—they seemed to hold the vastness of the entire desert in them. An energy pulsed through his body. Her teachings had helped them defeat their Shadows the last time they met. Mariano wondered this time what they would lead to.

"I am so happy to see you." Mariano took her hands. "I have lost it. I have lost the peace you gave to me." Noticing his desperation, he released his grip.

"I gave you nothing, and you can never lose anything. All is perfect here in this present moment."

"In Santiago, I felt like I was sinking in quicksand. Everything was pulling me into despair for no reason. I shouldn't have been feeling that way."

"Is it true that you shouldn't have been feeling this way?" the Alchemist asked.

Mariano chuckled and shook his head. "Not this again? I thought we defeated our Shadows. I saw mine disappear."

"It is easier to fight the Shadows you can see than those that are in the recesses of your mind. You must find these hidden Shadows and question them. They are the ones that lead you to the 'quicksand,' as you call it. They call you like a siren until you are drowning, and you never notice they are there. You must investigate these Shadows, these thoughts, and once again, see them for what they truly are. Come with me."

Mariano threw dirt on the small fire and followed the Alchemist through the grove of eucalyptus. He felt like the peeling bark of the tree. He would be exposed once more, stripped of his identity by the Alchemist's teachings. He was ready. He hated who he had become in Santiago. The others didn't understand him leaving, but it was either this trip, or his life. Many nights Mariano thought about suicide. Losing the sense of peace he had experienced was too much to bear, and he didn't know how to get it back. Besides that, he felt utterly alone. He had lost Alba, and now his best friend Gerhart was with Clair all of the time. The others thought he was fine, but as he told the Alchemist, he was drowning.

After some time, they entered a small cave. It was pitch black inside. Mariano kept one hand on the wall for reference and shuffled his feet cautiously.

The Alchemist spoke a word and several logs in the middle of the cave burst into flames. Mariano's eyes adjusted to the light, and from the blackness emerged a giant cavern. The walls stretched high and were dotted with crude paintings of animals. Mariano had heard of such a cave outside of Burgos, but he had never been inside.

"How did you do that?" Mariano asked. After his previous experiences with the Alchemist, he knew anything was possible. But he had to ask all the same.

"The art of Alchemy is turning one substance into another, but I am not here to teach you that. I brought you here to give you what my teacher gave to me. It was this that set me free."

"You had a teacher? I didn't think you were a person. I thought you were... Well, I don't know what I thought you were."

"Are any of us people?" The Alchemist's laugh reverberated off the walls. "My teacher gave me *The Work*,[18] which was four simple questions and a 'turnaround' that set me free. I woke up to the truth of what everything is. I see reality for what it is. I will give this system to you now, Mariano, for your salvation will lead to the salvation of many."

Mariano wasn't sure if he had heard her correctly. He looked at the pictures on the walls, avoiding her bright eyes and the question burning inside him. His shoulders slumped, and his head dropped. He would have to face the Alchemist sometime. He would have to face her last statement.

"How can someone who can't save himself save others?" Mariano brought up his eyes under his heavy brow to meet hers.

"None of us can be saved nor save. Echo!" The Alchemist shouted. Her powerful voice reverberated off the walls and bounced back to them. "The world is just an echo of *you*. It reflects back *you*." The Alchemist let out a hideous shriek. The sound tore through Mariano. He covered his ears. The tone caused a sharp pain in his body. When the sound subsided, he uncovered his ears and shook his head. But the ringing wouldn't stop.

"If you are suffering, the whole world will reflect suffering back to you. If you are at peace..." The Alchemist sang a beautiful song in a tongue Mariano did not know. Mariano savored each sound as it bounced off the walls and faded into oblivion. "...the world will reflect back peace."

"That was the most beautiful thing I have ever heard." Mariano's eyes welled with tears. He felt a heaving joy in his chest.

"The world isn't the problem—your thinking about it is. The world will only change when you change."

"And how do I do that?"

"With these four questions from *The Work:* 'Is it true? Can you absolutely know it's true? How do you react when you think that thought? Who would you be without that thought?' This is the first part of *The Work.* You experienced a taste of this on our first encounter. The second component to make it complete is to turn the thought around to the opposite."

"I remember. The thought that was giving me so much pain was 'Alba shouldn't have died.'"

"Yes, we questioned that thought, and it brought you clarity. Let's do another one. What is the thought that is causing you the most suffering? What is the Shadow that is secretly pulling you into the quicksand?" Mariano dropped his head again. He thought back to his time in Santiago and all of the sleepless nights he had. What thought had been keeping him up?

"I should be at peace."

"Isn't it funny that the Shadow whispers 'I should be at peace,' and it brings you to war with the world? Let us begin. I should be at peace. Is it true?"

"Yes, it's true. Of course I should be at peace. I was at peace before." Mariano was surprised at the anger in his response. The Alchemist smiled at him gently. It wasn't fair. She was at peace.

Nothing phased her. Mariano's fist clenched, and his muscles tightened.

"Can you absolutely know it's true beyond a doubt that you should be at peace?"

Mariano clenched his teeth. He didn't want to admit it, but there was no way he could absolutely know he should or shouldn't be at peace. He shook his head and said, "No. But—"

The Alchemist raised her hand. "It is a simple yes or no question. Anything else comes from the Shadow trying to justify its existence." She looked at Mariano with compassionate eyes. "Let's continue. How do you react when the Shadow whispers 'I should be at peace'?"

"I get angry. My body becomes tight. I feel like a failure. I feel like ending my life so I can be at peace once more. I hate myself for not being at peace."

"It must be very painful for you to believe that Shadow. Who would you be if there was no way possible for you to think 'I should be at peace'?"

The last time the Alchemist had asked this question, somehow she had washed the thought from his mind, but it had returned just as quickly as it had gone. This time, though, he remained conscious of his troubling thought.

"I would be at peace without the thought 'I should be at peace.'" Mariano laughed slightly. "That is really ironic. If I couldn't think that thought, I would have exactly what I am looking for—peace."

"Good, now let us turn it around. What is the opposite of 'I should be at peace'?"

"I shouldn't be at peace." Mariano crinkled his brow. This didn't make any sense. The Alchemist laughed at his expression and it echoed off the walls.

"That's right. You shouldn't be at peace because you aren't. It is when we fight against reality that we suffer. Also, if you were at peace, you wouldn't be sitting here with me. You would be back in

Santiago. That discomfort has led you here to me. It has led you to the next phase of your life.

"I see what you are saying. How could I ever be at peace if I am always thinking I should be? It just causes stress."

"Good. Now, let's go on to the second opposite; 'my thinking.' Or in this case, 'my Shadow.'"

"My thinking should be at peace; my Shadow should be at peace." Mariano smiled broadly. His body relaxed. "That is so true, if my thinking was at peace, I would be at peace."

"Can you think of a good reason to listen to the Shadow that says 'I should be at peace'?"

"I can't. Every time I think of it, I am taken out of the present moment and find only suffering. It is amazing that one thought was causing me so much pain, when I believed it was helping me."

"Excellent, now I want you to say, 'I am excited to not be at peace. I look forward to not being at peace.'"

After repeating back the phrases, Mariano asked, "I don't understand. Why did you just have me say that?"

"Because the next time it comes up, you can do this process again until you accept the reality of the situation and are at peace with it." The Alchemist produced a quill and parchment. "You will stay here until you have questioned every Shadow that has troubled you. Hold them up to the light of questioning, and your freedom will lead to the freedom of many others."

"I will question every negative thought that comes up. I will face every Shadow with inquiry." Mariano held his chest proudly.

"Good, there is one final task for you before I go—clean that spot off the wall."

Mariano walked to the spot she was pointing to. He rubbed it with the corner of his cloak. It didn't come out. He wet the cloak and scrubbed even harder. The edge became frayed, but the spot was still there.

"I can't. It won't clean."

"I said clean the spot!" Mariano's body obeyed her order. His knuckles scraped against the stone and he bled, but he continued to scrub.

"I can't!" A surge of anger rushed through his body. He scrubbed even harder, and his blood joined the smudge on the wall. "Agh!" Mariano picked up a rock and started chipping away at the stone wall, but the stain was still there.

"Clean it."

Mariano turned to throw the rock at the Alchemist, but stopped— in front of the fire was a log casting a shadow on the wall that Mariano had mistaken for a spot. Mariano put his back to the wall and sank to the ground.

"It was just a shadow on the wall, not a spot." The Alchemist nodded and sat with him.

"The wall is like the world, and the spot is all the *problems* it contains. Everyone tries to fix the *problems* by cleaning the wall. They make war with the wall, just as you did. But the truth is it isn't the wall that is the problem, it is your thinking. You must clear the perceived problems from the light of your mind, and the world will soon follow. See the Shadows for what they are. Goodbye, Mariano." The Alchemist walked to the entrance of the cave.

"How will I know when I can leave the cave?"

"You will know." The Alchemist disappeared, and Mariano was left alone with his thoughts.

CHAPTER 16

"Stefano, can I ask you a question?" Fransie quickened her pace to join him at the front of the group. They had left the grove with the old man a few hours before and began their ascent of the Pyrenees to rejoin the Camino at Roncesvalles—a large monastery on the western slope of the mountain range. On the hike, Fransie's breath had been taken away by both the views and the altitude.

"You just did, Sister Fransie."

"This isn't a time for joking; this is serious."

"Laughter is the best cure for seriousness. But of course you can ask me a question—what is it?"

"You said Molay sent you to protect us. Are you Templars?"

"We aren't Templars. You can say we are mercenaries who work for Molay when he doesn't want people to know it is Templar work."

"Why not just become Templars?"

"You have traveled with us for twenty days. You know we aren't Templar material, except Michael, but he made a promise to his mother on her deathbed that he wouldn't join the Templars."

"And you three—surely you fight well enough to become Templars?"

"My brother Luca and I like to be free to do what we want, with who we want, for as long as we want—and Emmanuel—well, let's just say he is Emmanuel. I think he cares more about coaches than people. I mean, look at that contraption he made."

Fransie didn't have to look. She could hear the squeaking wheel of Emmanuel's makeshift cart even though he was bringing up the rear. He had salvaged what he could of the wagons and made a cart of sorts in which he pulled the provisions. It was a lovely device, except for the squeaking.

"Look—there it is." Stefano pointed into the valley. Below, nestled between the trees, was a beautiful building made of white stones and a blue roof.

"That must be Roncesvalles," Luca said, wrapping his arm around Stefano's shoulders.

"Stefano, you found it." Emmanuel left the cart to come look.

Raphael cleared her throat.

"Are you all right?" Stefano turned to face her.

"Thank you for leading us here," Fransie said, bowing slightly to Raphael. "You have performed a great service to God."

"Right, right," Stefano said, taking Luca's arm off his shoulder. "Thank you for leading us. Now you and your bird can go back to where you came from." The falcon overhead dove, narrowly missing Stefano and landing on Raphael's outstretched arm.

"I didn't think you were so perceptive." Raphael fed the falcon a piece of dried meat.

"Well," Stefano puffed out his chest, "the bird appeared when you did and hasn't left us." Fransie had been too busy enjoying the sweeping landscapes to notice.

"Go be my eyes, Hokhmah." The falcon soared from her arm, narrowly missing Stefano once again, and let out a cry as she sped to Roncesvalles. Fransie's heart raced seeing the bird in flight. In the convent she had kept pigeons. She'd had names for each and had loved watching them fly. Fransie smiled back at Raphael and noticed that the tattoo on her shoulder was glowing red and her eyes were glazed.

"Raphael, are you—?" Sister Fransie asked.

Raphael nodded and smiled.

"Enough of these tricks. Let's go." Stefano walked in the direction of the Camino. The falcon screeched in the air.

Raphael cleared her throat again, and Stefano stopped dead in his tracks. He sighed and asked, "What is it?"

"I was ordered to lead you to the edge of our lands in safety. Hokhmah told me there is danger that way." Noticing his suspicious look, she said, "Think of it—if I was going to trap you, I would go to the next town on the Camino and wait until you arrived. I would wait for you to come to me instead of searching for you. If you go that way, you will be caught."

"She does have a point," Fransie said, and Sister Caroline nodded. "We will follow Raphael."

Stefano shook his head and kicked a small stone on the ground. "Since we are bound to protect you two, it seems we have no other choice."

"Good," Luca said, tapping Stefano on the chest. "I think this way is more beautiful." He winked at Raphael.

"That is quite enough, boys." Sister Caroline placed her hands on her hips. "I was glad that you returned to us, now I'm not so sure." Fransie was happy to see Sister Caroline returning to herself. Worrying for her old friend had put a strain on her body.

"This a-way, that a-way, it doesn't-a matter." Emmanuel picked up his squeaky cart and wheeled it to Fransie.

Suddenly, Stefano and Luca drew their swords and Raphael whipped around. Behind her, a horse with a single rider was streaming down the mountain. Fransie had never seen a horse move so quickly. The rider was bareback. Her red hair flowed behind her, interweaving with the horse's mane. Together, they looked like a flame.

Raphael lowered her bow and inhaled deeply. The rider leapt from her horse and ran barefoot to Raphael.

"How could you leave without me?" The rider was smaller than Raphael, but had fire in her emerald eyes.

"Little sister, calm yourself." Raphael said, slinging her bow over her shoulder. "Father asked—"

"I know what he asked, but my question is, why didn't you come to get me?" The horse brayed and stomped its hooves.

"Well, you are here now. But you can go back. I won't be gone for more than a day. I will take these guests to Pamplona and return."

"I'm coming with you!"

"No."

"Yes, and so is Binah." The horse snorted and shook its mane.

"No."

"There is nothing you can do to stop me. We are quicker than you... You will need us."

"Sisters? But, you look nothing alike. We are brothers. I look like Luca and Luca looks like me, but you two..." Stefano raised an eyebrow.

"You don't have to look alike to be family," the rider said with an edge of steel. "Besides, who would want to look like you?"

Raphael smiled at the comment. "Maybe you should join us after all. Auriel, this is Sister Fransie, Sister Caroline, Michael, Emmanuel, Luca, and Stefano." Raphael pointed at Stefano and Luca. "Watch out for those two, and I will let you come."

Sister Fransie and her companions followed a stream from high in the mountains, past Roncesvalles, and deep into the heart of the woods. It seemed Raphael knew every inch of the country as if it were a part of her own body. She belonged to the woods, and they belonged to her.

Fransie knew that sense of belonging. She felt the same way about the woods she had grown up in. She used to spend hours running through the deep forest, climbing the trees, and playing in the streams. She felt closest to God in nature. It was there, in those deep woods, that she had met the Virgin Mary.

Fransie remembered it like yesterday; it was just after her tenth birthday. She could still feel the moss under her as she lay on the big rock—her special rock. A light had shone brighter than anything she had ever seen. It was almost as if the sun had left the sky and had taken up residence below the trees. Fransie had had to shield her eyes, and as the glow had diminished, she'd seen a beautiful woman dressed in a blue robe with golden stars on it.

"Who are you?" Fransie had asked.

"Fransie, I am the Mother of the Word, the Immaculate Conception."

Fransie remembered being puzzled at the words. She hadn't had a religious upbringing. She had only stepped foot into a church twice in her life before then. She'd had no idea the beautiful woman was the Virgin Mary.

"Fransie, I will teach you to pray the rosary. I want you to pray it every day of your life—especially when you are afraid—and I will be with you. In the future you will become a nun. It is very important that you follow my directions. Can you do this?"

Fransie had nodded, and the Virgin Mary had given her a rosary. Since that day, Fransie had kept it on her at all times. The beads were smooth and almost chalky at the time. Now though, the oils from her hands had eliminated the chalkiness. Each small bead was pink, and they smelled of roses. Even after fifteen years, the rosary still smelled just as fresh as it had the day she had received it.

Fransie fondled one of the beads between her fingers and smiled gently at the memory. That single moment was why she had become a nun, why she had dedicated her life to the service of God. Sister Fransie supposed the stones she gave to the pilgrims in Santa Anna was her way of giving what the Virgin had given to her.

"I am the Phantom of the Camino!" Emmanuel shouted, jumping from behind a bush with a cloak over his head. Sister Fransie put both hands to her heart and breathed heavily.

"Why would you do that?" Fransie asked, still clutching her chest.

"I kid, I kid," Emmanuel said.

"Don't mind him," Michael said. "He always likes to joke around. We have almost been fired once or twice for it."

"Would you be quiet? We are approaching Zubiri," Raphael placed a finger to her lips and looked at Emmanuel sternly. She motioned for everyone to join her. Fransie stood beside Raphael and saw the little stream they had followed fed into a much wider river. The river ran swiftly to a bridge and a little town.

Stefano tapped Luca on the chest. "Look." He pointed to several young ladies splashing in the river. "You know, my feet hurt from all of this walking. I think we should go soak them down there."

"I think that is a good idea, brother." Luca raised an eyebrow and nodded his head.

"Oh, heavens me. Is that all you boys think about?" Sister Caroline asked, fanning herself. "Although resting our feet in the water does sound nice. Raphael, do you think we would be safe to do that?"

"I think we are past the danger, but I will go check it out—" Before Raphael finished her sentence, Auriel took off down the hill.

"I have this one, sis," Auriel said in the wind, once again looking like a flame zig-zagging full speed down the hill. It wasn't long before she reached the other ladies. They exchanged a few words and started splashing each other. Auriel flashed a large grin to her hidden companions.

"I think we will be fine," Raphael said. She looked sternly at Stefano and Luca. "It is the town's women I am worried about."

The water felt cool and refreshing on Fransie's feet. It was so cold it almost hurt, but it brought relief to her swollen feet and respite from the scorching sun. Caroline precariously walked over to Fransie, holding her habit up to just below the knees.

"My, this is refreshing." Caroline stumbled, and Fransie caught her arm.

"And entertaining," Raphael said, nodding to Stefano, Luca, and Emmanuel, who were chatting with the local girls, each trying to show off by outdoing the others and failing miserably. "What is wrong with these men?"

"Raphael, how far will you accompany us?" Fransie asked, changing the subject.

"I will take you just past Pamplona. After this, my service is done, and we can return home." Hokhmah let out a cry from above and dove into the trees. "Ah, we have dinner." Raphael sprinted out of the water, chasing the falcon. Moments later, she reemerged with two dead rabbits.

Fransie felt a slight ringing in her ears. She shook her head, but the ringing continued faintly.

Sister Caroline placed a hand on her shoulder. "Are you well, Fransie?"

"Yes, it's nothing."

"Dinner!" Raphael shouted at the Italians.

"I have a proposition," Stefano said, wading in the water to them. "The mothers of the beautiful young maidens over there have invited us to stay in the town for the festival tonight. There will be singing, dancing, and lots of food." Stefano eyed the dead rabbits in Raphael's hands.

"Suit yourself," Raphael said. "Auriel and I will stay in the woods tonight. You can do as you like."

"But..." Auriel protested. Raphael took Auriel by the arm and the two of them headed to the thick trees.

Stefano nodded to Fransie and Caroline. "Will you join us, or sleep in the woods?"

"Oh my word, I do love a good festival," Sister Caroline said. "Which saint are we celebrating?"

"Does it matter?" Stefano asked.

As day turned to night, the town square filled with people dressed in their finest clothes. On the side closest to the bridge, a wooden stage was erected and a band played merrily. Sister Fransie loved all of the decorations strung from building to building, and the dances the locals were doing were electrifying.

Sister Caroline locked arms with Fransie and they spun along with the others. Fransie found herself weaving from partner to partner, using one hand to keep her habit slightly raised. Fransie loved dancing. She felt it was one of the truest expressions a person could have. She hooked arms with Stefano and they twirled about. They locked hands with Luca and one of the maidens from the river, and they moved toward each other then back out again.

Sister Fransie turned to the stage and saw that Sister Caroline had somehow managed to find her way onto it. Fransie wondered what on earth she was doing up there. Sister Caroline said a few words to the drummer. He smiled and gave her the drumsticks one at a time as he kept the beat. Sister Caroline sat and nodded at Fransie as she picked up the tempo.

The townsfolk whirled and twirled faster and faster as Sister Caroline increased the speed. The world became a merry-go-round of colors and laughter. Fransie danced with person after person, everything a glorious blur. She didn't know how much faster she could go. Finally, Sister Caroline flipped a drumstick in the air and hit the last beat, and the crowd erupted in applause.

"Come," Stefano said, wrapping his arm around Fransie's shoulder. He led her to a table with the two maidens from the river and their mothers.

"See, I told you we were good Catholic boys. We even bring our own nuns," Stefano said, seating Fransie at the table.

"Sister," said all the women at the table.

"I brought one too," Luca said as he ushered Sister Caroline to the table as well.

"Where are Michael and Emmanuel?" Fransie asked.

"They are getting drinks." Stefano pointed at an outside bar. "Sisters, this is Maria, Theresa, Mary, and Elizabeth."

"My Maria is beautiful, no?" Theresa said, bursting with pride. "The most beautiful *señorita* in town."

"Mama," Maria said, feigning modesty.

"My Elizabeth is beautiful too," Mary said, straightening in her chair. Fransie noticed both Stefano and Luca were transfixed on Maria. She stroked her raven black hair as she looked at her reflection in her cup. She twirled her hair slightly on her finger and smiled at Stefano. Elizabeth's expression soured for a moment then returned to normal.

"There are more important things than looks," Sister Caroline said. She crossed her arms and sat back in the chair.

"Yes, yes. Both are beautiful. Too beautiful for this world," Stefano said. He continued to speak, but the ringing had returned to Fransie's ears. It was hard for her to make out the words he was saying.

Fransie shook her head, but the ringing continued. This time, though, it wasn't just one awful pitch, but several. The band started to play again, and Sister Fransie's heart raced, panic spreading through her body. The ringing got louder and louder—it was unbearable. She stood abruptly from the table and covered her ears. She bit down hard, but the ringing continued. Sister Fransie couldn't take the pain, and her body gave out.

CHAPTER 17

*I*sabella's dress swooshed as she walked to answer the firm knock on her door. *All dressed up and nowhere to go.* Matilda and her maids would come to dress Isabella in the mornings and then would leave her to sit in this room like a trapped bird.

"Gaston, thank God it's you." Isabella threw her arms around the captain's brawny neck.

"Petite Fleur," his voice grumbled. "The Camino has definitely changed you. I can only remember you hugging me twice since you became an adult. Once when you returned, and now." He was right. Isabella would have never shown a sign of affection like that before the Camino, but her companions had changed her.

"It did." She ushered him in and closed the door. "Any news from Sister Fransie and Sister Caroline? It has been over three weeks, and they haven't returned. Are they…" Isabella put her hands to her mouth.

"You can relax." Gaston sat in an ornately decorated wooden chair. "My sources tell me Jaques de Molay sent them back to the Camino."

"They're going back?" Isabella perched on the window ledge, wishing it was her returning instead of them.

"Yes, it was of great urgency that they deliver something to Etienne."

"What was it? Why them?"

"That, no one knows." Gaston paused and placed his forearms on his knees. "I do have some good news though—your father has given you permission to leave the tower under my supervision. Where would you like to go first?"

"That's wonderful news. Let's start in the rose garden."

Isabella and Gaston spent hours walking around the grounds. As they toured, she felt like a woman looking back on a young girl's life. She was not the same person she had been the last time she had stepped into the gardens.

"I have one final place to take you," Gaston said, as the day waned. He led her to the doors of the dungeon.

"Has my father changed my accommodations?" Isabella raised questioning eyebrows. She trusted Gaston and knew he wouldn't trick her like this, but she also knew her father.

"No." Gaston shook his head. "I want you to meet another prisoner." Isabella had never been in the dungeons before. Her father had said it was no place for a princess. That never stopped her from trying to get in when she was younger. Once, a young guard had let her see a man on the rack through a window. After that, Isabella never ventured to the dungeons again.

Isabella covered her nose. The dungeon smelt of putrefied flesh and feces. "Good Lord, Gaston. Is this how we keep the prisoners?"

"It is so, Your Highness." Isabella felt guilty as she saw the prisoners shackled to the wall. She kept her focus forward. She didn't want to see their suffering. Isabella wondered who Gaston wanted her to meet.

Gaston led her away from the main cells to an isolated door at the far end of the dungeon. The door was curved at the top and there was an iron slat that opened. Isabella supposed it was to give food to the dangerous criminal on the other side.

"Gaston, is this safe?"

"Absolutely." He placed a reassuring hand on Isabella's shoulder and opened the slot in the door so she could see for herself.

"Isabella, I would like for you to meet one of our longest term prisoners, Fatima."

Isabella braced herself on a wall. The woman in the cell had Etienne's eyes. Or was it that Etienne had her eyes? Isabella gasped and shook her head.

"My God, is she—"

"Etienne's mother." Gaston closed the slot and pulled out a large iron key ring. Isabella stopped his hand.

"Gaston, I can't. Not yet." Isabella wasn't ready to meet Etienne's mother—not like this. She wanted time to prepare.

CHAPTER 18

Etienne had enjoyed traveling with the Knights of Saint James. They didn't possess the humility of the Templars, but they did have the brotherhood. It felt good to be back among the ranks—to have a place and a purpose. Etienne had always been a part of an organization larger than himself, until he left it all for Isabella. He pulled up some grass and balled it in his fists.

"Etienne, come join us by the fire," Joseph said. He and James were the only other knights still awake. Etienne threw the grass and joined them. The warmth of the fire felt nice on his face. "So, tell us about this woman that was worth abandoning the Templars for?"

Isabella was the last thing Etienne wanted to talk about. He had tried so hard to forget her and reclaim his life. He had done it once before, and he would do it again. This time it felt different, though. This time they had entered into matrimony and shared a promise with their bodies.

Sensing his hesitation, the grand master said, "I have a wife. Her name is Mandy."

"And two fine young lads," interrupted James. The grand master's eyes lit up and his face became kind.

"Yes, and two boys, Sean and Maximus. I would do anything to provide for them and protect them. They are my life. They are actually why I joined the Knights of Saint James. I wanted to make these lands safe for them. I want my boys to grow up without fear."

"And what about you?" Etienne asked James.

"No, I'm a free agent. I like to keep my options open." James placed his hands behind his head.

"That's not necessarily true, James. He has his heart set on a widow and has been very kind to her children. They love him like a father, but she won't have him—not until he changes his lifestyle. I have given him my blessing to marry her and leave our order."

Etienne was shocked. A Templar master would never utter the words he just heard.

"But, I have refused," James admitted.

"Why?"

"My brothers—you have met them." James laughed heartily. "I need to make sure they stay alive. I promised my mother I would watch out for them."

"They are grown men now, James. You deserve a bit of happiness yourself. Plus, if you don't hurry, she will wed that wealthy merchant."

"I hate that guy." James made two fists, shaking them vigorously. "God told me she is the one for me, and I trust Him. It is on His time, not mine."

"So let it be," said the grand master. "Now that we have divulged our life stories, who is your fair maiden?"

"Her name is Isabella." The corners of Etienne's lips reflexively raised. "I grew up in her father's house, and we loved each other from a young age. We both were different from the others, and this brought us together. When her father found out about our love, I was banished and became a Templar. I never expected to see her again, but we were reunited on the Camino." Etienne felt all of his features soften. "We were wed in secret and were going to run away together, but God had other plans."

"I'm sorry, brother." Joseph put his hand on Etienne's shoulder. "I hope you meet in this life once again. What was she like?"

"She was the type of woman who would lead you to a cliff, show you the beauty of the world, then push you over the edge, only to show you that you can fly and achieve great things."

"She sounds like the type of woman who could launch a thousand ships, as the saying goes."

Etienne laughed. She was definitely the type of woman that nations would go to war over. The grand master didn't know the truth that was in his words.

A rumbling came from the bushes. Etienne drew his sword as James' brother Gino burst through the leaves. He was panting and bent down, placing his hands on his knees.

"What news, Gino?" the grand master demanded.

Gino raised a finger from his bent down position and continued to pant. He straightened. "They are close." He took a few breaths. "At least five hundred of them."

This meant that they were vastly outnumbered. Etienne would have taken these odds with the Templars, but he didn't know how well the Knights of Saint James fought. From his experience, not that well.

"Five hundred?" The grand master stood abruptly. "We weren't expecting that many. We were told— Who is organizing them?"

"Muhamad III[19] is with them," Gino replied.

"The Sultan of Granada? If we kill him, the last Moorish kingdom in Spain will fall. The Moors will be defeated. We must take this chance, but I fear it will come at a great loss."

"Unless someone was to get close enough to kill just him. If you cut off a snake's head, the rest of the body will soon die," Gino said.

"We would never make it into the camp undetected," the grand master said.

"We wouldn't be able to, but he might." Gino pointed a finger at Etienne. "He is dark-skinned, just like them."

"I can't allow him to take that risk alone. We must all fight."

"Sir, have you made peace with your family?" James asked.

"I have, and they know the nature of my work." The grand master put a hand on James's shoulder. "James, look after them if I should fall in the battle tonight. For we must strike when it is dark, and we have the element of surprise."

"I would be honored to, my old friend."

"I will do it," Etienne said, and all eyes turned to him. He was already dead inside. If his body followed, it would be no great loss. These men had families and loves. All Etienne had was the memory of Isabella.

"I couldn't ask you to. The responsibility isn't yours."

"I have infiltrated a Moorish camp before. I can do it again. I will just need a soldier's uniform."

"I left a scout dead just outside of their camp. No one will notice he is gone until after the third watch has finished." Gino rubbed his hands as he spoke.

"Take me there," Etienne said.

Gino led Etienne to the scout he had killed, and Etienne quickly changed.

Gino shook his head. "You look just like one of them. Don't let us down." Something about Gino's comment made Etienne feel unsettled rather than supported. He watched Gino disappear into the woods. Once he was out of sight, Etienne gathered some firewood and walked straight into the camp.

The one thing that had made Etienne conspicuous his whole life now made him invisible in the enemy's camp. He never *felt* different from others, but their reactions to him always reassured him of the fact that he was.

In Santiago, shopkeepers looked at him like a criminal. They had him followed around the stores—convicting him before a crime was ever committed. At the pubs, the bartenders would always warn him not to make any trouble. He had tried to convince himself that this behavior was normal. He tried to shrug it off and ignore it, but he couldn't. Maybe that's why he hated living in Santiago.

Etienne pondered defecting with the army of Moors to the south. He would never be looked at as different. He would be treated as an equal. He nodded to two soldiers as he passed. Why was he doing this? It wasn't for the love of his countrymen. It wasn't because he believed in expelling the Moors from Spain. For him, this would be a senseless killing. The automatic response of a soldier following orders. But he wasn't a soldier any longer, and he didn't need to follow orders.

If he failed and didn't return, Etienne bet the Knights of Saint James would retreat instead of fight. The grand master talked as if he were willing to fight no matter what, but Etienne's gut told him otherwise.

"As-Salamu Alaykum," a soldier said as he passed.

"Wa-Alaykum Salamu," Etienne responded. *Peace be unto you, And unto you peace.* Could a culture that greeted each other in this way be so terrible? Did these soldiers not have families, just as the Knights of Saint James? What made them any different? Everyone was just trying to provide for and protect their loved ones.

Etienne decided he would go through with the action, not for the Knights of Saint James, but for the soldiers on both sides. He would take a life, and sacrifice his own, so both armies could go home to their families.

Etienne approached a regal tent that had two guards posted at the entrance. *This must be the place.*

The grandeur of the tent was almost obscene. It looked as if the whole tent was made of red silk and pure golden threads. Etienne went to the rear of the tent and placed the firewood on the ground. He knew there was no way he was getting in through the front entrance. He pulled his dagger and slid it through the red silk to make a slit, feeling like he was destroying a beautiful piece of art.

The tent was lit by several hanging oil lamps, and there were furs covering the ground. Exotic fruit was on the table, and a cluster of grapes was dangling off the edge.

A ferocious snore startled Etienne. In the bed, the sultan lay on his back with his mouth open. He stopped breathing for a second, then let out another animalistic snore. He turned on his side facing away from Etienne and continued to slumber.

Etienne crept to his bedside and positioned his dagger to strike. He didn't like the idea of killing someone in their sleep, but his death would prevent the deaths of many.

A strong hand covered Etienne's mouth, and a blade pushed against his throat.

"Step back," a voice said in the common tongue. Held tightly by his captor, both men stepped away from the bed.

"I knew they would send someone to attempt this, but I never imagined it would be you, nephew."

The hand dropped away from Etienne's mouth, but the blade remained at his throat. His captor moved from behind Etienne, and Etienne saw with his own eyes that it was true—it was Nazir, his uncle. The last time they had met, Nazir was pursuing Isabella and had nearly killed him.

"This is very interesting." With that, Nazir struck Etienne between the eyes and the world went dark.

CHAPTER 19

"You must let me inspect your ears," Sister Caroline said, pulling at Fransie's veil. Sister Fransie's consciousness slowly came back to her. The sun was shining, and it was well into the morning. Her eyes stung from the light streaming in through the window. She blinked and tried to focus on the wooden beams on the ceiling.

"Where are we? What happened?"

"We are in the albergue, and you had an episode last night. You covered your ears and passed out. It reminded me of when one of the saints was tormented by demons. That's why I need to look at your ears. I need to make sure no little demon has taken up residence in the head I love so much."

Fransie pushed up onto her elbows. Besides a little disorientation, she felt fine. She sat up all the way and pulled back the veil of her habit, exposing her ears. Sister Caroline leaned in for a closer inspection. Caroline was the best healer that Fransie had ever met. She had a gift for the art. Fransie believed that it was because of this that Caroline was asked to leave the Convent of Santa Ana, not for the accusation of immorality. The local priest had been jealous of her abilities.

"Mmm, nothing in this ear." Fransie turned her head. "Sister Fransie, when did you get a tattoo?"

"What do you mean? I don't have a tattoo." Fransie's heart raced. It was a sin to have a tattoo. At least, that is what she had been told. It was impossible.

Sister Caroline held up a mirror, and just below Fransie's left ear was a tattoo shaped like an hourglass. She immediately recognized the shape—it was the same one that Raphael had on her shoulder.

"What is this witchcraft, Fransie? Surely the devil is after you!"

Fransie clutched her rosary and silently recited the Lord's Prayer.

"Do you feel well enough to walk? We must leave this wicked town before the demon strikes again."

Fransie nodded and the two nuns gathered their meager belongings.

As they walked the Camino, the sun beat down and the smell of the earthen forest rose. Fransie continuously rubbed the spot where the tattoo was. She wanted to erase the blemish. Plucking up her courage, she quickened her pace to walk in stride with Raphael.

"Good morning." Fransie wanted to ease into the conversation. She couldn't just come out and ask about a tattoo that could possibly be the mark of the devil.

"Good morning." Raphael looked her up and down. "The others told me what happened to you. These Italians gossip more than nursemaids." Fransie smiled timidly, and Raphael smiled back and continued. "Passing out is nothing to be ashamed of."

"Binah says you can ride on her if you need to," interjected Auriel, who jumped off the horse and hurried her pace to join them.

"I thought you said she was a free horse?"

"She is. She is free to choose who rides on her and who doesn't." Auriel nuzzled her face on the horse's snout.

"Why did you two sleep in the woods last night?"

"There were too many people," Raphael said, scanning the trees ahead.

"Yes, there were lots of people, but that is no reason for you to sleep in the woods. The evening was amazing until…"

"For us, there are too many without Binah, and Hokhmah." The horse snorted and shook its mane.

"You are so strong. Surely you don't need these animals as your security blankets?"

Raphael shot Fransie a half smile and raised an eyebrow. "Security blankets, no. They are our filters."

Fransie's brow furrowed.

"I know you don't understand—not yet anyway. I also know you came to ask me about the tattoo on my shoulder." Raphael's words stopped Fransie dead in her tracks.

"I have one too," Auriel said, raising her shirt to show the same tattoo just below her belly button.

"It means you have been touched by God and given a great gift."

"It is a gift that can kill you," Auriel interrupted. Raphael shot her a stern look.

"Our father has this gift too," Raphael continued. "And it did almost kill him, but he taught us how to use it."

"Use what?" Fransie asked, quickening her pace.

"We have been given the ability to sense as God does. My father and I have true sight and—"

"And I have true feeling." Auriel spread her arms wide as if she was presenting something.

"Feeling…like emotions?" Fransie asked.

"No, touch." Auriel stroked her horse.

"Are you sure it isn't the mark of the devil?" Fransie asked, remembering the excruciating pain she was in the evening before.

Raphael and Auriel smiled at each other. "Everything comes from God," Raphael said. "Sensing as God does is too much for a person to bear on their own. That is why you need a filter." Hokhmah screeched through the trees and landed on Raphael's shoulder. Her talons gripped just above the tattoo. "I was given true sight, as was my father. We see as God sees, but without a filter it will make one go blind."

"Just like your father is?" Fransie asked.

"Yes, the true sight was too much for him. He would have died had Keter not come to him." Fransie eyed the bird on Raphael's shoulder. "Keter is the name of our Father's falcon. Its eyes are our father's eyes. Just as Hokhmah's are mine. She not only filters the true sight, but she allows me to see as she does."

"Do you also have true sight?" Fransie asked Auriel.

"No, just true feeling." Auriel said, casually. "Binah is my filter. I can feel an earthquake a thousand miles away and sense any danger before it comes too close."

"What I heard last night didn't sound like God," Fransie said, remembering the pain.

"It wasn't. You heard the devil last night. Explain to me what happened right before this occurred." The falcon sprung from Raphael's shoulder.

"I was sitting at a table with Stefano, Luca, and a few locals when I first heard the tones." Raphael nodded her head and smiled. "What?" Fransie paused to ask.

"The devil pulls hard on those two, but in different shades."

"Shades?"

"Yes, you have true sound, so you hear different tones. For me, I see different shades. Before Hokhmah, I saw shades so terrible it made me want to tear my eyes out. I also saw shades so sublime I wanted to leave this world. Hokhmah filters both so I can see the shades but to a muted degree."

"For me I felt things, but not in the normal way. I experienced them to such a degree that it felt like my insides would tear out, or something so amazing it cannot be described. Each one affected me in a different way."

"I heard four different tones last night. Each was like a different note, off key and terrible. It started when Stefano and

Luca were looking lustfully at the two maidens. They weren't the same tones, though."

"No, because one was lust and the other gluttony. I have seen those shades many times around those two. That is the frequency the devil uses to tempt them." Raphael read Fransie's confused look and continued. "Since you have true sound, I will explain it in those terms. Imagine that the devil has a large pipe-organ and that each note is a sin: gluttony, pride, lust, envy, sloth, vengeance, greed, etc. He is always playing this organ, looking for a sympathetic ear for his music. When he finds a soul who resonates with a certain note, he plays it again and again until that person is controlled by it. You heard the notes of lust and gluttony."

"Gluttony?" Fransie asked, raising her eyebrows.

"Yes, one of them doesn't lust after women, he just wants to have as many as possible." Fransie nodded her head.

"This explains so much. When the beautiful young woman was looking at her reflection, I heard the third tone. This must have been vanity, which is an offshoot of pride, and the fourth was envy, I could see that emotion in the other woman's eyes."

"That is why we stayed in the forest," Auriel said. "There were too many people. We couldn't keep our animals close enough to filter the pull of the devil. As time progresses, you will sense more and more. Your true hearing will only grow from here."

"I don't think I would be able to survive another episode like that. How did you choose your animals?"

"They chose us," Auriel said. She jumped onto Binah's back and they sped ahead.

"Let's hope your animal finds you soon. Had Keter not found my father, the true sight would have burned out more than his eyes."

CHAPTER 20

Andy's eyes shot open. He was in his bed, and the light was streaming in through the window. It was well past noon.

"Ach, 'twas just a dream." Andy lay back down and turned onto his side.

"Noo!" Andy shouted as he tumbled out of bed. The severed head was staring at him from his pillow. Andy cautiously crawled back to the bed and looked eye to eye with the head.

The door flew open. "Andrew Sinclair. What in God's name is 'appening!" Before Clair saw the head, Andy threw his covers over it.

"Clair, 'tis nothin, just a bad dream." Andy picked himself up and joined her at the door. "What time is it?"

"'Tis just past noon. But everyone's just getting up. We had a new arrival last night."

"It wasn't the Templars, was it?"

"Na, just a lady named Acedia. She looks ta be a sickly thing, but who am I ta talk?"

"I'll just get dressed then and come join ya for the day's work."

"Actually, I think everyone is gonna take the day off. Ya ken we 'ave been working so 'ard."

"Will Chelsea be fine with that?"

"She was the one who recommended it last night shortly after our guest arrived." Clair leaned lazily on the door frame.

"But there is so much ta do."

"Ya can go off ta work if ya like, but we will all take the day off. I'll be in bed." Clair closed the door.

What is going on? Andy had never known Clair to act like this. Even as a child, she never took a day off to rest. Andy looked back to the lump on his bed. Since the head was here, that meant it wasn't a dream. Andy was in the trial. He pulled back the covers, revealing the gruesome severed head.

"Right then, if you are supposed to represent wisdom, what is this trial, and how do I overcome it?" Andy couldn't believe he was talking to a severed head, but he had experienced stranger things on the Camino de Santiago. He stared at the head, waiting for a response. Andy didn't know what to do, but this felt like the right action.

If I am not for myself, who is for me? And being for my own self, what am 'I'? And if not now, when? This quote from Hillel the Elder, a rabbi who lived before Christ, kept repeating itself in Andy's head. He couldn't remember when he had learned about Hillel, nor when he had first heard the quote, but now here it was. This happened to Andy often. Thoughts worked like worms in his mind and would dig until a solution appeared.

Feeling ridiculous that he was expecting an answer from a severed head, Andy covered it back up and walked downstairs for breakfast.

Sitting at the table was a woman with jaundiced skin and a sallow face. It seemed that her skin was barely hanging onto her bones. The woman had mousey brown hair that was unkempt and greasy.

"Good morning," Andy said cheerfully. The woman turned her beady eyes to him.

"What is good about it? The sun was too bright in my room this morning and the birds were too loud."

"Right... You must be Acedia, I'm Andy. Nice ta meet ya." Andy feigned politeness, but he didn't like looking at her. Those beady eyes were too close together; something about her just wasn't right.

"If you say so. Will you hand me that jug of water?" Acedia lazily motioned with her head to the counter. Andy couldn't believe the pile of dishes and food left over from the night before.

"Why didna' they do the dishes last night? And where is everyone else?"

"It was late. They were too tired to do the dishes. They didn't need to be done." Andy took the jug of water from the counter and brought it to the table. "Sit with me—you must be tired from standing." As Acedia spoke these words, it looked like a fine mist was coming from her mouth. Andy backed away from the table quickly.

"Na, I will start on these dishes."

"They aren't yours to do. Why waste the effort?" The fine mist from her words continued in his direction.

"If not me, then who? If not now, then when?" Andy said reflexively. He turned from Acedia and began to wash the dishes.

"The water is too cold to wash the dishes. Just let them be until later." Acedia's whisper came across the room and straight to his ear.

"If not now, then when," Andy repeated, scrubbing as hard as he could.

"Your loss. I will go join the others." With that, Acedia lurched away from the table. As she left the room, it was as if a cloud had passed.

Andy's blood ran cold. *The others.* What terror had he brought upon this house? How was he going to save those he loved?

CHAPTER 21

Approaching Pamplona felt like approaching an ancient Roman coliseum. From a distance, Fransie saw throngs of people streaming into the city, all dressed in white with red sashes.

"What is happening here today?" Sister Caroline asked as she motioned to the crowd.

"The running of the bulls," Stefano said. He looked as excited as a child at Christmas. "The villagers in Zubiri told me all about it. They release the bulls in the city, and you run in front of them. It's very dangerous. We're all going to do it." With his words, Stefano nodded at Luca, Emmanuel, and Michael. "You are welcome to join."

"You aren't going to do this as well, Michael? I thought you had more sense than the others," Sister Caroline said, hands resting on her hips.

"He is not a man if he doesn't do it," Stefano said, tapping him in the stomach. "This is a once in a lifetime opportunity. You can come watch and wave as we go by."

"No, thank you. We will stay here and pray for your safety," Sister Fransie said. She didn't understand why they were taking this unnecessary risk.

"If I die, will you look after my cart?" Emmanuel asked.

He was answered by a punch in the arm and a stern look from Raphael.

"What? I kid, I kid." Emmanuel rubbed his bicep.

"Come on, boys." Stefano wrapped his arms around Luca and Emmanuel. Michael followed reluctantly behind and looked back wistfully at the sisters.

Sister Fransie prayed silently with Sister Caroline for the safety of their companions as they sat by the pastures. She was happy to stay outside the city and not explain to the others why. She couldn't take another attack like the one she had in Zubiri. She wished her animal would choose her soon, so she could filter out the true sound.

Sister Fransie walked to a corral that had several cows grazing and one very large bull. Auriel came to her side, and Binah nuzzled into her.

"I can't believe the way they are going to treat these animals. What harm did they ever do to anyone?" Auriel said.

Fransie rested her head and arms on the fence and gazed ahead. She turned her head and the bull turned his head. Fransie turned her head the other way and the bull mimicked her again.

"Did you see that, Auriel? Do you think he is my animal?"

"I did see! Try something else." Fransie raised her head, and the bull raised his head.

"Bulls do have good hearing." Auriel encouraged Fransie to continue.

Fransie lowered her head and the bull did the same. Their eyes locked, and the bull brushed its hooves while snorting.

"Auriel, I don't think—" The bull lurched forward, and charged full speed at them.

"Run!" Auriel yelled. "Run!"

Fransie lifted her habit and ran as fast as she could. She heard a terrible crash and stole a glance behind, seeing a gaping hole in the fence and the bull still thundering after her.

"Fransie!" Auriel rode up on Binah's back and extended a hand to Fransie, lifting her onto the horse's back with ease. The two of them rode quickly, but two thousand pounds of pure muscle was chasing right behind them, and Binah was carrying two people.

"Oh, my Lord Jesus, protect us," Fransie said, gripping Auriel tightly.

"Sister Fransie!" She heard Sister Caroline calling in the distance.

Binah headed straight for a large stone ramp leading into the city. The crowd screamed and parted as Binah cut through them. The streets were blocked off with wooden planks and Binah only had one way to go—straight ahead. The crowd cheered as they passed and others ran alongside them.

"Stefano!" Fransie cried, catching sight of him. "Help!"

"Hey, hey! Over here!" Stefano shouted, waving his arms and a red sash. The bull took notice and looked between him and Fransie, who was galloping away. Stefano threw a rock, hitting the bull in the ear. The beast stomped the ground hard and ran full speed at him. Stefano hid behind a column and the bull chased him around it, nearly goring him.

"Hey!" Luca shouted, getting the bull's attention. The bull turned his sights on him and Luca slid between a narrow gap in a boarded fence, narrowly missing a horn as the bull slammed into the wood.

The bull shook its head and rammed the wood again. It then caught sight of Fransie and Auriel once more. They had reached the end of the run, but the gates to the bull arena hadn't been opened yet. They were trapped. The crowd hooted and hollered, but there was no escape.

Hokhmah screeched out of the sky and dove at the bull's head, pulling at one of the bull's eyes. The beast quivered in pain but continued its charge. Raphael jumped from a roof landing between Fransie and the bull.

Raphael charged and grabbed the beast's horns as it thrust its head upward, catapulting Raphael into the air. Mid-flight, she did a graceful turn and loaded her bow. She loosed an arrow and shot the bull through the back of the neck. Raphael landed, and the bull skidded to the ground, stopping a few feet away from Fransie.

The crowd erupted in applause, but Raphael shook her head. She walked to the beast and pulled her arrow from its neck. She stroked him as he took his last breath and said, "I am sorry, my friend."

"That was amazing!" Stefano shouted as he ran to Raphael. More people crowded around the bull, and Fransie heard a slight ringing. This time, though, the ringing was in tune, and the different pitches harmonized. She dismounted Binah and wanted to celebrate with the others who gathered around Raphael, but she was pulled in the opposite direction by the music. Her feet wouldn't obey her. The music lured her away from the crowd and down a lonely street.

CHAPTER 22

Andy spent the day doing all the chores he could outside the house. There was no way he could keep this up for long. In a matter of days, the weeds would overtake the crops and destroy the harvest. He needed to figure out how to save his friends, quickly.

Why had I been saved by saying 'If not me then who? If not now, when? And what was that fine mist coming out of Acedia's mouth?

Andy didn't dare go back in the house yet. He wasn't ready to face Acedia until he figured it out. That saying had acted like a shield, and the moment he started working, Acedia had left. Was it his words or actions that saved him?

Guilt weighed heavily on Andy. He was directly responsible for what had happened to Gerhart, Clair, and Chelsea. He hoped Mariano had left like he said he would. How many days ago was that?

The sun beat down, and Andy needed to take a rest. He had been working nonstop. He was too afraid to stop. He cautiously walked to the house and peered through the kitchen window.

"Thank the Lord, 'tis empty." Andy entered and poured himself a large glass of water. He sat at the table and wiped his brow.

"Now are you ready to stop this foolish work? Why bother doing it? Just sit." Acedia's words entered his unsuspecting ears.

"It does feel good ta sit. And the sun is hot," Andy parroted back unwittingly.

"Yes, the sun is hot. It's too hot to work today. Join the others. Why should you have to do all the work?" Andy was paralyzed to the spot. His arms and legs were heavy. It felt as if manacles were binding him to the table. "That's it, just rest a while."

"Aye, why do I need ta work anyway? 'Tis not important." Andy placed his head on the table, shifting its weight and spilling his water on him. "Ach, no! I am the one that has ta do the work—now!" Andy struggled his way out of the kitchen before Acedia could say another word.

Andy found refuge under the shade of the only tree in the fields. He absentmindedly combed Blueberry, the mule who had joined him.

Acedia had almost trapped him—he needed to figure out who and what she was. Obviously she was the trial of this door, but what were these trials all about? There was Charity, and the Shadows, now Acedia. What do they all have in common?

"What do ya think, Blueberry?" The mule just twitched its ears back and forth.

"Charity didna seem like much of a challenge, all we had ta do was be kind to her—no, that's not it, we had to give her something—we were charitable. Tristan was greedy, that is why he failed." Charity and greed—Andy knew he was onto something.

"And what about them Shadows, Blueberry?" The mule brayed loudly. "Shhhh, I donna want her to know where I am."

"Them Shadows were vengeful, and deadly, but they were a part of ourselves. They were wrath itself… That's it! They were Wrath!" Andy's body quivered. "We overcame them by being in the present moment but also by forgiving our past. 'Tis it! 'Tis it! I have an idea."

CHAPTER 23

Fransie followed the music. The closer she got to the sound, the more her soul was in rapture. She closed her eyes, letting the music envelop her. She trusted in the music to lead her.

Her foot hit a step, and she raised her gaze to see a magnificent church with pointed archways. The noise wrapped around Fransie again, and her feet were pulled forward. She entered through the doors below the ornately decorated archway, and the melody stopped.

"Welcome to San Saturnino, Sister. How may I be of service to you?" a young priest asked.

"What was that music just playing, Father? I must know."

"Sister, there was no music."

"Are you sure?"

The priest nodded.

"It must have been from the divine." Fransie made the sign of the cross.

"From the angels on high." The priest pointed at the ceiling. "I will leave you to your prayers."

Fransie walked to the left and knelt at the front pew. It felt so good to be in a house of God again. After the many trials she had been through, Fransie needed God's guidance and support.

My Lord, what is happening to me? Be my strength and my guide. Fransie closed her eyes and listened for God's voice, but in her heart, she was hoping to hear the music—she craved it.

"Sister Fransie, don't you ever do that to me again," Sister Caroline said, plopping down next to her, out of breath. "What has gotten into you, riding bareback, being chased by a bull... I don't know who is a worse influence on you, the Italians, or Raphael and Auriel. You haven't been the same since we met them. What is going on? Sorry to interrupt your prayer." Sister Caroline hastily made the sign of the cross.

"It's so hard to explain." Fransie took Caroline's hand. "I don't know if I'm cursed or blessed. Something happened to me when Raphael's father put his hands on my ears. I can hear things others can't. At first I thought it was just demons—now I know it is angels as well. Caroline, I can hear the angel's song." Sister Caroline looked at her blankly and shook her head.

"*Mamma mia*, would you look at this church?" Stefano said from the entrance. He was joined by Luca, who whistled. Michael made the sign of the cross, and Emmanuel looked from side to side.

"I asked them to give us a few minutes before entering." Caroline looked at them sternly. "I would have liked more time."

"They acted very bravely with the bull. Stefano and Luca risked their lives trying to save us." Fransie clasped Sister Caroline's hand.

"Hey, look at this!" Michael exclaimed from an alcove chapel in the northeast corner of the church. The other Italians joined him and began deliberating something.

"Let's go see what they found," Fransie said. Sister Caroline frowned, but followed Fransie, albeit reluctantly. Stepping into the alcove, the beautiful tones started again. Fransie felt her whole body lift, and joy emanated from her face.

"What happened to you?" Stefano asked.

"I don't know what is happening to me. Do you not hear that music?"

"Oh, my dear Sister Fransie," Sister Caroline said, wrapping her arm around her shoulder.

The music stopped when Emmanuel shouted. "No! I tell you, it's a sign of a secret society." He waved his hands vigorously at Michael.

"It's a sign of the trinity." Michael placed a hand on his chin and observed the large picture in front of them.

Fransie wouldn't call the picture beautiful, but it was impressive. It appeared to be a painting of the rapture. Several poor souls were being consumed by fire as angels lifted the chosen from the flames. Above, Jesus held his cross, and a dove, which represented the Holy Spirit, was in flight. Opposite Jesus was an image of God, with a golden triangle above his head containing an eye in the middle, blessing them.

"The triangle with an eye is a symbol of a secret society from Egypt," Emmanuel insisted.

"You mean the Eye of Providence, Emmanuel?" Fransie asked. "Surely you know the triangle with an eye in it represents the ever-watchful eye of God. Also, the triangle represents the holy trinity. The Father, the Son, and the Holy Spirit." Fransie crossed herself as she finished speaking.

"Sure, that's what they want you to believe." Emmanuel crossed his arms. "What is he pointing at then?"

"Emmanuel, surely you must pay more attention in church." Sister Caroline placed a hand on his shoulder. "The hand pointing up represents the hope of heaven."

"True, but, I think it is trying to tell us something else." Emmanuel smiled mischievously and walked out of the alcove, motioning for the others to join him. "Look what it's pointing to." Above the alcove was a bodiless hand pointing at a mounted knight with a cross on his shield.

"That doesn't prove anything." Michael shook his head.

"Look at the hand closely." Fransie strained her eyes and saw a Templar cross in a halo behind it.

"See, the hand points to the Templar Knight and his lance is pointing at—"

"An organ!" Fransie exclaimed.

Fransie heard the music again and ascended the stairs leading to the organ. She couldn't get the song out of her head. She needed to capture it—to play it, and all of the sweet harmonies. She hit the notes on the organ and tried to replicate what she was hearing—or was she feeling it, now? This didn't make any sense, but she knew she had to do it.

"Sister Fransie, honestly, what has gotten into you?" Sister Caroline panted, as she mounted the last step.

"I have to capture it... No, it's fading! I have to play it." The notes Fransie hit made no sense. She banged on the keyboard as the last notes left her. Fransie wanted to cry. The beautiful feeling of the music had left her body again. She craved that music. She *needed* that music.

"Are you possessed?" Stefano asked, cautiously holding his fingers in a cross.

Sister Caroline slapped away his fingers. "Of course she's not."

Emmanuel leaned over the banister. "How many keys are on an organ?'

"Usually, each keyboard has sixty-one notes." Caroline glanced over her shoulder at the organ. "It looks like this one has four keyboards. Why?"

"And how many is that all together?" Emmanuel motioned for them to keep going.

"That equals two-hundred and forty-four. Why do you ask?" Michael said, with questioning eyebrows.

Emmanuel motioned to the floor below. Fransie stood abruptly and ran to the banister. Carved into the large wooden floor planks were numbers ranging from one to 244. The numbers appeared to be at random and were interspersed between planks without numbers.

"I think someone or something wants us to play a song," Emmanuel said. Fransie gripped the railing tightly—she knew he was right.

CHAPTER 24

Andy crept back into the kitchen with a broom and dustpan in hand. Before the door closed behind him, he swept the floor vigorously. He continued to sweep down the hall into Clair and Gerhart's bedroom. Both lay on their beds, and Acedia sat between them, whispering. As she whispered, the mist strung from her mouth and bound both in a cocoon of her silken words. Clair and Gerhart's faces were drained, and their skin was the same jaundice color as Acedia's. She was sucking the life out of them. Andy swept vigorously, and Acedia whispered more intently.

"Clair, will ya 'elp me with this?" Andy put the dustpan in Clair's hand that was hanging off the bed.

"Why would you want to help him?" Acedia whispered. "You are comfortable. He can do it himself. You don't want to move anywhere."

"Clair, I really need your 'elp." Andy closed Clair's fingers tightly around the dustpan. Clair turned her head to Andy. Her eyes pleaded with him.

"Clair, all ya 'ave ta do is take hold and 'elp me out." Clair's fingers tightened around the dustpan, and Andy swept in the dirt. Acedia scowled at Andy with her beady eyes.

"See that was na so 'ard." Clair managed a smile and struggled to sit up.

"It is so much better to lie down. You are so much more comfortable in your bed," Acedia insisted

"Clair, do ya think ya can empty that in the bin?" Andy asked, sweeping more dust into the pan. Clair labored to stand and emptied the pan. The mist from Acedia's mouth still clung to her body.

"Come lay back down. Other people can do that work later." Clair was pulled back to the bed by the string of mist that connected her to Acedia.

Andy took Clair by the hand and said, "If not you, then who? If not now, when?" Clair continued back to the bed.

Andy's heart sank. Had he been wrong? Acedia shot Andy a cruel smile with her pencil thin lips.

"That's it, Clair, there is no need for you to do anything," Acedia hissed, as Clair bent to the bed.

"Aye, as my brother said, 'If not me, then who? If not now, when?'" Clair straightened the covers and made the bed.

Acedia scowled. It looked as if she had eaten a whole lemon. She turned her full attention to Gerhart. "Isn't it nice not doing farm work? That work was never meant for you. Actually, no work was ever meant for you."

Andy continued to sweep the floor until he was next to Gerhart. "'Aye, big fellow, I need your 'elp reaching something." Andy produced a feather duster from behind his back. He placed it in Gerhart's hand and closed his fingers around it. "'Tis just behind your head." Andy lifted Gerhart's hand above the cocoon of mist and moved it back and forth, dusting above the headboard. Gerhart's hand came to life and started to move on its own.

Andy released his hand and started sweeping. "That's it. Thank ya, Gerhart."

Acedia began to speak, but Gerhart's feather duster made its way to her mouth, blocking the stream of mist from issuing forth. Clair shook the blanket vigorously, sending a gust of wind that pushed the rest of the mist off Gerhart. He stood and dusted Acedia even more. Catching his drift, Andy moved behind her and swept as hard as his hands could push. Acedia tried to escape to the side, but Clair continued to shake the dust from the blanket. Acedia was trapped; she only had one way to go. Andy and the others flanked her down the hallway and out the kitchen door. The moment Acedia passed the threshold, she vanished.

"Now that's what I call taking out the trash," Andy said, brushing his hands.

Clair and Gerhart embraced Andy tightly. Gerhart twirled his feather duster, putting it in his belt. "How did you know how to defeat her?"

"With the wise words from a rabbi; and I took personal responsibility. 'If not me, then who? If not now, when?' I ken that a body in motion tends ta stay in motion. I just 'ad ta get ya movin'. It just takes one small act of integrity ta overcome Sloth. Each time you repeat that act, your integrity becomes stronger—soon, industry takes ya over, and destroys the sloth that has kept ya trapped." Andy looked around. "Where's Chelsea?"

"I donna ken, but you have some explaining ta do, Andy Sinclair. Who—or what—was that?"

"I have ta confess, I havena been goin' ta work."

"What!" Clair rolled up her sleeves.

"See...Etienne and I...well, there is a Templar treasure..."

CHAPTER 25

Fransie was mesmerized by the markings on the floor. This was the key to hearing the music again, and she needed to hear it— every fiber of her being craved it.

"We must figure this out. This is what God wanted to show me." The excitement drained from Fransie's body as she received a stern look from Sister Caroline.

"We should leave this church and never come back."

"Caroline, I have to hear it again."

"Fransie, you are talking like someone who is obsessed." Fransie rubbed her arm. She had never felt so compelled in her life.

"You can leave if you want to." Fransie couldn't believe she had just said that to her closest friend and companion. But, there was no taking it back. Sister Caroline placed her hands on her hips, and it looked as if she was about to say something, but she shook her head.

"I agree, we must figure this out. If only to prove my point," Emmanuel said, smugly.

"The blank spaces must be pauses in the music—that makes perfect sense. But, where do we begin besides that?" Fransie leaned over the railing to get a better look.

"We begin at one," said Caroline. "I'm still not sure about all of this, but I will trust you, my friend. If you say this is from God, I will believe you. One will be the base note and will match the lowest key on the keyboard. On this organ it looks like a C. Also, the numbers are all facing the same direction. Reading music is just like reading a book; you start at the top of the page on the left and work your way down." Caroline was an accomplished musician. She played the lute, the harp, drums, and of course, the organ. "If I'm going to play these notes carved in the floor, then I will need sheet music."

The Italians sprang into action, leaving Caroline and Fransie alone on the balcony.

"Fransie, I will trust you with this, but if I see it is harming you in any way, we will stop immediately. I feel like I don't understand you anymore."

"Raphael and Auriel would understand."

Caroline pounded the base notes on the organ. The sound reverberated in the church and made Fransie jump.

"That may be so, Fransie, but they aren't here—I am, and I always will be." Fransie covered her ears as a penetrating screech accompanied Caroline's words.

"I see that you are envious. Please, Caroline, for my sake, show them kindness."

"Sister Caroline, we have it. All of the numbers from the floorboards are written out." Stefano said, mounting the stairs followed by the others. Caroline took the paper from Stefano and, within a matter of minutes, she had all the numbers and spaces transposed into proper sheet music.

"Are you boys ready to hear the concert of your life?" Sister Caroline sat at the organ and cracked her knuckles.

Fransie loved her friend so dearly. She didn't know why she hadn't told her about the true sound. She knew she could trust Caroline with anything. Why couldn't she tell her about this?

Sister Caroline hit the first notes, and a warmth spread in Fransie's body. This was it. This was the music that had drawn her to the church. The music wrapped around Fransie as Caroline played. It enveloped her and fed her craving.

"*Mio Dio,*" Michael murmured from the balcony's edge. Fransie peered down and didn't know if the music was making the world turn, or if the floorboards were actually moving.

Caroline hit a high C and descended down the scale, and as she did so, ten round energy centers appeared on the floor, all glowing a different color. Lines soon appeared, connecting the energy centers. Caroline hit the last note, and a beam of green light shot like a lightning bolt from the farthest glowing ball to the closest—which, to Fransie's surprise, opened into a glowing hole.

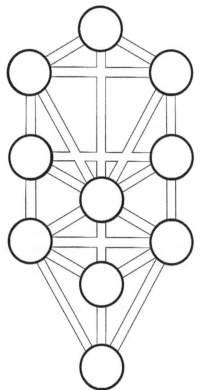

"What is that?" Michael asked.

"I don't know, but I was right," Emmanuel said with a smug look on his face.

"Who cares what it is? I will be the first to discover it," Stefano said, rushing down the stairs of the balcony.

"Oh, no you won't." Luca pulled him back, and they fought all the way down the stairs to be the first to look at the mysterious portal.

"Who do you think should go first?" Fransie asked as she and Caroline joined the others at the gaping hole in the floor.

"Who should go first? What on earth are you talking about? You can't even see the bottom. We have no idea what this is. We must close it immediately. Forgive me, Father." Sister Caroline made the sign of the cross.

"I think Emmanuel should go first, since he was right," Michael said, smirking.

"No, no, I-a couldn't." Emmanuel waved both hands. "Stefano is our fearless leader. He should go."

"I couldn't take all the glory," Stefano said. "Luca?"

"No, you must go, big brother."

"Do you hear it?" Fransie asked, and everyone shook their heads. "The music. It's calling to me." Fransie stepped over the edge. Sister Caroline wrapped her arms around Fransie to stop her, but they both fell into the abyss.

Fransie gasped for air and opened her eyes. She and Caroline were standing on a pedestal inside a cylinder of golden light. In front of them was a path leading to a door with a face that had a slot for a mouth. There wasn't a door handle or any hinges, only that face staring at them.

"We're not dead. Thank the Lord. Where are we?" Sister Caroline asked. "Ahh! What is that?" Sister Caroline hid behind Fransie as she noticed the door.

"I think we are inside the image that was on the floor, and I don't know what that is." Fransie looked above. She could hear the Italians, but couldn't see them.

"Are you coming or not?" Caroline called up to the others. "We need you down here."

Moments later, Stefano, Luca, Emmanuel, and Michael all appeared in a knot. They continued to wrestle until they realized where they were.

"Mamma mia," Emmanuel whispered.

"Where are we?" Michael asked.

"I don't know, but there is an obvious path." Fransie pointed to the door straight ahead.

"Step back. I'll go first this time," Stefano said, drawing his sword. The other Italians did the same, surrounding Fransie and Caroline. Stefano walked cautiously to the door and knocked on it with the hilt of his sword. A hollow sound reverberated back. He hit the door harder, and a deep sound wave responded, knocking them all to the ground.

"I don't think we can force it." Fransie brushed herself off and walked to the door. She wasn't afraid of it; the door was calling to her. "I hear it. Thank the Lord, I hear it." Fransie crouched and placed her ear to the slot. The melody filled her ears and overflowed to the rest of her body.

"Sister Fransie, step away from that thing at once—it might bite your head off." Sister Caroline tried to pull Fransie away, but the pull of the music was stronger.

"I have to, Caroline." Fransie pressed her head as hard as she could against the door. She wanted to force herself through the slot, even though she knew it was impossible. Momentarily regaining her senses, Fransie tried to push away from the door, but the music called her back. She clawed at the door until her fingers became raw.

"Fransie, you are hurting yourself, stop! You are bleeding." Caroline struggled with Fransie's hand, which zig-zagged down the face. The mouth of the face on the door rapidly expanded from a slot into a gaping hole, and Fransie fell through head first.

"Restrain her," Stefano ordered. Everyone rushed through the door. Emanuel and Michael lifted Fransie to her feet and held her fast on each side.

"I am better now," Fransie said. "This isn't necessary."

"We are bound to protect you—even if that means protecting you from yourself," Stefano said. "Luca, come with me. You four wait for us on the other side of the door." As soon as the words left his lips, the mouth of the door closed to a slot once more, trapping them all.

"Well, brother, looks like the only way to go is forward, and I'm up for an adventure." Luca wrapped his arm over Stefano's shoulder. "I suggest we head for that purple light."

It wasn't as if they had a choice. The only option was to continue forward on the narrow path to where a purple sphere beckoned them. Every other direction led only to darkness and the sense of a steep drop.

Luca and Stefano took the lead, while Fransie and the others were a few paces behind. When they reached the sphere, Stephano and Luca stepped through with their swords at the ready and were swallowed by the purple light.

"This is impossible. Come join us. It is safe." Stefano's words led Fransie and her companions through the purple light. On the other side, Fransie found herself back at the festival in Zubiri. Sitting at a table in the distance were the two maidens, Maria and Elizabeth.

"Stefano, Luca, come join us." Maria lifted her dress to show her ankles then flicked her long black hair. "We are so lonely."

"This isn't right," Fransie said, clutching Sister Caroline's habit with both hands. She looked around in desperation. "We have to get out of here." Fransie was afraid that she would hear the piercing tones that had almost shredded her the last time they were at the festival. She looked around the square frantically again. Diagonally to the left was a passage of light closing quickly. Fransie broke free from Emanuel and Michael and ran. She was too afraid to be concerned about the others.

"I'm with you, Fransie." Sister Caroline's heavy footsteps and voice came from close behind.

"She's right. Stefano, Luca. We have to go." Michael said, trying to pull their friends, but it did no good. They were caught in the sirens' spell.

"Let's finish what we started the other night. Don't you want us?" Maria stuck out her bottom lip in a pout.

"Get off of me!" Stefano shoved Michael. He tapped Luca in the chest. "Let's go, brother." Luca shrugged off Emmanuel, and the two brothers ran to join the maidens at the table.

Emmanuel tried to grab the brothers, but Michael restrained him. "They have made their choice. We must protect Sister Fransie."

Emmanuel and Michael joined Fransie and Caroline in the passageway and the purple sphere shut behind them.

"Agh!" Michael screamed, clearing tears from his eyes. "They are lost to us forever."

"We don't know that for sure." Sister Caroline patted Michael on the shoulder.

"Michael...I..." Fransie started, but the music pulled her forward down the path. Before she got too far ahead, Caroline and Emanuel hooked her arms. She struggled to get free, but their grip was too tight.

"Let's all do this together," Caroline said, and they walked four abreast to an orange sphere at the opposite end of the passage.

"Are you sure about this? We don't know what's on the other side," Emanuel said as they approached.

"I don't think we have another choice," Sister Caroline replied.

"I'll go first. It is my fault that we are here," Fransie said, but everyone else shook their heads. "Together then." All stepped through at the same time.

The orange sphere was empty except for a passage that led to the right. They followed the passage to a green sphere and once again found it empty.

"I don't like this, Fransie. Why did you lead us down here?" Sister Caroline clutched at Fransie's arm tightly.

"It wasn't me—it was the music." Fransie still heard it—with each step, it was more defined. Her body craved the vibration of the notes.

Diagonally to the left was another passage that led to an illuminated yellow sphere. The passage was smaller, and they had to break off into groups of two to enter it. Sister Caroline and Emmanuel stepped through first, closely followed by Fransie and Michael. The sphere opened up to a mountain meadow.

"Sister Fransie, look!" Sister Caroline pointed to a chiseled man working on a beautiful carriage. "Gerhart. I would know those muscles anywhere." Sister Caroline rushed forward and wrapped her arm around Gerhart's bicep. "What on earth are you doing here?"

"Waiting for you." Gerhart flexed his mighty muscles, and Sister Caroline nearly lost her grip.

Emmanuel whistled and shook his head. "Look at that carriage. It has the latest axel design...and those wheels."

"Do you like it? It's yours." Gerhart threw Emmanuel the keys to the carriage door. Emmanuel rushed to the carriage and unlocked it. He rolled around on the velvet seats. Diagonally to the left a red corridor shone.

"Sister Caroline, we must go." Fransie pulled at her friend.

"I think we can stay here a while. Right, Gerhart?" Sister Caroline batted her eyelashes up at Gerhart.

"Sister Caroline, he is married to Clair!"

"Who?"

"Fransie, we must go." Michael grabbed Fransie by the arm. "It is just like what happened to Stefano and Luca. I think the only way to save our friends is for us to continue."

"No, I can't leave Caroline—" The music started again, and Fransie's body no longer obeyed her. She was pulled forward to the passage with the red light.

"Don't interact with anything," Michael said, stepping into the red sphere at the end of the passage. It was empty, just like the other two. They ran to the right, down a corridor with blue light, and into a blue sphere. Once again, nothing.

The music grew louder, and Fransie's body became ecstatic. "Michael, it is calling to me—I can't resist it. I want it. I want to be consumed by it."

"What are you talking about?"

"The music—don't you hear it?" Michael shook his head.

Diagonally to the left there was a black corridor. "We must trust in God." Fransie clutched her rosary tightly as she and Michael ran forward hand-in-hand.

Fransie felt a stinging pain, as if she had run into an invisible wall, and she crumpled to the ground.

"Michael, where are you? Michael!" Fransie's voice disappeared into the abyss, and the music started again just on the other side of the invisible wall. Fransie tore at the wall, kicking and punching; she needed to reach that music and be covered in it. She *lusted* after the music. She rammed herself into the invisible wall again and again. She kept silent through the pain—she didn't want her cries to corrupt the music.

Fransie backed up and ran full speed in the darkness to the invisible wall. She braced her shoulder for the impact, but this time it was her shins that gave out. She toppled onto a pew and rolled to the ground of the church. Pain shot through Fransie's body, and the music was gone.

She turned her head from side to side—her companions were strewn on the floor as well, except for Michael. He helped Fransie to her feet, and in his right arm was a golden harp.

"Fransie, I believe you. This is what you heard. I think it is David's harp.[20] When I reached it, I also heard the secret chord that pleased the Lord."

"How is it that you passed every trial and we failed?" Fransie stared at the harp, willing it to play one more time.

"I am chaste. The only thing I lust for is to do the will of the Lord. Each of you faced your greatest temptation—the thing you lust for and desire most in the world." Fransie's heart dropped. Until this afternoon, she could have said the same thing. Hearing the divine was almost as bad as hearing the devil.

CHAPTER 26

A streak of silver darted across the starry sky as Sister Fransie and her companions left Pamplona. God had sent streak after streak since she awoke. Fransie didn't know if it was a good or bad sign. What had happened in the church the day before was not of this world.

"Did you see that one, Fransie?" Caroline asked, gripping her arm.

"This is a bad omen," Raphael said, from the front of the group. "Those are the tears of God. You never should have taken that thing from the church."

Fransie and the others had told Raphael the story, and she was not pleased. Fransie could see in her eyes that Raphael was just as attracted to the harp as she was. Raphael had kept Hokhmah perched on her shoulder since they had returned to camp with it. She needed him as a filter. Likewise, Binah hadn't left Auriel's side.

In the distance, Fransie heard the revelers in Pamplona still playing music and celebrating. The party had gone on all night, but Fransie had slept through it. The events of the day had drained her.

The first flames of morning crept in behind them, and the strands of silver in the sky became less distinct. Dawn was approaching.

"Our lands end there at Alto del Perdon." Raphael pointed to a high mountain ridge in the distance. "We will lead you over the peaks and then return to our father."

Emmanuel's cart creaked loudly. "If only I had been able to keep that carriage. You should have seen it, Luca. She was beautiful."

"Not as beautiful as our señoritas." Luca continued on in Italian. Fransie was happy for the language barrier. She had had quite enough of them talking about the women. She blocked them out and focused on the first birds' singing.

She pretended that Stefano and Luca were two birds singing their song as well. Who was she to judge them? They lusted after women, and she lusted after the harp Michael was carrying. Fransie needed to talk to Raphael and Auriel about what had happened to her, but the moment hadn't presented itself.

"Why are they stopped?" Michael pointed to a backlog of pilgrims at the entrance to the next town.

"That is a Hospitaller flag." Stefano motioned to a large fortress to the left of the Camino that proudly flew the black flag with the eight-pointed cross.

"Is that a problem?" Raphael asked.

"Yes, when we were first attacked, two of the riders with the priest were Hospitallers."

"Hokhmah," Raphael said. The falcon took flight from her shoulder and circled the Camino ahead. Fransie noticed Raphael's tattoo glowing red. "There are several knights examining the pilgrims as they pass. I see them pulling back the women's hoods. They just separated a nun from the crowd and let the others pass." Sure enough, the band of pilgrims ahead moved forward.

"There is a way around." Raphael's tattoo glowed again. "To the right, if we follow the city wall around the crest of the hill, we can pick the Camino up on the other side. We must move quickly before the sun rises and we are spotted." Everyone ran in the direction Raphael had indicated, Emmanuel's cart squeaking the whole way.

"Leave the cart, Emmanuel," Raphael urged.

"No, she is my baby. I cannot-a leave her."

"Emmanuel." Stefano shot him a look. "They will hear us."

A flaming arrow struck the ground a few feet ahead of Raphael, who was leading the group.

"Hold," a voice shouted from the north tower. "and await inspection!" Raphael continued forward, and another arrow landed closer. She turned and, in one swift movement, let loose an arrow from her bow. The soldier fell from the tower, letting out a hideous wail as he met the ground.

"Emmanuel, leave the cart!" The fire of the arrows flashed in Raphael's eyes.

"Okay, okay!" Emmanuel lowered the cart to the ground.

"It's too late." Luca pointed at several riders heading their direction.

Sister Fransie's insides turned. Instinctively she ran around the north corner of the wall. In the distance was a vast field of sunflowers, all facing the now-risen sun.

"Quickly, let's hide in there. We have no other choice." Auriel jumped off Binah's back and joined the others by foot. "I love you, girl, now go!" Binah whinnied and took off to the north.

"Oh, Sister Fransie, we will be caught for sure." Sister Caroline clutched Fransie's arm as they disappeared into the field of sunflowers. Fransie's heart was racing faster than her feet.

"Ahh!" Sister Fransie let out a little squeal as a black and yellow face met hers. She skidded to a stop and her feet gave out from underneath her. Sister Caroline caught Fransie and helped her to stand.

"It's just a sunflower." Stefano chopped the sunflower head from the stalk and the yellow eyes and mouth drawn on the face of the flower fell to the ground. They were now in the center of the field, and everywhere Fransie looked, she saw drawings etched from the small yellow flowers on the face of the sunflowers. Fransie heard horses race to the far side of the field. They were surrounded.

"Undress," Stefano said.

"What! You are…why you… How could you ask such a thing at a time like this?" Sister Caroline scowled at him, hands on her hips in her signature move.

Stefano smiled and shook his head. "They are looking for two nuns—so let's give them two nuns." Stefano motioned to Raphael and Auriel. "They don't know how many are in our company."

"He's right, we must switch clothing," Raphael said grudgingly. "We are bound to protect you to the end of our lands, and our land ends over there." Raphael pointed to the mountain. "Continue on to Point de la Reiana. The Hospitallers have one more stronghold there, but after that, you should be able to disappear with the other pilgrims along the Camino."

"Luca, Michael, I want you to accompany them." Stefano put his hands on their shoulders. "I will miss you."

"No…" Luca threw Stefano's hand off his shoulder.

"It is the only way, brother. Keep them safe. Now hide and we'll draw them away."

Fransie and Caroline quickly took off their habits and gave them to Auriel and Raphael. Even though the men were facing the other way, Fransie felt naked and exposed. She put on Raphael's cloak as quickly as possible. Her body was screaming to run. The soldiers were getting closer by the second. She could see the tops of the sunflowers rustling with their movements.

"It is done," Raphael said.

"Protect them, brother," Stefano said. He shot up from the sunflowers and ran toward the nearest soldier, followed by Raphael, Auriel, and Emmanuel. They disappeared, and the shouts of the soldiers chased after them.

Fransie wanted to see what happened, but she knew she needed to remain hidden. Caroline clutched her arm tightly, and Fransie felt Caroline's fingers trembling.

"We give up!" Stefano shouted from the far end of the sunflower field closest to the Camino.

"Sir, there are two nuns with them," a soldier said in the distance.

"We must bring them to the priest. I hope these are the two the Pope is looking for," a sharp voice said. "Hospitallers to me!"

Fransie swallowed a scream as a boot stepped a foot away from her hand. She held her breath until the soldier passed. She clutched her rosary tightly and recited the Lord's Prayer. It wasn't until she had prayed the entire rosary that Luca gave them the signal to rise. They stood in a crouch and made their way to the edge of the sunflower field. A group of pilgrims approached, and they joined them. The pilgrims were light hearted and eager to talk, but that was the last thing Fransie wanted to do. Her *gift* was a liability. Without her animal, she was afraid she would lose control again, being around so many people and their temptations.

CHAPTER 27

Etienne tasted the metallic tang of blood and spat before opening his eyes. He wiped the blood from his nose and smelled the damp forest. He vaguely remembered being in the Moorish camp, but nothing after that.

"Ah, so you are awake. Back from the dead twice. Praise be to Allah." Etienne tried to move, but found he was restrained to a tree. "My apologies, nephew, for the broken nose and the restraints. Before I untie you, there are some things we must discuss."

Etienne spat again. "I have nothing to discuss with you. You poisoned me the last time we met and nearly killed me."

"Technically, it wasn't I who poisoned you. The man who did has been killed. Poison is a woman's weapon." Etienne would have liked to see him say that to Clair. She would have given him an earful. Etienne smiled at the thought.

"What is this—you agree?"

"No, I am just thinking of your arrogance."

"As I said in the woods, you are blood of my blood. I would never kill my kin. The soldier was only supposed to maim you. I did not know the blade was poisoned."

"Why should I trust you?"

"Are you dead? I could have left you to a very painful death with the Moors." Etienne hated to admit it, but there was truth in his words. Why had he saved him?

"Is the sultan dead?"

"No, he is traveling safely back to Grenada as we speak."

"The Knights of Saint James didn't attack?"

"The Knights of Saint James aren't foolish like the Templars—they would have never tried to take on an army of that size—their tactics are more cunning. They used you, nephew. Once again, you are doing the bidding of a people who aren't yours. They care nothing for you." Etienne struggled with the ropes, but they were too tight.

"You are angry because you hear the truth in my words."

"They only discovered the army last night. They had no idea the sultan would be there, nor that there would be so many soldiers."

"Do you really think a sultan traveling with five hundred plus guards would go unnoticed? Think, nephew."

"I see the truth in what you say." Nazir was right; there was no way an army that size could travel undetected.

"So you must ask yourself, what was the sultan doing in this part of the land?"

"I had heard there was a peace treaty between the kingdoms of Castile and Granada in 1303. But, with the Moors chasing after Isabella and our company, I didn't believe it."

"Who do you think gave the Moors permission to venture on the Camino? King Ferdinand IV of Castile[21] himself—at my request, that is."

"And now why are they here?"

"The Moors took the town of Ceuta, giving them complete control of the Straights of Gibraltar—giving them complete control over trade. This has made Ferdinand and many other kingdoms very unhappy. The sultan was here to try to repair that relationship. But, obviously that didn't work—otherwise you wouldn't have been sent to kill the sultan."

"But, the Knights of Saint James don't work for King Ferdinand."

Nazir raised his eyebrows. "Everyone works for someone, nephew. As I said before, they used you. I knew they would send someone to kill the sultan, but I didn't think it would be you."

"It was my choice to go. I volunteered. The death of one for the lives of many."

"You truly are an Assassin." Nazir placed a hand on Etienne's shoulder. "That is our creed. For generations we have been taking the lives of a few to spare the masses."

"How could trying to kill Isabella spare the lives of the many?"

"We have much to discuss."

CHAPTER 28

"Sister Fransie, you heard that Hospitaller—the Pope is looking for us. We should turn ourselves in and be done with it." Sister Caroline had slowed their pace to be out of earshot of the other pilgrims.

"Sister Caroline, I can't do that."

"What did Molay say to you? How has what he spoke changed you so much? I feel like I don't know you anymore." Sister Caroline's words pierced Fransie's heart.

"I am still Fransie." She patted Caroline's hand. "Things have just changed so much. I wish I could explain better what's going on, but you wouldn't understand."

Sister Caroline stopped and placed her hands on her hips. "I may not understand, but I want to be here for you. I want to help you bear your burden, just like Jesus does for all of us."

"That is why I love you so dearly, Caroline. I didn't accept this task because of Molay, the Templars, Isabella, or Etienne—I took it because the Virgin Mary visited me as a child." Sister Caroline's jaw dropped.

"Sister Fransie, you never told me that before." Caroline hurried to her and took her arm.

"I have never told anyone before. I'm doing this because of something she told me as a child."

"What did she tell you?"

"It's a secret, but I trust you—" Before she could continue, Michael and Luca ran back to join them, their brows furrowed. Fransie felt her chest constrict.

"Michael, what is it?" Fransie asked.

"The Camino is shut ahead at Puenta la Reina." Fransie's chest constricted even more.

"Is it because of us?"

Luca shook his head. "It's the plague. They have shut down the gates to the city. Now there is no way to access the only bridge that crosses this river. The Camino is closed."

Fransie felt like sitting on the ground and crying. Her friends' sacrifice would have been in vain. The Hospitallers would find them out and come chasing after them.

"Are you sure there is no other way to cross the river?" Fransie looked at them desperately.

"No." Michael shook his head. "Let's set up camp off the Camino. There is a group of pilgrims ahead who have contracted the plague. Thank God we got the message before we got any closer." The others started off the Camino, but Fransie stood firm.

"What is it?" Sister Caroline asked.

"I was naked, and you gave me clothing. I was sick, and you cared for me. I was in prison, and you came to visit me."

Sister Caroline nodded. "Whatever you did for one of the least of these brothers and sisters of mine, you did for me."

"Michael, Luca, we must tend to the sick," Fransie said. "Besides, the Hospitallers would never search for us among those who have the plague."

"Sisters, we can't let you. We are supposed to protect you," Luca insisted.

"That is God's job, not yours." Caroline took Fransie by the arm again, and they walked together to the death camp.

CHAPTER 29

Etienne wanted to coax Nazir into talking more. It would give him time to plan his escape. Even though Nazir had spared him, Etienne didn't trust him.

"So explain—how could killing Isabella spare the many?"

"For you to fully understand, I must start at the beginning." Nazir rested his back on a tree opposite Etienne and placed his hands behind his head.

"You can say that the Order of the Assassins[22] is an equalizer in this world and an insurance policy for the treasure the Templars currently possess."

Etienne hated that treasure. It had robbed so much from him. First his mentor Ronan—the old Templar who had become like a father to him—then Isabella. It had even robbed him of his identity. Before Isabella and that treasure appeared in his life, he was content to be a sergeant in the Templars. His life was simple—he knew who he was and what he had to do. Ever since the treasure appeared in his life, it had only brought change and destruction.

"Our order was founded in 1090 by your great-great-grandfather, Hassan-i Sabbah,[23] after he and his followers took Alamut Castle.

As I said before, you have the blood of the Assassins in your veins."
Etienne looked at Nazir with wide eyes. His ancestor was the
founder of the Assassins?

"It is true," Nazir said, reading his expression. "My great-
grandfather's disciples were first called Asasiyyun." Etienne
raised his eyebrows. "Of course, you don't speak our language.
It means, 'people who are faithful to the foundation.' Over the
past two hundred years, we have killed the few to save the many.
Seeing our noble cause, an angel came to my great-grandfather
in a dream. He told him that soon Jerusalem would fall to
infidels from the west, and a powerful treasure would be found
below the Dome of the Rock in the ruins of Solomon's Temple.
He was given a charge to help protect this treasure and to make
sure it was never used."

"Why are you telling me all this?"

"I want you to know who you truly are. I want you to know that
the task you have been handed was in your blood long before you
were born."

Etienne dropped his head. Once again, he knew there was truth
in Nazir's words. He felt it down to his bones. The souls of his
ancestors swirled inside of him. This man was his uncle. He was
of his blood.

"Untie me, Uncle." Etienne held out his bound wrists.

"I see that you feel the truth in my words." Nazir cut Etienne's
bonds. Etienne was tempted to lunge for his sword and run, but he
wanted to hear what Nazir had to say. This was his only chance to
figure out where he came from.

"Continue; I want to know everything." Etienne rubbed his
wrists, willing the blood to return to his hands.

"Allahu Akbar! Your ears have been unplugged." Nazir
squeezed Etienne's shoulder tightly. "I will continue then, now
that you have ears to hear."

Nazir pressed his fingers together. "Jerusalem fell to the crusaders in 1099, and our ancestor watched the Templars rise to power. Knowing that they were the ones who had discovered the treasure, my great-grandfather infiltrated the Templars and delivered the message the angel had given him. He warned the first Grand Master of the Templars, Hugues de Payens, under the penalty of death, never to use the treasure they had discovered. Hugues told our ancestor that he had received the same warning from an angel as well. In that moment, an alliance was formed that superseded all religious and political ties."

Nazir chuckled. Etienne hadn't realize it, but his jaw was gaping. Etienne shook his head and asked, "So the alliance held until the Battle of Montgisard?"[24] Ronan had told him about the battle where Templar Grand Master Odo de St. Armond had used the treasure to wipe out an army of 26,000 Saracens with five hundred Knights Templar.

"That is correct, and I think you know the rest of the story."

"All of it except for how my mother came to be in France."

"As I have told you in the past, the Order of the Assassins has eyes everywhere. After King Philip and Joan of Navarra were wed, he discovered a rumor that Grand Master Arnold of Torroja had hidden the Templar treasure in Spain. He was obsessed with finding this treasure. Your mother was sent to kill him. Bad things happen to many when men of great power search for the treasure."

"There were women Assassins?"

"Of course, some of the best Assassins are women. There are secrets women can pry from men's lips that no amount of torture would reveal."

This was so true. Etienne thought of all Isabella had discovered from him before he found out she was after the treasure. Etienne was surprised at the half smile on his face. He respected Isabella for all that she had accomplished.

"As I said before, your mother never returned. She must have fallen in love and had you. That part is still a mystery to me. When an Assassin doesn't want to be found, no one can find them. So it has been with your mother."

"How did you know Isabella was looking for the treasure on her pilgrimage?" Etienne asked, trying to take in all the information he was receiving.

"One of our eyes in the palace was Tristan. He was bought for a very low price."

Etienne's jaw clenched. Even in death, Tristan still managed to betray those he loved.

"He was to escort Isabella and report to us if she found anything. My hope was that she would discover nothing and her father would be satisfied that it was just a rumor. But, she discovered a door in Burgos, and we had to take action."

"I understand why you had to try to stop Isabella." Etienne felt the hate he had once had for Nazir disappear into a sort of admiration.

"We would have succeeded, too, had it not been for you." Nazir rubbed the knee that Etienne had displaced in their fight.

"Sorry about that." Continually the world had shown Etienne that what he thought was bad was actually good, and that what he thought was good was actually bad. It all depended on the perspective. Everyone is fighting a good fight for what they believe in. Everyone is the hero in their own story, and those who don't agree with it are the villains. Even Philip believes he is the hero in his story.

"Traitor!" Came from the woods, followed by a dagger flying straight for Etienne. Nazir lunged forward and shielded Etienne's body with his own. Etienne caught Nazir in his arms and felt the dagger sink deep into his back.

"We should have never trusted you." James stepped into view, followed by Gino. "This explains why the Moors left in the middle of the night. We missed our only opportunity to kill the sultan."

"You are one of them!" shouted Gino. "I knew it the whole time." He spat on the ground. Both knights pulled their swords and charged forward. Nazir swept James's feet out from under him, and they grappled on the ground.

Etienne tried to draw his sword from nearby, but his hands were covered in Nazir's blood. Gino swung his sword. Etienne ducked, and the blade lodged itself into the tree. Gino pulled with both hands on the blade, and Etienne delivered an uppercut to Gino's jaw, toppling him to the ground, unconscious.

Etienne pulled James and Nazir apart. James's stomach was split open, and he screamed out in agony.

Nazir grabbed Etienne's tunic and pulled him to the ground. "Etienne, remember who you are. The key lies inside you," he whispered, then gave up his spirit.

"Aggh!" James cried out again. He cradled both hands over the wound on his stomach. "I will never see my love, nor her son again... I don't want to die! It hurts!"

"Chew on this." Etienne pulled some white willow bark from his leather pouch. He always carried a bit for pain relief. "This will help."

"Why should I trust you?"

"If it is poison, you will just die more quickly." James nodded his head, and Etienne placed the bark in his mouth.

"You dropped something," James said, and Etienne followed James's eyes to a rolled-up piece of cloth that had fallen from his sporran.

The sliver of the True Cross—the treasure Charity gave us Astorga. Etienne picked up the small object and unrolled it. He felt a sudden urge to place it over James's wound. He remembered Andy's hand had healed incredibly quickly after they had taken the blood oath, and his own wound took many days to heal. Andy had held this shard in his fist and wouldn't let it go.

"May the Lord Jesus Christ heal you," Etienne said, holding the small shard of wood to James' stomach. The blood stopped flowing.

"I don't feel the pain. This bark must be working." James removed his hands from his stomach. The cut was healed. "My God, what just—how?"

Strong arms wrapped around Etienne's neck. "I will kill you!" Gino pulled Etienne away from James and held him in a choke hold.

"Gino, stop! Let him go. He saved my life!" James sat up.

Gino slowly loosened his grip, and Etienne backed away from the two knights.

"How can I ever repay you? I am in your debt, sir," James said, as Gino helped him to his feet.

"You can leave and tell everyone I am dead." Both James and Gino bowed and left. Etienne rushed to Nazir and placed the shard of the cross on his wounds, but it did no good—his spirit had already left his body. Etienne let out a primal scream, and the birds flew from the trees above.

CHAPTER 30

Fransie felt safer amongst the dying than she had for the entirety of their journey. She was happy to be in the service of others, happy to take her mind off the changes she was experiencing. Fransie placed a damp rag on a pilgrim's forehead. Plus, she only heard the gentle hum of compassion. There wasn't any room for the devil to pull on a dying person's heart.

"These poor souls, Sister Fransie." Sister Caroline placed a new bucket of water next to Fransie. Both she and Caroline had taken the proper precautions by covering their faces with cloths and saying their prayers, before treating these pilgrims.

"They will be with God soon." Fransie dabbed the pilgrim's face with the cloth. "So will we, if we can't figure out how to get past the wall of the city. It won't be long until they figure out that Raphael and Auriel aren't us."

"I am still thinking we should turn ourselves in. I hate going against the church."

"We may be going against the church, but we are heading for God. We don't even know if the Pope sent that priest here."

"I hadn't considered that." Sister Caroline poured a hot tincture down a pilgrim's throat. "I wish we could do more here."

"Thank you," the pilgrim groaned. "They just left us all here to die. We don't have the plague. We have the Fire of San Anton.[25] We are trying to reach the Arc of San Anton to be cured."

"I know, I know," Caroline crooned. "The Fire of San Anton mimics the symptoms of the plague. We can pray to Saint Anthony here as well." The pilgrim grimaced, trying to smile through excruciating pain.

"It's so cold," he managed through small convulsions of his body. Sister Caroline split open an onion and rubbed it on a swollen nodule on his neck.

"Fransie, what happened to you in that church?"

"I told you—I heard as God hears. It had to do with that harp. It was calling to me. I craved that sound more than anything in my life. It scared me how badly I wanted it. I thought the dissonance I heard in Zubiri was bad—this was much worse. It was as if I wanted to die just to hear that sound again. Even as we sit here with these pilgrims, I hear a sweet gentle hum."

"Are you sure you aren't going mad?" Sister Caroline continued to rub the onion on the pilgrim's body.

Fransie shook her head. "Raphael and Auriel have the gift too. However, Raphael sees it, and Auriel feels it. Somehow, Caroline, we have the senses of God in our bodies."

"Ouch!" the pilgrim wailed.

"Oh my, I'm so sorry," Sister Caroline said. There was a distinct red mark where she had rubbed the onion too hard.

"Caroline." Fransie took the onion from her hand. "I think this will kill me if I don't find my animal."

"Now I know you have gone mad! Your animal? What are you going on about?"

"Hokhmah and Binah serve as filters for Raphael and Auriel. They said the gift would kill me if I don't find my animal." Fransie lowered her head.

"You *are* serious." Caroline heaved an arm around her shoulder and pulled her close.

"Caroline, I am afraid. Please, keep me away from that harp at all costs." Caroline nodded.

"Fransie, Caroline, come quickly! I have great news," Michael shouted from a distance.

"I'm sorry, we must leave," Fransie said tenderly to her patient. "You must get to the Arc of San Anton. They will be able to heal you there. We will continue to pray for you."

Caroline and Fransie washed and followed Michael. Fransie didn't like the idea of leaving the sick, but they had done what they could. She agreed; these pilgrims didn't have the plague, they had the Fire of San Anton. They needed to make it to the Arc of San Anton to be treated properly.

"What is it?" Fransie asked Luca, who stood smiling up at the wall.

"Not what, but who." Luca pointed to a woman with sun-kissed skin and a curl to her hair. "Sister Fransie, Sister Caroline, I would like you to meet Gaia." The woman smiled and waved at them enthusiastically.

"Who is she?" Sister Caroline asked, crossing her arms.

"The love of my life, and our ticket out of here." Luca blew her a kiss, and she pretended to catch it.

CHAPTER 31

Alexander waited patiently in Sanjuanista, the Hospitaller headquarters just outside of Pamplona. Patience was one of his finest qualities. Alexander pressed the tips of his long fingers together hard. The Hospitallers had brought him many nuns in the past few days, but none were the ones he was looking for. He would be patient. He would pray. He was doing the bidding of the Pope. God would deliver them into his hands.

This Hospitaller commandery was the largest in the Navarre region. It was impressive, with its many towers, a monastery, a hospital for the pilgrims, and the church in which he now stood. The chapel was simple, just the way he liked it. The shafts of light coming in from the far window behind the altar were reminiscent of the Holy Spirit filling the church.

The gray stone walls stretched up to a vaulted ceiling, and the only decorations were the flags hung from the walls. Besides that, it was humble, just like him, only fulfilling one purpose—God's purpose.

The Hospitallers had served the church well. They were renowned for their many good works and loyalty to the Pope. They could be trusted, unlike the Templars.

The Hospitallers had been faithful, and they would be rewarded for their fidelity. In his few days at the Commandery, Alexander had learned of the numerous good works the Hospitallers had achieved on the Camino. They had established many resources to aid the pilgrims, and their healing arts were renowned. They truly were God's servants.

The door at the back right of the church swung open, and the sound of the heavy wood hitting the back wall echoed through the chapel. Alexander rose and walked to the altar slowly. He bowed and said a small prayer that these nuns would be the ones he was looking for.

The sound of footsteps approached and he turned—Four Hospitaller knights presented two dirty pilgrims whose hands were bound, and two nuns who kept their heads down.

These are the same habits that the sisters in Paris had worn— perhaps God has smiled on us.

"Father, we caught these pilgrims avoiding our blockade. They tried to sneak around the Commandery and killed one of our guards at the northern tower." The Hospitaller dug his hand firmly into one of the pilgrim's shoulders. "We caught them cowering in the sunflower fields." The guard punched the pilgrim in the side.

"Come now, Diego, let's not treat them too harshly before we have heard what they have to say. Sisters, why did you, women of God, try to avoid the blockade?"

"We were so full of the spirit we didn't want to stop," said the pilgrim who had been struck.

"I wasn't talking to you." Alexander nodded, and Diego struck the pilgrim again. "Sisters, I know you must be afraid, but raise your heads, and tell me why one of our guards is dead."

"We didn't kill him. It was the rider who went to the north," said the other pilgrim. Alexander nodded, and Diego punched the pilgrim in the stomach. The man wheezed and doubled over.

"I will ask you one last time, Sisters, why did you avoid the blockade?"

"Because I don't like you." One of the nuns, with dark skin and cold, dark eyes, looked up at him. In a movement so fast it couldn't quite be seen, she took the sword from one of the Hospitallers' sheaths and split him up the middle. The other nun slammed her captor in the groin with her elbow, dropping him to the ground.

Diego, the lead Hospitaller, drew his sword, as did the other standing guard, and they attacked. Diego swung at the dark nun, but the pilgrim he had first pummeled stuck out his foot and tripped him. Diego stumbled, but regained his footing quickly.

"Stefano!" The dark nun threw the pilgrim a dagger, and he cut his bonds. A few more Hospitallers entered the room and attacked, as did a falcon. The bird swooped on the Hospitallers, its talons ripping one soldier's eye out.

The two nuns and the other pilgrim fought their way to the door. But Stefano was cornered by Diego and another Hospitaller. A horse whinnied in the courtyard, and Diego saw the dark nun and Stefano exchange a look that said goodbye. Stefano nodded his head, and the others disappeared out the door.

Alexander walked to Stefano, who was now pinned, and wrapped his long fingers around his neck.

"How dare you bring this destruction inside God's house." Alexander squeezed tightly. He had killed before and had enjoyed it. He had given confession many times for the feeling of joy it brought him. Alexander squeezed even tighter, and Stefano's eyes rolled upward as the struggle left his body.

Just one more sin to confess. Alexander dropped the dead man and knelt at a pew, allowing the Hospitallers to clean up the mess.

CHAPTER 32

Night fell, and as promised, Gaia let down a rope from the high wall. Luca had told Fransie that when Gaia and he first saw each other, it was love at first sight. She had agreed to help them into the city if they would take her with them out of the town.

"Luca and I will climb first, then we will pull you up the wall." Michael tugged on the rope to make sure it was secure. "Just put the rope around yourself like this and tie it." He demonstrated the knot and had them practice. Being satisfied, he climbed up with the harp strapped to his back. Once he reached the top, Luca followed close behind.

"Caroline, do you want to go first, or shall I?"

"I'll go. You will be down here to catch me if anything happens." Caroline gave her a nervous smile. Sister Fransie said a small prayer that she wouldn't have to catch her friend.

Once Caroline was secure, Michael and Luca hoisted her to the top. It wasn't long before they threw the rope down, and Fransie secured it around her waist. She became giddy as her feet left the ground. It felt as if she was a small child on a ride. Halfway up, something swooped at her. Fransie covered her face, but the creature just hovered in front of her. She peeked through her fingers.

"Hokhmah!" Fransie shouted. The falcon let out a cry. Luca and Michael lifted Fransie the rest of the way up. From there she could see three riders tearing down the Camino, and just behind them, Hospitaller Calvary.

"Why are there only three of them?" Michael asked.

"My love," Luca said, wrapping his arms around Gaia. He went in to kiss her, and she pushed him away.

"How dare you!" She crossed her arms firmly. "Just because I love you doesn't mean I will kiss you or—"

Fransie turned back to the riders. They were now headed to the wall. Michael lowered the rope. The first rider climbed, and the second was quick to follow. The third rider continued out and around the city. Michael and Luca helped Emmanuel onto the ledge. Moments later, Raphael appeared and they helped her up as well.

"Where is Stefano?" Luca peered below. "Where is he?"

"Luca, see… He sacrificed…" Luca grabbed Emmanuel by the cape. Emmanuel threw up his arms. "We don't know if he is dead." Luca released Emmanuel and prepared to climb down.

"Where are you going, Luca?" Fransie asked.

"I have to get Stefano." Both Michael and Emmanuel held him back. Luca struggled ferociously, but the two of them were stronger than he.

The Hospitallers reached the wall. Seeing no way to follow, they circled to the gate of the city.

"Open up! By order of the Hospitallers!" the lead rider shouted.

"There is plague on the Camino. We won't open these gates, even for you!" a voice shouted back.

"Quickly," Gaia said, "Follow me before it's too late."

They rushed down the stairs to a canyonous street with buildings stretching high on either side. The sound of their footsteps bounced off the walls and up to the sky. With each step, the towered entrance to the city slowly faded into the distance.

Within minutes, they reached the opposite side of town, and were met by a twin tower matching the entrance of the city. However, this tower opened up to a bridge wide enough for two carriages across.

"Gaia, what are you doing?" A man's voice came chasing after them down the streets. "Close the gates!" A large portcullis dropped just feet away from Fransie, blocking the path.

"Papa!" Gaia shouted.

"Papa?" Luca raised both eyebrows.

"He will be excited to meet you, my love." Gaia took Luca's hands in hers. "He is the mayor."

A portly man, in his night clothes, came into range of the torch light, accompanied by guards.

Luca shook his head. "This night just gets worse and worse."

"We don't have time for this." Raphael bounded up the wall and through a small window above the closed gate. There was the sound of something breaking, and a man screamed. Moments later, the portcullis raised just enough for Fransie and her companions to pass. After everyone was safely on the other side, the portcullis crashed down, and Raphael jumped out the window on the opposite side of the tower to join them on the bridge.

"*Adios*, papa! I love you. I will return as a married woman!"

"Gaia!" the old man bellowed, shaking his fist.

Auriel and Binah met them on the far side of the bridge. Binah shook the water from her body. Fransie was amazed that they had waded across the mighty river. She couldn't help but wrap her arms around Auriel. She was so happy to see her. But, what about Stefano? Was he dead or alive? Even with all of his faults, Fransie had a certain sort of love for Stefano. Fransie could only imagine the anguish inside Luca. She didn't know what she would do if she lost Caroline.

CHAPTER 33

"Andrew Sinclair, ya canna leave this house." Clair stood with both hands on her hips, blocking the door.

"I'll be careful. 'Tis dark out, and no one will ever recognize me in this." Andy pulled a large black hood over his face. "See, even ya cuddna tell I am your own brother."

"And how do ya suppose y're gonna get around town with that thing over your eyes?"

"I can see just fine."

"Prove it. Walk ta the kitchen and back. If ya make it without running in ta anything, I'll get out of your way."

Andy smiled. He knew this house like the back of his hand. This would be simple, even if he could only see the ground right in front of him. Andy walked cautiously down the hallway to the kitchen door.

"See 'tis easy."

"Ya walk like old Auntie Mable. If ya can walk back here properly, I'll move."

"Walking like old Auntie Mable..." Andy muttered. He would show Clair that he could walk at a normal speed. He walked down the hallway briskly.

Andy fell hard as he ran into something as firm as a tree limb. Clair burst into laughter. Andy pulled back his hood and rubbed his head. Gerhart extended the same arm that had knocked Andy down and helped him to his feet.

"Now why did ya have ta do that?" Andy accepted Gerhart's hand and stood.

"She made me do it." Gerhart pointed at Clair, who was still bent over laughing. "I just put out my arm, and you ran into it."

"See?" Clair cleared a tear. "I told ya ya culdna see in that thing. I win."

"That wasna fair."

"Neither is life, Andy. 'Tis too dangerous for ya out there with them Templars looking for ya. Ya shouldna even be seen in the fields."

"What am I suppose ta do during the days?"

"I'm sure Chelsea will find something for ya." Andy was happy they had found Chelsea curled up in her bed after Acedia had disappeared. To the best of his knowledge, she couldn't remember Acedia ever being there. However, she had been working them extra hard.

Andy walked to his room, muttering the whole way. He slammed the door. He hated feeling trapped. He needed to be free. He needed to go back to the cathedral.

Actually, I donna need ta go back.

Andy walked to the chest at the bottom of his bed and took out the diagram he had been working on. Andy had cataloged every symbol on every pillar in the church. It was all there, waiting to be decoded.

PLANTA DE LA CATEDRAL DE SANTIAGO.*

Andy looked at the lump on Etienne's bed, where he had hidden the severed head. He had hoped it would look just like another pillow—and it did, for the most part.

"Maybe ya can 'elp me with this as well." Andy pulled down the covers and took two steps back. The head had sprouted branches that were budding and growing into the headboard.

"What the 'ell? Well, never mind." Andy tossed the blanket back over the head with trembling hands and walked back to his bed.

He laid out the gridded codes from the Keystone Church next to the diagram of the cathedral. One by one, he laid out the grids he had drawn for each pillar. Comparing them, he noticed that the pillars in the north wing of the church contained the highest concentration of symbols from the code among the marca de cantera,[26] which indicated the quarry the stones come from.

Andy placed the grids in sequential order according to his diagram of the church and noticed that every other pillar contained the code amongst the mason's marks. He quickly consulted the cypher from the Keystone Church and wrote out the letters descending clockwise. He started at the first symbol he saw and worked his way around and down the diagram of the column. Sometimes there was only one symbol per level of blocks and on others there were several. However, each pillar contained seven characters.

PILLAR 1	ZKYTANL
PILLAR 2	AGPOPTC
PILLAR 3	GNAIOMR
PILLAR 4	VSDBSFK
PILLAR 5	AFMDWTC
PILLAR 6	OAHGDUP

So, there is another level to this code. Andy rubbed his hands together. There was no way there would be six words containing seven letters each. Andy paced the room back and forth.

After half an hour of pacing, Andy had run through every scenario he could think of. He had noticed he kept glancing over at Etienne's bed. He tried to convince himself that he was just wishing Etienne was there to help him—but, deep down, Andy knew he wanted to ask the head for help.

"Fine." He sighed heavily. He uncovered the head. "Well, um-a, thank ya for your 'elp before. Sloth was a nasty piece of work." Andy twiddled his thumbs. "I was wondering if ya could 'elp again. Since ya are here, ya probably know we are looking for the treasure. We're the good guys. We need ta protect it from the baddies. I am stumped on this code from the cathedral. Any 'elp would be appreciated." Andy twiddled his thumbs again.

He scrunched his face, waiting for the message from the head. He sat patiently listening to his thoughts, but they were all his own.

"Right then, let's just go ta bed." Andy covered the head, cleaned up the papers, and tucked himself in. "Goodnight, creepy head."

CHAPTER 34

Fransie's eyes were heavy from their journey through the night, but she was enjoying the sunrises. Every time they crested a hill, the sun would rise again behind them before descending back into twilight. By the time the sun had fully risen, they had reached Estella. Sister Fransie and her companions climbed the steps of a monastery at the entrance of the city and looked out over the town.

"This is the farthest that I have made it," Gaia said, triumphantly.

"What do you mean?" Fransie asked.

"Every time I run away, my father catches me before I reach Estella. This is the first time I have made it this far. They must have had trouble opening the portcullis."

"And, how many times have you run away?" Sister Caroline placed her hands on her hips.

Gaia counted on her fingers, amusing herself with internal stories of each escape. "I think this makes eight." Gaia laughed to herself. "Oh yeah, this is actually nine. This one time—"

"Let's get breakfast," Raphael said.

The town square was bustling with merchants and the smell of baking bread filled each street leading to this main hub of the city. Fransie admired the balconies of the tall buildings that surrounded the square. Each balcony was slightly different—some had plants, and others laundry drying in the morning sun. Fransie loved watching the interactions of the townsfolk. Everyone had their purpose for the day.

"So, Raphael, I thought you would only be joining us until the edge of your lands. Didn't that end just outside of Pamplona?" Sister Caroline rested her elbows on the table. Behind Caroline's voice, Fransie heard one of the dissonant tones slightly.

"Plans changed." Raphael placed her quiver of arrows on the table.

"Yeah, it would be difficult for us to go back unnoticed," Auriel said.

It was true, no one in the whole town looked like these two, Raphael with her dark skin and warrior's body and Auriel with her fiery red hair, emerald eyes, and porcelain skin. They were a unique duo.

"We can't go back, at least not for a while, but you can, Gaia." Raphael stared down the young woman, who took no notice.

"Now that I have found my love, why would I ever leave him?" Gaia tightened her grip on Luca, who looked like a frightened animal wanting to escape.

"You don't expect us to believe that?" Sister Caroline said, giving her a concerned look.

"And why wouldn't you believe that?" Gaia pouted her lip and crossed her arms.

"Have you looked at him?" Emmanuel asked. Everyone laughed except for Gaia, and Luca, who gave Emmanuel a menacing look. Emmanuel raised his hands in surrender. "I kid, I kid, you know that, Luca."

"And were the eight, oh no, wait, nine other times you ran away for love too?" Auriel rolled her eyes.

Gaia's gaze dropped. She shook her head. "No, they were just to get away. I want to live a life of adventure, on the road, and my father won't let me leave the house. I only saw Luca because I was on the roof. I'm sorry, Luca, I was just using you."

"It was mutual." Luca drew back. "We used you to get over the wall—and you used us to escape. Let's just say we were helping each other instead of using each other." Gaia shot him a nod.

"See, doesn't it feel better to be honest?" Sister Caroline sat back in her chair, glancing at Fransie.

"You don't want this life," Raphael said. "You will never be happy in your life unless you are satisfied wherever you are. You will always be looking for something just over the next hill and ignoring the beauty around you."

"That may be true, Raphael, but this young woman should have a choice." Sister Caroline leaned forward again. "Every woman should have a choice."

"We grew up outside of society and have always been free." Auriel's emerald eyes reflected the green hills of the Pyrenees Mountains. "My sister and I could never fully understand what that must be like for you. Raphael was the only one who ever tried to tell me what to do." Auriel pushed her sister then placed her hand to the side of her mouth and whispered, "I never listened either. You can join us if you like—the choice is yours."

"And where are you going? Also, why were the Hospitallers chasing you?" Gaia questioned.

"Luca, are you all right?" Fransie interjected before anyone could answer. His eyes looked hollow, and his smile lines drooped.

"I am concerned about Stefano. Did he die?"

"We can't say for sure," Raphael said.

"It is the uncertainty that is eating at me. If I knew he was dead, I could deal with it. But the thought that he is alive, imprisoned, tortured..." Luca hit his fist on the table, splashing the water from the glasses.

"We will continue to pray for him." Fransie placed a reassuring hand on his fist. "If you would like to go back, we would understand." Fransie had prayed nonstop for both Stefano and Luca. She hoped God had heard her prayers.

"I can't." Luca shook his head. "His last request to me, perhaps his dying request, was to watch out for you two." Luca threw his napkin on the table and stood. "Let's continue."

CHAPTER 35

Isabella had repeatedly refused Gaston's requests for her to visit Fatima. Being seen with a secret prisoner wouldn't help her to get on her father's good side. Finally though, Isabella's curiosity and boredom got the best of her, and here she stood, at the prison door.

"Does my father know about her?" Isabella raised an eyebrow at Gaston, and he put a reassuring hand on her shoulder.

"Isabella, I have entrusted you with one secret. I feel this one will be safe with you as well. I was supposed to kill Fatima after we extracted the information we needed. But, just like with Etienne, I couldn't do it."

Isabella wondered what other secrets Gaston was keeping from her father. He was supposed to be his most trusted guard, the person in charge of protecting him. Even though Isabella was mad at her father, and wanted to stop him, she still loved him. Isabella took a deep breath—she had to prepare herself before entering.

"I'm ready." She nodded at Gaston, and he led her in. Fatima's cell was clean and furnished. Light poured in from a large window at the far end, almost making it cozy.

"Isabella, I would like you to formally meet Etienne's mother, Fatima." Isabella gave Fatima a curt nod, and Fatima returned it, her eyes scanning Isabella the whole time.

"How is this possible? Etienne is an orphan. Both of his parents died." Isabella crossed her arms. She felt uncomfortable to be meeting Etienne's mother. So many petty thoughts ran through her head.

"It is true, my husband is dead, but I am yet still alive. Praise Allah."

"My father would never tolerate this blasphemy in his castle." Isabella wished this was going better. The words just came out of her mouth.

"We tolerate certain things for special guests." Gaston's body sighed.

"You're in love?" Isabella turned her head between the two. Their body language gave it all away.

"It is so," Fatima said, taking his hand. Fatima looked at Gaston exactly like Etienne looked at her. Isabella didn't trust Fatima. Even though parts of her reminded Isabella of Etienne, other parts reminded her of her captor, Nazir.

"Why did you bring me here, Gaston?"

"I thought you would like to meet the mother of the man you love. I know Fatima wanted to meet you." Fatima looked Isabella up and down, sizing her up. Isabella stood proudly, holding her ground. She wouldn't let this prisoner intimidate her. She was the princess of France and soon to be queen of England.

"How is my child?" Fatima asked. Gaston looked at Fatima with hurt eyes, and she took his hand. "How is our child?"

"Are you Etienne's father?" Isabella gasped.

Gaston shook his head. "No, but he was like a son to me. He was part of our deal."

"Deal?" Isabella's brow furrowed.

"Yes, Fatima was captured trying to kill your father." Isabella's blood boiled, and her hands closed to fists. "Her husband, Etienne's father, worked here at the palace. We caught him letting Fatima into the throne room. Fatima killed three of our guards, and it took another four to restrain her—my type of woman." Gaston beamed a smile at Fatima. Isabella couldn't believe what was happening. "They tortured her, but she wouldn't talk. That is until we discovered she had a son, Etienne. He was her one weakness."

"And still is," Fatima interrupted. "I promised to tell them all that I knew if they would find Etienne and protect him."

"It didn't take long for us to find Etienne on the streets and bring him back to the palace. Look out the window."

Isabella walked cautiously to the window. On the other side was the training yard for the young squires.

"I got to watch my Etienne grow up," Fatima said proudly. "I also saw the two of you together when you thought no one could see." Isabella felt vulnerable and bit her lip.

"What did my father get out of the deal?" Isabella asked, wanting to regain her power.

"Everything I knew," Fatima said. "I told him about the Order of the Assassins and our mission to kill the few to spare the many. Had I succeeded in my mission, and killed your father, many lives would have been saved. But, the life of my Etienne was worth more than all of theirs combined."

"Isabella, your father used the information we got from Fatima to turn France into what it is today. We won many victories because of the knowledge she had."

"If you were so useful, why did my father want you dead?"

"I outlived my usefulness. When your father found I had no more information to offer, he ordered me executed."

"That sounds like my father." Isabella tried not to brush against the wall in the beautiful gown she was wearing.

Gaston chuckled. "By the time he had ordered the execution, Fatima and I had fallen deeply in love. We had become a sort of strange family with Etienne. I couldn't kill Fatima, so I moved her here."

Isabella took a step back—she couldn't believe what she was hearing. Everything she knew about Gaston was unraveling before her eyes. In a short time he had gone from her father's protector to a traitor and a spy. She shook her head. How could she judge him—hadn't she done the same? Isabella felt wretched inside.

"Come closer." Fatima motioned to Isabella with both hands. "I want to see the beauty my son has fallen in love with." Isabella had been so taken aback by what Gaston was telling her that she almost forgot that Fatima was Etienne's mother. A lump formed in Isabella's throat. She wanted to please this woman for Etienne.

Isabella walked closer and stood in a shaft of sunlight. Fatima raised her hand to Isabella's chin, moving her head from side-to-side.

"You are beautiful and powerful, I will give you that, but I can't approve of you for my son." Isabella clenched her fists and narrowed her gaze. She pushed Fatima's hand from her chin.

"And why is that?" Isabella had fury in her eyes.

"Because you're not too smart." In one swift movement, Fatima pulled Gaston's dagger and slit his throat. She then placed the blade under Isabella's chin. Isabella felt the sharp point push through her skin, and her blood joined Gaston's.

"I thought you loved Gaston?" Isabella said, trying to make sense of the situation and to buy some time. She needed to think her way out of this.

"Love." Fatima's laugh echoed Nazir's, and Isabella's blood turned cold. "He was my captor. I did what I had to do to survive—to protect my child. Now, you will help me to fulfill my mission." Fatima pulled Isabella in front of her and held the dagger to her neck. Isabella stole one last look at Gaston bleeding out on the floor as they exited the cell—leaving her father's strength dying on the floor.

CHAPTER 36

*J*ust outside of Estella, Fransie and her companions came to a blacksmith's shop. The sound of the smith's hammer hitting steel shot onto the Camino, along with sparks. A hiss sounded and steam wafted into their path as the smith placed the metal into a bucket of water.

"*Hola, peregrinos.*" The smith pulled the blade from the bucket and placed it on the table. He took off his apron and beckoned them to enter. "Would you like to buy anything?"

Gaia rushed into the shop and rummaged through the metal goods. "How much is this?" She held up a metal scallop shell on a leather string.

"One copper," the smith said.

"Will you sharpen our weapons as well? Who knows what dangers we may face ahead." Luca unsheathed his sword.

"I will sharpen them." The smith took Luca's sword and inspected it. "But, the only dangers on the Camino are the ones you bring with you." He took the sharpening stone and began the work.

Fransie admired all of the beautiful things in the smith's shop as he worked on the swords. The smith was a true artist.

"There, that does it." The smith handed back the weapons in exchange for a few small coins. "Gracias, make sure to visit the fountain ahead—you can fill your gourds there with either water or wine."

Just as the smith said, five minutes down the road was the fountain. Fransie was relieved—her gourd was almost empty, and the Spanish sun was punishing. The metal fountain was set back inside a masonry of tan stones. Fransie wondered if the metal smith had constructed the fountain—the work was excellent. There were two spigots protruding from decorative scallop shells. Below each was a basin—one was clean, and the other was stained with red wine. Between the basins was a sculpture of a staff with a scallop shell. Above that was the cross of Saint James. At the top was a crest with a lion encapsulated with the words *Fuente de Xrache* and *Bodegas Irache.*

Emmanuel headed straight for the spigot labeled *vino* and filled his scallop shell with red wine before taking a tentative sip "It's-a good," he said, taking a more generous swig.

Fransie approached the fountain and heard a soothing sound. It was as if someone had dipped their finger in water and ran it along the edge of a glass. The noise reverberated through her.

"Do any of you hear that?" She looked at the others.

"Oh no, not this again." Sister Caroline crossed her arms.

"I feel it. Binah, come closer." The horse obeyed orders and nuzzled into Auriel.

"I see it." Hokhmah screeched out of the sky and landed on Raphael's outstretched arm. "Fransie, leave it alone."

"I—I can't." Fransie tried to restrain her hand, but it moved without her will. In the stones surrounding the fountain was the same pattern that appeared on the cathedral floor. Without thought, her finger automatically tapped the descending lightning bolt pattern from top to bottom.

"Oh, no you don't." Sister Caroline grabbed Fransie's wrist. The two of them struggled, but Fransie managed to push the last stone. As it decompressed, there was a bright light and they tumbled through the rocks.

Fransie's landing was softened by Sister Caroline. She rolled off her old friend and stood in front of a large wooden door. Carved deep into the wood was a face with a slot for a mouth.

"Sister Fransie, help me up immediately. Where are the others? Can you hear me? Help! Help!" Fransie looked around; they were alone in the darkness, except for the strange door emanating light. Fransie put her ear to the door, and behind it, she heard a gentle hum. It poured into her ears and made her feel whole.

"Step away from that door! You remember what happened last time. We must find another way out of here. There has to be a way out. How do you keep getting us into these situations?"

"Sister Caroline, I don't know. But I fear the only way out is to go forward." Fransie's hand moved instinctively once again. Remembering the last door didn't open until she bled, Fransie dipped her index finger in the blood from a small cut from her landing, and drew a backward Z on the forehead of the face. The mouth on the door expanded until it was a gaping hole large enough to walk through. Fransie took Caroline by the hand, and they stepped across the threshold.

CHAPTER 37

For many days Mariano sat in the cave just looking at the parchment and quill. He didn't know where to start. The more time that passed, the more helpless and angry he became. It wasn't fair; the Alchemist shouldn't have left him like this. She should have given him more instruction. He wished it would have been like the last time they met. Just being with her had brought Mariano into the present moment—it had ended his suffering. Why wasn't it like that this time? He wanted it to be easy.

"She shouldn't have left me!" Mariano shouted.

"She shouldn't have left me, left me, left me...," his own voice echoed back.

Mariano laughed uncontrollably. His own voice was telling him where to start. The thought that had been giving him so much trouble—the Shadow that had been secretly attacking him—was the thought *She shouldn't have left me.*

Mariano rushed to the parchment and wrote:

She shouldn't have left.

1) Is it true?
- *Yes! I need more instruction. I'm not ready for this...*

Mariano laughed again. He remembered the Alchemist telling him that the first two questions are simply yes or no. Anything else is the Shadow trying to justify itself. Mariano saw that. This thought was using those beliefs as justification for its existence. He continued with the second question.

2) Can you absolutely know it's true?
- *No.*

There was no way Mariano could know beyond a doubt that the Alchemist shouldn't have left him. This answer felt truer in his body than his first, and he decided to continue with the third question.

3) How do you react when you think that thought?
- *I feel sorry for myself. I feel helpless. I get angry and want to give up. I feel abandoned and unwanted. A knot forms in my stomach and pushes itself up to my throat, and I hold back tears.*

Mariano didn't realize this one thought was causing him so much suffering. He saw a chain in his thinking for the last few days, and all of his self-pity led back to this thought. Excitement grew in him, as he continued on to the fourth question.

4) Who would you be if you couldn't think this thought?
- *I would have started this work many days ago. I would be confident in my actions. I would be independent, happy, and at peace. I would be free to do what I am here to do.*

"This thought has been preventing me from doing what I am here to do," Mariano whispered.

One single thought had defeated him in a cave for days. Mariano saw how this had happened before in his life in other situations. He had put his personal responsibility on others, blaming them for his inaction. Mariano wasn't as clear on how to do the next part, but he continued.

Turn around

1) The opposite:
- *The Alchemist should have left me.*

That statement felt truer in his body than the original statement. Just for good measure Mariano decided to give some examples of how this statement was truer:

The Alchemist should have left me:
- *She did leave me.*
- *Had she not left, I wouldn't have been able to discover this on my own.*
- *I am capable of doing this on my own.*

Mariano took a deep breath. *She did leave.* There was no arguing with that. Mariano would have been insane to fight against that. It was a fact that she did leave, and that's exactly what she should have done because she did it. Who was he to argue against that?

2) The self:
- *I shouldn't have left me.*

Boy, that had some truth to it. Mariano had been so busy hating the Alchemist for leaving that he had neglected himself. He hadn't eaten, nor slept well. *He* had left himself alone in the cave, not the Alchemist. Mariano gave himself a hug. *I am here with you now.*

He moved on to the third turnaround. Here, he was supposed to insert his thinking into the turnaround.

3) My thinking:
 * *My thinking about the Alchemist shouldn't have left me, or*
 * *My thinking about the Alchemist should have left me.*

That's interesting. Both of these statements were true. Had Mariano trusted the Alchemist like he had before, he would have seen clearly that her leaving wasn't done to hurt him. He also saw that his current thinking about the Alchemist should have left him—he was blaming her for his inactivity. The invisible Shadow *should* was what was stopping him from having peace in the moment. It wasn't his circumstances—it was his thinking about his circumstances.

"She shouldn't have left me!" Mariano shouted. Before the cave had a chance to echo back, Mariano's laughter left it dead in its tracks.

Mariano tried to find the anger he once had at the Alchemist for leaving, but he couldn't. She did what she did, and there wasn't anything he could do to change it. The only thing he could change was his thinking about it. Mariano realized in that moment that he couldn't control anyone, he could only question his thoughts to see that they weren't true.

He was thinking with a clear mind now. Of course she should have left him, because she did. He would have never been able to discover these truths for himself if he was always relying on her. Mariano was so thankful that she had left him; so thankful for the gift of self-discovery. Mariano knew exactly which concept to question next. He looked at the top of his paper and laughed again. He would take away all of the legs that once had supported this belief.

I need more instruction.

1) Is it true...

CHAPTER 38

Fransie stepped through the door into a land unlike any she had experienced before. The best way she had to describe it was empty: a wasteland. Even though there was a large lake with a castle in the middle, the whole land was desolate. Everything seemed to have a green-gray hue to it.

"Where have you taken us, Fransie?" Sister Caroline made the sign of the cross. "I don't like this place. I feel like it is eating me from the inside out."

"I don't know, Caroline, but I hear it coming from that castle—we have to reach it."

"Reach what? I don't understand you."

"It's like a hum calling to me. It is the only thing nourishing me in this land—everything else is draining me—an emptiness consuming me."

"Oh, Fransie, I am scared."

"Me too, Caroline. But we must be brave."

"How can I be brave when I am so afraid?"

"Bravery isn't the absence of fear, it is acting in spite of those very fears. Let's take action and figure out how to cross this lake."

"Maybe he can help?" Caroline pointed to a solitary boat on the lake with a lonely lantern, and a hooded figure. "Let's call him over. If he is the boatman of death, it's better to find out sooner rather than later." Fransie nodded her head. "Oy!" Caroline shouted, sending little ripples out over the water.

"That was very brave, Caroline." The two of them exchanged a smile.

The boat pulled up onto the pebbled shore where the water gently lapped.

"How may I be of service to you?" the boatman said from just outside the radius of lantern light.

"We must reach that castle." Fransie recognized the desperation in her voice and wished she would have said it more calmly.

"Why must you reach that castle?"

"Because, it's calling to me."

The boatman motioned for them to enter the boat. After Fransie passed the lantern, her eyes adjusted, and she saw the boatman clearly. His face matched the desolateness of the land. It looked as if all the blood had been drained from his body, yet, he still clung onto life.

"Oh, goodness me," Caroline murmured as she saw the boatman as well. He pushed off from shore and ferried them to the middle of the lake, where he ceased rowing, and the vessel came to a complete stop.

"What are you doing?" Fransie's voice was shaky.

The boatman placed both hands on his groin and, in the dim light, Fransie saw that he had a large wound.

"Let us help you." Fransie moved forward, but the boatman held up a hand to stop her.

"What do you seek?"

"I don't know, but it is in that castle. I can hear it calling to me." There was a long pause, and Fransie felt as sheepish as her voice had sounded. The boat gently rocked like a metronome on the dead lake, as the seconds passed.

"We seek the grail," Sister Caroline said, triumphantly.

"What are you talking about, Caroline?"

"He is the Fisher King."[27] Caroline read Fransie's blank stare. "From Arthurian Legends—surely you must have read them." Fransie shook her head and Caroline sighed heavily. "You must keep up with the times. They are very popular now."

"I am he," said the Fisher King.

"Ha, I knew it." Sister Caroline sat back, and the boat rocked again. "Oh my, sorry."

"Caroline, how did you know?"

"According to the legend, the Fisher King protects the Holy Grail."[28] Fransie made the sign of the cross. "He was wounded as the result of his own ethical failings. His wound doesn't heal and the land withers with him. So, a once rich life has now become a wasteland." Sister Caroline motioned to the land around them, and the Fisher King lowered his face behind his shroud.

"Well, what can heal his wound?"

"Only the healing question." Sister Caroline and the Fisher King said in unison.

Sister Caroline put her hands over her mouth. "Oh, sorry. I'm sure you only get to say that every couple of hundred years." The Fisher King nodded his head.

"Well, what is the question?" Sister Fransie gripped the side of the boat hard, trying to contain her anticipation. Through the whole conversation there was the constant hum coming from the castle, pulling her to it.

Caroline looked from Fransie to the Fisher King. "I love that part of the legend... I mean, your legend." She smiled politely at the Fisher King.

"Well, what is the question?" Fransie wanted Caroline to get on with it.

"Whom does the grail serve? That is the healing question." Caroline smiled triumphantly.

Fransie believed the Fisher King would have smiled if he had the ability. "No!" he said, hunched over, and holding his wound.

"I must have messed up the words. It was something like that." Sister Caroline crossed her arms.

"What is the healing question?" The Fisher King placed his full attention on Fransie. Caroline had had her guess, now it was Fransie's turn.

She hated seeing him suffer—she wanted to end it. The hum came skipping across the water; it had the same cadence as speech even though there were no words. Fransie nodded her head to the sound. *What words have that rhythm?*

She let the rhythm wash over her and guide her. "Who is served by the grail?" Fransie's mouth spoke on its own.

"The old king whose heir you are." This Fisher King continued rowing. The blood from the Fisher King's wound dried up, and the mist was blown from the land. The greenish haze left, and radiant sunlight bathed them.

They reached the shore of the castle and the Fisher King stood. The shroud dropped from his shoulders, revealing a white mantle with a golden cross and belt. His slumped shoulders were now broad and strong. He was healed.

"Sister Fransie, you are now my heir and protector of the grail. May your moral fortitude serve you better than mine served me."

He opened the large doors to the castle, and Fransie's ears were filled with the hum that nearly vibrated her. She didn't need him to lead her—she knew exactly where the grail was. The way the sound bounced off everything made a visual representation in her mind of the whole castle.

They followed the Fisher King up a large set of stairs, and at the top was the grail. The humble cup sat on a pedestal and seemed to glow. Fransie looked back at the Fisher King.

"Take it. The burden is now yours to bear." Fransie nodded and wrapped her hands around the Holy Grail.

CHAPTER 39

The doors to the throne room flew open, and the faces of all those present reflected Isabella's fear. Fatima's hair brushed Isabella's neck as she turned her head from side to side, sizing up the room. Fatima dug the blade closer into Isabella's throat. Her skin threatened to pop open again at any moment.

"What is this!" her father demanded, standing from his throne. "Where is Gaston?"

"He is dead." Fatima cackled. Guards lined up in front of her father's throne as they approached.

"That is close enough," Philip ordered. Fatima hesitated for a moment, but continued forward.

"I am the one making the rules here, unless you want your precious daughter dead." Fatima drew a little of Isabella's blood for emphasis. The blade stung as it cut a thin slice in her neck. The blood ran down her chest and stained her dress.

"What is it that you want?" Philip barked.

"A life for a life," Fatima said. "I must finish what I have started."

"You are that woman I captured years ago for plotting against me." Philip sat and waved away the guards. Isabella felt a slight stutter in Fatima's step. Her father's display of confidence had affected Fatima's courage.

"You have done well with the information I gave to you."

"I had you killed. Have you come back from your grave to take revenge?" Philip clasped his hands together. "Pierre." Philip beckoned for his advisor to come closer. Pierre looked from Philip to Fatima then back to Philip again. Philip gave him a stern look and Pierre obeyed. Isabella couldn't make out what her father had whispered in his ear.

"Stop it, or I will kill her. I am the one giving orders now!" Fatima demanded.

"Go ahead, kill her. She is a traitor as well. The moment she dies, you will die too." His words drained all of the blood from Isabella's face—had he just said what she thought she heard?

Fatima stopped at the foot of the steps leading to the throne. Isabella heard Fatima smile behind her.

"I am already dead." In a breath, Fatima took the blade from Isabella's neck to throw at Philip. As Fatima began to move, Isabella rammed her head into Fatima's face and felt the woman's nose crunch. The force of the blow was enough to send the dagger off trajectory. It made a hollow sound as it sunk into the wood of the throne.

"Guards!" Philip shouted. Ten guards surrounded Fatima and attacked. She took out three of them before the others were able to subdue her. Philip took the dagger from the throne and walked to Fatima.

"This time, you will stay dead." Philip plunged the dagger deep into Fatima's heart.

"This is a good death," Fatima said with her last breath. Philip nodded, and his guards dragged Fatima's corpse from the throne room.

"Pierre, have someone clean this mess up." Philip demanded. Pierre bowed and scurried away. "Leave us. All of you!" Philip roared. It wasn't long until it was just Isabella and her father alone in the opulent hall.

Isabella sat on the steps leading to the throne and tied a piece of cloth from her underskirt around her throat to stop the small trickle of blood. Her father paced back and forth for a moment, then sat by her side. It was the first time he had ever positioned himself as an equal with her.

"Daughter, you saved my life." Philip took Isabella's hand in his. "Perhaps I have misjudged you and treated you too harshly."

Isabella's childhood desire for approval welled up inside of her. She had searched for this sort of affection from him for years. She savored the moment, not knowing how long it would last. She hated feeling like a failure in his eyes.

"Where is Gaston?"

Isabella had almost forgotten about him. Would she tell her father that Gaston had betrayed him for so many years, or would that secret go to the grave with him?

"He died an honorable death." Isabella couldn't tell her father the whole truth. Gaston had filled a role in her life where her father had fallen short. He had been kind to her, and kind to Etienne. What difference did his betrayal make now that he was dead?

"You may return to your normal quarters, but I still can't have you leave the palace." Isabella nodded. "Now that I know I can trust you, you will rejoin the small council. As you will be the queen of England one day, you will have a large role to play, and there is much to discuss. Are you willing to accept that role? And are you through with these silly thoughts of that boy? What was his name, Etienne?"

Isabella paused for a moment, and her father retracted his hand—Isabella grasped it before it left hers. She looked at him with large eyes and nodded her head.

"Good, because there is going to be a ball in your honor, and I need you to do something for me."

CHAPTER 40

Everyone was staring down at Fransie. Turning to her left, she saw Sister Caroline grasping her hand tightly. In Fransie's other hand was the grail. She could feel its gentle hum, as she clutched it tightly to her body.

"What happened?" she managed.

"You just disappeared! It was like magic," Gaia said excitedly. Fransie sat up and her head spun. She clasped her legs in and rested her forehead on her knees.

"What is that?" Luca eyed the grail.

"Something she shouldn't have taken." Raphael crossed her arms.

"Fransie, do you still have the grail?" Sister Caroline shot up as if rising from a dream.

Michael's mouth dropped. "The *Holy Grail?*" He made the sign of the cross, and the other Italians followed suit.

"I'm sorry, Raphael. I couldn't stop myself. You know how hard it pulls. Do you remember the time before you had Hokhmah? It felt as if the vibration from the sound would explode my body if I did nothing."

"As I said before, the voice of the angels can be more tempting than the voice of the demons. We have two treasures now that emanate the purest forms of divinity I have ever experienced. You won't be able to control the temptation. Pray to your God that he sends your animal soon."

"What is going on here?" Gaia asked.

"It is hard to explain, young lady. Now if you don't mind..." Sister Caroline extended her hands for the others to lift her.

Sister Fransie did the same. Luca reached for her, but instead of taking her hand, he took the grail. He ran to the fountain of water, filled the cup, and drank. Fransie's heart sank. She was the protector of the grail, and she had already lost it.

"You fool, what have you done? Give that cup back to Fransie!" Raphael pointed her bow at Luca.

"Go ahead, shoot." He walked to her and put the tip of the arrow on his chest. "I have eternal life now."

"Do you want to test that theory?" Auriel placed a dagger in his back at the level of his heart.

"There is no need to test it. I already feel it in my body." Luca casually gave the grail back to Fransie. "Now, no one can stop me from avenging Stefano. I will kill that priest and all of the Hospitallers." Fransie didn't like this change in Luca. Standing next to her, she heard a dissonant tone coming from deep in his stomach.

"My body needs food for the changes happening inside of me. Gaia!" He motioned for Gaia. She came close to him, and he clasped his arm around her tightly.

CHAPTER 41

It had been two days since they found the grail. Sister Fransie had kept it close to her body. She loved the gentle hum of it. Now, however, it felt as if the hum was a part of her—it almost felt as if it was inside her. There was one problem through—Fransie had missed her moon. Ever since she became a woman, her cycle followed the moon. It should have come two days prior, but it hadn't.

Raphael and Auriel had been ignoring Fransie. They mainly kept to themselves, watching Luca at all times. Fransie was sure they were sensing what she was—the dissonant tone inside Luca grew louder as the time passed. Something else strange was happening with him—he wanted more of everything and was never satisfied. First it was water. Every stop they came to, he would drink all the water from his gourd, and refill it, only to drain the liquid once more.

Fransie also noticed it with women, as well. He kept Gaia on his arm at all times, but every female pilgrim or villager they passed, his eyes would soak up. If Gaia hadn't stopped him, it would have been more than just his eyes. He even looked at the women in their company with the same hungry eyes. Fransie wondered what the grail had done to him.

"Sister Caroline, I'm worried about Luca." Fransie took Caroline's arm as they continued on the Camino. The dusty road stretched on for miles in front of them, with vineyards as far as the eyes could see.

"Me, too, Fransie. He keeps looking at me like I will be next on the platter, and he hasn't stopped drinking. Have you noticed how swollen his belly is?" Fransie had made note of it. His stomach had nearly doubled in size. "I'm worried about you, as well. You have barely eaten or drunk anything."

"I am fine. I actually feel more satisfied than I have my whole life. I feel as if I have the word of God inside me, sustaining me. It is just a gentle hum."

Sister Caroline cocked her head. "What are you talking about? You do look a little rosy."

"I missed my moon. It has only been a few days but..." Sister Fransie instinctively placed her hands on her lower abdomen.

"Well, that doesn't seem like much...being a few days late happens to women all of the time. Surely it's happened to you before?"

"It has, but this time it's different. I feel something inside of me."

"How is that possible?"

"I don't know. I have never lain with a man." Sister Caroline marched to Luca, Michael, and Emmanuel and began pushing them.

"All right, which of you did it? Which of you took advantage of my poor Fransie?" She shoved Emmanuel hard.

"What? I didn't-a do anything." Emmanuel raised his hands in surrender.

"Was it you?" She placed a finger in Michael's chest. "Always acting innocent."

"What are you talking about?" Michael shook his head.

"Of course it was you." Sister Caroline shot Luca a death-look and rolled up her sleeves.

"Sister Caroline, come back here immediately!" Sister Fransie ordered.

Sister Caroline continued to stare at Luca and raised an eyebrow. "I am watching you." Sister Caroline backed away from the group and joined Fransie.

"What was that all about?" Michael asked.

"I think the sun has gotten to her," Luca scoffed.

The Camino led the company to a beautiful bridge whose underbelly dove in and out of the water like a serpent. It was a magnificent feat of architecture. On the other side of the river was a colorful city teeming with life.

"This must be Lagrono," Gaia said. "The food is supposed to be amazing here. I have always wanted to try it. My father has told me many stories about this town. I think we should stay here for the whole night."

"Raphael, will you join us in the city?" Fransie looked at Raphael and Auriel expectantly. They had avoided all of the other cities, just passing through quickly, except for last night— they stayed with the group at the alburgue, ever watchful of Luca.

"I would prefer that you stay with us outside the city; it isn't safe for you yet." Raphael looked at Fransie sternly.

"This is a once in a lifetime opportunity." Luca wrapped his arm over Fransie's shoulder. "You heard Gaia—this city has the best food on the Camino. We have to go through the city either way— why not stay the night?"

"He's right." Fransie looked at her road-weary companions. "We have been pushing our bodies so hard. I think an afternoon and evening of rest will do us good. I think if we all stay together, we will be safe."

"If you insist, we will join you." Hokhmah flew from the sky and landed on Raphael's shoulder. "You must stay close." Raphael stroked the falcon's beak.

They followed the scallop shells marking the Camino to the main plaza. The large square opened wide, and to the left was a giant cathedral. Sister Fransie had the overwhelming urge to pray. She left the others and headed for the church entrance.

"Oh no, not this again," Sister Caroline said, hooking her arm.

"No, Sister Caroline, I want to speak with God." Everyone followed Fransie into the cathedral except for Raphael and Auriel. They waited outside with their animals.

Sister Fransie sat in a pew and bent her head. *My dear Lord, I pray for Luca and for myself. Help us to make it through this task.* Fransie gripped her rosary tightly. *Our Father, who art in heaven...*

Fransie looked around and saw it was just herself and Sister Caroline in the church.

"My dear Sister Fransie, I am here with you until the end. You know that." Caroline looked at her tenderly and patted her hand. Fransie nodded, not sure why Sister Caroline had made such a proclamation.

As they exited the church, the whole town was opening up from the afternoon siesta. Emmanuel ran up to them excitedly.

"It is time to get some *pinchos*. I have never seen anything like this." He kissed his fingers. "Mamma mia."

Sister Caroline and Sister Fransie followed Emmanuel across the square to the entrance of a small alley, which was a cornucopia of smells, colors, and tastes. The small street was lined with bars; each had a small window to the street, presenting their finest pinchos. The small plates of food looked like fine art.

"Look at the prosciutto," Emmanuel said. "Just look at it."

He was right, it was a thing of beauty. The prosciutto ribboned down on a stick, which was stuck into a large fried ball of polenta. Fransie salivated at the sight. Next to this was bread with goat cheese and wild berries on top. On the next plate were artichoke hearts and more prosciutto. Next to this was *tortilla*. All of this was just on one bar window. There were dozens of these windows stretching the length of the street.

Michael waved at them from a bar halfway down the alley. They weaved through people with drinks in their hands and food in their mouths, all laughing, intoxicated with the sensations.

"I think we died and went to heaven," Michael said, wrapping his arm around Emmanuel's shoulder.

"It is one of the most beautiful things I have seen." Emmanuel took a moment of silence with his hand over his heart.

"Let's join the others." Michael ushered them into the bar, and Fransie was hit with the aroma of many different foods that all blended into a perfect bouquet.

Raphael and Auriel sat on either side of Luca and Gaia, with a giant pile of plates on the table between them.

"Wa? You didn't wait for us?" Emmanuel said, with a hurt look on his face.

"I was just so hungry—I couldn't wait," Luca said, releasing a large belch.

"Are all of these plates yours?" Michael asked. "You know we were only given so much money." He crossed his arms and looked down his nose.

"Ahh, it's nothing." Luca waved him off with a mouth full of food. "Join us," he said, still chewing.

Emmanuel rubbed his hands together and walked to the bar. He took several pinchos and indicated that he wanted two glasses of wine. Fransie looked at the smorgasbord and didn't know what to take. She had never seen food so beautiful in her life. She took a small plate with baked cheese sitting on bread topped with raspberries and blackberries. There were swirls of red and dark blue on the plate as well.

Fransie thanked the Lord silently and took the first bite. The tastes combined into physical sensations in her body. She felt relaxed and euphoric at the same time. The feeling trickled down from her head and spread all the way to her toes. She had to shake her body to bring herself back. The hum grew stronger in her stomach, and it was more satisfying than the food she had just eaten. At the same time, she heard a shriek come from Luca's stomach.

Fransie looked around, but no one else noticed. The more food Luca stuffed himself with, the louder the shriek became. Fransie purposely dropped her napkin and looked under the table. Luca's lower abdomen was bleeding. The wound was almost in the same spot the Fisher King's had been. Fransie shot back up.

"Luca, you are bleeding." Luca waved her away and continued to stuff his face. "Your stomach—feel for yourself." Luca reached a hand down and, sure enough, it was returned with blood on it.

"It's nothing," he said, taking a large gulp of wine.

"We need to attend to you—"

Luca pushed back the table, silencing Fransie.

"More, I need more," he demanded. Luca lifted his shirt, and where the blood originated was a hideous mouth that had eaten through his flesh. Luca leaned forward and the mouth took a bite out of the table.

The bar erupted in screams, and the patrons stormed out. Fransie was shoved back and fell hard against the bar. In a stupor, she tried to hide herself from the monster Luca had become. The teeth of the mouth gnashed loudly. Gaia fainted and lay on the bench next to Luca. He picked her up and dragged her arm to the ravenous mouth.

Raphael elbowed Luca in the face, stunning him momentarily, but the mouth continued to chew and drool blood. As the sharp teeth came down on Gaia's arm, Sister Caroline bravely stuck a leg of a chair in the mouth, propping it open. The screech it let out was worse than looking at it. Fransie covered her ears, but all the others seemed unaffected.

"Run!" Michael shouted, taking Sister Fransie by the arm. They tore out into the street and were met with a hundred wide eyes from all those who had heard the horror inside. Everyone backed away from the door as more patrons exited. There was a loud snapping noise and splinters bulleted out of the door.

Luca exited, the mouth at his belly leading the way. The screams shot up the sides of the buildings, and people ran in all directions—any direction to get away from the monster.

"More!" Luca shouted. The mouth bit off one of the bar window ledges that had the pinchos on it.

"Only you have what will satisfy me, growing in your belly." Fransie looked around for who was speaking, but saw no one.

"Did you hear that?" Fransie asked as her friends placed her and Sister Caroline behind them, but none responded.

Raphael let loose an arrow, pinning one of Luca's hands to the wall. She let another fly, pinning the other hand.

"We have to kill it." She drew another arrow.

"It is Luca." Michael stepped in front of her arrow. "We can't kill him."

"You're right, you can't kill me." Luca lurched a hand free then pulled the other one. "I am immortal." He held up both hands as his wounds healed.

"Run!" Michael shouted. "Run!"

Sister Fransie ran hand-in-hand with Sister Caroline. Her lungs sucked in all the oxygen that they could as she pressed her body hard. She ran blindly through the small alleys. Somehow she and Caroline got separated from the others.

"I can't run anymore." Sister Caroline clutched at her side. She placed her hands on her knees and breathed heavily. Fransie touched Caroline's back, and she retched.

"We have to keep going, our lives depend on it." Fransie heard the sound of gnashing teeth before she saw Luca round the corner. His whole body was arched backward like a bow as the mouth protruding from his stomach led the way.

"Run!" shouted Sister Caroline. She rolled up her sleeves and charged Luca. Fransie reached for her friend, but just barely missed her arm.

"Caroline!" Fransie turned—she couldn't watch her best friend die. Fransie heard a god-awful crunch and Caroline's scream. Fransie's body trembled all over, and her eyes were blinded by tears as she desperately searched for an escape. She tripped on a small stone and felt her ankle twist. She tried to put weight on it, but she crumpled to the ground as pain seared through her body.

More! I want more! Fransie heard as Luca came into view. The voice wasn't his—it was as if the mouth in his stomach was talking. Fransie looked up. The terrible mouth was covered in blood—Sister Caroline's blood. Fransie curled into a little ball and grabbed her rosary tightly. Fransie wept bitterly for her friend, and prayed that the Lord would deliver her.

Dogs barked all around her. Fransie stole a glance and saw street dogs lined up between her and the monster, led by a massive gray shaggy dog. The pack of dogs charged Luca, toppling him to the ground.

Pain be damned. I won't let Caroline's sacrifice be in vain, she thought, standing gingerly on her sprained ankle. She inched her way past Luca, who was being mauled, and slipped down another alley, bracing herself against a wall. Horse hooves echoed from the other side of the small street as a rider approached. *Auriel and Binah, thank God,* she thought, but it wasn't them.

"If you want to live, come with me." The stranger on the stallion extended his hand, and Fransie took it without question.

CHAPTER 42

Fransie clutched her arms tightly around the stranger as they sped through the countryside, the land disappearing almost as quickly as the day had. Fransie kept playing Sister Caroline's death in her head again and again. Every time she saw those bloody teeth, she wanted to retch. Fransie had no idea where she was going, nor who she was with. At this point, she didn't care. The only thing that gave her comfort was the gentle hum coming from deep inside her.

"We are approaching Santo Domingo de la Calzada. We will stop here for the night. There should be enough distance between us and that beast." These were the first words the stranger had spoken. His voice was soft yet powerful.

Fransie didn't respond. Her jaw was locked as tightly as her arms around her companion. Her body was frozen—the aching had given way to numbness several miles ago.

The dust of the Camino was replaced with cobblestone as they entered the city. The sound of the horse's hooves clacked up the buildings on either side. Torches lined the street, and pilgrims dined at tables outside the inns.

"Sephirah," the stranger said, and the huge shaggy dog from the alley walked in stride with them. Fransie hadn't noticed that the dog had followed them. She hadn't looked behind the whole ride. She was afraid she would see those awful bloodstained teeth gnashing at her again. Seeing the dog gave her comfort. However, its sheer size made those dining at the tables appear nervous—or was it her companion?

The stranger was tall and broad shouldered. He wore all black and had rune tattoos on his neck. Fransie was sure the tattoos spread further than his neck, but she couldn't remember his face. The whole ride, she had only seen the back of his head.

Her companion stopped the horse before the main cathedral in the city and dismounted. His face wasn't what Fransie had expected—he had a strong jaw and dark eyes. Had it not been for the tattoos, and his heavy brow, he would have looked like a prince from a faraway land.

"I'm Gabriel," he said, reaching up to assist Fransie.

"Sister Fransie," she said, accepting his help. "Thank you both for your help." Fransie looked from Gabriel to the dog sitting obediently at his side.

Gabriel patted Sephirah on the head. "She says, 'You're welcome.'"

"Good evening, pilgrims, how may I be of service to you?" the innkeeper asked as they entered the large alburgue. When he noticed Gabriel's tattoos, he took a step back.

"One room for my companion." Gabriel handed the guest master a small amount of money.

"And where will you sleep?" Fransie asked.

"I will stay in the stables with my horse and dog." Relief spread across the guest master's face at Gabriel's remarks.

"That is a dog?" The innkeeper pointed out the window at Sephirah. "I thought it was a pony. Of course we can't have a beast like that inside." Gabriel nodded at the innkeeper, and a rooster crowed in the background.

"A little late for roosters, isn't it?" Fransie asked.

"They are considered holy here. You get used to them after a while," the innkeeper said. "Have you heard of the great miracle that happened in this very town?" Both Fransie and Gabriel shook their heads. Gabriel seemed uncomfortable, but Fransie was eager to hear the story. She wanted anything to take her mind off Sister Caroline.

"Do tell us," Sister Fransie said.

"Several years ago, a German pilgrim named Hugonell came through town with his family. They stayed the night in the city, and the daughter of their host made improper advances on Hugonell. He refused her advances, and the girl was deeply hurt. In her anger, she placed a silver cup in Hugonell's bag and accused him of stealing it. In accordance with the law, Hugonell was sentenced to hang in the gallows." The innkeeper lowered his head and raised his eyebrows in a dramatic pause. Fransie could tell he had told this story more than once.

"Hugonell's parents were heartbroken, and not knowing what to do, they continued on to Santiago de Compostela. On their return, they visited their son's body, and to their amazement, he was still hanging, but alive. As they examined his body, they heard Hugonell's voice saying that Saint Dominic had saved his life."

Sister Fransie made the sign of the cross, and the innkeeper followed suit. Fransie was surprised to see Gabriel cross himself as well.

"His parents immediately went to see the magistrate, who was dining on a rooster and hen. When they told him the miraculous news, the magistrate said, *Your son is as alive as this rooster I have been dining on.* Immediately, the dead bird regained its feathers and crowed as it came back to life. This is why roosters are revered here."

"Thank you for sharing that miracle with us. I will think of the graciousness of Saint Dominic every time I hear the rooster crow,"

Sister Fransie said. She smiled, but inside she prayed that Saint Dominic would restore the life of her best friend.

After Fransie settled into her room, she went to the stables to see Gabriel. She had to know why he had helped her, and why he was there at exactly the right moment. Fransie knocked gently on the wooden post of the stall Gabriel was in.

"Come in," he said, in his soft, but powerful voice. His back was against his horse, and Sephirah had her head on his lap. "I don't think I introduced you to Cash." The horse seemed unfazed by the introduction.

"Thank you for your help. How did you—?"

"—know that you were in the alley and needed help?" He raised his weighty brow. "The same way I knew you would come here to ask me that." Fransie took a step back. "We Druids[29] can see the future."

"You're a pagan?" Sister Fransie stammered. "A sorcerer?"

"If you would like to call me that, you can. Or perhaps, I sensed that beast just as you did." He pointed to the marking beside Fransie's ear. "I saw it glowing when I lifted you onto Cash." He raised his chin to show the same marking. "How do you sense?"

Fransie felt as if the wind was knocked out of her. She braced herself against the coarse wood of the stable.

"I... I have true sound," she managed.

"And is that little one your filter?" Gabriel pointed to Fransie's shoulder.

Fransie gripped the rosary in her pocket for strength and stole a glance. An adorable mouse, with large ears turning in all directions, returned her stare.

"I...I guess she is."

"What is her name?"

Fransie fondled the rosary in her hand. "Um... Rosalita, yes, that's it. Rosalita." When had this mouse become her filter? She had noticed that the terrible shriek coming from Luca turned into words. With Rosalita as her filter, she could understand him.

"Nice to meet you too, Rosalita." The little mouse brushed its face with the back of both paws.

"Is Sephirah your filter?" The large shaggy dog raised her head at the sound of her name.

"She is my nose," Gabriel said. "We could smell that thing a mile away. We were hunting it, but something more important came up."

"What was that?" Gabriel nodded to Fransie's midsection. Fransie grabbed the grail tightly behind her back. She had fastened it to her rope belt, and hid it under her long habit.

"Not the cup." Fransie placed a hand on her stomach, and the gentle hum resonated even louder. Gabriel nodded again. "You don't know what's inside you—do you?"

Fransie shook her head.

"I take it you met the Fisher King?" Fransie timidly nodded. "The land you saw was the land of my birth. It was a thriving kingdom until the Fisher King's moral depravity." Gabriel slammed his fist on the ground. Sephirah didn't react, but Cash blew her lips and shook her mane.

"Depravity?" Sister Fransie slid down the wooden wall until she was seated on the floor.

"Yes. His gluttony led to the depletion of our land. The wound he had, the same wound that monster had, is the curse of more. It will continue to fill itself with anything, and anyone, eternally unsatisfied until all life is consumed."

Sister Fransie shook her head, trying to forget the image of the monster Luca had become. She saw the gnashing teeth again.

"The only thing that can stop the curse of more is the realization that you always have enough in the present moment and need nothing more, or, what lies inside you." Gabriel pointed to Fransie's stomach.

"And what is inside of me?" Sister Fransie cradled her lower abdomen with both hands.

"I will tell you of a legend. In the land of my people there once lived a king named Bran the Blessed, whose sister married the King of Ireland. There was some strife between the two families. To make amends, Bran gave a magical cauldron to the King of Ireland, which could bring people back from the dead, giving them eternal life. Sound familiar?" Fransie repositioned the grail to her side. "Yet there was strife again between the two kingdoms, resulting in a great war. King Bran pretended he was dead so he would be revived by the cauldron. He then destroyed the cauldron from the inside out, but suffered a mortal wound. His followers chopped off his head, but because he had eternal life, his head lived on forever.

"Part of that legend has been intertwined with the grail legend. But, do you know what the true grail is?"

Fransie shook her head

"It is the word made flesh–Jesus's bloodline." Sister Fransie felt her consciousness leaving her, but she regained her composure before hitting the ground.

"The Fisher King was a member of an order that was supposed to protect the bloodline and keep it pure. However, the sin of gluttony led him to the bedchamber of many women. This gluttony grew within him until it opened up into a wound that swallowed the land. Now, it would appear you are the protector of this bloodline, and your companion's gluttony has caused him to adopt the curse of more. Fransie, *you* are now the Holy Grail. You carry the bloodline of Jesus in your womb."

It is just as the Virgin Mary told me. Fransie cradled her stomach. In her vision of the Virgin Mary, she had told Fransie she would bear a great task, perhaps the same task she had. Fransie hadn't understood what that task was until now. She thought it was delivering Molay's message to Etienne, but this felt like something even greater. Fransie clutched her rosary tightly and silently thanked God.

"You aren't surprised?" Gabriel read her expression.

"One must accept the fate God has given them. Good night, Gabriel."

Fransie returned to her bedchamber and listened to the hum inside of her. This child would protect her from Luca and make the world right again.

CHAPTER 43

"Andy, wake up!" Clair shook Andy vigorously, and he opened his sleep-crusted eyes.

"Settle ya down, Clair. What's happenin'?"

Clair scrunched both of Andy's cheeks between her hands and turned his head to look out the window. Just outside the front door, Gerhart was blocking a host of soldiers led by a young man with billowy pantaloons and a puffy cap. Andy thought he looked ridiculous, but he must have paid a fortune for the clothes.

"You 'ave ta hide." Clair tugged Andy out of bed.

"Can I hide under my covers?"

"Andrew Sinclair." Clair placed her hands on her hips. "'Tis not a joke. I donna think they are here for Gerhart and me."

"I donna think they are here for me either. I 'ave never seen them before."

"Well 'tis too late now." Clair let go of Andy.

The man in the pantaloons pushed past Gerhart and walked into the house. Moments later Andy's bedroom door flew open.

"I am looking for Etienne LaRue, and you shan't stop me." The stranger in the pantaloons had an arrogance in his voice that matched his clothing.

"And who might you be?" Andy struggled to put something over his sleeping clothes.

"Your executioner, if you question me again." The young man pulled a fancy sword that looked like it had never seen battle. "This is His Royal Highness Prince Charles the Fourth of France."[30]

Andy looked at the soldiers who now filled the room, and the prince, who stood puffing out his chest. The boy couldn't have been more than fourteen years old.

"Your Highness." Andy bowed so low that the ball of his sleeping cap touched the floor. "Thank the heavens you are here."

"You may rise. Your civility has spared you. Whatever do you mean, commoner?"

"Well, ya see, we do know Etienne. He is actually a dear friend." Clair shot daggers out of her eyes at Andy. "Ya see…the thing is, you're a little too late. The pixies came and got em. Ain't that right, Clair?"

"Aye." Clair crossed her arms still glaring at Andy.

"Pixies?"

"What, have ya never heard of the fair folk?"

"I can't say that I have."

"You're lucky then. Nasty they are. They run wild in our country—ain't that right, Clair?"

"Aye."

"The pixies came about a week ago and put an awful curse on Etienne. They stole his body and left his head. The only way to restore him is to return his body."

"Surely you jest. This can't be so. Where is this head?"

"'Tis here." Andy pulled back the covers on Etienne's bed, revealing the severed head with its branches growing into the headboard. The prince gasped, and all the soldiers pulled their swords.

"I wouldna go too close. 'Tis nasty magic. I thanked the Lord them pixies didna take me too. I woke up in the morning, and this was all that was left of Etienne." Andy removed his sleeping cap and put it over his heart. He glanced out of the corner of his eye to see if the prince was buying his story.

"Well, the skin tone is close." The prince ventured a step nearer. It was true—time had made the skin of the head dark and leathery. "How can I know this is Etienne and not some parlor trick?"

"Have you ever seen a severed head do that before?" Andy pointed to the flowers on the branches that were opening to meet the morning sun.

"I can't say that I have."

"And ta prove 'tis Etienne, look in that chest… Go on." The prince nodded to one of his guards who slowly walked to the chest and pulled out Etienne's Templar mantle.

"Would a Templar ever leave behind his mantle? They took him in the middle of the night. Thank the Lord, they didna come for me." Andy crossed himself.

"Where is his body?"

"That we donna ken, but if you want to speak with Etienne, you will 'ave ta find his body and bring it back here. We've been looking for it since them pixies took him. Ain't that right, Clair?"

"Aye."

"How important is your mission?"

"Very important. My father the king sent me here himself." The prince puffed out his chest.

"Well, ya better find that body then. We're na going anywhere."

"How will I know it's him? And where should I look?"

"Well, besides the obvious of a decapitated body, he will have a lot of scars. Etienne was a great warrior."

"How can a great warrior have lots of scars? I would think he would have none if he really was so great."

"Your body is your biography, Your Highness. His most recent scar is on his shoulder right here." Andy touched his own shoulder. "A nasty wound from a poisoned Moorish blade."

"And where should we start looking for the body?" Andy smiled. He knew he had the prince at this point.

"That is the question we have been pondering. It depends on what type of spell the pixies put on him. It could be a slumbering spell or a walking dead spell. Ain't that right, Clair?"

"Aye."

"If it is a walking dead spell, my guess is you will find him haunting the Camino, walking at night, searching for his head. I would ask the pilgrims coming in if they had seen anything like this. If it is a slumber spell...that one would be harder. His body could be asleep in any cemetery or in any grove of trees. It would appear to just be another dead body."

The prince walked to Andy and struck him across his face. "If you're mocking me, let that be a reminder to you of the consequences. Much worse things will happen to you and your family."

"Well," Andy moved his jaw back and forth. "Ya will know where ta find us. I wouldna' waste any more time though. The longer a pixie's spell lasts, the harder it is to break. Ain't that right, Clair?"

"Aye."

The prince pointed to the door, and the guards moved allowing him to pass. One by one, the guards followed the prince until they had all left the house.

"Andrew Sinclair, what the 'ell was that?"

"It would appear that was Isabella's brother."

"No, that!" Clair pointed at the head, which now had budding antlers growing into the headboard.

"Oh. That, my dear sister, is one of the Templars' secret treasures."

CHAPTER 44

Etienne had buried his sword along with Nazir. He was done with a life of violence—he wanted to leave it all behind.

It had been several days since Etienne had eaten, and the pains of hunger gnawed away at his stomach. Etienne had no idea what he was doing, nor where he was going. For once, though, he knew who he was and where he came from. He let himself grieve for the passing of an uncle he barely knew, and for a life he was leaving behind.

Etienne found a small stream and washed the blood from his clothing. He still wore the tunic of the Knights of Saint James. As soon as he didn't need it for warmth at night, he would burn it. Etienne followed the stream to the north. It provided subsistence for him, and its babbling was a constant companion. He couldn't remember the last time that he had spent this much time alone. Since he had left the streets, he had always been around the guards, Templars, or his companions. He had never truly been alone.

The stream joined with a large river, and Etienne continued to follow it north until a bridge appeared with a town on the other side. Etienne approached and recognized the bridge. *This is Portomarin.*

The last time he was here, he and Andy had met an old fisherman who'd showed him where the Keystone Church was. Not knowing what else to do, Etienne decided to visit Brother Philip.

Etienne had an echo of a memory as he approached the Keystone Church. He saw himself cradled in Isabella's arms on the ground where the wolves had attacked him. Etienne shook his head.

Why do places hold memories? Etienne turned to leave—there were too many memories here he didn't want to face.

"Etienne? Why, Etienne, it is you," Brother Philip said.

Etienne's shoulders slumped. He took a moment, then faced the church again.

"I thought that was you. It is so good to see you, my boy. Where are the others?" Etienne hesitated. "Well, no matter, come inside and you can explain it all to me."

Etienne was hit with a wave of deja vu as he entered. This wasn't just reminiscence from his last time here. This was something different. Once again, it was as if he had lived this before.

"I will go prepare some food," Brother Philip said.

"Do you need any help?"

"No, you rest, my boy. It looks like you have had quite the journey."

Philip disappeared from the chapel, and Etienne sat in a pew. He thought of Andy as his eyes scanned the coded wall. He wondered if Andy had been able to crack the code in Santiago with the symbols they had discovered here. He missed Andy's companionship—he was annoying at times, but he was always able to make Etienne laugh. To the left of the altar was the room Isabella had slept in. His heart welled at the thought of her appearing again. She had looked so radiant in the sunlight.

"Etienne, come join me, supper is ready."

CHAPTER 45

Andy smiled to himself. *Pixies—I canna believe he fell for that.* After the prince and his companions left, Andy rushed over to the head. There was something different about it—one of the branches had a green vine coiling around it tightly. Andy was sure it wasn't there two days before when he was trying to solve the code.

This must be it. He is trying ta tell me something.

Andy hurried back to his bed and laid out the papers he had stashed in his trunk. He studied the chart with the letters he had decoded and looked back at the coiled vine.

PILLAR 1	ZKYTANL
PILLAR 2	AGPOPTC
PILLAR 3	GNAIOMR
PILLAR 4	VSDBSFK
PILLAR 5	AFMDWTC
PILLAR 6	OAHGDUP

"What's the relationship?"

At the top of the vine, Andy noticed another branch had sprouted that was about the thickness of one of his letters and appeared to have six sides.

"'Tis it. Andy tore a thin strip of parchment and wrote out the seven letters from the first pillar, in a straight line. He took the slender piece of paper to the twig and wrapped it around like the vine. "Sorry for intruding, head—this will only take a minute."

"That's na it." Andy loosened the paper.

His letters fit perfectly onto each side, but none of them lined up. Andy sighed heavily. "I 'ave ta figure this out."

The end of the vine moved slightly and curled into the shape of a symbol.

"I know that symbol!" Andy rushed back to his bed and looked at the symbols on the first pillar. The symbol the vine had made was the same as the first mason's mark on the pillar.

"Of course, how cudda I been so daft? I 'ave ta include the masons' marks as well ta make it work." Andy drew out another grid and placed a dot where each masons' mark was as a placeholder.

PILLAR 1	Z-K-Y--T--AN---L
PILLAR 2	AGPO----P-T---C
PILLAR 3	-GN-----A-I-O-M-----R
PILLAR 4	V-S-D-BS-F-K
PILLAR 5	A-----F-----MDWTC
PILLAR 6	O-A---H-----G---D---U-----P

Andy walked back to the head and wrapped the thin piece of paper with the full code around the six-sided branch. Andy smiled broadly as two letters matched up. He repeated the process with all of the pillars until he had singled out the letters of the new code.

Andy felt the anticipation rise in his stomach only to be met by disappointment. The code still didn't make any sense.

PILLAR 1	YA
PILLAR 2	PPC
PILLAR 3	NAMR
PILLAR 4	VB
PILLAR 5	AFM
PILLAR 6	OHGUP

"Are ya sure this is it?" Andy looked around. He couldn't believe he was getting advice from a severed head with vines growing out of it. He must be going mad. He could have sworn the leathery head winked at him.

Andy quickly threw the covers over the head again and made haste back to his bed. He decided to try the oldest cypher he knew, the Caesar Cypher. He had learned it in his schooldays to pass notes back and forth with his friends. Not that they ever had anything to say. They just liked that the teacher couldn't figure out what they were writing. The cypher was appropriately named after Julius Caesar, who'd used it to send encoded messages.

The cypher worked by offsetting the alphabet by one to twenty-five letters. If it is offset by one, A would become B and so on. Since Andy didn't know how many letters it was offset by, he would have to do it the hard way.

He drew another grid and took the two-letter word from pillar one, *YA*. He thought of all the two letter words he could: it, at, in, to, on, no, of... That gave Andy several options to start with—that should be easy enough.

Decryption Shift	Text	Decryption Shift	Text
0	YA	13	MO
1	ZB	14	NP
2	AC	15	OQ
3	BD	16	PR
4	CE	17	QS
5	DF	18	RT
6	EG	19	SU
7	FH	20	TV
8	GI	21	UW
9	HK	22	VX
10	IL	23	WY
11	KM	24	XZ
12	LN		

**

"Well, tha didna work."

Andy tried the process with the other two-letter words and met with the same fate. He crumpled up the parchment with the Caesar Cypher and threw it into the fire. This was going to take much more work and thought.

"Any suggestions?" Andy yelled at the covered head. "I didna think so."

CHAPTER 46

Fransie and Gabriel left Santo Domingo de la Calzada before the sun rose. Gabriel wanted to put as much distance as possible between them and the beast Luca had become. He said Luca would stop at nothing to kill both Fransie and her child before she gave birth. Fransie looked back at the Camino snaking through the land behind them. She hoped her companions had survived Luca and that they had given Sister Caroline a proper burial.

At sunset, they reached the grand entrance into the city of Burgos. The turret of the city wall stretched high, and the whole edifice was decorated with sculptures. Fransie entered the arched mouth to the wall and was met by a beautiful song from a group of French pilgrims. The melody echoed off the ceiling, creating a haunting canon as it rose.

They passed into a grand courtyard filled with pilgrims, and just opposite them was the cathedral. The immaculate structure reflected the setting sun so brilliantly Fransie had to shield her eyes.

"Fransie, do you sense that?" Gabriel asked, as they dismounted Cash.

Rosalita, Fransie's newly adopted friend, climbed to Fransie's shoulder and twitched her ears in all directions. Fransie still wasn't sure how this worked. Gabriel noticed her look of uncertainty.

"Close your eyes and focus on the sound."

Fransie took a deep breath and focused. She only heard the chatter of pilgrims and wagons. She took another breath, releasing her consciousness, and a deep bass voice emerged into her awareness. Fransie concentrated on the sound until it formed into words. *You are special and have been chosen. Fransie, you are equal to her.*

Fransie's eyes shot open, and she took a deep breath. "It... It was calling to me from inside the church. The words sounded kind, but there was something menacing in the tone. I don't understand."

"We only sense something terrible as well." Gabriel nodded to Sephirah, who sat obediently at his side.

"I can resist it this time though—before I was pulled so much, it was as if I had no control over my body."

"You have her to thank for that." Gabriel nodded to Fansie's shoulder.

Fransie smiled at Rosalita. The small brown mouse was cleaning herself on Fransie's shoulder. Fransie broke off a small piece of bread and fed it to her new friend. The mouse took the bread and ran back inside Fransie's garments.

"Usually when I sense something like this, Sephirah and I hunt it down before it can do too much damage. But, as I said, you are now my first priority. The choice is yours: do we go into the church to see what's calling you, or ignore it and rest?"

"I think the voice has something to do with the child inside of me. We must go see." Gabriel nodded at Fransie, and he tied Cash at a watering trough. They ascended the steps to the cathedral and were stopped at the door.

"No animals allowed." A pompous looking guard blocked their path. Fransie was surprised someone would try to stop Gabriel; he was such an intimidating looking person.

"She will enter with me," Gabriel demanded.

"This is a house of God; I wasn't talking about the dog, I was talking about you, pagan." Two other guards joined the first.

"How dare you talk to a new convert like that!" Sister Fransie said, emulating Sister Caroline's righteousness.

"I'm sorry, Sister. I didn't know he was with you. His dog will still have to stay out here. You can understand." Fransie was glad she and Raphel had exchanged clothing after they'd reconnected. Being a nun provided certain privileges.

"There were animals present at our Lord's birth—or do you not remember his humble beginnings?" Fransie didn't know where this was coming from. It was so unlike her to speak like this.

"What is all this?" a priest said, coming to the door.

"Father, we were just stopping this animal from coming inside." Both Sephirah and Gabriel bared their teeth.

"So I see. You are absolutely right to do so. You cannot enter this house of God with that dog."

"Have you never heard of Saint Francis of Asissi, Father? He would have allowed animals in the church." Fransie put her hands on her hips.

"His feast day isn't until October, and until then, there will be no animals in this church."

"If you knew who I am…" Fransie glared at the priest. "You would be bowing now."

"Sister, where is your humility?"

"We will be fine." Gabriel placed a strong hand on her shoulder. "Sephirah, stay with Cash." Sephirah looked at Gabriel with pleading eyes for a moment then turned tail and joined Cash by the watering trough. The guards and priest moved, allowing Fransie and Gabriel to enter.

"Are you sure you will be all right without Sephirah?" Fransie asked.

"Yes, I think I know what we are up against." Gabriel scanned the cathedral. He chuckled and walked to a pillar to the right. Fransie followed his gaze to a statue of a man holding his detached head, inset on an ornately decorated pillar. Fransie lowered her gaze.

"Why are you showing me this?" she asked, reading the placard below the statue. "It is just Saint Victores."

"Is it?" Gabriel raised an eyebrow. "Or is it Bran the Blessed, from the legend I told you last night?" Fransie didn't want to think about severed heads or death. It triggered the memory of Caroline's murder.

"I need to go pray." Fransie left Gabriel and knelt in a pew in the middle of the cathedral, clasping her hands together. "Father, I pray that you will take the soul of my dear friend Sister Caroline. She was a devout servant of yours." The melody in Fransie's womb began to hum again, and she placed both hands on it in a motherly fashion. "Thank you for all the gifts you have given me. I am your willing servant." The hum grew louder, and Fransie looked to the ceiling. "Thank you."

Fransie made the sign of the cross but continued to look upward. Above her was a giant, domed, stained-glass ceiling. It contained a flower within a flower composed of many different colors. On all sides of the beautiful centerpiece were vaulted ceilings, each containing an intricate carving.

"My God," she said. She quickly found Gabriel and brought him to where she had been sitting. "Do you see it?" She felt so proud of her discovery.

"It's a beautiful sight." He placed his arms behind his head as he looked up.

"No, the pattern. One, two, three, four, five, in the middle, and one, two, three, on each side."

"What on earth are you talking about?"

Fransie's heart raced. Maybe he didn't know about the pattern they had found at the fountain, and at the church. She really didn't know much about him. Maybe he wasn't saving her, maybe he was using her.

"Never mind." Fransie shook her head. They rose and walked the length of the cathedral. Fransie saw the pattern repeating itself again and again on the ceiling. They stepped into a chapel by the western entrance of the cathedral. Fransie braced herself on a pew. Behind the altar was a carving of the Root of Jesse.

"'And in that day there shall be a Root of Jesse, which shall stand for an ensign of the people; to it shall the Gentiles seek: and his rest shall be glorious,'" Fransie quoted.

"What was that?" Gabriel asked.

"The passage from Isaiah that describes that carving." Fransie pointed at the sculpture. "It is the family tree of Jesus, stemming from Jesse. The man lying at the bottom with the vine growing out of his stomach is Jesse, and the branches stretching out are the family tree leading to Jesus. Fransie pointed to the infant at the top of the sculpture.

"I guess you are a part of that lineage now."

You are the mother of God... said a voice that came wafting into the room.

"Did you hear that?" Fransie asked, looking around the chapel.

"No, but I smelled something terrible." Fransie wondered how that message could be something terrible.

Mother Fransie, the immaculate conception.

Fransie chased after the voice down the long corridor of the church.

You are special, you have been called.

At the opposite end of the cathedral, behind the altar, was a beautiful chapel with two tombstones. Fransie could have sworn that the voice was coming from that chapel, but it was completely empty. She looked around once more, and in the far right corner was a door. Not just any door—it had the bust of a man with a slot for a mouth carved into it, just like the doors at the fountain and in Pamplona.

Instinctively, Fransie ran to the door and drew a backward Z on the forehead as she had at the fountain. Nothing happened.

"You can't open a door backward," a raspy voice cackled. To her left was a hag, bent with time.

"What do you mean?" Fransie asked.

"Fransie, step away from her." Gabriel entered the chapel, covering his nose. The hag cackled loudly.

"And, what will you do, Druid?" She turned back to Fransie. "All hail the mother of the word made flesh." She came closer to Fransie and took her hand between her clammy palms.

"Fransie, step away from her. Don't let her touch—" In a swift movement, the hag stood below Gabriel and extended a cruel nail, touching the marking under his chin. Immediately Gabriel dropped to the ground and started convulsing. In an instant, the hag was back at Fransie's side.

"The last girl's pride caused so much glorious death. How much will yours bring?" Fransie looked at Gabriel, who was now foaming at the mouth.

Fransie clutched her rosary and recited the Lord's Prayer. She prayed so loudly it drowned out the hag's words. As she continued to pray, Sephirah bounded into the chapel and stood between Fransie and the hag.

"You will return to me." Fransie heard over her prayer, as the hag disappeared.

The chapel quickly filled with pilgrims and clergy alike.

"What is going on here?" the priest they had met at the front entrance asked. Seeing Gabriel, he continued, "This man is possessed." Everyone stepped away from Gabriel. Fransie ran to him and cradled him in her arms.

"Only Joshua the Healer can help with this," the priest said.

"Take us to him," Fransie demanded.

CHAPTER 47

A local merchant attached a cart to Cash, and the town's folk heaved the convulsing Gabriel into the back. Fransie knew enough to put a thick stick between his teeth to prevent him from biting off his own tongue.

She tried to hold Gabriel still as the small cart wound through the streets of the city. They turned left behind the cathedral and skirted the hill with the magnificent castle. Burgos was the capital of Castile, and the castle boasted of the city's greatness. The look of the people changed as the cart found its way to the far side of the castle. They first passed through a Moorish quarter where the people were as dark as Raphael, then they entered the Jewish quarter.

Sister Fransie hadn't met many Jews in her life, but she recognized the yellow horned skullcaps they often wore. She thanked God that they were getting close. The foam in Gabriel's mouth was thick. The cart stopped in front of a cozy building with a wooden sign that read *Joshua the Healer, All are welcome.* A bell rang as the door opened, and a kindly man with a broomed mustache greeted them.

"How may I be of service—" He stopped mid-sentence, seeing Gabriel foaming at the mouth, supported by two villagers. "Put him in that bed immediately." Joshua pointed to a straw bed next to a large window. He busied himself making a decoction of herbs in a cauldron on the fire.

"Thank you," Fransie said, as the villagers placed Gabriel in the bed.

"It is the least we can do for peregrinos, Sister," one villager said.

"Hold him steady. Hold him steady," Joshua said. He hummed merrily as he worked and danced from one large glass cylinder to the next, collecting herbs. Noticing Fransie watching, he said, "It's all part of the cure, Sister. There is so much healing power in music and dance." He spun and put a dash of what looked like mint in the pot.

Joshua ladled the decoction into a mug and blew on it to cool the liquid. After the steam had subsided, he joined them at the bed. Up close, Fransie could see all the smile lines that surrounded his eyes. His kindness was written on his face.

Joshua smiled, and his mustache rose on both sides. "We will be able to heal your friend. Don't you worry. Great thinking about putting the stick in his mouth. Now, I need you to take it out and hold his head back." Fransie followed directions and held Gabriel's head, as Joshua poured the liquid down his throat. "Now, that should do it."

Joshua stepped back and the two villagers released Gabriel as his body became still. Fransie's shoulders relaxed—she hadn't noticed how much tension she was holding. Fransie thanked the villagers as they left, and Sephirah came bounding through the door. The pony-sized dog sat vigilantly at Gabriel's side.

"I'm sorry about the—"

Joshua raised a hand stopping her. "Did you read the sign over my door?" Fransie nodded her head. "It says *All Are Welcome*. I meant that when I wrote it. All are welcome here, even dogs—and mice." He shot a glance to Rosalita who was poking her head out from Fransie's cloak.

"Thank you," Fransie said.

"You can thank me when you get the bill."

Fransie hadn't thought about payment. The only thing she had of value was the grail. She was sure that Gabriel had coins someplace, but she didn't know where he kept them. Joshua read her face— his eyes clearly absorbing her worry.

"The price will be one dance." His mustache moved side to side. "It has been a while since I have had a dance partner, and as I said before, dancing has healing powers." Joshua extended his hand, and Fransie took it.

Joshua hummed a sweet melody, and she saw joy spread across his body as they danced. His joy was infectious, and she was soon laughing and smiling as well. The dance made her forget all of her worries. She never in a million years would have imagined she would have so much fun dancing. He spun her around, and they grapevined around the large wooden table. As his song came to an end, he dipped her, and they both laughed.

"You are all welcome to rest here tonight. Your friend should be fully recovered by the morning. I will have to keep an eye on him throughout the night."

"Thank you. We will stay only if I can have another dance with you."

"With pleasure."

Sister Fransie enjoyed Joshua's company throughout the evening. They laughed and told stories. Joshua was kind and very attentive to everything she said. Had Fransie not taken her vows, she would have allowed herself to be attracted to him.

"Is he the father?" Joshua directed his gaze at Gabriel.

"No… Wait, how did you know?" Fransie placed her hands on her abdomen. It had swollen since the last time she had touched it.

"I'm a healer." Seeing Fransie's concerned face, Joshua smiled kindly and raised both eyebrows. "What are you, three, maybe four months along?"

"I...I don't know." That was impossible. It had only been a few days since she received the grail and missed her moon.

An awkward silence filled the room. Fransie picked up a piece of charcoal, and unconsciously drew the symbol that had followed her since first seeing it in Pamplona.

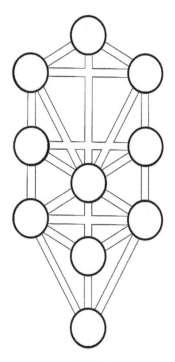

"How do you know that symbol?" Joshua stared at her, deadpan. His whole demeanor changed.

"I have seen it again and again on the Camino." Fransie was happy to change the subject. She continued to draw, connecting the dots and ending with the lightning bolt moving from the top to the bottom.

"I don't believe this." Joshua leaned back in his chair and shook his head. "No, you can't know this... It's forbidden. Only Kabbalists know this."

"Kabbalists?" Fransie stopped drawing and looked directly at him. He was as uncomfortable as she had been when he asked her about her child.

"Kabbalah."[31] Joshua looked from the drawing to Fransie and sighed heavily. "Kabbalah is a form of Jewish mysticism, and that drawing is an important part of it. It is secret, forbidden knowledge. Who showed you this?"

"God," Fransie said, honestly.

"God showed you this?" Joshua pushed his broom mustache from side to side.

"Joshua." Fransie took his hand. "God has shown me this again and again. What is it?"

"But, you are a gentile... Why would God—?" After saying a silent prayer, Joshua leaned forward and placed both elbows on the table. "That symbol is the tree of life. I shouldn't be telling you this." Joshua looked around, even though they were the only two people in the room.

"It's all right. I have been inside it."

"You have what?"

"I will explain if you tell me more about the tree of life." Joshua took the paper and charcoal from Fransie.

"The tree of life is made up of ten sephiroth." At the sound close to her name, Sephirah walked from Gabriel's bed and placed her large head on the table. "Do you want some food?" Joshua said, pushing a plate toward her. The dog didn't accept, she just stared at Joshua from behind her bushy brow.

"You called her."

"What?"

"Her name is Sephirah." Sephirah placed her large head in Fransie's lap, and she stroked the giant dog gently.

"Amazing! Sephirah is the singular form of sephiroth! Is he Jewish?" Joshua motioned to Gabriel and Fransie shook her head. "Ahh, I see. I will definitely continue and hold nothing back. But first…"

Joshua stood and placed another log on the fire. He took more of the decoction and brought it to Gabriel. Fransie assisted once more by holding Gabriel's mouth open. He accepted the liquid easily, and he groaned.

"Through these ten sephiroth, God reveals itself, and continually creates this physical realm and higher spiritual realms," Joshua continued as they sat.

"But, there are eleven circles, five in the middle and three on each side." Fransie pointed to the drawing.

"I will get there. One can study the Kabbalah for many years and barely scratch the surface of the deep knowledge it contains. I will give you a brief overview." He took the charcoal and darkened the dot at the top of the drawing. "This Sephirah is called Keter, it is the divine will—beyond consciousness. It is the *I am that I am.*"

Fransie put a hand to her mouth. "Keter was the name of the old man's falcon."

"You will have a lot to explain." Joshua shook his head. "The next one down is Hokhmah, the creation from nothingness. It represents the masculine in creation and is the idea before it takes on any limitations."

"But, Raphael is a woman?"

"What?"

"Raphael, her falcon is named, Hokhmah."

"These sephiroth have nothing to do with gender—they are energies. It has to do with the will to bestow and the will to receive."

Fransie traced her finger across to the next sephirah. "Let me guess, this one is called Binah"

"How do you know this? This knowledge is one of the most closely guarded secrets of the Jewish people."

"Binah is Auriel's horse. She and Raphael are the daughters of the old man." From the blank stare on his face, Fransie could tell Joshua didn't know what to say. "I'm sorry, continue."

"Yes, that is Binah—it represents understanding. It is the feminine vessel that gives birth to emotions and brings a return to God." Joshua traced his finger to the next sephirah. "This is Da'at—the invisible sephirah that represents knowledge and is the central state of unity in the tree of life. This is the hidden eleventh Sephirah of which I spoke earlier."

Fransie remembered running through the tree of life in Pamplona—she had gotten stuck in Da'at. It was invisible yet everywhere. Its boundaries had held her and didn't allow her to continue.

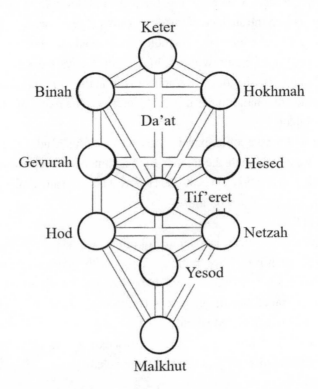

Joshua quickly traced his finger down the tree of life in the zig-zag pattern Fransie had drawn. "Hesed—kindness, Gevurah—discipline, Tif'eret—beauty, Netzach—eternity, Hod—splendor, Yesod—foundation, and finally, Malkuth—kingship. It is in Malkuth that all of our reality takes place. All of the sephiroth flow into our world. It is exaltedness and humility. The final revelation of the divine, both the receiver and the giver."

Sister Fransie took a deep breath. This was too much information for her to take in. She looked at the drawing. What was God trying to tell her? Looking at the zig-zag pattern coming down from the top to bottom, she remembered the way the light traveled down the image the last two times they opened the door. It was the divine expressing itself on the earth. That energy was straight from God.

"Are you well?" Joshua asked with raised eyebrows.

"Yes, I am just recounting the last times I encountered this image."

"Ahh, so it is my time for a story. I want you to start at the beginning and tell me everything."

"I don't know if I can tell you everything, but what God allows me to tell, I will."

CHAPTER 48

"Etienne, wake up." He felt Isabella's hand on his shoulder. "Wake up. What are you doing out here?"

"Isabella!" Etienne startled from bed and looked around wildly.

"What are you doing, silly?" Isabella asked, smiling.

"You're here." Etienne felt Isabella's arm. "You're really here!"

"Of course I am. Where else would I be other than at my husband's side?"

"Mornin', sleepin' beauty. Did ya 'ave a domestic last night? What are you doing out here with us?"

"I was just trying to figure out the same thing, Andy." Etienne looked around; they were all here in the chapel: Clair, Gerhart, Mariano, Andy, and most importantly, Isabella.

"I, ahh…I must have sleepwalked. What day is it?" Everyone laughed, except Isabella.

"A very special day," Brother Philip said, entering the chapel. "It has been one year since you first arrived. And what a blessing you have been."

What is going on? That is the exact amount of time that had passed since he was last at the Keystone Church. Etienne couldn't believe his senses. Isabella was in France and the others Santiago. Yet, here they were all laughing.

"Isabella."

"Etienne?" Isabella arched an eyebrow. Etienne knew he should stop speaking. He brought both arms around her and grasped tightly.

"Uck! Ya spend one night apart and 'tis like you are first in love again," Andy said, making kissing faces. Etienne didn't care. He was holding Isabella in his arms again and wouldn't let go. She was here. With him.

"All right, Etienne, you can let go now." Etienne released Isabella and sat up straight.

"Who's hungry?" Brother Philip asked.

As the day carried on, Etienne questioned if he had died and gone to heaven. Life here was perfect—he had everyone he loved in one place—he had his family back.

The sun beat down, and Etienne had his shirt off as he chopped wood. He enjoyed the simplicity of this task, and it worked different muscle groups than he was used to. He could already feel the strain on his body and loved it. He split another piece of wood and rested his chin on the handle. He couldn't help but grin.

"Taking a break already?" Isabella walked by and nudged him in the side. Etienne feigned pain and gave her a half smile. "Are you all right?"

"Yes, you didn't hurt me." Etienne straightened up.

Isabella punched him in the arm. "Not that—you have been acting strange all day." Etienne took her into his arms and kissed her.

"I just love you, all of you, so much. You are my family." He kissed her again.

"I think the sun is getting to you." Isabella took a finger and dragged it across his chest. "Although, you do look good when you are chopping wood. Come with me." Etienne reached down for his shirt. "Oh, you can leave that."

Isabella led him into the woods to a little waterfall with moss-covered rocks. There was a little pavilion with pink roses climbing in and out of the lattice work. Etienne took a rose from the vine and stroked Isabella's lips with the petals then kissed her.

"For you, my lady," Etienne said, placing the rose behind her ear. "This place is beautiful. Thank you for bringing me here."

"You remember what happened here? Don't you?" Isabella smiled and raised her eyebrows. Etienne leaned in to kiss Isabella again, but he felt a blade to his throat. "No, I'm serious. What happened here?" Isabella stepped back, still holding the knife to his throat.

"I...I don't know." Etienne felt the life drain from his face. Isabella's features hardened, and she pushed the knife harder into his throat. Etienne felt a little drop of blood stream down his neck.

"How can you not remember? We were married here, properly. After we decided to stay, Philip married us where you stand. You are not my husband. What have you done with him?"

"I am your husband. I can't explain... You were gone and now you are here. All of you are here."

"What are you talking about?"

"Calm down, lassie. I donna ken what 'appened between you two last night. But, I think ya can settle it without a dagger," Andy said, approaching.

"Andy, stay out of this." Isabella said, with venom in her eyes. She pressed the knife even harder into Etienne's throat. "Where is my husband?"

"I may not have my recent memories, but I do know when we were young in France, our secret dream was to run away together," Etienne said, holding up his hands.

"What are ya talking about, laddie, ya met Isabella on the Camino just before ya met Clair and me." Etienne's heart raced. He didn't know how to explain what was happening. He had loved Isabella since his youth. This wasn't right.

"There they are!" shouted a gruff voice. "There are the two deserters. Molay will be happy we found you." Five Templars approached with their weapons drawn. "Kill the woman, and bring the other two with us."

Isabella stabbed a Templar in the eye as he approached. Etienne took the Templar's sword and finished the job. Etienne felt searing pain as an arrow shot him in the shoulder, sending him back a few paces. Another arrow shot Isabella in the chest, and Etienne caught her as she fell.

"You did this," Isabella said, as she sunk her dagger into Etienne's chest.

CHAPTER 49

Fransie awoke to Sephirah whining and thumping her tail from side to side. Across the room, Gabriel sat up and placed a hand on his head. He looked around in a daze.

"Where are we, girl?" He placed both hands on Sephiarah's face and brought her forehead to his.

"Thank God." Fransie sprung from her covers. "You are all right. He saved you."

"It would appear so." Gabriel raised his head from Sephirah's and managed a smile.

"What happened to you? She touched your chin…and…?"

"I couldn't face my own pride without Sephirah. It was too much—it was too powerful." Gabriel shook his head.

"Pride?"

"I have sensed pride before, but that witch embodied it in its purest concentrated form. It overwhelmed me. I saw the change in you as well. I thought I could overcome it, because I knew what we were facing, but I was wrong."

Fransie thought of her actions at the church. She hadn't realized it at the time, but there was a pull that was telling her she was equal to the Virgin Mary. A voice telling her that the others should respect her.

"Lord, forgive my self-righteous pride." Fransie clasped her hands and closed her eyes.

"Ahh, it is good to see that you are awake. My name is Joshua."

"I'm Gabriel, and this is—"

"Sephirah," the two said at the same time.

Fransie opened her eyes to see Joshua standing by Gabriel's bedside. He gave Gabriel a steaming cup of liquid then looked over his shoulder.

"Oh, I'm sorry to disturb your morning prayer. I just finished my prayers and thought you could use some breakfast. He pointed to the table that had several long squiggly pieces of dough on a plate. "They are called churros. They are my favorite. Usually I only eat them as a dessert, but I thought they would help with the healing process."

"Thank you, Joshua. Your kindness is unparalleled," Fransie said, walking to the table. Below the plate, the drawings from the previous evening were strewn across the old wood. Joshua helped Gabriel up, and the two of them joined her.

Gabriel looked from the pictures to Fransie and back at the pictures again.

"So you *do* know about the tree of life?" Fransie asked. "Why didn't you say you recognized the pattern in the church?"

"Perhaps we should discuss this another time?" Gabriel heaved himself onto the bench, and looked cautiously at Joshua.

"You can trust him—he saved your life. Just like I trust you for saving my life."

"Sister…" Fransie looked at him sternly. He shook his head. "I didn't tell you, because as I said before, my main purpose is to protect you now."

"I understand," Joshua said. "If she was carrying my baby, it would be my first priority as well. Eat, eat."

Gabriel raised questioning eyebrows at Fransie and managed a half smile as he reached for a churro. He crunched down hard on the fried bread. Fransie took one as well—it was unlike anything she had ever tasted before. She chewed slowly, savoring the flavors.

"Ah. I knew you would like them." Joshua took a bite. His eyes closed as the taste became a visible sensation on his face. "I love these so much. They are a delicacy to this region. I have almost worked out the recipe."

"I think it's perfect." Fransie took another small bite.

"So, Gabriel, how is it that you know about the sephiroth?" The dog walked to the table and sat obediently. Joshua broke off a piece of the churro. "Do you mind?" Gabriel nodded, and Joshua fed the small bite to Sephirah.

"I have lived many years and traveled many lands," Gabriel responded.

"But, you can't be older than thirty."

"As you say." Gabriel shot Joshua a smile.

"I was thinking about our conversation from last night." Joshua pulled the drawing of the tree of life from under the plate. "Have you ever heard of Jacob's Ladder?" he asked Fransie. Of course she had. She was a nun. She had dedicated her life to the service of God and studying the bible.

"Yes. It is in a story from Genesis 28. In it, Jacob has a dream that a ladder appears, reaching from the earth to the heavens, with angels ascending and descending. Here, God tells Jacob that he will give him the land he is laying upon and that his seed will spread throughout the world."

"Very good," Joshua said. "Do you know how many rungs were on Jacob's ladder?" Fransie shook her head. She had never thought about that before. "According to the oral tradition, there were four steps. Each step embodies one of the four worlds of the Kabbalah."

"For the Kabbalist, stories in what you call the Old Testament are written in a language of roots and branches. When the Kabbalists wrote these stories, they used this language to describe states and forces with a language people could understand, but there is a deeper meaning behind it.

"Take for example the story of creation." Joshua pointed at the top sephirah. "Keter represents the divine will of God to bestow. This is the will of the universe. This is the unknowable force behind everything." He traced a line down to the right.

"Hokhmah is Adam, the first creation. Created in God's image, this is the force to bestow. So your friend Raphael being a woman doesn't matter. Even though Hokhmah is related to the masculine energy, it primarily is the will to bestow.

"This leads us to Binah." He traced his finger across the drawing to the left. "Binah represents the divine will to receive. The story of creation is to explain how these forces work together. They describe the different aspects of God.

"The story of Jacob's Ladder is also written in a language of roots and branches." Joshua drew lines, which divided the tree of life into four parts. "The tree of life can be divided into four different worlds—it is said that Jacob's Ladder is a metaphor for these worlds, and the experience of prayer. Prayer is the ladder that allows one to climb from earth to deeper states of consciousness."

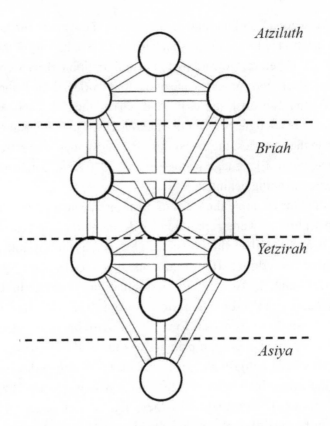

Atziluth

Briah

Yetzirah

Asiya

"Until you reach the soul," Gabriel said, leaning forward to get a better look at the drawing. His body language told Fransie he was just as interested as she was. Joshua wrote the word *Asiya* under the line closest to the base of the tree of life. It separated the lowest sephirah from the others.

"If you remember from our conversation last night, Malkuth"— Joshua pointed to the bottom sephirah—"represents the physical world. Everything you have ever experienced with your senses has happened here."

"So, what is Asiya? And how does that relate to prayer?" Fransie asked.

"Good question. Asiya, which is the world of action, is where the first steps to growth happen. It is here that one must take control over their actions. It is recognizing your patterns of behavior and making the necessary changes. These changes can occur in all areas. It could be dishonesty, slander, addictions, immoral sexual behavior, and so on. The first step on the ladder is a commitment to change these patterns on a behavioral level."

Fransie thought of her obsession to the music from the harp in Pamplona. She had never been obsessed with anything before, and never wanted to be so again. She also thought of Luca, Stefano, and the others. She shook her head.

"And how does that relate to your prayer?" Gabriel asked.

"Ah, in this first section of our morning prayer, we read many verses about sacrificing animals to God in the temple. This is symbolic of us confronting our own beast and sacrificing its desires to God. Surrender to God is the first stage of growth. Before spiritual development can be obtained, you must sacrifice the desires of your inner beast."

"And what about the second world, Yetzirah?" Fransie pointed at the second line. Fransie wanted to avoid talking about her inner beast. She had lived a chaste life until she developed her obsession. She didn't have the tools yet to tame that beast. She knew if she heard that song again, she couldn't resist it.

"Yetzirah is the world of formation. It is here that you examine your attitudes and beliefs that give rise to your daily actions. It is these beliefs that feed your actions. It is through introspection, humility, and brutal honesty that you can restructure your thoughts.

"In the second part of our morning prayer, we read beautiful psalms about God's relationship with nature. Meditation on these psalms helps us to realign ourselves with our true nature. It is here that we weed through the garden of our beliefs, pulling out every thought that feeds the beast of desire. It helps us to see deeper into the true nature of reality."

Fransie thought of Raphael's father. He had told them the story of the two forces that live inside every person. Was Joshua talking about starving the beast that feeds on negative thoughts?

"The third world is Briah. It is the world of creation. It is here that you recreate yourself. It is here that you surrender all that is yours to the divine will of life. You allow God to recreate your identity from nothing."

"When I became a nun, I renounced everything of the world and gave it over to God, even my birth name." Fransie had been re-created into a new person at the convent. She had given everything to God. She felt humbleness enter her body, and the hum inside of her grew louder.

"I sensed that you had attained that level." Joshua's mustache moved back and forth. "However, there is something deeper here. In Briah, we realize God creates existence anew every day, every moment. It is a continuous metamorphosis from something into nothing. In this part of the prayer we declare, '*Hear O Israel, God is one,*' which means God continually recreates us as an expression of his one reality."

"Joshua, continue. I want to hear about the last world." Gabriel leaned forward, putting more of his weight on the table.

"So, the Druid doesn't know everything about Kabbalah?" Joshua and Gabriel exchanged a smile.

"At this stage there is still an *I* trying to experience oneness. The awareness of an *I* is what creates separation from true reality. I love dancing, as Fransie knows, so this is the best metaphor I have for it. When I dance there comes a moment when there is no separation from me, my partner, and the music. I am lost in the moment and we are one; there is nothing but that connection. When I become one with the music, and my partner, I'm not experiencing 'oneness'—we just are one. All artists experience this. There is a moment when they disappear and become a conduit for something greater."

Fransie replayed their dance the evening before. There was a moment when she had truly lost herself in it. She had felt exactly what Joshua was talking about. It was that moment of flow. It felt like a deep prayer.

"This is the fourth world, Atziluth, the world of intimacy. It is here that you completely melt away into the all-encompassing God. Your entire being becomes a conduit through which the oneness with God shines through. It is in this moment of the prayer that we stand in silence."

"Where did things go so wrong in this world that we are so disconnected?" Gabriel leaned back in his chair. Fransie sensed that his mood had become melancholic.

"Fransie, hand me that tapestry on the wall." Fransie took a beautiful tapestry of a garden with a unicorn from the wall and handed it to Joshua. "This tapestry is beautiful, isn't it?"

"Yes, I have admired it all night. It must have taken so many hours to make. The stitching is superb." Fransie touched the tapestry, and the threads felt soft under her fingertips.

"And what about now?" Joshua asked, turning the tapestry over. On the reverse side, threads of all colors shot in different directions.

"It is total chaos," Gabriel said.

"Yes, so it would appear, yet they are the same thing. It all depends on your perception of it. All of these threads that are seemingly misplaced and chaotic in life actually create the most beautiful tapestry in the world. Kabbalah helps us to see this tapestry: the reality of God."

CHAPTER 50

I "I feel that I must return to the Cathedral," Fransie said as she and Gabriel left Joshua's.

"I don't think that is a good idea. We have already wasted a day. Luca could show up at any time—he will hunt you ceaselessly. Also, God only knows what will happen if I face that crone again without Sephirah." Gabriel fastened the saddle tightly on Cash.

"We can't run away from our sins forever." Fransie gently placed a hand on his arm. "We have to face them."

Gabriel put both hands on the saddle and took a deep breath.

"I have to go back. I know I have to."

"If they won't let Sephirah in, I can't join you."

"We each must face our sins alone. No one else can do it for you." Rosalita squeaked from Fransie's shoulder. "Besides, I won't be totally alone."

They rode to the main entrance of the church, and Fransie admired the stained-glass window, which contained the Star of David. This made Fransie think of Joshua. She had seen the symbol in his shop. She smiled at his kindness and words of wisdom.

"The dog can't come in. Don't you remember from yesterday?" said the priest whom they had met. "Besides, a church is no place for the possessed."

"Father, forgive me. But, Jesus came for sinners, not the righteous. 'It is not the healthy who need a doctor, but the sick. I have not come to call the righteous but the sinners.' He has the same right to be here that you do." Fransie felt her pride swell. Jesus's words would prove this priest wrong.

"Sister, don't quote scripture to me. We have rules, and they will be obeyed. They stay out here, or I will call the guards to remove both of you."

Fransie was about to speak, but she felt a hand on her shoulder.

"It's all right, Sister Fransie, we will stay out here. If you need anything, we will come."

Fransie was so frustrated. She wanted to continue arguing with the priest. Who was he to turn away anyone from God's house? What gave him the authority to do that? She felt hot inside her habit.

"Be careful, pride is the most dangerous sin." Gabriel looked at her sternly.

"You're right." Fransie thought about her words. Pride was already affecting her. She could hear the subtle whispers telling her she was better than the priest—that she knew scripture better than him—that God was on her side of the argument.

The priest let Fransie pass, and she avoided his gaze. To the left of the entrance was the side chapel that housed the sculpture of *The Seed of Jesse*. This is where she was called the last time. This was where she had heard the voice the strongest that had led her to the door.

Fransie entered the chapel and made the sign of the cross as she knelt in a pew. The sculpture behind the altar stretched from the floor to the ceiling and was magnificent. At the bottom was a carving of Jesse with a giant tree trunk coming from his abdomen. The trunk branched off into limbs on either side of a framed carving of Joseph and Mary. Both limbs that came from the central trunk had branches on which sat Jesus's family tree. Each side had two sets of three patriarchs, and crowning the sculpture was baby Jesus in Mary's arms.

A bell rang, and everyone emptied the small chapel to attend Mass at the main altar, except for Fransie. What was happening to her? She would never miss a Mass. Anytime she entered a church, and those bells rang, she was always in the front row. Now, though, she would figure out how to open the door that the hag said could only be opened from the other side.

"It's the tree of life," a voice said from behind her. Her breath startled out of her, and she turned to see Gabriel.

"What are you doing here?"

"I couldn't let you face this alone. I left Sephirah right outside the door. She is close enough to filter for me if I don't go too far."

"I can do this on my own. You didn't need to come." Her words surprised her. She was happy he was here, but did she need him?

"Did you see the pattern?"

"What pattern?"

"As I said before, it's the tree of life."

"But there are two Sephirah missing on the center column."

"Remember Da'at is invisible."

Fransie looked to where the fourth sephirah would be and there was a triangle at its exact location. "And below Jesse is Malkuth." Fransie hadn't considered the relief carving to be part of the main sculpture, but it made sense. Jesus stood amongst people—it was a perfect representation of Malkuth, the bottom sephirah, which represents our earthly world.

"Gabriel, he is standing on a ladder with four rungs. It's *Jacob's Ladder.*" Fransie rushed to study the carving. "You are right—this has to be it. I would have figured it out without you."

"This part you wouldn't have been able to, though." He pointed to the statue to the right of baby Jesus. It was a statue of a woman, blindfolded, holding a tablet. Fransie couldn't read the language it was written in. "It says, 'The will to bestow and the will to receive are both the lock and key.'" For some reason Fransie felt annoyed at this. The quest was hers, not his. She was the chosen one, not him.

"I bet you don't know how to unlock the tree of life—do you?" Fransie said, wanting to prove her superiority. "Hand me that chandelier lighter."

Gabriel handed her the long brass stick which had a curved bell to extinguish flames. Fransie extended the stick and traced the lightning pattern down the sculpture, depressing the pedestals on which the saints stood. Finally she depressed the bottom rung of Jacob's Ladder, and a green light flashed down the carving.

Fransie stood back and watched Mary and Joseph separate, opening a central passage. There was a loud clank behind her. Gabriel had sealed the gate to the chapel, locking them both inside.

"What are you doing?" Fransie asked.

"I told you, you were the chosen one," a raspy voice answered back. Gabriel disappeared and the hag stood at the gate. "All hail the immaculate Fransie," she hissed.

"Rosalita, why didn't you warn me?" Fransie chastised the mouse.

"That's right. It is her fault. You are infallible. It is always someone else's fault." The hag walked closer, and Fransie backed up against the wall. The opening above her had an ethereal glow.

"You are worthy to enter. Go ahead, climb up and take your place amongst the heirs of Jesus. You belong up there too." The hag's voice seemed to fill all the space in the room, except for a gentle note that sounded like the way a summer's breeze feels.

In desperation, Fransie looked around for an escape route. To her left, she noticed the sculpture that contained Jacob's Ladder had also opened to a black tunnel. She heard the note faintly coming from it, and seeing no other option, Fransie dove in.

The black passage was only large enough for her to crawl forward on her forearms—the space was suffocating. Fransie hated being in small places. She had just left one nightmare and entered another. Her forearms scraped as she clawed herself forward.

"You should be walking, not crawling. You are special." The hag's voice sounded like a thousand cockroaches chasing after her.

Fransie followed the sound that was like a wind. It was her lifeline. All was pitch black. Everything was closing in, and the crawl space was narrowing. Fransie's heart pounded hard—it was trying to escape her body, like she was trying to escape this hole. Finally, Fransie gave up and laid her head on the cold hard stone.

"God, I can't do this myself. I need your help!" she yelled.

The floor opened and her stomach rose to her mouth as she fell. Fransie hit the ground hard. She couldn't raise her head. She didn't want to. Fransie wasn't sure if the warm liquid around her face was blood or tears. Turning to her side, she retched and spat the last remnants of the bile from her mouth.

"Rosalita, Rosalita," she said, patting her body frantically. The small mouse climbed down to Fransie's hand and nibbled her finger playfully. Fransie was in too much pain to smile. Every part of her ached. She lifted her gaze from her hand to the room around her. An ethereal blue light poured in from a door that stood ajar.

Fransie passed the door and noticed the blood-stained Z between the eyes of the face. This was the door she'd tried to unlock the day before—but now, it was already opened. Fransie cautiously walked into a mirror image of the cathedral. Everything here was backward. In the center of the cathedral, a pillar of blue light shot up to the domed stained-glass window.

Fransie approached the light cautiously, ducking from pillar to pillar. She peered over the altar, and her gaze rested on a prostrate body in front of the light. The figure's arms were outstretched, and its head was pressed to the floor. The sound

Fransie heard in the tunnel wrapped itself around her and pulled her closer to the figure.

"Your faith in God has saved you from being devoured by your pride," the figure on the ground said.

Fransie dropped to her knees and lay prostrate next to the figure. She looked under her arm at the figure, and a strikingly beautiful face stared back at her. She couldn't tell if the figure was a man or a woman, but its face was radiant.

"You are so beautiful," Fransie let out unconsciously.

"I am what God made me, nothing more." The angelic face turned to the ground once more. Fransie mimicked its action.

"If the hag was Pride, then you must be Humility."

"I am only what God made me."

"I'm not worthy to be in your presence. I don't deserve to be here." Rosalita cuddled up to Fransie's face.

"Humility isn't thinking poorly of yourself, it's *not thinking of yourself.* Pride is the attitude of esteeming yourself better than other people, but the truth is, everyone is special. No one is a mistake."

Fransie thought of the tapestry Joshua had shown her. It was true. Each of those little threads was special, and necessary to make the whole, no matter how ugly they looked on the back of the tapestry.

"Pride is the most dangerous of the seven deadly sins. It was this sin that caused Satan to fall from heaven. His pride led him to believe he was equal to God. His pride separated him from God. Pride also separated man from God, as if such a thing was possible." Fransie thought she saw the angelic being smile.

"Adam and Eve were expelled from the Garden of Eden due to their pride. The devil tricked them into eating from the tree of good and evil. He said that they would be equal to God if they ate from it. Their pride also led to the fall of mankind."

"Did I overcome my pride today?"

"Your pride was overcome by your plea for help. You can do nothing yourself, but everything through Christ. If you take the focus away from yourself, and let God work through you, anything is possible."

"Why was the door open when I arrived?"

"Another was here before you. Pride led him to the treasure, and she allowed him to take it. The crown of thorns is now in his possession. His pride has led to the destruction of many and will lead to the destruction of many more. Pride will consume him until it kills him. Because you overcame your pride today, should you encounter the crown of thorns, it is yours to do what God wills you to do with it.

"The trick isn't realizing you are special. The trick is realizing everyone is special. To remember this, and to ward off pride again, take my cloak of humility and wrap yourself in it."

"I couldn't..." Before Fransie finished her sentence, Humility disappeared, and all that was left was the weight of the invisible cloak in her hands. Fransie hesitantly lifted the cloak and wrapped it around herself. In an instant, she was back in the chapel, and the priest was banging on the locked gate.

CHAPTER 51

"No!" Etienne's eyes shot open in the pitch-black chapel. "Isabella, no." Brother Philip's door opened, flooding the chapel with torchlight. Etienne curled up in a ball of agony, as he heard Philip's footsteps approach. Etienne hid his face. He was too proud to let Philip see him crying.

"Are you all right, my son?"

"No, I think I'm going mad." Etienne sniffed reflexively and stifled his tears.

"Whatever do you mean?"

"Every time I am in this church things happen in one way, then in another. They are the same for the most part but with slight differences, and I have memories of both.

"Ah, I see. Let me ask you a very important question—what color is Isabella's hair?"

"Brunette, of course."

"I definitely remember her as a blonde." Etienne's brow furrowed, and he turned to face Philip. How could he mistake Isabella for a blonde? Her hair was so dark it was almost black.

"Are you color blind?"

"By no means," replied Brother Philip. "Let's try another one. What are the names of my two adopted wolves?"

"Bennie and Moira."

"Good, good, and did they look like this? Benedict, Moira!" The two wolves came bounding into the room, playing as they entered. Etienne couldn't believe his eyes. Moira put her front paws on Etienne and licked his face, her purple eyes smiling at him.

"This can't be—Moria died. Is this the place of rebirth?"

"Ah, I see. Here, Raphael was the one who passed." The corner of Brother Philip's lips turned down and the light in his eyes diminished slightly. "What did you mean when you asked, is this a place of rebirth?" Etienne felt shame crawling under his skin. He didn't want to answer that question, but he needed to know what was going on.

"The last time I was here, I had what I thought to be a dream... but it felt so real. I went to the garden to talk to Isabella and I..." Etienne rubbed his arm up and down. "I killed her. But, then I woke up, and the day started exactly the same, but finished differently. Just now I had another dream, and once again, Isabella died, saying I had killed her. What is happening?"

"You killed her, and you didn't kill her, both are true. You have awakened to a gift that all humanity has but hasn't realized yet."

"What do you mean?"

"Come to the garden, and I will explain."

The last thing Etienne wanted to do was go to the garden. He couldn't face what he had done and said to Isabella there. Brother Philip reached the door, and Etienne hadn't moved.

"I understand you have painful memories there. I will begin my daily work, and when you are ready, you can join me."

Etienne knew he had to face what he had done. He had to face who he had been. He was no longer that person anymore. Moira playfully bit Etienne's pant leg and dragged him to the door.

"You want me to go too?" Moira whined and tugged harder. Etienne reluctantly walked out the door and was met by the first rays of daylight.

Moira walked by Etienne's side, past where he had confronted Isabella, to a log that Brother Philip was sitting on. Etienne was grateful for Moira's company; it lessened his self-loathing.

Etienne sat next to Philip. "I thought you were going to be working." Moira placed her head at Etienne's feet, and he stroked her.

"I have been." Brother Philip smiled broadly and held up a book. On the first page was a picture of a butterfly on a flower. "What direction will this butterfly fly?"

"What?" Etienne raised his eyebrows.

"Do you want to know what has been happening?" Etienne nodded. "Good, then what direction will the butterfly go?"

"To the left," Etienne answered.

Philip turned to the second page, which already had a flower drawn, and drew another butterfly to the left of the first.

"And now?"

"To the left again."

Philip flipped the page and proceeded to draw another butterfly where Etienne had indicated.

"What about now?"

"Up." Etienne thought that if he answered differently, Philip would get to the point.

"And now?"

Etienne brushed his hands on his pants. He didn't like playing games, and the more times Philip asked him the more it felt like a game he was playing.

"To the left." Etienne sifted his fingers through Moira's fur, her head still at his feet.

"I see you are getting impatient. Let me reveal the secret of life to you." Philip winked and flipped the pages quickly. Etienne's jaw dropped—it looked as if the butterfly was actually flying.

"How did you…what magic is this?" Etienne asked.

Philip flipped the pages again. "This isn't magic. It is only part of the lesson I want to reveal to you. "You are the butterfly, my friend, and each piece of paper is a moment in time. Life is made up of present moment after present moment. All seem to connect, yet each is individual and is the only thing to exist. You are the sum of all the choices you have made in your life so far."

Philip turned to the last page.

"Just as the butterfly sits in this position on the last page, so do you sit here with me now. Every decision you have ever made has led you to this moment, here, now. You could have chosen to go in any direction, yet you chose this one." Philip flipped the pages for emphasis.

"May I?" Philip handed Etienne the book, and he flipped the pages for himself. Once again the butterfly took flight. "Amazing." Etienne handed the book back to Philip.

"You could have chosen to fly here." Philip drew another butterfly on the second page. "Or here, or here, or here." He continued to draw until the page was covered with butterflies. "All of these possibilities exist in this present moment, an infinite number of realities happening now." Philip turned the page. "And now again." Philip filled up the page with butterflies and continued to do so with each page. "Flip the pages now."

Etienne turned the pages, and the butterflies appeared stationary because they occupied all the spaces on each page. "There is no movement."

"It is through conscious choice and the illusion of time that we appear to live in reality. What you have experienced was a jump from one reality to another. You killed Isabella in one reality, in another you all stayed here, and in our current reality, you and your friends proceeded to Santiago. All are true, and all are happening at this very moment. Sometimes just one consciousness shifts, sometimes a whole group. That is why I asked you Isabella's hair color. In this reality it was blonde, and in the one you came from, it was brown."

Moira jumped on Etienne, sending him to the ground behind the log. She lovingly licked his face.

"Moira seems pleased you are in this reality." Brother Philip helped Etienne to his feet and read his look of confusion. "Come, I will show you in another way."

Brother Philip led Etienne to a small pond. He picked up a stone and said, "You are this stone." He threw the stone into the pond and it sent out ripples in all directions. "You create the ripples—each is a different frequency—a different reality. Your consciousness matches the frequency of the ripple and you exist in that reality, but all frequencies exist simultaneously. You are the source and the ripple, all at the same time."

"If everything happens at the same time, does that mean my consciousness can go back in time?" Etienne's mind was reeling at all the possibilities.

Philip smiled broadly and clasped his hands together. "The butterfly can fly in all directions. Come, walk with me."

Etienne didn't know if he liked being called a butterfly, but he joined Brother Philip, who was walking incredibly slowly. Etienne tried to match his pace but found it difficult.

"Steady your mind. Feel each part of your foot as it rolls through the ground."

Etienne stepped slowly and rolled through the heel of his foot to the ball. He felt twigs and small clumps of dirt give way as he applied pressure. It took all of Etienne's focus to move so slowly, to feel each part of the step. Etienne's breath slowed along with the pace of his feet, and soon his mind slowed as well. It came to a point where Etienne wasn't sure if he was moving any longer, breathing any longer, or thinking any longer.

"Focus your mind on the energy of the reality you desire to be in."

Etienne focused on the feeling of Isabella. The love he had for her moved through his body. He could almost feel his arms around her. His love for her was a beacon pulling him to a different place. Now he felt her hand in his, the softness, the way it sent energy through his body. He slowly gazed at his hand and found Isabella's nestled in it. He squeezed her hand tightly and looked into her eyes. She was here, but dimly, as if a filter covered her.

A horse brayed loudly, and Etienne's awareness was pulled back away from Isabella's hand. The world came into focus, and Etienne felt the wind knocked out of him. His spirit was still catching up with his body.

The horse snorted and turned in a circle. "Etienne, Etienne, thank God we found you!"

Etienne stretched his eyes wide. There were two riders on the horse. The first was a man with rune tattoos, and the second was Sister Fransie.

"It appears you chose to stay in this reality," Brother Philip said, patting him on the back.

"Thank God, we found you first," Sister Fransie said as the stranger helped her down.

"First? What do you mean?" Etienne furrowed his brow.

"Oh, heavens me. King Philip has sent soldiers to capture you, the Templars have Molay's old orders to kill you for deserting, and the Pope has sent a psychotic priest who has been working with the Hospitallers to prevent me from delivering this message—I think they are after you too!"

"What is going on? Who sent you?"

"Isabella, and Jaques de Molay."

Etienne felt he must have awakened yet again to another reality. He couldn't imagine Isabella and Molay working together. "Isabella wants to save you from Philip, and I have something from Molay that I can give only to you."

"Who is this?" Etienne sized up the other rider. "I never expected to see you riding with a man covered in tattoos. Maybe Sister Caroline..." Etienne stopped as Fransie's eyes filled with tears. "Where is Sister Caroline?"

"I am Gabriel, and Sister Caroline died in the service of finding you," answered the stranger on the horse.

Etienne felt a sharp pang of sadness. "I'm so sorry, Fransie."

"She is with God now." A small mouse crawled up Fransie's arm and perched on her shoulder.

"Wolves approaching," Gabriel said. Etienne could have sworn that a tattoo under his chin glowed.

A large, charcoal-colored dog with scraggly fur rounded the church and stood next to the horse, almost reaching the height of its neck. The dog bared its teeth as Bennie and Moira approached with bristled fur. The dog was slightly smaller than Bennie, but not by much.

"Benedict, Moira," Brother Philip said. The two wolves split and walked on either side of the horse, keeping their eyes on the dog. They passed Etienne and sat at Philip's feet.

"Sephirah," Gabriel said, and the dog sat.

"Now that we are all acquainted, what is going on here?" Brother Philip asked.

"They know...they all know, Etienne," Fransie said, grasping his tunic.

"They know what?" Etienne asked.

"That you are the key to finding what God has entrusted to the Templars. Molay said you must find it before King Philip or the Pope, otherwise the world will be in grave danger," Sister Fransie said.

"And why can't Molay find it himself?"

"He and Isabella are both trapped in Paris. You are the only hope."

Etienne froze, and everything became silent. "I gave up the quest for the treasure and never wanted to be a part of it in the first place."

"Etienne, Molay is risking his life so you have a chance to find it before King Philip and Pope Clement. As we speak, they are planning to arrest all of the Templars and take their treasure."

"It would be impossible for Philip to do that, let alone find the treasure."

"Molay didn't think so. He feared that with what Isabella had told him—and what might be revealed through torture—King Philip would have all he needs to find the treasure. Etienne, even a small stream can tear apart a mountain, given enough time. King Philip's persistence will allow him to succeed." Fransie straightened her garments.

"Do you know the kind of trials you have to face to find the keys that unlock the one true treasure?"

"I think so." Sister Fransie pulled the grail from under her habit. Etienne's eyes widened.

"Is that what I think it is?" Fransie nodded. "You have to put it back."

"I can't. I don't know how. Plus, the Hospitallers and much worse things are after us."

"How many doors have you unlocked?"

"Three, but we only have one treasure. A companion has David's Harp, and the treasure from the Cathedral of Burgos had already been taken."

Etienne turned and walked away. He paced back and forth, a war rising inside him.

"Please, Etienne, Sister Caroline gave her life so I could reach you. This is bigger than all of us. Quit being so selfish."

Etienne stopped. Sister Fransie's words struck a chord. Was he being selfish? He just wanted to live in peace. He didn't want anything to do with this treasure, but it just kept coming back into his life.

"How did you find the other treasures?" Etienne faced Fransie again.

"I sensed them." She glanced at Gabriel. "*We* sensed them."

"What do you mean, sensed?"

"I have true sound and Gabriel has true scent." Etienne looked at Fransie blankly. "It is too hard to explain now."

"Did you sense me and that's how you knew I was here?"

Fransie shook her head. "No, we sensed another door that leads to the treasure." Etienne's body turned to ice. He had spent time in this chapel and had never seen a tree of life.

Brother Philip laughed robustly and the wolves howled. "So it is...so it is." He wiped tears from his eyes and placed a hand on Etienne's shoulder. "You can't avoid what God has called you to do. That path leads to much suffering for you and others. Jesus accepted what the Father had planned for him. Do you think yourself better than Jesus? Could you imagine the world had He not died for our sins?"

A wave of humility came over Etienne. Fransie was right. He had been trying to run away from what God had called him to do. He was being selfish. All he had thought about was Isabella. He hadn't considered his purpose in life. Even after all this time, he didn't feel worthy to have a calling. Why would God choose him?

Etienne took a deep breath. "Very well then, where is the tree of life that leads to the last door?" Etienne asked Brother Philip.

"As Fransie said, you are the key." Etienne scrunched his brow.

"What?"

"Sephirah," Gabriel said. The large dog walked to Etienne, and the wolves bared their teeth.

"Bennie, Moira, peace." Brother Philip placed a hand on each wolf.

Sephirah continued to Etienne and sniffed him vigorously. As she did, Etienne noticed Gabriel's tattoo glow once more. Sephirah sniffed below Etienne's feet causing him to move to his left. She followed her nose on the ground back to Etienne. Satisfied with what he had found, Sephirah walked to Gabriel and sat obediently at his side.

"It is so." Gabriel looked Etienne squarely in the eyes. "What we have been sensing lies inside you. You must be a portal."

Etienne couldn't believe his ears. What were they talking about? He was a human being, not a portal to a door that harbored a great treasure. He looked desperately at Fransie.

"It is so. I heard it. I don't know how it is possible, but it is true. The way to this treasure is through you, Etienne."

"This is exciting! Remember the butterflies, Etienne. All possible realities occur at exactly the same time and moment. You just need to step into one where you open this door." Brother Philip smiled reassuringly at Etienne.

Etienne wanted to say *you are all mad,* but he restrained himself. He thought of the words from before. Who was he to run away from the life that was laid out in front of him?

"Very well—but, I go alone. How did you defeat the last trials?" Etienne asked.

"We actually haven't defeated all of them. Remember when I said there were worse things than the Hospitallers after us...?" Fransie's eyes glossed over. Etienne could tell she was reliving a painful memory.

"I see. How do I open this portal?" Etienne looked at Brother Philip.

"Continue the exercise from before."

Etienne nodded and walked very slowly. He became conscious of the smallest movements in his body. He was aware of every single inch of his foot as it left the ground. Etienne's consciousness fluctuated.

"Focus on the feeling from the last time the portal was opened," Brother Philip's voice penetrated Etienne's inner silence.

Etienne focused on Astorga. He watched as Charity touched the symbol of the tree of life in a lightning bolt pattern. He felt the hairs on his arms stand up as the electricity came from above and worked its way down the door, unlocking it.

Etienne felt this same powerful energy above his head—emanating from the source, it moved to the left of his head, then the right. Etienne felt the balls of light glowing even though he couldn't see them. The energy traced across him to his left shoulder, followed by the right. His head and neck tingled as the energy rushed through him. The energy continued from his shoulder to his left elbow then his right. Etienne felt his whole body pulsing. The light was alive in him. The energy moved from his elbow to his navel. Etienne could feel his body pulsating at almost the same vibration as the light. The energy dropped from his navel to his groin, and there was a bright flash.

Etienne felt smooth cold marble under his hands before he regained his sight. He placed his forehead on the ground to join his hands. The coolness of the floor was a relief to the heat he was radiating.

"Rise," a regal voice commanded. Etienne lifted his head, and he could make out two blurry figures sitting on thrones. He pushed up onto his knees and stood.

Etienne rubbed his eyes and blinked. The figures slowly came into focus. It was a man and a woman. No, a king and queen. Etienne saw the crowns, then the faces below the crowns.

"Isabella!" Etienne shouted with joy. She was sitting on a throne with a large, jewel encrusted crown. She was absolutely radiant. She was clothed more beautifully than the night sky—a million diamonds made her shimmer.

"Who is this, and how do you know him, my love?" Etienne's blood boiled as the king took Isabella's hand.

"This is Etienne," Isabella said, sweetly. "I knew him long ago, but now, he is just another one here for the test."

"What test?" Etienne clenched his jaw as he spoke. How could Isabella just sit there and pretend she was happy? This must be King Edward, her betrothed. Had they been married already? Etienne had clung to the vain hope that somehow Isabella would be brought back to him, her rightful husband.

"Very well. Any friend of yours is welcome to the test, my queen." Edward kissed Isabella's hand.

Etienne was more than just a friend—he was her true love.

"You may try to pull the sword from the stone." Edward motioned to a rock in the middle of the throne room with a sword thrust deeply into it.

"What happens if I succeed, or fail?" Etienne eyed the sword cautiously.

"We don't know." Isabella sat up excitedly. "No one has ever been able to pull it out before—though, many have tried."

"Some believe the one who is able to pull the sword will be the true king of England. That is a ridiculous notion though, as I am the true king. Isn't that so, my love?"

My love. Those words coming from him frayed every one of Etienne's nerves. It should be him sitting up there with Isabella. Not this pompous king. She was his wife first. She was his love first. Etienne knew Isabella felt the same way, even though she didn't show it. How could she have left him for this handsome, rich king? Etienne knew he had answered his own question. Who was he to compare to a king? He was a poor nobody.

"I accept." Etienne had enough anger and adrenaline in his body to do a great feat. He would show Isabella that he was better than this king. He would show her that she belonged with him.

God, give me the strength to do this one thing. Etienne took the hilt of the sword in both hands and placed his foot on the rock. As his fingers clasped around the hilt, he felt the same strange energy in his body. With all of his might, Etienne pulled hard on the blade. He felt his muscles strain. He wasn't going to be able to do it.

He took a deep breath and cleared his mind. He would resonate with a world where he pulled the sword. He felt what it would feel like for the sword to be out of the rock. He felt its weight in his hand, and the sound it made when it sliced the air. Etienne felt a current of energy shoot down his body, and he went flying backward as the sword left the stone.

"See, Isabella, I am just as good as he is," Etienne said, regaining his footing. Both Isabella and Edward looked at Etienne with amazement. Etienne followed their eyes to the sword and nearly jumped back as he realized it was covered in flames.

"How...how is this possible?" Edward stammered. Etienne loved seeing his cocky face in utter shock. Edward fumbled around, trying to form words, but none came. Etienne smiled broadly and approached the throne.

"It is possible, because I am the true king of England, and Isabella is my wife." Etienne thrust the sword hard, and felt the metal point hit the back of the throne, as he ran Edward through.

Etienne opened his eyes. He was laying on the ground facing the sky. He felt the weight of the sword and scabbard in his hand. He was back, and he had the sword.

"Etienne." Fransie and Philip rushed to his aid, helping him to his feet.

"How long was I gone?" Etienne looked around in a daze.

"You never left. The sword appeared and you fell to the ground." Fransie made the sign of the cross.

Etienne gripped the scabbard of the sword tightly and loosened the blade. Everyone took a step back as its blue flames licked the night sky.

"I have heard two legends of a flaming sword," Gabriel said, looking at the blade curiously. "The first comes from the Celtic tradition—the flaming sword is said to have belonged to Rhydderich Hael. It is said that when a worthy person drew the sword it would burst into Flames."

"And the second?" Etienne asked, sheathing the sword.

"The second is from the Bible." Fransie responded before Gabriel could answer. "In Genesis, it is written that God entrusted the cherubim with a flaming sword to guard the gates of Paradise after Adam and Eve were banished."

CHAPTER 52

"Stop the horse." Fransie had been fine riding on the back of Cash, but the breakfast Philip had given them a few hours ago was rushing back up.

"Are you well, Sister Fransie?" Etienne asked as he helped her down.

Fransie ran past him and bile spewed out of her mouth. This wasn't her first bout of morning sickness, but it was definitely the worst so far. The back of her throat burned as she wiped the spittle from her lips. She reminded herself that it was a small price to pay for the honor bestowed on her.

"How is it you knew Sister Fransie needed help in Logrono?" Etienne asked Gabriel. Fransie noticed that Etienne didn't quite trust Gabriel. She didn't know if she fully did either. He hadn't said much about himself, but he had saved her life.

"As Fransie said, I have true scent."

"What exactly is that?

"I can sense virtues and sins. Virtues smell sweeter than the most potent rose—each virtue a different fragrance. The smell is intoxicating, almost addicting." Fransie thought of her own addiction to the sound of the harp in Pamplona. Even the thought of it sent a craving through her body.

"And sins," Gabriel continued, "are the worst smell in the world. Once again, each has a different odor. If I didn't have Sephirah, a fate much worse than what happened in Burgos would befall me. She is my filter. Through her the scents are tolerable, and I can distinguish one sin from another. Since I left my land, I have followed these scents and put a stop to whatever sin was happening."

"So you help others, just like a priest?" Fransie asked as she rejoined them.

"Yes, I feel if God gives you a gift, you have to use it for the betterment of others. I usually don't track down gluttony, but in Logrono, the stench was worse than any other time I had experienced it"—Gabriel paused—"except with the Fisher King. I have searched in many lands for him and my former home, but they have been hidden from the world."

"Who is the Fisher King?" Etienne asked.

"He is the one who led me to the Holy Grail." She turned to Gabriel. "Why would you want to find him?"

"Because he is my father—at least, I think he is." Gabriel's face became grim, as if a shadow was passing over him.

Fransie nearly stumbled backward. "What do you mean?"

"As I told you before, the Fisher King's wound was caused by the sin of gluttony, just as your Luca's was. The man who became the Fisher King was supposed to be chaste and a protector of the bloodline, but gluttony overtook him, and he had many women— my mother being one of them."

"Bloodline?" Etienne raised questioning eyebrows.

"The bloodline of Jesus. The true Holy Grail." Fransie unconsciously rubbed her pregnant belly.

"Your child?" Etienne couldn't even finish his sentence. Fransie smiled and nodded. Etienne dropped to his knees and made the sign of the cross.

"You didn't bow to the cup, and you won't bow to me." Fransie helped Etienne up. The sense of false pride she felt in Burgos had totally abandoned her.

"How did you know he was your father?" Etienne asked, trying to overcome the awkwardness of his kneeling.

"His curse was passed onto me. I was born with the curse of more." Gabriel raised his tunic to reveal a massive scar across his midsection. It looked like a giant mouth that had been sewn shut.

Fransie gasped and put both hands to her mouth. Her brain re-lived being in that small alley, facing the terrible mouth that consumed Sister Caroline.

"That is enough." Etienne put his arm around Sister Fransie.

"My apologies; I needed you to see the truth in my story. I was a slave to gluttony from my birth. I always wanted more. I could conceal this abomination"—Gabriel pointed at his stomach—"but my ambition and desire had no disguise. This is why I was banished from the land you visited. I have been trying to get home ever since."

"How did you defeat this curse?" Etienne asked.

"I traveled many lands, devouring all that I could. People didn't realize what I was doing until their lives had been sucked away. One day I met an old man with a falcon who said he wanted to give me something. Of course I accepted, not knowing what I would receive." Gabriel lifted his chin and pointed to the marking, the same one Fransie had behind her ear. "He gave me this."

"He gave you true scent, just as I have received true sound." Fransie pulled back her habit to show Etienne and Gabriel her marking.

"It is so," Gabriel said with a heavy sigh. "But, it wasn't this gift that directly saved me. This gift nearly killed me. The putrid smell overwhelmed me. The stench became worse every time gluttony overtook me, or I was around the other sins. I would drop to the ground, convulse, and foam at the mouth. Everyone thought I was possessed."

"Just like the priest in the cathedral." Fransie put a hand on Gabriel's shoulder.

"After one episode, when I was passed out, the townsfolk bound me and took me to a Benedictine monastery. I will be forever grateful to them for doing that. At the monastery, the sweet smell of the virtues balanced the stench of my sins. It was also there that I met Sephirah. The monks told me she appeared the same night I did and never left my side." Gabriel looked kindly at the dog and petted her head.

"Was it she who cured you? I am still trying to figure this out." Etienne raised questioning eyebrows again.

"No, but she did act as my filter and made both the sins and virtues bearable." Gabriel looked at Fransie's stomach. "It was the Word of God that healed me. I tried to fill myself with many things, but I was only truly content when I found the word of God."

"That is beautiful. I didn't know you were Christian." Gabriel smiled at Etienne and nodded his head.

"Philippians 4:11-13 became my mantra: 'Not that I speak from want, for I have learned to be content in whatever circumstances I am. I know how to get along with humble means, and I also know how to live in prosperity; in any and every circumstance I have learned the secret of being filled and going hungry, both of having abundance and suffering need. I can do all things through Him who strengthens me.'"

"My grace is sufficient for you," Fransie quoted.

"Those who seek the Lord lack no good thing," Etienne said, rubbing his chin.

"It is so," Gabriel said. "I was saved by the grace of God. The more I accepted these words, the more I was filled. Eventually the

curse of *more* left my body, and I was healed." Gabriel placed a
hand on Fransie's shoulder. "There is still hope for your friend."

"I hope so." She took his hand. She never wanted to see the horror
she had witnessed in that small alley. A chill ran up her spine.

"My heart changed from a will to receive more and more to a
heart that would give whatever it received. I have searched these
many long years to find a way back to my land to help my father. To
share the Word with him and remove the curse from his kingdom."

"That is why you knew so much about the tree of life."

"In my travels, I heard rumors that this was the only way to reach
my former home. I learned everything I could about it and other
mysteries—with the will only to save my father. But from the
sound of it, I must thank you."

"Why is that?" Fransie asked, a little taken aback by the statement.

"You set my father free. Your question enabled him to give up
the one thing he cherished most and restored the blood line. This
is why I had to save you in that alley. I owe you a great debt. You
fulfilled my quest."

Fransie didn't know what to say. She looked at the ground and
pulled the invisible cloak of humility around her tightly. After a
long moment she looked up. "It was God's will."

CHAPTER 53

Mariano had spent days, months, years, in the cave; there was no passage of time. Each present moment was spent unraveling all of the thoughts that had caused him so much suffering. Every day he drew water from the stream, and every day his reflection looked younger. Mariano was more present than he had been his whole life. After facing each of his *shadows*, there was only one final thought binding him to the cave. He took the parchment, which now was completely full of the thoughts that had once kept him captive, dipped the quill, and wrote:

The Alchemist told me I shouldn't leave the cave.

1) Is it true?
  • *Yes.*

2) Can you absolutely know it is true?

Mariano thought for a moment about what the Alchemist had told him—what were her exact words? Mariano laughed heartily and the cave joined him, echoing back his laughter. He often did this when he saw a thought that was giving him trouble for what it was—a lie. *The Alchemist never said I shouldn't leave the cave. She said, "You will stay here until you have questioned every Shadow that has troubled you."* Mariano let out another thunderous laugh. *She never said I couldn't leave—my thinking said that.* Mariano wrote out *No* to answer question two.

Mariano had done the process so many times, now every thought he had was automatically met with *Is it true.* The process was alive in him and worked automatically. He decided to continue writing to see where this Shadow was leading him.

3) *How do you react when you think that thought?*
  • *I feel trapped. I feel obligated to do something that I don't want to do. I get angry at the Alchemist for trapping me in this cave. I miss my friends. I feel lonely.*

These words and concepts that were once so charged with emotion were now met as old friends. Mariano saw the fallacy in each. He saw how each one of these thoughts lead to its own suffering.

4) *Who would you be without that thought?*
  • *I would be free to leave the cave anytime I wanted, or to stay; the choice would be mine.*

Mariano smiled gently. He knew the choice had always been his. He could have left anytime he wanted to. Without that thought, he would have been able to stay, or leave the cave, and been at peace either way. Both were good options.

Turn around

1) The Alchemist didn't tell me 'I shouldn't leave the cave:'
  • *She actually never said that. She said, I will stay in the cave until I have questioned every Shadow that has troubled me.*

Mariano had discovered this truth above, but to actually see it on paper brought a whole new reality. *Was she predicting the future? Had she seen that I would stay here until I finished?* Mariano had taken her words and twisted them. He had heard something that wasn't said.

2) I told me that I shouldn't leave the cave:
  • *I took her words and gave them that meaning. I have been my jailer this whole time and blamed her for keeping me captive. I could have left anytime I wanted to. I kept myself here.*

3) My thinking told me I shouldn't leave the cave:
  • *That one thought—that one Shadow—has kept me trapped here. I was held ransom by what might have happened to the world if I didn't stay. Now, I see this is a lie.*
  • *Had I not had that thought, I would have been free to stay, or go, and both would be the right choice.*

Mariano lit a small fire and burned the parchment. As his limiting beliefs went up in smoke, so did his reliance on the Alchemist. Mariano knew he didn't need her any longer. He was responsible for his own peace. Looking for it outside of himself was insanity and would only lead to more suffering.

After the parchment was nothing but ash, Mariano rose and left the cave. The sun was blinding and felt amazing on his skin. As the Alchemist had predicted, he knew it was the right time to leave.

Now was always the right time. Reality was showing him exactly where to go, and he didn't try to fight it any longer. The only thing that existed was the present moment, and he would love whatever it brought. Mariano knew life would lead him to his friends, or it wouldn't. Either way it would be the right thing. He was excited for the adventure ahead. For all he knew, he wouldn't make it as far as the stream, and that was all right as well.

CHAPTER 54

Etienne thanked God as they entered the familiar streets of Santiago de Compostela. He focused all of his efforts on taking the next step. His body burned in a way he had never experienced before. It had started slightly after they had left Brother Philip and the Keystone Church. At first, it just felt like a slight irritation in his joints, but over the miles, the irritation became an aching, and now as they entered Santiago, it was an intense burning.

"Why are you walking like an eighty-year-old man?" Gabriel asked, as Etienne tried to descend the steps leading to the courtyard in front of the cathedral. Pilgrims were passing him quickly on either side. Etienne's leg joints felt like they were fused together. He couldn't bend his knees and took every step with a straight leg.

"Pain," Etienne managed through a jaw that was quickly tensing up. The pain spread through his body and burned all of his joints. Etienne had fought it to this point, but now he needed help. He was nearly frozen to the spot.

"Help him," Fransie implored. Gabriel struggled to drape Etienne over Cash. The horse waited patiently until Etienne was hanging off either side of the saddle. The pain was excruciating.

"Where are the others?" Fransie asked, bending down to the same level as his head.

"Ahead...left....down alley," Etienne said, without moving his now fused jaw. Etienne felt the stares of onlookers as they passed the bar he and Andy frequented.

Cash turned down the small alley, which soon gave way to the fields they had tended all year.

"Etienne, my God, what 'as 'appened ta you!" Andy popped up from behind some tall stalks of wheat.

"We don't know," Sister Fransie said. "What were you doing hiding down there? You nearly gave me a heart attack jumping out like that."

"Sister Fransie, is that really you?" Andy ran out from the wheat and embraced her. Seeing Gabriel from the other side of Cash, Andy stepped back. "Who is he?" Andy said suspiciously. "I'd expect Sister Caroline to show up with a man covered in tattoos, but not you, Sister Fransie." Andy shook his head.

"Andy Sinclair, quit your blubbering and let's get Etienne inside. Can ya na see he needs 'elp?" Clair crossed her arms and raised an eyebrow at Andy.

Even though Etienne couldn't move his face, he smiled on the inside—it was good to be home.

Cash moved forward and a large pair of hands lifted Etienne from the horse. "You have gotten heavier since the last time I carried you," Gerhart's voice boomed as he carried Etienne inside.

"What's wrong with him?" Clair lifted one of Eitenne's arms then dropped it. Etienne groaned at the movement. "Sorry 'bout that," she patted him gently.

"We don't know," Fransie said. "His body just stopped working as we entered the courtyard.

"This isn't Etienne's sword." Andy pulled the sword from the scabbard and the flames on the blade lit the room. "Son of a...," Andy said, fumbling to put the sword back in its sheath.

"Don't ya touch tha. It could be poisoned." Clair took the sword away from Andy.

"The sword, of course," Fransie said. Etienne's eyes darted from friend to friend. He wished he could speak, but most of all, he wished the burning in his body would cease. "There is a treasure, but also a trial. Etienne, what was the trial you faced?"

Etienne hadn't told them what had happened inside the throne room. He was embarrassed by his actions. He didn't want them to know he had killed an unarmed man, even if that man had his wife. Etienne's body burned at the thought.

"You are talking 'bout *the treasure*. Aren't ya?" Andy asked, and Fransie nodded. "How do ya know?"

"It's a long story," Fransie interjected.

"Figures," Andy huffed. "I'll let you in on a little secret." Andy looked squarely at Gabriel. "Can we trust him?"

"He saved my life and is helping us with Etienne now. I trust him."

"Good, good. I figured out that the trials are related to the seven deadly sins," Andy said. Etienne knew Andy's face well enough to know he wasn't convinced. He saw a small squint in Andy's eye that told him everything. "Well we 'ave to save Etienne. We need ta figure out what sin he is facing. So far we 'ave faced the trials of Wrath, Greed, and Sloth." Andy shook his head. "She was trouble, that one."

"I have faced Lust, Gluttony, and Pride," Fransie said.

"What? You have?" It looked as if Andy was about to pass out when Sister Fransie nodded. "Well, I bet being a nun that was quite easy for ya. Anyway, that only leaves envy."

"Of course, 'A heart at peace gives life to the body, but envy rots the bones,'"

"What was that?" Andy raised both eyebrows.

"Proverbs 14:30—Etienne must be facing Envy or faced Envy."

"Makes sense. Isabella is married ta another man." Etienne's body contorted in pain. "Yep, 'tis it."

"She's not married yet," Fransie said.

Etienne closed his eyes. *She's not married yet? That means what I saw didn't happen. It was a test of my envy, and I failed.* Etienne scrunched his eyes tightly and breathed through the pain. He needed a second chance.

Etienne focused on the feeling of the light traveling through his body. He kept his breath steady and tuned out his friends speaking. He was going inside to that place of stillness and silence. He focused on the feeling of the first ball of energy appearing above his head and pouring into the others that met at each joint.

In the darkness of his mind's eye, he saw the light. The radiant white light coursed through the tree of life, easing the pain at each joint, and as it reached the last ball, he was transported back to the throne room.

Etienne panted heavily with the cold tiles beneath his palms. He raised his head and saw King Edward, alive, holding Isabella's hand. At first sight, rage filled his body, but he calmed his heart. It was his envy he was here to face. He failed last time, but this time he would succeed. His envy only led to pain for himself and others. He had to let it go.

"Rise, Etienne. You have returned?" Isabella raised one eyebrow.

"Isabella, Your Majesty, I want a second chance." Etienne forced himself to watch as Edward lavished affection on Isabella.

"Can you truly face us with joy in your heart instead of rage?" Edward asked. "The last time you were here, you thought your envy killed me, but really you were its only victim."

He was right. All of the hours Etienne had spent being envious of Edward only left Etienne feeling ungrateful for what he had. His envy had emptied the hours from his life.

"I can find joy in Isabella's happiness," Etienne said. It was true.

"Good, her joy is my joy." Edward kissed Isabella's hand. "You may have a second chance." Edward motioned to his right where the sword was still in the stone.

"Thank you." Etienne placed both hands on the hilt of the sword and prayed that this would be good for all of them. He pulled hard, and the blade came out easily, sending Etienne flying backward.

"Very good, Etienne. You have been found worthy without forcing it," Edward said. "You now have a choice—you can envy after what I have..." Edward motioned to the extravagant palace and exchanged a look with Isabella.

Etienne saw the love in her eyes and something inside his heart released. He examined her face. Isabella looked genuinely happy with Edward. It was the life that was meant for her. It was the life she was born into, her purpose. It was the life she had chosen. He was the intruder bringing destruction and sadness due to his desire to possess Edward's life.

"Or you can appreciate the unique plan God has for your life. Trust that God will deliver all that you desire when the time is right and if it serves his will. Remember, your value is not in what you do, but who you are in Christ. We can do all things through Him."

Etienne looked at the sword. It was true, he had been called to a great purpose. Perhaps one of the greatest purposes of mankind. He may not have a palace or Isabella, but he would protect thousands and change the world. Etienne placed the sword at the foot of the throne.

"I lay this sword at your service and harbor no ill will towards you. God has called me to a great purpose, and my only desire is to fulfill that purpose. I do not covet what you have."

Etienne bowed his head, and when he opened his eyes, he was back in the room with his friends, and his pain was gone.

CHAPTER 55

After regaining consciousness, Etienne asked for a moment alone with Andy. He trusted Fransie and knew her intentions were true, but he was still uncertain about Gabriel.

"Andy, have you made any progress on the code?"

"I thought ya didna want me to look for the code." Andy crossed his arms in a huff. "Ya 'ave ta make up your mind, laddie."

"I did want you to stop—that is until I found out the Hospitallers, the Pope, and King Philip are all after the treasure and know we are the key." Etienne looked at the ceiling from the bed. "And Molay ordered us to find it."

"That explains so much." Andy pressed his back against the wall. "First the Templars tried ta get me, then some of Philip's soldiers came here offering a handsome reward for you. I almost turned you in, mind ya."

Etienne smiled. He was so thankful to have Andy as his best friend. Molay had been right in Ponferrada, there was a need for Andy to know about the code and treasure. Etienne needed Andy; he was the only one he could trust. Etienne couldn't do this on his own.

"I'm so happy to have you, my friend."

"I'm 'appy ta 'ave ya back as well. 'Twas na the same without ya." Andy pulled up a chair and joined Etienne at his bedside. "Since ya want me ta find the treasure, I can tell ya now—I found one of the treasures. I found Baphomet."

"It's real!" Etienne sat up a little too quickly, and his head spun.

Andy nodded. "Sloth put up a vicious fight, but in the end, we overcame it." Andy's body shook to brush away a bad memory. "Do ya want ta see it?"

"Yes." Etienne said excitedly.

"I thought ya might." Andy walked to the other bed and pulled back the covers, revealing the decapitated head.

"Is that—"

"Yeah, 'tis the head, complete with leaves and vines."

On the wooden headboard where the head was touching, leaves and vines spread out in all directions. It made Etienne think of the carvings he had seen in Leon of the man with antlers.

"I canna figure out how ta make it stop. I even found a flower the other day, and ya donna want ta see the legs of the bed. They have become roots." Andy threw the covers back over the head.

"What about the code in the cathedral?" Etienne asked.

"I made some progress there as well, but I still canna figure it out. Hold on." Andy walked to the trunk at the foot of the bed and pulled out some papers. "This is a diagram of the whole cathedral." Andy smiled triumphantly. "And this is every marking on every pillar in the main sanctuary." Etienne marveled at Andy's detailed drawings.

"And exactly how many days did you actually go to work?"

Andy's face flushed.

"This was work. I can tell ya that. See 'twas a good thing I didn't go ta that job. 'Tis far too dangerous for us ta go anywhere in Santiago now. Clair told me the Templars are still searching for us. And Philip's men are still here as well. I 'ave been cooped up at home since the day I found him." Andy nodded to the lump on his bed. "I'm happy I had this ta keep me busy."

"What have you found so far?" Etienne looked over Andy's detailed diagrams.

"Well...'tis quite difficult." Andy pointed to the diagram. "The cathedral has eleven pillars on both the north and south wings, twenty-three on the west wing, and four giant ones around the main altar. That's forty-nine pillars in all. 'Twas no small feat."

"I'm sure you enjoyed every minute of it."

"That's beside the point." Andy straightened up. "At first the task seemed daunting, but I realized the code was hidden amongst the masons' marks." Andy pointed to a grid he had made. "See here, pillar N3."

Etienne looked at the grid and saw several symbols that matched those from the Keystone Church. But there were other symbols interspersed among them as well.

"At first, I thought those other symbols were another coding system, but a kindly priest told me they were the marcas de cantero, or masons' quarry marks in the common tongue. 'Tis how the quarries were paid when they were constructing the cathedral. See that is the brilliant part of this code. 'Tis hidden in plain sight. Everyone just thinks the symbols are simple mason's marks. Once I made that discovery, it became much easier."

"How so?"

"I was able to eliminate all of the pillars that only had one or two symbols from the code, which led me to the north wing. It had the highest concentration of symbols from the Keystone Church." Andy pointed to a piece of paper with eleven tables filled with symbols. "What do you notice about those grids?"

"Andy, we don't have time for this." Andy gave Etienne puppy-dog-eyes. "Fine." Etienne looked at each grid and compared it to the symbols from the Keystone Church. "Every other column contains symbols from the code."

"Correct!" Andy said, beaming. "What next?"

"I don't know. Maybe go around clockwise or counter clockwise until things line up."

"I tried that and many other things, none of which worked, until I found this." Andy produced a stick. Etienne loved Andy's eccentric genius, but he really wasn't in the mood for this.

"Enough with the theatrics."

"Settle down, settle down. I'll show ya." Andy took a long thin strip of paper that contained all of the code from the last column and wrapped it around the stick. "There ya go. They line up." It was true—the symbols lined up perfectly to form a seven letter code.

"What does it say?"

"I donna ken. It just spells gibberish. We are still missing one key to the code." Andy showed Etienne his findings: pillar one YA, pillar two blank, pillar three QQD, pillar four blank, pillar five OBNS, pillar six blank, pillar seven WC, pillar eight blank, pillar nine BGN, pillar ten blank, pillar eleven PIHVQA. "There is no pattern I can see. It has me stumped."

"I don't see a pattern either. But, I think Sister Fransie might have something to help. She said Jaques de Molay gave her something that we would need to solve the code. She was instructed to give it to me only."

"Well, what is it?"

"I don't know, but let's find out."

CHAPTER 56

Fransie sat in the kitchen with Clair, Gerhart, Chelsea, and Gabriel. She wrapped her fingers tightly around a warm mug and blew gently, sending ribbons of steam in all directions. Gerhart kept looking at her pregnant belly then at Gabriel. It looked as if he wanted to say something, but he was biting his tongue. He looked at Clair.

"Go on. I know ya want ta ask." Clair motioned with her head to Fransie.

"Are you pregnant?" The words burst like a broken damn from Gerhart's mouth.

"Ya, could 'ave done it more gently," Clair chastised him.

"Right, gently." Gerhart squinted an eye and nodded his head. "Is he the father?" Gerhart asked gently. "I thought you were a nun—" Clair covered his mouth before he could say anything else and looked at Fransie apologetically.

"It's all right. I'm still a nun, but I am pregnant, and I don't know who the father is." Clair placed her free hand over her mouth. Fransie didn't feel ashamed; she was proud of the child in her womb. "It isn't what you think. It's complicated."

"Well, congratulations!" Chelsea said, topping off Fransie's tea.

Andy appeared at the entrance to the hallway. "Fransie, Etienne would like ta see ya."

"How's he doin'?"

"He's fine—fit as a fiddle. I think he was just fakin'." Andy winked at Clair and they exchanged a smile.

"Can we see him?" Gerhart stood.

"I think 'tis best if ya keep our guest entertained."

"Right, right," Clair said. "Gabriel, let's get your horse ta the stable. I reckon she is hungry."

"As you wish," Gabriel said.

Fransie followed Andy down the narrow corridor to the sleeping chamber. As they entered, Etienne looked to be in perfect health. The color had come back to his body, and he was alert. Andy closed the door, and they both sat at Etienne's bedside.

"Fransie, I understand Molay gave you something to give to me?" Etienne propped himself up on his elbows.

Fransie nodded and looked at Andy.

"I was instructed to give it only to you."

"I will tell Andy after you tell me. So you might as well tell it to us at the same time. Thank you for taking on such a brave mission. I am sorry for your losses."

"Etienne, it was worth it to keep the treasure out of the hands of King Philip. You should have seen what he did to Isabella—his own daughter. That man has no love in his heart."

Etienne's features hardened. "What did he do to Isabella?" He balled up the covers in two fists. The love he still had for Isabella was evident, and she knew that Isabella loved him the same.

"He tortured her to get information about..." Fransie didn't know if she should let Etienne know he was part of Isabella's suffering. Etienne looked at her expectantly. "...about you. She was trying to protect you." Etienne threw back his head, hitting the headboard hard.

"Enough about Isabella. What did Molay tell ya?" Andy said. Fransie looked from Andy to Etienne.

"He gave me the master word of the Templars."

"No, ya donna say?"

Etienne slowly straightened his head. "Why would he give it to you?"

"He had no other choice. He can't leave Paris"—Fransie looked at both of them nervously—"and he suspects there is a traitor in the Templars, so he couldn't have one of them deliver it.

"That makes sense; only a high-ranking Templar would have known enough to take the treasure of Burgos. Did he say who it was?" Etienne's body was at attention now, hanging on Fransie's every word.

Fransie shook her head. "No, he didn't know, but Molay told me you are the only hope for protecting the treasure now, Etienne."

"We are the only hope." Etienne looked at Andy, and they exchanged a nod. "What is the information you traveled over a thousand miles to give to me?"

"10,565." Fransie hoped that Etienne would understand it, but from his blank stare, she could tell he was as confused as she was. "He said you would need it to find what God entrusted to the Templars."

"Does that mean anything ta you?" Andy asked.

"No." Etienne shook his head and looked up at the ceiling. His eyes darted back and forth, deep in contemplation. "We have to go back to the cathedral. I am sure there is something there to guide us. Did you look for the sign of the triangle? Ronan told me this is how the wisdom is revealed."

"I was too concerned with the code." Andy looked at Etienne apologetically. "But we canna go back now, 'tis too dangerous."

"We will have to take that chance. I know some people who can help." Etienne stood.

Fransie thought she would be happy to deliver the message, but now, she felt like she had lost the purpose she had been holding onto during the long, difficult miles she had traveled.

CHAPTER 57

Isabella was happy to be back in her own quarters again. She looked out her large windows over the gardens to the bathhouse at the very tip of the Île de la Cité. The Seine River split in two as it met the island. What strength; what fortitude.

"Everyone will be at the ball tonight!" Matilda spun with a dress in her hand and flopped on the bed.

"Yes, and I will be shown off like livestock."

"You are the prettiest cow I have seen."

Isabella took a pillow from a chair and threw it at Matilda. She gazed back out the window at the setting sun. Paris was stunning this evening.

"Who is coming tonight, anyway?" Matilda asked.

"Two knights from England; a Sir David and Sir Richard."

Isabella walked to the bed and sat next to Matilda.

"Ooo, I do love knights so." Matilda sighed heavily. Isabella hit her friend lovingly.

"Matilda, you don't want to mess around with British knights. Find yourself a good French lord."

"You sound just like my mother." Matilda flopped over onto her stomach. "I want to come to London with you. I want some adventure." Matilda sounded like Isabella had before her Camino. Isabella had had her fill of adventure and was ready to accept the life that had been planned for her. At least, that's what she told herself.

"If my father will let me"—Isabella placed a hand on Matilda's back—"I will take you to London with me as long as you promise not to lose your virtue to a British knight." Matilda hit Isabella with the pillow she had thrown at her.

A few hours passed, and a knock came at the door. Matilda smiled and mouthed the words "It's time."

Isabella wished she had more time, but she didn't. This would be her grand entrance back into court. Reluctantly Isabella rose and they followed their escorts to the ball.

Isabella took a deep breath as she entered La Grande Salle. The enormous hall was one of the largest in Europe, and tonight it was filled with people, all of whom stopped when she stepped into the room.

"Princess Isabella of France, and Lady Matilda from the House of Baux," Pierre announced. The last of the echoes from conversation died off in the high ceiling. It was so quiet Isabella could almost hear her heart beating.

Matilda took Isabella by the arm, and they entered the Grand Hall. The chatter and music started again.

"I am so happy that part is over," Isabella said, straightening her golden gown.

"You were radiant."

"We both were." Matilda's blue gown brought out her deep sapphire eyes, and her porcelain skin complimented both of them beautifully. "Come, we must go see my father."

The two belles of the ball dodged conversation left and right as they made their way through the crowd. At every turn, someone was bowing or curtsying to Isabella. She tried to enjoy it, but she longed for her days on the Camino when she was anonymous—just a pilgrim.

King Philip sat on a raised platform above the crowd, and two brawny knights stood below, along with the Pope.

"Ah, daughter," Philip motioned for Isabella to join him on his perch. He took Isabella's hand in his. "The flowers of the field would be jealous of your beauty tonight. I wish your mother could have seen you." Isabella felt a warmth in her body. Her father was still treating her with affection. He approved of her.

"Your Highness." Both knights bowed.

"This is Sir David and Sir Richard from London," her father said.

"Your Highness, you are even more beautiful than your reputation suggests. Our prince will be pleased," Sir David said. His words, that were meant to be a compliment, had the opposite effect. They reminded Isabella that she was only a commodity, a price for peace.

Isabella smiled demurely. "I have seen paintings of Edward. He looks to be quite handsome as well." It was true, in the paintings he was pleasing to the eye. Her father had said all of the British were beastly, but these two knights in front of her were quite the opposite.

"Grand Master Jacques de Molay." At the announcement, the ballroom fell silent once more. It seemed as if the room was holding its breath...but then the moment passed like a collective exhale, sending the ballroom into a chatter again.

"What is he doing here?" Pope Clement shot Philip a questioning gaze.

"He is my guest." Philip's fingers drummed the armrests of his throne. Philip leaned over to Isabella and whispered, "He is here because I want you to gain his confidence."

"How?"

Philip silenced her with a look, and she nodded. She needed to regain her father's trust if she was to dissuade him from his plan.

Isabella watched the guests in the ballroom part as Molay made his way to the throne. Each step he took seemed to tip the balance of power in the room. She had never seen this before in her father's presence—he always commanded the room, but Molay had a gravity of his own. Molay stopped at the foot of Philip's pedestal, and instead of addressing Philip, he turned to the Pope, knelt, and kissed the papal ring.

"Most Holy Father," Molay said on rising.

"Shouldn't you address your host first?" Philip's fingers tightened on the armrest, but his face remained calm. Isabella was the only one to notice.

"One should always address God before man." Molay smiled at Clement then at her father. "Your Majesty."

Was Molay conspiring with the Pope now? Were they going to turn on her father and take Paris? Isabella's mind spun in all directions as a knot formed in her stomach.

"Your Highness, may I have a dance, with your father's permission?" Molay bowed to Isabella. She looked to her father, and he nodded.

Molay was the last person in the room Isabella wanted to dance with, but it would seem she had no choice. She needed to discover his motives and regain her father's trust.

They walked to the center of the ballroom and a waltz began. Molay had an air of dignity that preceded him on the dance floor. Every step was precise—his form perfect—his movements true and honorable.

"I owe you an apology," he said, as they whirled around the floor. "I misjudged your character. Thank you for your warning."

"I did it for Etienne, not for you." Isabella ducked under his arm as she turned in a large circle.

"I think you did it for more than just that. I think you did it because you realized your father's character and feared what he might do."

"Do not insult my father in my presence."

"My apologies once again." They narrowly avoided a portly duke who spun wildly with his partner. The effects of alcohol were clearly grasping him tighter than his partner.

"Why are you here tonight?"

"Your father invited me, and I needed an opportunity to speak with you. I haven't heard from Gaston in quite some time." Molay scanned the room. "I fear the worst, as I do not see him here tonight." Molay lowered Isabella into a dip. On rising, her features hardened.

"Your fears are confirmed. He is dead."

"Did your father...?"

Isabella spun out again; on returning, she said, "No, it was Etienne's mother. My father doesn't know Gaston was your spy.

"Gaston was a good man. Many will grieve his loss."

"Yes, he was."

"Isabella, I need to know what day your father is going to execute his plan."

"I do not know, and even if I did, I wouldn't tell you. I only sent that message so you could help Etienne, and you took away two other people who are dear to me. I do not know why I am even talking to you. Why would my father invite you here? Unless this is a test." Isabella separated from Molay and curtsied. "Thank you for the dance."

Screams erupted at the entrance to the ballroom, and there was chaos. Isabella grabbed the arm of a servant as he tried to pass. "What is happening?"

"A rebellion." The servant looked back at the door fearfully.

"Come with me." Molay took Isabella by the arm, and they rushed back to her father. "Your Holiness, Your Majesty. If the castle has been compromised, I insist you allow me to escort you to the safety of our Templar commandery."

"I will come with you," the Pope said shakily.

"As will we." Her father's voice was calm, and Isabella could have sworn she saw a smile behind his eyes.

CHAPTER 58

Etienne itched from the hay he was hidden under, and he could have sworn he had a radish poking him in the back. It had been much more comfortable the last time Etienne was hidden in a cart—Katsuji's fabrics were soft, and Isabella was close by. Isabella had kept true to her word. She was trying to stop her father. Fransie's presence was proof of it.

"Whoa, Blueberry," Gerhart commanded the donkey. The rhythmic vibration of the cart as it went over cobblestones stopped. This meant they were ready for the next part of the plan. Etienne and Andy would slip into the cathedral, as Gerhart and Clair set up a food stand in the square to sell vegetables. Etienne chuckled to himself thinking of Gerhart the Destroyer selling vegetables. He must really love Clair.

"Are you ready?" Gerhart asked, pulling a crate from the cart.

"Aye, this hay is itchier than bed bugs." Andy scratched himself vigorously.

The main square and cathedral were probably the most dangerous place in the city for Etienne and Andy. The Hospitallers had a commandery on the north side of the square, and a host of

Templars had taken up residency at the alburgue on the west side of the square. Clair had been keeping an eye on them every day as she went about her business in town. And then there were the Knights of Saint James—their main commandery was inside the cathedral. Etienne wasn't sure if they would be happy to see him again. Clair hadn't been able to locate King Philip's soldiers yet, but Etienne hoped that they had left Santiago.

"Comma on, ya big lug. Are ya gonna 'elp me?" Clair busied herself turning the cart into a food stand.

"The coast is clear." Gerhart raised a large crate from the back of the wagon, concealing Etienne and Andy as they slipped off. Etienne brushed the hay from his long cloak and cast his hood low over his face. Andy and he joined the steady stream of pilgrims, slipping into the cathedral unnoticed.

"This way, laddie." Andy led Etienne to the north wing of the cathedral. Andy had done an amazing job cataloging the symbols on the pillars. The markings were just as he had drawn them.

"We need to find triangles. They will lead to the wisdom of this cathedral." Etienne surveyed a large pillar.

"Right." Andy nodded. "I'll go left and you go ta the right." Andy, blinded by his hood, turned and almost ran into a pilgrim.

"I think it's fine if we pull back our hoods now."

"Right." Andy pulled back his hood and walked to the left.

Etienne laughed and continued down the right side of the column. He looked every pillar up and down, but there was no sign of a triangle. As he reached the last pillar, to his right was the chapel Clair and Gerhart were married in.

Etienne took a deep breath and ascended the stairs. A wave of nostalgia hit him as he entered the chapel. He replayed Clair's marriage and looked at the pew where Isabella had sat. Instead of sorrow, he felt giddy. Something inside of him had changed when he faced his own envy. He was happy for Isabella. This happiness gave him a new sense of meaning. He was ready to let her go and accept the life God had planned for him.

Etienne bowed to the altar. As he rose, his jaw dropped. Above the cross was a blue triangle with gold trim, and in the center, were four Hebrew letters.

"It's one of the most sacred symbols in all of Christendom," a raspy voice said from behind. Etienne hadn't noticed the tall priest sitting in the back of the chapel when he entered. "Do you know what it is?"

"It is the sacred name of God, YHWH." Etienne crossed himself.

"Good. When it is found inside a triangle, it is called the Tetragrammaton." The priest clasped his long fingers together. "The name of God holds in it the secret of all of creation, my son."

Etienne was happy he had learned Hebrew in his time with the Templars. It had served him more than once. He had never heard about the name of God holding the secret to all creation, though.

"What do you mean, Father?"

"I see you have learned the Hebrew alphabet, but not the deeper meaning of it. Creation speaks in the language of numbers, and in Hebrew, each letter also represents a number. I wear this to remind me of that." The priest pulled a chained necklace from under his clothes, revealing a crucifix and a small nautilus shell. "The pilgrims have their shells, and I have mine."

"Forgive me, Father, but I am lost." Etienne sat at the pew in front of the priest and turned his body to face him.

"Both the Tetragrammaton and this shell depict the golden ratio—the building blocks of creation." The priest turned the shell over and, drawn with gold, there was a thin line that mimicked the shape of the shell, as well as a set of boxes.

"What is that?" Etienne traced the markings on the shell.

"That is the Fibonacci Sequence. If you lend me some of your parchment and charcoal, I will show you." The priest pointed to Etienne's bag that had the diagram of the church in it. Etienne placed a protective hand over the bag. "I will only need a small piece, not the whole parchment."

"This belongs to a friend, but I'm sure he wouldn't mind if I tore off a small corner." Etienne handed the priest a small square of parchment and some charcoal.

"The Fibonacci Sequence is a remarkable thing. If you add one plus one what do you get?"

"Two," Etienne answered, and the priest drew two boxes with the number one in each, then he drew another rectangle to the right of it equaling the two squares.

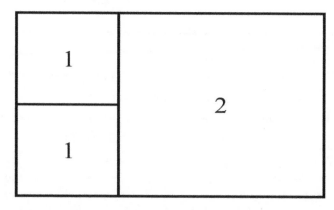

"And two plus one?" The priest drew a rectangle above the rectangles with the ones and two.

"Three."

"Very good." The priest drew the number three in the box and proceeded to draw a rectangle to the left of it. "And three plus two is five." He wrote the number five in the rectangle and repeated the process below. "And what is three plus five?"

"Eight."

The priest smiled and wrote eight inside the rectangle. He drew another rectangle to the right of those he had drawn, its height was equal to that of the combined rectangles. He wrote the number thirteen inside.

He drew another rectangle above, its length equal to all the rectangles below. "And what number will this be?"

Etienne thought for a moment and answered, "Twenty-one." The priest drew a final rectangle whose height was equal to all the rectangles before and wrote thirty-four. Below the drawing, he wrote out the Fibonacci sequence 0,1,1,2,3,5,8,13,21,34.

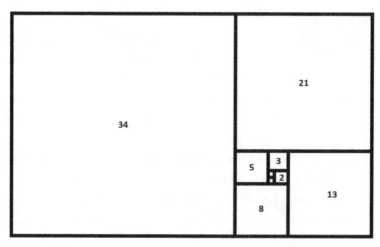

0, 1, 1, 2, 3, 5, 8, 13, 21, 34

"Now for the miracle of God." He drew a spiral starting at the division of the two smallest boxes and finishing in the farthest corner of the last rectangle. The image he drew perfectly mimicked the nautilus shell on his necklace.

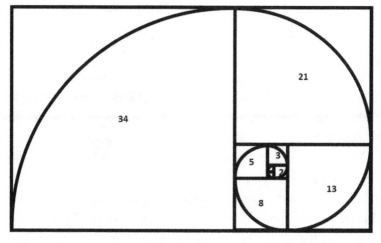

0, 1, 1, 2, 3, 5, 8, 13, 21, 34

"That is amazing."

"You can find this golden ratio in all things in creation: your hand, your face, a flower, this shell. If you look for it, you will see it." The priest put away his necklace. "You may be wondering how this relates to the Tetragrammaton?"

Etienne nodded. He thought of all the flowers he had seen that mimicked this pattern. He wanted to learn more.

"In Hebrew, each letter is assigned a number as well." The priest turned the paper over and drew a table. "The numbers assigned to the letters in the Tetragrammaton are: Yud equals ten, Hey equals five, Vov equals six, and Hey equals five." He filled in the table.

YUD	10	י
HEY	5	ה
VOV	6	ו
HEY	5	ה

Etienne's insides jumped. 10, 5, 6, 5 was the master's word Molay had given to Sister Fransie. This was the clue they were looking for.

"I see the excitement in your face. Do you understand where this is going?"

Etienne composed himself and shook his head. "I don't. I just feel like I am receiving something important."

"Ah." The priest placed his long fingertips together. "That is interesting. I suppose I shouldn't have expected it. I haven't told you what the golden ratio is. I had a vain hope you might have figured it out." The priest leaned his tall torso over Etienne's pew and whispered. "A plus B is to A as A is to B." Reading Etienne's blank stare he continued. "What is five divided by three?" He pointed at the numbers in the boxes.

"One point…"

"One-point-six-six etc. What about eight divided by five?" The priest pointed to the consecutive numbers in the Fibonacci Sequence and looked at him expectantly, but when he didn't answer he said, "One-point-six. This is the Golden Ratio and its reciprocal is point-six-one-eight."

"So the Tetragrammaton contains the golden ratio?" Etienne wanted to avoid math. He could do arithmetic, but he hadn't mastered division.

"It is so." The priest wrote again on the table.

YUD/VOV	10/6	1.666
VOV/YUD	6/10	0.6
$\frac{(YUD+VOV)}{(HEY+HEY)}$	16/10	1.6
$\frac{(HEY+HEY)}{(YUD+VOV)}$	10/16	0.625

Etienne studied the table for a moment and looked back at the triangle with the Hebrew letters.

"Thank you, Father. I must be going now." He wanted to get back to Andy as quickly as possible. He had found what they were looking for, and Etienne didn't know if he could take much more math.

"I insist you stay." The priest grabbed Etienne's wrist. "The Fibonacci Sequence also works with occurrences with distance and time." Etienne took a seat again. He didn't like the way the priest had grabbed him, but he wanted to hear this.

"How so?"

"I will give you an example. Thirty-four days ago, I met a particular nun a few miles before St-Jean-Pied-de-Port. The Pope gave me a special message to give to her, but before I could, there was a fire and she disappeared. On day two, I saw her outside Roncevaux. It was about thirteen miles from where we met." The Priest circled the number thirteen inside the drawing. "But, by the time I reached her she was gone."

"We next crossed paths outside Pamplona on the third day. Remember one plus two equals three. Where we met again was thirty-four miles from the last place I had seen her." The priest circled 34 on the picture.

"Give me a moment." The priest wrote the numbers 55, 89, 144, 233 below the picture of the nautilus shell. "I had to continue the Fibonacci Sequence so you could see the divinity in what I speak. The next time I saw her was on day five." He circled the number five on the drawing. "I reached Logrono just as she was leaving."

0, 1, 1, 2, 3, (5,) 8, 13, 21, 34, 55, 89, 144, 233

"It sounds like she didn't want to see you."

The priest shot Etienne a cruel smile. "When you're doing God's work, you don't care about the preferences of others."

Something wasn't right about this priest. He was cold and calculating and had a look in his eye that Etienne didn't trust.

"I really must be going." Etienne stood again, but the priest pulled him back to the pew with his long cruel fingers.

"You will leave when I say you can leave. Plus, your friend is right here." Etienne looked to the doorway where Andy was being accompanied by four Hospitallers. Andy waved sheepishly.

Etienne wished he hadn't buried his sword with Nazir. There was no way Etienne could take on five enemies unarmed. He had thought about bringing the flaming sword with them.

"In Logrono," the priest continued, "I performed an exorcism and did more of God's work, which we will come back to. Logrono is fifty-five miles from Pamplona." The priest circled fifty-five on the sheet of paper.

"I lost her trail for a few days, but on day eight, I was told of a strange occurrence in the cathedral of Burgos involving a nun and a tattooed Druid. I had found them once more." The priest circled the number eight in the drawing. "Also, Burgos is around eighty-nine miles from Logrono."

Even though Etienne and Andy were captive, Etienne found the occurrence intriguing. There was too much evidence here to be a coincidence.

"Once again she eluded me, but I could see the pattern now and knew the next divine appointment for us would be on day twenty-one. I consulted the map and discovered that Leon was the city for our appointed meeting. I sped to Leon, making it there on the eve of the twentieth day. I am sure your companion told you about this meeting. I would have been able to deliver my message, but her tattooed companion used his magic, and they escaped once more." The priest circled the number twenty-one on the drawing.

"Knowing it traditionally takes thirty-four days to walk the Camino, I knew our paths would cross here, in Santiago. We have been waiting for you."

"What does this nun have to do with us?" Etienne hoped his question sounded convincing.

"Everything. Knowing that she would arrive here on the thirty-fourth day, I had the Hospitallers set up a watch for anything suspicious. Yesterday, they saw you enter the town, and followed you to your house. They already had you all under surveillance as suspicious individuals in town."

"Why didn't you come yesterday?"

"It wasn't the thirty-fourth day." The priest circled the number thirty-four. "Now we shall go to collect her, and dispatch her friend."

"Ya will 'ave ta dispatch us too if ya think we will let you take her!" Andy yelled from across the room.

"As you like. You can stay here and claim sanctuary, or you can come with us, and we shall see what God has planned for you."

Etienne lunged at the priest, but he was restrained by two Hospitallers.

"I was hoping if you understood God's divine plan in the numbers, we could do this peacefully." The priest pulled a dagger and pressed it firmly against Etienne's side. "I changed my mind. You will come with us."

Held at knife point, the priest led Andy and Etienne to the southern exit. All of the passing pilgrims looked at Etienne as if he was a criminal. He had been looked at like this for most of his life. Etienne caught the eye of a young man with a graceful lady on his arm.

"James!" A wave of recognition hit Etienne. The priest dug the blade into his skin. "Help." James turned his head and continued into the cathedral with his lady.

"There will be no more of that," the priest said, twisting the blade for emphasis.

"Ahh, Etienne..." Andy nodded to a group of Templars at the fountain. "Oye!" he yelled, getting the Templars' attention.

"Those are the two we have been looking for," a ginger Templar said. His six comrades stopped what they were doing and they approached. "These two are Templar deserters. We have been ordered to bring them to the Templar castle in Ponferrada for a trial."

"We have our own orders," a Hospitaller said, knocking shoulders with a Templar as he made to pass.

"I must insist that you give them to us." The ginger Templar put a hand on the Hospitaller's chest and pushed him back.

"I am an emissary of the Pope. He has a direct need of these two. Unless your orders are from a source higher than him, I command you to move out of our way." Etienne felt the priest's hand grip tightly on his shoulder as he spoke.

"Our orders came from Jaques de Molay, and I would say he is higher ranking than this pope." The ginger Templar ground his feet.

"Blasphemy!" yelled a Hospitaller, drawing his sword. The Templars drew their swords, and the square became silent. All of the pilgrims scurried away, as the prospect of blood hung in the air by a thread.

Should it come to blows, Etienne had planned his escape with Andy. His mind was already working out their moves and the action he needed to take.

Heavy footsteps and the sound of armor came from behind Etienne. The Knights of Saint James filed out of the cathedral, clad for war. They formed ranks on the steps. Etienne guessed there were thirty, perhaps more. James caught Etienne's eye, and they exchanged a nod. The last to exit was the grand master.

"What is this that you bring onto the steps of this great cathedral? Are we not all soldiers of God?" He boomed. "Release those two at once. One of them is a Knight of Saint James and the other his companion."

"I cannot release them, by order of the Pope." Etienne felt the point of the blade on his back and the priest's vise grip on his shoulder.

"Let me see this order. I do not know you from Adam, sir," the grand master retorted.

"Joseph, we are neighbors. If you take any action on us, our brothers across the courtyard will have words with you," a Hospitaller said to the grand master. "You cannot side with these Templars." He spat, and the Templars pressed forward.

"Good. Fetch the master of your commandery and we can settle this matter immediately. These two are neither leaving with the Templars nor the Hospitallers." He drew his sword and Etienne heard the sound of thirty swords unsheathing.

"Ach, this is killin' me. If ya donna mind we will just be on our wa—" Andy's words were choked off by an arm around his neck. Etienne had no idea what was going to happen, nor who he wanted to win. For all he knew, the Knights of Saint James wanted to kill him and find out about the treasure as well.

The sound of many hooves came echoing up the alley as a stream of Templar Calvary rode into the courtyard. Etienne couldn't believe what he was seeing. This wasn't going to be pretty.

The ginger Templar smiled and said, "Etienne La Rue and Andrew Sinclair, you will be coming with us."

"Etienne? That's exactly the man we are looking for. Happy you found his body and saved him from the pixies," said an arrogant voice.

"Ach no, they are 'ere too." A new group of soldiers appeared at the entrance to the left of the courtyard.

Etienne nodded to the new arrivals. "Who are they?"

"King Philip's son and his men. I liked Isabella much better." Andy shot Etienne a side glance. "I'll explain about the pixies later," he muttered.

"That will be all. We will take Etienne from here by order of King Philip the IV of France, my father." The prince looked as arrogant as he sounded. He was wearing ridiculous striped pantaloons and had a feather coming out of his puffy cap. His soldiers, on the other hand, looked war hardened.

"Wow, we are quite popular, aren't we?" Andy said, winking at Etienne. He didn't seem to understand the gravity of the situation.

"Well, why aren't you moving? I am Prince Charles the Fourth of France." Etienne grimaced. It appeared that time had not improved Charles's humility.

Paying no attention to the prince, the lead rider of the Templars asked, "You are Etienne? Isabella's Etienne?" He moved his horse closer.

"I once was. That life has passed me now," Etienne responded.

"Templars! Salute your new senechal!" the riders shouted. All the Templars banged their shields and let out a guttural call. "We must protect him and his companion at all costs."

Etienne couldn't believe what he was hearing. Was he now the second in command of the Templars following Jacques de Molay himself? Sister Fransie hadn't told him that.

"You mean Isabella, my sister?" The prince's voice drew Etienne from his thoughts. Etienne nodded and smiled at the prince. He couldn't help himself. He had never liked Prince Charles.

Fury swept across the prince's face. "I demand satisfaction, sir." The prince drew his sword.

Andy shook his head. "Ya better put that thing away before ya hurt yourself."

"I am a prince! You shan't speak to me like that. I challenge you to a duel, as well."

The whole courtyard erupted in laughter, breaking the tension.

"Knights of Saint James, will you help us to liberate these men?" asked the leader of the Templar Cavalry.

"We will," responded the grand master. "I ask you Hospitallers again to release these men!"

"It will be known to the Pope that you are all enemies of the church." The priest sheathed his blade, but before his hand left Etienne's shoulder, the priest leaned forward and whispered, "Tell Sister Fransie that I have her friends held captive in Hospital de Orbigo. I will expect to see her there in twenty-one days, or her friends will die. The Fibonacci Sequence continues."

The priest nodded to the Hospitallers, and they sheathed their swords then left the courtyard.

The leader of the Templar cavalry dismounted and walked to Etienne. "I'm Captain Anton," he said, extending his arm.

"Etienne." The two shook hands. "Thank you for your help.

"Isabella was on my ship—I bore her from Finisterre to Paris."

"Ach, then you know Sister Fransie as well." Anton nodded. "Well ya better go get her before them Hospitallers do."

"Andy is right. We should all be together, and it seems that the cathedral is the safest place in Santiago."

"Very well, where is she?"

"In front of the cathedral, there is a giant and a fiery Scottish woman," Etienne said.

"I know them. She tried to sell me a radish."

"They are with us—tell them we sent you, and they will lead you back to our lodgings. Have them gather all of our things and make haste back here."

"As you command." Anton put his hand on his stomach in a sign of fidelity. "We have much to discuss when I return." The two shook hands again, and Anton departed along with most of his soldiers.

"Did that really just happen?" Etienne looked to Andy for confirmation, and he nodded.

"It looks like you are the second in command of the Templars now." Andy mockingly placed his hand on his stomach and bowed.

"I still demand satisfaction! Looking at you now, I can see you were that runt Gaston brought to the palace all those years ago. I bested you then, and I will do it again." The prince put his hands on his hips.

Etienne sighed heavily. Of course he let the prince win—what else would have he done?

Etienne smiled at the prince. "I accept." He turned to James. "May I borrow your sword?"

James handed Etienne his sword. It was lighter than his own, but it would do. The prince took his stance—it was the standard one taught to all young squires. The two bowed, and the prince attacked. He swung his sword carelessly, and Etienne easily avoided each stroke. This only made the prince angrier.

"Come on, fight like a man."

"No offense, your Highness, but your sister fights much better than you."

The prince ran at Etienne, who extended his foot, sending the prince into the fountain. Everyone erupted in laughter.

"Quit laughing at me. I order you!" He pounded his fists against the water. "I order you to stop." Etienne placed the point of his sword on the prince's chest.

"You are not in the position to be giving orders." Etienne dug the blade in for emphasis. "Yield."

"Guards!" The prince's guards sprang into action, but the remaining Templars and Knights of Saint James prevented them from approaching.

"Yield, return to France, and wish your sister our congratulations on her wedding from everyone, including me. We all love her dearly. Do you think you can do that?" The prince nodded. "Good, then take your guards and go back to Paris."

"I will not forget this."

"I hope you never do. Humility is a virtue."

The prince stomped out of the fountain and signaled for his soldiers to follow.

"Thank you." Etienne handed James back his sword.

"It was the least I could do. You saved my life in the forest and gave me a second chance. I haven't wasted a single day. When I returned to Santiago, I proposed to my true love."

"Congratulations." This warmed Etienne's heart. He searched for any hint of envy or thoughts of Isabella, but there were none.

"Ya sure gave it ta him, Etienne," Andy said, swinging his fists in the air. "And ta think I was afraid of them."

"Settle down, settle down." Etienne placed a hand on Andy's shoulder. "We have much work to do."

CHAPTER 59

Fransie's heart raced as she peered out the window. A line of Hospitallers turned up the small alley leading to the house.

"We should go now, Sephirah smells wrath." Gabriel took the flaming sword and wrapped it in their things. "Fransie."

"I know. I hear it and can see them coming up the lane now." Fransie moved so Gabriel could see the Hospitallers, who were making no attempts to hide as they marched.

"We must go."

"Where shall we go?" Fransie's swollen belly had her back aching, and her feet hurt. She didn't know pregnancy could be so uncomfortable. "Gabriel, I have completed my mission. If they must take me, they can. I can't travel in my condition."

Pounding rang through the house, as the Hospitallers battered the door. "Come out. We know you are in there," a taunting voice called. Sephirah answered with a growl and a loud bark.

Gabriel drew the flaming sword, and its light brightened the room.

"Ouch." He dropped the sword immediately, cradling his hand. Fransie took his hand in hers and saw a blistering burn through his leather gloves. She carefully placed the sheath over the blade, extinguishing the flame.

The pounding started again and mixed with Sephirah's barking. Now the pounding was coming from the rear of the house as well. They were surrounded.

"I'm sorry I couldn't—" Gabriel's words were cut off by the sound of horses and metal clashing. Screams rang out through the air. Fransie stole a glance out the window. A host of Templar Calvary was now on the grounds, engaging with the Hospitallers. A splash of blood painted the window and Fransie cringed away, the sight making her feel nauseous.

"Gabriel, it's the Templars."

Soon, the sound of fighting died down, and there was a knock at the door. Fransie peered out the window and saw a single Templar standing on the porch. Gabriel joined her as they walked to the door.

"Anton?" Fransie wrapped her arms around the Templar's neck. "I am so happy it's you. How did you know we were here?"

Clair and Gerhart appeared with their wagon. "We showed him the way, lassie."

"We don't have much time. They will return with reinforcements. My men will help you to pack what you need. It is no longer safe here," Anton said, removing his helmet.

"Come with me, lassie." Clair took Fransie by the wrist and led her into Andy's bedroom. "Donna say a thing about the sword, grail, or the head. We still donna ken who ta trust."

Fransie nodded. "But, I know Anton. He is a good person."

"I'm sure he is, but we canna take any chances—not now."

"How do you suppose we take care of this?" Fransie nodded to the bed that was in full bloom.

Gerhart appeared at the door with his axe and a pair of pruners. "Ah, just in time." Clair took the pruners from Gerhart. "I'm 'appy this will be the last time I use these."

"What do you mean?" Gerhart's eyebrows raised.

"I just canna be domesticated. I canna pretend ta be something I'm not any longer."

Gerhart wrapped Clair up in his arms, and said, "I know—me neither. I have been waiting for months for you to say that. Let's get back on the road—back to a life of adventure. Now, you go first." Gerhart pushed Clair to the severed head whose vines were intertwined with the bed, boasting little white flowers.

"Na, you go."

Gerhart hesitantly joined Clair at the bed and raised his axe. "What if...what if we hurt it?"

"'Twill be just like givin' it a haircut, that's all."

Gerhart shrugged and brought down his mighty axe. On impact, he flew back, hitting the wall.

"Or not." Clair helped him to his feet. "Do ya ken how this thing works?" Fransie shook her head. "I didna think so. Well, we will just 'ave ta improvise."

Clair picked up Gerhart's axe and instead of hitting the vines, she chopped away at the bed until the headboard came loose.

"Donna just stand there, 'elp me with this." Gerhart sprang into action and lifted the headboard as Clair wrapped the head in a sheet. "Now we can be going."

Fransie quickly gathered her things and took the flaming sword from the floor. It was lighter than she expected. It felt as if she was holding nothing at all. She put the grail, the sword, and a few of Andy's belongings into his trunk. Gerhart reappeared and hoisted the trunk with the ease of picking up a stick, and they were off.

CHAPTER 60

"What da ya mean we have much work ta do?" Andy asked, after the Knights of Saint James had left.

"That priest helped me figure out Molay's message." Andy raised questioning eyebrows at Etienne. "Follow me."

Etienne led Andy into the chapel where Clair and Gerhart had been wed. A part of him was excited that he had discovered the clue, not Andy. Granted, he had some help from that deranged priest. Etienne bowed at the altar and made the sign of the cross.

"What do you notice about this chapel?" Etienne asked, mimicking Andy when he knew something Etienne didn't.

"Can't ya just tell me?" Etienne shook his head. "Fine." Andy scanned the chapel. Etienne repressed his smile and stole a glance at the triangle with the Hebrew letters.

"I saw that."

"Saw what?"

"Ya looked above the altar at…" Andy's words faded as his gaze lifted. "'Tis a triangle, just like in Leon. I see 'tis the marker for wisdom in this church, but I donna ken what it is."

"I didn't either, until the priest said something that made me understand. Andy, each letter in Hebrew has a number assigned to it." Etienne pointed to the letter on the right. "Yud equals ten, Hey equals five, Vov equals six, Hey equals five."

"10,565. 'Tis the message Molay sent...amazing! Did ya figure out what it has ta do with the code?"

"Not yet."

"Good." Andy rubbed his hands. "Let's figure this out together." Andy took out the papers and drew a four by four grid. In the first column he placed the Hebrew letters, the second contained the name of the letter, the third was the number, and the fourth was the common letter the symbol represented.

י	YUD	10	Y
ה	HEY	5	H
ו	VOV	6	W or V
ה	HEY	5	H

"YHWH, 'Tis the holy name of God." Both Andy and Etienne crossed themselves. "Let's see how this works with the other codes." Andy spread out the parchment with the code he had figured out from the pillars, the description shift, and the grid from the Keystone Church.

PILLAR 1	YA
PILLAR 2	PPC
PILLAR 3	NAMR
PILLAR 4	VB
PILLAR 5	AFM
PILLAR 6	OHGUP

Decryption Shift	Text	Decryption Shift	Text
0	YA	13	MO
1	ZB	14	NP
2	AC	15	OQ
3	BD	16	PR
4	CE	17	QS
5	DF	18	RT
6	EG	19	SU
7	FH	20	TV
8	GI	21	UW
9	HK	22	VX
10	IL	23	WY
11	KM	24	XZ
12	LN		

"What is this?" Etienne pointed to the paper with *Decryption shift* at the top

"'Tis a Caesar Cypher. Each number represents how many letters a letter is shifted in a code. In shift one, B becomes C, etcetera." Andy pointed to the second cell in the table.

"So it's exactly like this?" Etienne held up the cypher from the Keystone Church.

	A	B	C	D	E	F	G	H	I	K	L	M	N	O	P	Q	R	S	T	U	V	W	X	Y	Z
A	A	B	C	D	E	F	G	H	I	K	L	M	N	O	P	Q	R	S	T	U	V	W	X	Y	Z
B	B	C	D	E	F	G	H	I	K	L	M	N	O	P	Q	R	S	T	U	V	W	X	Y	Z	A
C	C	D	E	F	G	H	I	K	L	M	N	O	P	Q	R	S	T	U	V	W	X	Y	Z	A	B
D	D	E	F	G	H	I	K	L	M	N	O	P	Q	R	S	T	U	V	W	X	Y	Z	A	B	C
E	E	F	G	H	I	K	L	M	N	O	P	Q	R	S	T	U	V	W	X	Y	Z	A	B	C	D
F	F	G	H	I	K	L	M	N	O	P	Q	R	S	T	U	V	W	X	Y	Z	A	B	C	D	E
G	G	H	I	K	L	M	N	O	P	Q	R	S	T	U	V	W	X	Y	Z	A	B	C	D	E	F
H	H	I	K	L	M	N	O	P	Q	R	S	T	U	V	W	X	Y	Z	A	B	C	D	E	F	G
I	I	K	L	M	N	O	P	Q	R	S	T	U	V	W	X	Y	Z	A	B	C	D	E	F	G	H
K	K	L	M	N	O	P	Q	R	S	T	U	V	W	X	Y	Z	A	B	C	D	E	F	G	H	I
L	L	M	N	O	P	Q	R	S	T	U	V	W	X	Y	Z	A	B	C	D	E	F	G	H	I	K
M	M	N	O	P	Q	R	S	T	U	V	W	X	Y	Z	A	B	C	D	E	F	G	H	I	K	L
N	N	O	P	Q	R	S	T	U	V	W	X	Y	Z	A	B	C	D	E	F	G	H	I	K	L	M
O	O	P	Q	R	S	T	U	V	W	X	Y	Z	A	B	C	D	E	F	G	H	I	K	L	M	N
P	P	Q	R	S	T	U	V	W	X	Y	Z	A	B	C	D	E	F	G	H	I	K	L	M	N	O
Q	Q	R	S	T	U	V	W	X	Y	Z	A	B	C	D	E	F	G	H	I	K	L	M	N	O	P
R	R	S	T	U	V	W	X	Y	Z	A	B	C	D	E	F	G	H	I	K	L	M	N	O	P	Q
S	S	T	U	V	W	X	Y	Z	A	B	C	D	E	F	G	H	I	K	L	M	N	O	P	Q	R
T	T	U	V	W	X	Y	Z	A	B	C	D	E	F	G	H	I	K	L	M	N	O	P	Q	R	S
U	U	V	W	X	Y	Z	A	B	C	D	E	F	G	H	I	K	L	M	N	O	P	Q	R	S	T
V	V	W	X	Y	Z	A	B	C	D	E	F	G	H	I	K	L	M	N	O	P	Q	R	S	T	U
W	W	X	Y	Z	A	B	C	D	E	F	G	H	I	K	L	M	N	O	P	Q	R	S	T	U	V
X	X	Y	Z	A	B	C	D	E	F	G	H	I	K	L	M	N	O	P	Q	R	S	T	U	V	W
Y	Y	Z	A	B	C	D	E	F	G	H	I	K	L	M	N	O	P	Q	R	S	T	U	V	W	X
Z	Z	A	B	C	D	E	F	G	H	I	K	L	M	N	O	P	Q	R	S	T	U	V	W	X	Y

"No, no...wait a minute. Yes! Yes! 'Tis just a series of Caesar Cyphers. Why didna I see this sooner?"

Etienne's stomach leaped to this chest. "Excellent! So you know how to decode this?" The anticipation was killing him. Instead of resisting his destiny, he was embracing it. He had been ordered to find the treasure, and he would.

"Not quite yet."

Andy looked from the papers to the triangle with the Hebrew letters then back at the papers. Etienne could see the wheels turning behind Andy's eyes.

"Thank you, YHWH." Andy and Etienne crossed themselves. "'Tis it—the key ta the cypher. Our lord's name lets us know how many letters ta shift." Andy went to work writing out another table. "Let's see if this works!"

YA	PPC	NAMR	VB	AFM	OHGUPZ
YH	WHY	HWHY	HW	HYH	WHYHWH

"If I draw a line from Y to Y on the grid I get W." Andy circled the W on the grid "Let's try it with the second letter. "If I draw a line from A to H I get H. WH...that canna be right."

	A	B	C	D	E	F	G	H	I	K	L	M	N	O	P	Q	R	S	T	U	V	W	X	Y	Z
A	A	B	C	D	E	F	G	H	I	K	L	M	N	O	P	Q	R	S	T	U	V	W	X	Y	Z
B	B	C	D	E	F	G	H	I	K	L	M	N	O	P	Q	R	S	T	U	V	W	X	Y	Z	A
C	C	D	E	F	G	H	I	K	L	M	N	O	P	Q	R	S	T	U	V	W	X	Y	Z	A	B
D	D	E	F	G	H	I	K	L	M	N	O	P	Q	R	S	T	U	V	W	X	Y	Z	A	B	C
E	E	F	G	H	I	K	L	M	N	O	P	Q	R	S	T	U	V	W	X	Y	Z	A	B	C	D
F	F	G	H	I	K	L	M	N	O	P	Q	R	S	T	U	V	W	X	Y	Z	A	B	C	D	E
G	G	H	I	K	L	M	N	O	P	Q	R	S	T	U	V	W	X	Y	Z	A	B	C	D	E	F
H	H	I	K	L	M	N	O	P	Q	R	S	T	U	V	W	X	Y	Z	A	B	C	D	E	F	G
I	I	K	L	M	N	O	P	Q	R	S	T	U	V	W	X	Y	Z	A	B	C	D	E	F	G	H
K	K	L	M	N	O	P	Q	R	S	T	U	V	W	X	Y	Z	A	B	C	D	E	F	G	H	I
L	L	M	N	O	P	Q	R	S	T	U	V	W	X	Y	Z	A	B	C	D	E	F	G	H	I	K
M	M	N	O	P	Q	R	S	T	U	V	W	X	Y	Z	A	B	C	D	E	F	G	H	I	K	L
N	N	O	P	Q	R	S	T	U	V	W	X	Y	Z	A	B	C	D	E	F	G	H	I	K	L	M
O	O	P	Q	R	S	T	U	V	W	X	Y	Z	A	B	C	D	E	F	G	H	I	K	L	M	N
P	P	Q	R	S	T	U	V	W	X	Y	Z	A	B	C	D	E	F	G	H	I	K	L	M	N	O
Q	Q	R	S	T	U	V	W	X	Y	Z	A	B	C	D	E	F	G	H	I	K	L	M	N	O	P
R	R	S	T	U	V	W	X	Y	Z	A	B	C	D	E	F	G	H	I	K	L	M	N	O	P	Q
S	S	T	U	V	W	X	Y	Z	A	B	C	D	E	F	G	H	I	K	L	M	N	O	P	Q	R
T	T	U	V	W	X	Y	Z	A	B	C	D	E	F	G	H	I	K	L	M	N	O	P	Q	R	S
U	U	V	W	X	Y	Z	A	B	C	D	E	F	G	H	I	K	L	M	N	O	P	Q	R	S	T
V	V	W	X	Y	Z	A	B	C	D	E	F	G	H	I	K	L	M	N	O	P	Q	R	S	T	U
W	W	X	Y	Z	A	B	C	D	E	F	G	H	I	K	L	M	N	O	P	Q	R	S	T	U	V
X	X	Y	Z	A	B	C	D	E	F	G	H	I	K	L	M	N	O	P	Q	R	S	T	U	V	W
Y	Y	Z	A	B	C	D	E	F	G	H	I	K	L	M	N	O	P	Q	R	S	T	U	V	W	X
Z	Z	A	B	C	D	E	F	G	H	I	K	L	M	N	O	P	Q	R	S	T	U	V	W	X	Y

YA	PPC	NAMR	VB	AFM	OHGUPZ
YH	WHY	HWHY	HW	HYH	WHYHWH
WH					

"'Tis na working. Why isn't it working?" Andy scratched out the letters with a heavy hand, and his head turned tomato red.

"It's all right." Etienne patted him on the shoulder. "I seem to recall you saying you wanted the Templars to come up with a harder code."

"So I did, laddie—so I did."

Etienne and Andy sat in the church for about fifteen minutes, pouring over the papers.

"The others will be here soon. We should clean these up." He started to move the papers, but Andy grabbed his hand.

"I can't stop, not yet. I haven't gotten the code yet." Andy tapped his leg incessantly.

Etienne knew that when Andy was fixated on something, he couldn't rest until it was resolved. It was what made him brilliant, but it also took its toll.

"Andy." Etienne placed a hand on his leg, and Andy quit moving. "It is time to stop."

"I just canna help but think that the triangle has something ta do with it." Andy held the paper up so it was aligned with the triangle behind the altar. "I see it now. Let me just try this one last thing." Andy looked at Etienne with pleading eyes.

"How can I say no to a face like that?" Etienne joked.

Andy placed a sheet of parchment diagonally from the Y in row Y to the Y in row Y and he wrote the letter A in the grid. "I think I am on ta something, laddie." Etienne leaned in for a closer look. "Let's try the next one."

Andy placed the paper diagonally on the letter A's until he reached row H. "That makes this T. And here we have the word *At*." Andy wore a triumphant look on his face.

	A	B	C	D	E	F	G	H	I	K	L	M	N	O	P	Q	R	S	T	U	V	W	X	Y	Z
A	A	B	C	D	E	F	G	H	I	K	L	M	N	O	P	Q	R	S	T	U	V	W	X	Y	Z
B	B	C	D	E	F	G	H	I	K	L	M	N	O	P	Q	R	S	T	U	V	W	X	Y	Z	A
C	C	D	E	F	G	H	I	K	L	M	N	O	P	Q	R	S	T	U	V	W	X	Y	Z	A	B
D	D	E	F	G	H	I	K	L	M	N	O	P	Q	R	S	T	U	V	W	X	Y	Z	A	B	C
E	E	F	G	H	I	K	L	M	N	O	P	Q	R	S	T	U	V	W	X	Y	Z	A	B	C	D
F	F	G	H	I	K	L	M	N	O	P	Q	R	S	T	U	V	W	X	Y	Z	A	B	C	D	E
G	G	H	I	K	L	M	N	O	P	Q	R	S	T	U	V	W	X	Y	Z	A	B	C	D	E	F
H	H	I	K	L	M	N	O	P	Q	R	S	T	U	V	W	X	Y	Z	A	B	C	D	E	F	G
I	I	K	L	M	N	O	P	Q	R	S	T	U	V	W	X	Y	Z	A	B	C	D	E	F	G	H
K	K	L	M	N	O	P	Q	R	S	T	U	V	W	X	Y	Z	A	B	C	D	E	F	G	H	I
L	L	M	N	O	P	Q	R	S	T	U	V	W	X	Y	Z	A	B	C	D	E	F	G	H	I	K
M	M	N	O	P	Q	R	S	T	U	V	W	X	Y	Z	A	B	C	D	E	F	G	H	I	K	L
N	N	O	P	Q	R	S	T	U	V	W	X	Y	Z	A	B	C	D	E	F	G	H	I	K	L	M
O	O	P	Q	R	S	T	U	V	W	X	Y	Z	A	B	C	D	E	F	G	H	I	K	L	M	N
P	P	Q	R	S	T	U	V	W	X	Y	Z	A	B	C	D	E	F	G	H	I	K	L	M	N	O
Q	Q	R	S	T	U	V	W	X	Y	Z	A	B	C	D	E	F	G	H	I	K	L	M	N	O	P
R	R	S	T	U	V	W	X	Y	Z	A	B	C	D	E	F	G	H	I	K	L	M	N	O	P	Q
S	S	T	U	V	W	X	Y	Z	A	B	C	D	E	F	G	H	I	K	L	M	N	O	P	Q	R
T	T	U	V	W	X	Y	Z	A	B	C	D	E	F	G	H	I	K	L	M	N	O	P	Q	R	S
U	U	V	W	X	Y	Z	A	B	C	D	E	F	G	H	I	K	L	M	N	O	P	Q	R	S	T
V	V	W	X	Y	Z	A	B	C	D	E	F	G	H	I	K	L	M	N	O	P	Q	R	S	T	U
W	W	X	Y	Z	A	B	C	D	E	F	G	H	I	K	L	M	N	O	P	Q	R	S	T	U	V
X	X	Y	Z	A	B	C	D	E	F	G	H	I	K	L	M	N	O	P	Q	R	S	T	U	V	W
Y	Y	Z	A	B	C	D	E	F	G	H	I	K	L	M	N	O	P	Q	R	S	T	U	V	W	X
Z	Z	A	B	C	D	E	F	G	H	I	K	L	M	N	O	P	Q	R	S	T	U	V	W	X	Y

YA	PPC	NAMR	VB	AFM	OHGUPZ
YH	WHY	HWHY	HW	HYH	WHYHWH
AT					

"Wouldn't it be easier to do it like this?" For the next word Etienne found the letter P in row W, which led to T on the top line. Next, he found the letter P in row H, which led to column H. Finally, he found the letter C in row Y, which led to column E.

	A	B	C	D	E	F	G	H	I	K	L	M	N	O	P	Q	R	S	T	U	V	W	X	Y	Z
A	A	B	C	D	E	F	G	H	I	K	L	M	N	O	P	Q	R	S	T	U	V	W	X	Y	Z
B	B	C	D	E	F	G	H	I	K	L	M	N	O	P	Q	R	S	T	U	V	W	X	Y	Z	A
C	C	D	E	F	G	H	I	K	L	M	N	O	P	Q	R	S	T	U	V	W	X	Y	Z	A	B
D	D	E	F	G	H	I	K	L	M	N	O	P	Q	R	S	T	U	V	W	X	Y	Z	A	B	C
E	E	F	G	H	I	K	L	M	N	O	P	Q	R	S	T	U	V	W	X	Y	Z	A	B	C	D
F	F	G	H	I	K	L	M	N	O	P	Q	R	S	T	U	V	W	X	Y	Z	A	B	C	D	E
G	G	H	I	K	L	M	N	O	P	Q	R	S	T	U	V	W	X	Y	Z	A	B	C	D	E	F
H	H	I	K	L	M	N	O	P	Q	R	S	T	U	V	W	X	Y	Z	A	B	C	D	E	F	G
I	I	K	L	M	N	O	P	Q	R	S	T	U	V	W	X	Y	Z	A	B	C	D	E	F	G	H
K	K	L	M	N	O	P	Q	R	S	T	U	V	W	X	Y	Z	A	B	C	D	E	F	G	H	I
L	L	M	N	O	P	Q	R	S	T	U	V	W	X	Y	Z	A	B	C	D	E	F	G	H	I	K
M	M	N	O	P	Q	R	S	T	U	V	W	X	Y	Z	A	B	C	D	E	F	G	H	I	K	L
N	N	O	P	Q	R	S	T	U	V	W	X	Y	Z	A	B	C	D	E	F	G	H	I	K	L	M
O	O	P	Q	R	S	T	U	V	W	X	Y	Z	A	B	C	D	E	F	G	H	I	K	L	M	N
P	P	Q	R	S	T	U	V	W	X	Y	Z	A	B	C	D	E	F	G	H	I	K	L	M	N	O
Q	Q	R	S	T	U	V	W	X	Y	Z	A	B	C	D	E	F	G	H	I	K	L	M	N	O	P
R	R	S	T	U	V	W	X	Y	Z	A	B	C	D	E	F	G	H	I	K	L	M	N	O	P	Q
S	S	T	U	V	W	X	Y	Z	A	B	C	D	E	F	G	H	I	K	L	M	N	O	P	Q	R
T	T	U	V	W	X	Y	Z	A	B	C	D	E	F	G	H	I	K	L	M	N	O	P	Q	R	S
U	U	V	W	X	Y	Z	A	B	C	D	E	F	G	H	I	K	L	M	N	O	P	Q	R	S	T
V	V	W	X	Y	Z	A	B	C	D	E	F	G	H	I	K	L	M	N	O	P	Q	R	S	T	U
W	W	X	Y	Z	A	B	C	D	E	F	G	H	I	K	L	M	N	O	P	Q	R	S	T	U	V
X	X	Y	Z	A	B	C	D	E	F	G	H	I	K	L	M	N	O	P	Q	R	S	T	U	V	W
Y	Y	Z	A	B	C	D	E	F	G	H	I	K	L	M	N	O	P	Q	R	S	T	U	V	W	X
Z	Z	A	B	C	D	E	F	G	H	I	K	L	M	N	O	P	Q	R	S	T	U	V	W	X	Y

YA	PPC	NAMR	VB	AFM	OHGUPZ
YH	WHY	HWHY	HW	HYH	WHYHWH
AT	THE				

"Well, I'll be." Andy scratched his chin. "Nice work." They continued to decode the message until the table was complete.

YA	PPC	NAMR	VB	AFM	OHGUPZ
YH	WHY	HWHY	HW	HYH	WHYHWH
AT	THE	FEET	OF	THE	SAINTS

"Where five become one. Here I lay under a field of stars at the feet of the saints." Etienne recited the whole riddle. "Any ideas on where it could be?"

"I donna ken, but there is only one saint around here that I know of—Saint James."

CHAPTER 61

Etienne and Andy snuck into the small passageway below the altar. The last time Etienne had been down there, Saint James had appeared to him. He knew for sure this had to be where his tomb was.

"Are ya sure he's down here?" Andy asked, staring at the stone wall in front of them. It could just be a passage from one side of the altar ta the other."

Etienne placed his hand on the cold stone wall—he knew that just on the other side was Santiago and possibly the treasure they sought.

"I am certain of it." Etienne ran his hand over the wall, searching for a way to enter, but all he felt was the coarse stone.

"What about one of these?" Andy tugged on a candle holder on the opposite wall of the narrow passage.

"Andrew Sinclair! What on God's earth are ya doin'?" Clair's voice came shooting down the stairs.

"I…ah….we—"

"Never ya mind. Why donna you and Etienne come up here before ya break somethin'. Anton needs ta talk ta ya."

Etienne was relieved that Clair and the others had made it. Her words reminded Etienne that he was now the second in command of all the Knights Templar. A huge responsibility was thrust onto his shoulders, but he was willing to take it.

Etienne's eyes adjusted as they reached the ground level. Gerhart stood next to Clair at the top of the steps with his arms crossed, Anton leaned against a wall looking at the ceiling, and Sister Fransie sat next to Gabriel, who had Sephirah at his feet.

"'Appy ta see you lot," Andy said, emerging from the stairs.

"We are happy to see you as well. Thank you for sending Anton and the Templars for us," Sister Fransie said.

"We got everything you asked for. Including the decorative headboard." Gerhart winked indiscreetly at Etienne. It took a minute to realize Gerhart was talking about the severed head. He wondered why they had taken the whole headboard.

"Where is everything?"

"Your Knights are guarding it," Anton said, placing his hand on his stomach in a sign of fidelity. Etienne stood straighter, trying to look more authoritative. "I must convey Molay's orders. There isn't much time. Will you walk with me?"

Etienne nodded and placed his hands behind his back. The two of them left the others and rounded the nave. The golden statues in the alcove chapels glinted merrily in the sun. Anton stopped and faced Etienne when they were out of earshot from any pilgrims.

"Etienne, the Templars are disbanding." Etienne felt like a bucket of cold water had just been poured over his head. Hearing these words from a fellow Templar made the reality of the situation sink in.

"What? Why?"

"Molay discovered the Pope and King Philip are plotting to arrest the Templars. They want to confiscate our lands and treasure."

"Why disband? Why not fight?" Etienne's blood was boiling.

"Molay doesn't want blood on his hands when there is another option."

"Where will the Templar fortune and knights go?"

"The Templar fleet will sail to every country that has a Templar commandery, to collect its wealth. They will then sail to Portugal. It has long been a contingency plan for the Templars to convene there should anything happen. King Denis of Portugal has signed an accord with Molay. However, our fate is up to you."

"I don't understand, why did Molay make me his seneschal?"

"For the same reason he made me admiral—there is a traitor in the Templars at a high level. Also, he said your mission was of the utmost importance. He wanted you to have the full force of the Templars to aid you in accomplishing it. Every Templar who has received the order to evacuate has also been informed of your position."

"And, what is my mission?"

"Molay didn't say what it was, but you don't have much time. Fall will be upon us soon. Once I have delivered my cargo to Portugal, I am to await you at the port of Santander. Do you know it?" Etienne nodded. He had once been to the port city in the north of Spain. "Good, from there you will choose our destination."

"Why am I to choose?"

"Molay didn't want to know where to find you, should his wits be compromised."

"You mean should it be tortured out of him?" Anton avoided Etienne's gaze.

"Yes, he is staying in Paris to buy us time until the mission is complete. Molay believes all of our wealth can be moved by October first. He has ordered all of the Templars around the world to disappear on Friday, October thirteenth. Once this is done, he will try to escape Paris to rejoin us, but there is a good chance Philip will strike before then. With your leave, I must depart. You only have until October. Make haste with your mission. Oh, I almost forgot." Anton handed Etienne a neatly folded garment.

"What is this?"

"Since you are Seneschal of the Knights Templar, and no longer a sergeant, you must look the part."

Etienne unfolded the white tunic and saw the red Templar cross staring back at him. He never in his life thought he would wear this garment and embrace all that it meant. He was a full-fledged Knight Templar now, something he thought was impossible after coming from his humble beginnings. This meant more to him than being senechal. He embraced the garment tightly in his hands.

"I must go now. The days of summer are slipping away quickly. Remember to meet me in Santander, and after the twelfth of October, the Templars will be no more." Anton placed his hand on his stomach, bowed slightly, and took his leave.

Etienne was dumbstruck. It was as if the only world he had ever known was slipping through his fingers, like sand through an hourglass.

A world without the Templars? Etienne shook his head. He squeezed the mantle in his hands almost as if he was trying to hold onto a memory.

This Templar has one last task to do. As Etienne donned the mantle, it was as if he became a new person. An inner confidence glowed inside of him as he walked to the others.

"He sure left in a hurry," Gerhart said, following Anton with his eyes.

"There is much to do and little time. Fransie, Gabriel, come join us. I have news of your companions."

"Did the Templars find them?" Fransie's entire being lightened, but the glow faded as Etienne shook his head.

"The priest who was leading the Hospitallers told me he is holding them captive in Hospital de Orbigo."

Fransie inhaled deeply and focused her gaze on Etienne. "What? Why?"

"He wants you and the knowledge you have. He said he would start executing them if you didn't arrive there in twenty-one days."

"We must go immediately to save them." She looked pleadingly at Gabriel. "I can't have them die at my expense. My mission is over. I delivered the message. What value would it be to him now? Gabriel, will you join me?"

"Where you go, I go," he said. They both turned to leave.

"Wait!" Etienne's words sounded more like an order than a request. The authority in his voice surprised him. "We will all join you. That priest is not to be trusted. If we hurry, we can make it to Hospital de Orbigo in eighteen days. That gives us three days to finish our business here. If we help you with that task, will you help us with one more thing? I know the quest you have accepted took so much from you, but we need your help once more."

"What is it that you could need from me?"

"I need to know how you located the other treasures. We need to find one more that we think is here in this cathedral."

"I'm afraid I can't help you." Fransie's answer shocked Etienne.

"Why is that?"

"It isn't because I'm not willing to, but it's because I can't. All of the other treasures called to me. I hear nothing here. The treasures were all protected by a sin which could be overcome by a virtue. What I heard, what was calling to me, was either this sin or virtue. Here, in this cathedral, all I hear is the virtue of the pilgrims."

"'Tis impossible, it has ta be here," Andy piped up.

"All the same, will you stay and help us?"

"If you agree to help liberate my companions. It will be to your benefit, as well, since they have the treasure we found in Pamplona."

"I understand," Etienne said. "This is grave news."

"I think to find what you are searching for, all seven treasures must be brought together—why else would they be here on the Camino? Sensing the four treasures we have together is unlike anything in this world. They almost seem to sing in perfect harmony." Fransie looked to Gabriel for confirmation.

"I believe so too," Gabriel said. "We possess four treasures here, the priest has Fransie's friends who had the harp, and the treasure from Burgos is missing. That only leaves one more to find."

"We never collected the treasure from defeating them Shadows. Where did Isabella open tha door?" Andy asked.

"It was in Castrojeriz—we will go there after we help Fransie free her friends." Etienne placed a hand on Sister Fransie's arm. "You will have us and the full force of the Templars to aid you, Sister." Etienne couldn't believe he had just said that—but it was true—the Templars were at his beck and call now.

"And we will remain here with you for the next three days," Sister Fransie said.

"Good, now that that is settled, Gerhart, go and get the treasures from the wagon. Clair, prepare our beds on the upper level with the other pilgrims—"

"Now just a minute." Clair placed a sharp finger in Etienne's chest. "Just because you're senechal of the Templars, dosna' mean ya can boss us around."

"I'm sorry." Etienne clasped Clair's hand between his. Clair squinted her right eye and cocked her head. "Clair, will you become a Knights Templar?" Clair's eyes widened, and she took a step back.

"What do ya mean? I'm a woman, I canna—"

"You are stronger and braver than most Templars I have met. You have kept our secrets and protected both pilgrims and Templars alike." Etienne placed a hand on Clair's shoulder. "I don't see any reason why you shouldn't be able to be a Templar. I am the senechal now, second only to Grand Master Jacques de Molay. Who is going to stop me from making you a Templar? The same goes for you, Gerhart—and Fransie and Gabriel. If we are to continue on this mission, we must take an oath here and now, dedicating our lives to protecting this secret."

Gerhart looked at Clair for guidance, and they both nodded at the same time.

"I will take such an oath," Fransie said.

"As will I." Gabriel stood straight.

"Good. Do you, Clair, Gerhart, Fransie, and Gabriel, wish to become Templars?" All responded in the affirmative. "Follow me and fear no evil." Etienne led them to the chapel with the Tetragrammaton, and they circled around an open Bible on the altar.

"Kneel—place your right hands on this holiest of holy books and raise your left in the air." Everyone followed his instructions, even Andy.

"It was not I who called you here today, but God. He has brought each of us together for this purpose, for this task, and we will swear to complete it. We will be a new sect within the Templars, protectors of its most guarded secret. As each of you know, this task is not easy, nor one to take lightly." Etienne looked at each of his companions, and their eyes reflected the earnestness he felt in his heart.

"Repeat after me: I swear to defend with my life, my strength, and my speech the treasures and secret knowledge of the Templars." Each repeated the oath.

"I promise to be obedient and submissive to the grand master, and to travel by land or sea if need be, to defend this knowledge." Once again everyone parroted back the words.

"My right hand and sword shall be dedicated to the service of protecting this treasure, and I will never fly from the enemy whether they be physical or spiritual." After they all finished the last sentence, Etienne smiled widely.

"Having taken the oath of a Templar, I now ask you to rise, not as a common man"—Clair shot Etienne a look—"a common person," Etienne amended, "but as a sister and brother Templar."

Etienne couldn't remember the proper Templar oath, but it didn't matter. This was a new order of the Knights Templar with only one purpose: to find and protect the treasure at all costs. Etienne looked at his new knights—the last hope to protect the treasure from the evil in the world.

"Having taken the oath of a Knights Templar, I will now entrust you with the grip and word of our most holy order." One by one, Etienne took his companions' hands and whispered in their ear.

"Usually, I would entrust you with the garments of a Templar. But as you know, I possess nothing."

Sister Fransie touched Etienne's arm and smiled. She motioned as if she were removing an invisible cloak from her shoulders and cast it over them. The moment she did, Etienne felt a humility he had never sensed before. Tears welled in the back of his eyes as his body absorbed the feeling.

"May the cloak of Humility cover us to protect us from our pride," Fransie said, casting her eyes to the floor.

"Aye, and the industry of our hands keep us safe from sloth." Andy placed his arms round Clair and Etienne. The others joined in and they formed a tight circle.

"May sweet charity always be in our hearts, giving more than we could ever take." Etienne glanced at Andy, and they exchanged a smile.

"May we only be gluttonous for the word of God, which is the only thing that can make us whole," Gabriel said solemnly.

"Aye, and 'tis forgiveness that is our shield against wrath," Clair said.

"And acceptance is our sword to destroy envy." Gerhart took the flaming sword from his belt and gave it to Etienne.

A voice rang out. "And may chastity be the light that reveals the snares of temptation and the fallacy of our thinking." At the back of the church, a hooded figure approached.

"Who are you? State your business." Etienne pulled the sword slightly from the scabbard and the light from its flames filled the chapel.

"I am someone who knows the way back home." The figure removed its hood, revealing Mariano. He ran to them, and they all embraced.

They were together once more. This time they were more than a family: they were a brotherhood, their oath running deeper than blood. Etienne glanced at Mariano. His skin was radiant. At first, Etienne thought it was the glow from the sword, but up close, he realized Mariano was radiating from the inside.

What did Mariano mean by saying he knows the way home? Could he know where the treasure is?

To be Continued...

EPILOGUE

Philip lay in his bed, but was too excited to sleep. His plan couldn't have worked better. The *rebellion* he had started served its purpose. He had discovered who was still loyal to the insurrectionist he had killed last year. But, more importantly, he had gained entry to the Templars' heavily guarded compound.

He'd noted every fortification and defense of the compound. He knew all of the weaknesses that could only be observed from the inside. In one month's time, he would lay in this bed again, as his army arrested the Templars. They would take the compound by surprise, and Philip would be the first to enter their vaults, seizing what belonged to him.

NOTES IN CLOSING

If you enjoyed this novel, please consider leaving a review wherever you discovered and acquired the book. Reviews are the lifeblood of independent authors, and can often make an enormous difference in how successful we are at making sure our stories are read or heard by the people who need them most. We would be incredibly grateful for your help in sharing this story as far and wide as possible.

For more information about the Through a Field of Stars series, including the upcoming release for book three, visit www.throughafieldofstars.com.

Thank you for reading.
Buen Camino,

B. J. S.

P.S. You can use the cyphers in the novel to decode hidden words and messages on the cover!

APPENDIX

The Knights Templar were a Catholic military order that operated from 1119 to 1312. The order was among the wealthiest and most powerful orders in Christendom. They were renowned fighters and never left a battle until their flag left. They also were arguably the first organization to be a multinational corporation, with over a thousand commanderies and fortifications across Europe and the Holy Land. They also served as the first banking system for pilgrims. The Templar legacy is shrouded in speculation, secrecy, and legend. Part of the Templar leadership was imprisoned in Paris in 1307. However, a majority of the Templars and their wealth disappeared and has yet to be found. The order was officially disbanded by Pope Clement V in 1312.

Princess Isabella of France was born to King Philip IV and Joan I of Navarre sometime between 1290-1295, and died in 1358. She was their youngest child and only daughter. Her nickname was the She-Wolf of France. She was notable for her intelligence, beauty, and diplomatic skills.

The Camino de Santiago was one of the most important pilgrimages in the Middle Ages, along with the Roman and Jerusalem pilgrimages. In English it is known as the "Way of Saint James." It is a system of pilgrimages that spread across Europe, leading to the remains of the apostle Saint James the Greater, which are housed in the Cathedral of Santiago de Compostela. Pilgrims would walk thousands of miles on the

Camino to receive a plenary indulgence for the forgiveness of their sins. Today the Camino de Santiago is still incredibly popular, attracting over 250,000 pilgrims a year.

Jacques de Molay was born in 1243 and died March 18th, 1314. He was the 23rd and final Grand Master of the Knights Templar. He led the Templars from 1289 to 1312. His main goal as Grand Master was to rally support for another crusade in the Holy Land.

The Order of Knights of the Hospital of Saint John of Jerusalem (*AKA: Hospitallers*): The Hospitallers were a Catholic military order formed in the 11th century. Originally, they were associated with an Amalfitan Hospital in Jerusalem. During the first crusade in 1099, they received their own papal charter and were charged with the care and defense of pilgrims. After the Templars were disbanded, they were charged with the care of many of the Templar properties. In 1530 they took up residency in Malta and became known as the Knights of Malta.

King Philip the IV of France was born in 1268 and died in 1314. His nicknames were Philip the Fair, and the Iron King. He reigned as king of France from 1285-1314, and was married to Joan I of Navarre. Philip waged many wars and expanded the power and territory of France. He borrowed heavily from the Templars for these wars and became very indebted to them. In 1307, Philip arrested the Templars, which in turn cleared his debt and eased his fears of them creating a state within France.

The Moors, a name that was first applied to the Maghrebine Berbers from North West Africa, was latter applied to the Muslim inhabitants of the Iberian Peninsula, Sicily, and Malta during the Middle Ages. In 711 the Moors first crossed over from

Africa to the Iberian Peninsula (Spain), conquering and ruling most of it until the Christian Reconquista. The attempts by the Christians to reclaim Spain began shortly after the Moorish i nvasion. But in 1212 the tides turned and the northern Christian Kingdoms pushed back the Moors. In this time they were aided by Christian military orders like the Knights Templars and Knights Hospitaller. By 1252 the Moors were pushed down to the Kingdom of Granada, where they ruled until 1492.

The Knights of Saint James, also known as the Order of Santiago, is a Christian military order founded in the 12th century to defend pilgrims on the Camino de Santiago and to remove the Moors from the Iberian Peninsula.

The Cathedral of Santiago de Compostela is the culminating spot for the Camino de Santiago. The Cathedral of Santiago was constructed to hold the remains of Saint James the Greater, an apostle of Jesus.

Santiago de Compostela: The city of Santiago de Compostela was built up around the cathedral, and is now the capital of the Galicia region in the northwest of Spain. It is believed the word Compostela comes from the latin Campus Stellae, which translated means *Field of Stars.*

Santiago (*also called St. Jacob or St. James the Greater)* was born around 3 AD and died 44 AD. Saint James was one of the 12 apostles of Jesus, along with his brother John. They were the sons of Zebedee. James was the first apostle to bemartyred. St. James is the patron saint of Spain. According to the 12th century Historia Compostelana, St. James preached the gospel in Spain as well as the Holy Land. After he was martyred by King Herod, his disciples brought his body back to Galicia, Spain.

Pope Clement V was born Raymond Bertrand de Got in 1264 and died in 1314. He was Pope from June 1305 – 1314. He is known for suppressing the Knights Templar and for moving the Papacy from Rome to Avignon, which started the Avignon Papacy. When elected Pope, he was neither a cardinal nor Italian; this caused many to speculate that he was tied with King Philip IV.

St-Jean-Pied-de-Port is a town in the foothills of the French Pyrenees. It is also one of the traditional starting points of the Camino Fransés, or The French Way, which is the most popular pilgrimage route of the Camino de Santiago.

Prisca Sapientia is the belief that there is one "lost pure knowledge" that would connect all sciences.

The Tree of Life is the central image of Kabbalah. It is made up of ten interconnected energy centers, the Sephiroth. Each energy center represents a different attribute God reveals itself through and the creation process of the physical realm and the higher metaphysical realms.

Baphomet is a deity that the Knights Templar were accused of worshipping. The name appeared in the Templar trials in 1307, and was subsequently incorporated into occult and mystical traditions. It first came into popular English usage in the 19th century during debate and speculation on the reasons for the suppression of the Templars.

The Alchemist: Alchemy is an ancient branch of philosophy practiced throughout Europe, Africa, and Asia. An Alchemist attempts to purify metals, turning base metals into pure metals (ex: lead into gold). They also work on purifying the soul in the process, and creating the Philosopher's Stone.

The Work is a system of four questions and a turnaround developed by Byron Katie. This section, and others in the novel, were inspired by her philosophy. The author highly recommends you visit her website www.thework.com and read her debut novel *Loving What Is*.

Muhamad III was ruler of the Emirate of Granada from 1302 to 1309. At one time he controlled both sides of the Strait of Gibraltar.

David's harp: According to the book of Samuel, in the bible, God sent an evil spirit to plague King Saul. The king summoned David to play his harp to soothe him. David later succeeded Saul as the king of Israel

King Ferdinand IV of Castile ruled over Castile and Leon from 1295 to 1312. He was a big supporter of the reconquest of Spain from the Moors.

The Order of Assassins was a military order that began in the mountains of Syria and Persia. The order was founded in 1090 and lasted until 1295. However, there are rumors that they never fully disbanded. In their time, the order of assassins killed hundreds of key Muslim and Christian leaders, possibly avoiding the deaths of many by killing one person. Our modern word "assassin" comes from this medieval order, which was originally labeled with the Arabic word "hasisin" (pronounced "hashishin" in English).

Hassan-i Sabbah lived from 1050 - 1124 and founded the Order of Assassins in 1090.

The Battle of Montgisard was on November 25th 1177 between the Kingdom of Jerusalem and the Ayyubids. In this battle, eighty Knights Templar helped 2,500 - 4,000 infantry, and 375 other knights, defeat the feared leader Saladin, and his army of over 26,000 soldiers.

The Fire of San Anton was a disease that spread during the Middle Ages because of an undetected fungus that grew on grains. People would travel to the Arc of San Anton in the hope of being cured. It was later discovered that the grain in this region didn't have the fungus that caused the disease.

Las Marcas de Cantería, or **Stonemasons' Marks,** in English; There are many hypotheses about the meaning of these marks that are found on both religious and secular buildings from the 11th - 15th centuries. The most popular hypothesis is that the marks indicated the quarries the rocks came from, as well as positioning of the stones. Up until the 20th century they were thought to be magical signs carved into the stones.

The Fisher King is a staple in Aurtherian legend. According to the stories, he is the last in a bloodline that protects the Holy Grail. In the legends he is wounded in either the leg or groin and can't stand. All he can do is fish in a boat outside his castle and wait for someone to heal him by asking the right question.

The Holy Grail is believed to be the Holy Chalice that Jesus used at the last supper, and that Joseph of Arimathea used to to catch Jesus's blood at the crucifixion. It is intertwined with Aurtherian legend and believed to bring eternal youth or immortality. In recent years, it has been believed that the Holy Grail refers, not to a cup, but to the blood-line of Jesus.

Druids were prominent members of Celtic culture. They were not only religious leaders, but also healers and judges. The Druids passed on their knowledge in oral form, even though they were literate. The first mention of Druids is from the fourth century, and it is often reported that they practiced human sacrifice. In Irish folklore, Druids also had magical abilities and could see the future.

Prince Charles the Fourth of France lived from 1294 - 1328. Charles was the third son of King Philip IV and the last in the direct line of the House of Carpet. He ruled from 1322 – 1328

A Kabbalah is a form of Jewish mysticism that is believed to date back all the way to the Garden of Eden and is still practiced today.

* This image is in the public domain in its country of origin and other countries and areas where the copyright term is the author's life plus 100 years or fewer. {{PD-US-expired}}

** The letter J came into existence in 1524 so all of the codes are based on a twenty-five-letter alphabet.

SUGGESTED READING LIST

There are many experiences, books, and
conversations with friends (both new and old)
all over the world,that have inspired my
philosophies and ideas in my life. As I wrote this
novel, and walked the Camino, some of the books
that have inspired me are listed below. I highly
recommend reading these books if you found the
concepts in this story interesting or meaningful to you.

Buen Camino,

~ *B.J.S.*

1. ***THE WAY: THROUGH A FIELD OF STARS***
   Book one in the Through a Field of Stars series.
   www.throughafieldofstars.com

2. ***THE BIBLE***

3. ***LOVING WHAT IS,* by Byron Katie**
   "The Work" is a system of four questions and a "turnaround" that
   Katie created to help you question your thoughts, which can
   ultimately help you escape from damaging or painful patterns of
   belief and thinking.

   To learn more about "The Work," read *Loving What Is,* or go to
   www.thework.com to discover how to use this process to confront
   and overcome your own thoughts.I have personally gotten some
   really life-changing results from engaging in "The Work,"
   and I know many others who have as well. I highly recommend it.

4. ***THE POWER OF NOW, by Eckhart Tolle***
   This book is amazing and really helps you to be in the present
   moment. It is perfect for those who want to explore meditation.
   https://eckharttolle.com/

ACKNOWLEDGMENTS

I like to say God has a sense of humor. When I was young, I was obese and I became a dancer; I have dyslexia, and now I am an author. You can never tell what you will be called to in this life. I would like to thank God for inspiring this novel and helping me to achieve a task that I thought was impossible.

Writing this novel has been an exciting and humbling journey. It forced me to face a lot of my fears and to turn something that was my weakness into a strength. It has been a long road, but I have been fortunate enough to have had many companions along the way.

"Every Camino is like a lifetime: some people walk with you for a day, others a few cities, still others come in and out at the perfect moment. But, there are a rare few, who will walk with you until the end of the world."

My journey as an author has paralleled my journey on the Camino. Many people influenced and helped this novel along the way, but I feel blessed to have found a partner willing to walk to the end of the world with me. My wife, Chelsea, has not only helped me with every aspect of the novel, but she also walked over 500 miles on the Camino with me until we reached Finisterre— the end of the world.

Chelsea has been with me since I wrote the first draft. I thought it was perfect, but she kindly let me know it needed a little work. Here we are, four years and many versions later, and she is still my constant companion and support. I hope everyone has the opportunity to feel as loved and supported by their partner.

I would like to thank all of the pilgrims who walked countless hours with me and inspired the characters in this novel. I would like to thank all of the mentors that led me down the path of becoming an author. I would like to thank all of my beta readers and editors. You took this novel from an ordinary book into an amazing novel.

To get this novel out into the world, there were numerous individuals who mentored and encouraged me along the way. They were generous with their time and helped to give feedback, or edit. I am so appreciative and grateful for these individuals.

There were also a whole slew of people who believed in me enough to support my Kickstarter campaign. Thanks to their generosity we have funded all the costs of editing, creating an audio book, printing, and distributing the first set of novels! To thank those individuals who financially supported the novel, I'd like to give a special shout out here! Oh, and of course a big thanks to my supportive family who planted adventure and spirituality into my heart.

KICKSTARTER BACKERS

Abigail and Alain Acosta-Roots, Abigail Ingram and
Christopher Ingram, Aidan Leonard, Alee Reed, Amanda
Li-Sai, Amanda McLearn-Montz, Andolie Marten, Andy Lewis,
Angela T. Beck, Angie Steward, Anna Takkula, Anne Marie
Marsiglia-Talon, Aunt Christine and Uncle Chris, B Garcia,
Ben & Beth Davies, Beth Allen, Beth Steffan, Biggest Ray Ray,
Billy Barnett, Bob Rodgers, Brien Crothers, Bryan and Cherie
Spellman, C. Corbin Talley, Carl and Beverly Seese, Carol
M. Pfeiffer, Carol Scheppard, Carole Raines, Carolyn Arthur,
Cassandra Van, Celia Frost, Chandra Isabell Fulton, Channie
Wright, Chelsea 'the best wife' Skillen, Chris and Hannah
Middlebrook, Chris Meeson, Chris Ransdell, Christina
Culligan, Claudia Kroon and Lucie Körber, Collin M. Johnson,
Corbett J. K. Stern, Cris and Ryan Sand Crystal Sutherland,
David Lars Chamberlain, Dawn Crosby, Delia Armstrong,
Denice Ogburn, Dennis Ingram, Edwin and Diane Weader,
Elaine "Lainey" Silver, Emanuele Falla, the barrow man, Eric
and Sandy Faw, Ethan and Akari Okura, Eron Wyngarde,
Francesco Tehrani, Ginny Heatwole, Graham Hallett,

Guilherme Ribeiro, Harrison Taylor, Hazel Squire, Helen Dickinson, Howlin' Whale, Ian Glendon Caldwell, Isabella Jagannath, Jack 'sprat' McKenzie, Jacob Crouse, Jamie and Aimee Doyle, Janet Goss, JayKub KolTun, Jeff and Carol Goss, Jeff Kellem, Jenn Rosenthal, Jenni, Jennifer L. Pierce, Jessica Fabling, John Idlor, John Miyasato, Jonathan and Ashley Wu, Jordan Bles, Jordan Kotzebue, Josh Lieberman, Joshua Perryman, Karma Raines, Kate & Nathan Hollenberg, Kathleen Quetin, Kathy Weibel, Kay Perret, Ken Heatwole, Kevin & Michelle Skillen, Kimberli Hudson, Kyle & LeAnn Tucker, Lark Cunningham, Larry and Barbara McCann, Laura Martineau, Leigh Brennan, Lindsay Clipner, Lou Pierce, Maia Linnea Wejdling and Thorbjørn Wejdling, Malina Dravis-Tucker, Mandy Matsumoto, Margot Konitzer, Maria Seco, Mark Clerkin, Marko, Martina Komerički, Matthew J M Everton, Melody Domanico, Michele Gibbel, Michele Rutherford, Michelle and Mike Giffin, Michelle Domanico, Nancy Cox, Nancy W Martin, Niels and Ari Bogardus, Pat Gangwer, Paul & Alaina Pfeiffer, Paula Ziegler Ulrich, Receive Joy, Renira Rutherford, Rhoni Blankenhorn, Richard Gilmore, Robert C Deming, Rod Simpson, Rosie Vincent, Sarah Ann Martin, Sherry Mock, Skip Spellman and Sue Pope Spellman, Sofia & Jerry Shronce, Stacy Harty, Stephanie Yamamoto, Steve Dulle, Suellen Khoury, Susanne Nunn, Susie Karasic, Suzanne Goode, Tammy Halaburda and Charlie Hamowy from YSBD...! Dance Studios, Tenae, Tina Grim, Tom Clancy, Tony Pierce, Tyler Goss, Victoria Berry, Yliander Ainslie

CPSIA information can be obtained
at www.ICGtesting.com
Printed in the USA
FSHW010814211021
85595FS